Ruby's Slippers

Leanna Ellis

B&H
PUBLISHING GROUP

Nashville, Tennessee

978-0-8054-4698-2

Published by B&H Publishing Group,
Nashville, Tennessee

Dewey Decimal Classification: F
Subject Heading: SHOES—FICTION \
ADVENTURE FICTION \ PROVIDENCE AND
GOVERNMENT OF GOD—FICTION

1 2 3 4 5 6 7 8   •   13 12 11 10 09

"There's no place like home."
DOROTHY IN *THE WIZARD OF OZ*

To the three Dorothy's in my life:

Dot Wilson
Dorothy Smith
D. Anne Love

I love you all!

Acknowledgments

The journey from idea to published book is long and often arduous and should not be attempted alone. In the *Wizard of Oz*, Dorothy had a few helpers along her path as I did. Thank you all. I hope I haven't forgotten any who made my steps sure and helped ease any burdens.

As always, thanks, David, for your enthusiasm and insights! You are an editing wizard. It's always a joy to work with you and the team at B&H Publishing. Julie, you're a marketing lion! Karen, thank you for all you do! Kim, Pat, Diana, Matt, the sales team, and all the rest who do so much for each and every book, I so appreciate you! You are the best!

Natasha, thanks for always believing, for seeing straight to the heart of a book or character, for your honesty and for you patience. You have a great big heart!

Thanks to Jane and Hock for wading through this story with me. Sometimes it was more like slogging through the muck to find that road again. I appreciate you guys so much! Jennifer Archer, what a friend you are! Thanks for reading a snippet for me. Cyndi Scott, thanks for being my Latin guru! Julie Eller, thanks for information on the Northwest. Magician Brad Brown, thank you for graciously allowing me to come to one of your fun performances!

As always, thanks to my prayer buddies who are such a blessing. Leslie and Maria, I love you guys!

Thanks to the reviewers and readers who have been so supportive and encouraging. Your notes have uplifted my spirits and reminded me when the going gets rough why I sit at my computer for such long hours.

Last, but never truly last or least, thanks to my sweet husband and children who picked up the slack when I forgot to cook dinner or didn't get the house cleaned. I love you all more than you will ever know. I am so proud of each of you and am delighted we are all on this journey through life together.

Chapter One

Some people wish on candles, others on stars. When I was a girl, nose pressed against the passenger window of our Vista Cruiser, I watched truckloads of hay bales rumbling down the highway near our Kansas farm. Weather-beaten farmers drove thirty miles an hour (or slower), traffic piling up a mile behind them. Momma would ease the station wagon into the left lane to pass the snaking line and say, "Make a wish, girls, and don't look back."

My younger sister, Abby, always made a production out of her wishes. She squeezed her eyes closed, pursed her lips toward heaven, and proclaimed to all who were within hearing, "I'm gonna . . ." She leaned forward, her hand on Momma's shoulder. "Can I wish on every hay bale?"

"Why not?" Momma shook her head with bewilderment as if my sister was a novelty act in the circus. To me, she was.

Puckering up again, Abby rattled off her litany of wishes. "I'm gonna be famous! I'm gonna be on the big screen! I'm gonna fly around the world."

Like any good big sister, I rolled my eyes and let out a long, loud huff of irritation. Looking back on it now, I realize I was jealous that Abby knew what she wanted and wasn't afraid to throw her dreams out there for all the world to see.

Cynical, even at age nine, I never wished on candles, stars, or hay bales. Maybe I've always been looking back rather than forward. Nowadays I've become a moderately healthy realist at age thirty-five. But sometimes in the dark of a lonely night, I do imagine wishes coming true.

Otto's barking first signals something amiss on this damp, overcast afternoon. He's my loyal, scruffy black dog, not more than ten or twelve pounds soaking wet. He follows me everywhere and will defend me if so much as a crow flies too near. Crouched on my knees in the garden, holding a prickly weed, I watch a strange sedan clip along the forlorn drive at an unsafe pace and feel a catch in my chest.

Squinting against the afternoon glare, I shield my eyes and push to my feet. Hope overrides any childhood cynicism. I decided long ago to hope for the best, prepare for the worst.

Ever since I was young, I've kept watch on the drive to our small Kansas farm. "Momma," I would shout, "somebody's comin'!" She would stop whatever chore was occupying her—folding laundry, drying dishes, balancing the checkbook—and we'd stand on the porch, my hand in hers, tracking the approaching vehicle. "Momma, do you think it's—"

"No, Dottie. Don't say anything to Abby, all right?"

Ever the protective big sister, I nodded, keeping my disappointment to myself. My little sister by two years tended to be more emotional than Momma and me. Momma never acted sad, and I took my cue from her. But she never hesitated when I called out again, "Visitors!" Hope would crest, soon to be dashed by disappointment. Still, even after all these years, when Momma is no longer here to stand beside me, there's that smidgen of hope at the sight of a strange vehicle coming up the drive.

Rolling my shoulder forward, I swipe my face with my sleeve, wiping away bits of dirt and sweat, and blink at the pale-gray four-door as it stirs up a whirlwind of dust in its wake. None of my neighbors drive this type of car. Craig Hanson, my lawyer and friend, drives a conservative dark-blue 4-Runner. Rhonda Cox, the preacher's wife, drives a white Expedition to haul her three children along with Pampered Chef wares to parties in the adjoining counties. Homer Davies, from the feed store, drives a battered and weary Chevy truck he's had since the seventies. Most come to drop off donations for the annual Easter egg hunt I'm organizing again this year, or if their kid needs help with math, or if they're in need of a third on yet another church committee.

The darkened windows of the strange sedan veil the driver's identity as it comes to a screeching halt in front of my house. I dust my hands off on the back of my overalls. My muddy Crocs leave a depression in the soft earth. Otto prances around me, yipping and barking. "Easy now. Let's go see who it is." I lift Otto over a chicken-wire fence I strung up last summer to keep out a family of rabbits that had been nibbling on my beets and sugar snap peas. The sedan hasn't moved. No door opens. No window slides downward. Is the driver lost or confused? Reconsidering? My footsteps quicken.

The driver's door swings open and a tall, shapely woman in a form-fitting white dress emerges. I keep my head upright as Momma always did, my footsteps steady. This woman is definitely lost, like she's looking for the pages of a *Vogue* magazine to crawl into. She has long black hair and dark sunglasses that make her eyes appear as big as a grasshopper's. It isn't until she swings her hair over her shoulder in a familiar way that recognition causes a whoosh of air to escape me.

"Abby!" I holler.

She turns, raises her sunglasses to the top of her head, and spots me.

"Come on, boy!" I slap the side of my leg. "Abby's home!" I break into a loping jog, unable to run at full speed with these shoes that want to slide off my feet with every step. It's been over a year since I've seen my sister, when she came home for Momma's funeral. Abby hasn't been around often enough for Otto to remember her. With his hind legs propelling him forward, my trusty little dog quickly covers the fifty yards or so and launches himself at the intruder.

"Get back!" Abby screeches, stepping sideways, wedging herself between door and car. His quarry cornered, Otto sounds the alarm and stands firm, tail straight up with its fringe like a flag and pointy ears flat against his head.

"Otto!" I yell and clap my hands. "Come." He doesn't. It takes another sharper command before he backs down, circles around, his hackles raised like bristles on one of Abby's many hairbrushes.

"Crazy dog." I push back a limp strand of hair that's fallen into my eyes. I keep it too short for a ponytail. "Don't worry about him," I say. "He wouldn't harm a flea." I hug my sister tight and breathe in her pricey perfume like it's a salve to ease the ache of an old wound. "Good to have you home."

I step back, releasing her, and she wobbles on impossibly high heels. Between the spiky white shoes and a newly enhanced bust no doubt manufactured in Hollywood, I'm surprised she doesn't tip over. I reach a hand out to steady her. Those breasts are definitely not coded in the family genes, and I find I'm a little self-conscious. "What brings you back to Kansas?"

Abby brushes from her dress a smudge left by my overalls. Her heavily lashed green eyes give me a once over. "What have you been doing, Dottie? Digging in the dirt?"

It's an old joke between us. Fact is, as a kid, I liked to dig in the dirt. Momma had shown me how to take a tiny seed, push it into the moist spring earth, and cover it with dirt, water, and prayer. Together, we would watch each day for the little shoots to poke through, unfurl, and reach for the sunshine. It didn't take pie-in-the-sky dreams to grow something; it just took water and sunlight. Abby, however, preferred daydreams and play-acting. Still does.

"Nothing's changed here." I say. That simple fact comforts me. I cling to what I know, to the past and tradition. Abby has always reached toward something she doesn't yet have.

"I can see that," she says, her tone indicating she's not amused.

"Look at me, standing out here gabbin'." I feel goofy grinning at my sister, but I'm truly thrilled by her sudden appearance. "Come on in!"

She presses a button on the car key and the trunk to what appears to be a rental car pops open. She picks her way over the gravel drive to the back of the car, then peers down at her oversized suitcase as if measuring it for the first time. Waggling her long, fake nails at me, she asks, "Think you can help?"

"Sure." I grab the suitcase, which weighs almost as much as I do, and a couple of heaves later it teeters on the brink of the trunk. I may be small, but I'm strong. The bag hits the drive with a thunk. "I hope there isn't anything breakable in here."

When she doesn't answer, I turn and realize she's already gone inside. Checking the luggage over for some sort of a handle or a way to roll it up to the door, I traipse back to the house. Otto sits outside the door, lifting one paw, his nails scratching the wood where he's already worn through the white paint. If I look close, I can see the layers of paint, like tree rings telling of years past, the colors Momma experimented with, from bright and hopeful white to anemic yellow to barely-there beige. I often imagine the house as it was when I was a girl, vivid and dazzling, a shimmering safety net among fields that routinely changed from summery green to autumnal gold and wintry barren.

The house belonged to my grandparents, then Momma, and now Abby and me. Even though it probably seems small and inconsequential to most passersby, it is my inheritance. More than weather-beaten wood and rusted nails, old-fashioned furniture and out-of-date equipment, it is full of significance and memories for me.

Otto looks up at me, his paw rising midair. His muzzle has turned gray over the last couple of years. I'm not sure how old he is. He was a stray lurking around the steps of the middle school where I taught. He looked part terrier, part anything goes. I fed him scraps of leftover peanut-butter-and-jelly sandwiches from my sack lunch. I posted signs around the school, but no one claimed him. I've had him nine years now, but he still has plenty of get-up-and-go. Forlornly he looks at the house and barks again.

"Abby's not used to having a pet around." Not in L.A. I reach for the doorknob. "Give her a little time."

I wrestle the suitcase through the narrow doorway, scraping the behemoth against the door frame. I give one last push and it flops over on its side, lying as if swollen and bloated from the heat.

Abby stands in the bedroom we used to share. The window unit blasts her with the coldest air it has to offer. "It's hot!"

"Tell me about it." I plop down on the bedside table. The doilies Momma once kept there have long since been put away to make dusting easier and more efficient. After I left for college in Wichita and Abby staked her claim in Hollywood, Momma kept the twin beds and lilac-covered spreads that suited Abby more than me. When I moved back home to take care of her, I never bothered remodeling or redecorating. It seemed like a waste of money. Momma used to say I'd inherited her ability to stretch a dollar to its breaking point.

Abby primps in front of the oval dresser mirror, fluffing her hair, which makes the bracelets on her arm jangle. She leans close and examines her makeup. "It's not easy, Dottie."

"What's that?"

"My job. There's always a younger actress. Someone more talented. Someone prettier."

"I doubt that. Besides, you're not old." After all, Abby had been Miss Maize her senior year. She could out-dance, out-sing, out-act anyone.

"You have no idea." Exhaustion deepens her voice. "Thirty-three is *ancient* in Hollywood. I've been turned down for parts that once were a slam dunk for me. Now they want me to audition for the part of a *mother*." She turns sideways, sucks in an invisible stomach, which only makes her curvaceous top protrude further. "Do I look matronly to you?"

7

I shake my head. "Not at all."

Her features relax. She focuses again on the mirror, forming an O with her mouth and stretching her jaw to the side. She taps the back of her hand under her chin twice. I can see my own reflection, small behind hers. It doesn't seem possible that we're from the same gene pool. She's tall and statuesque; I'm short, petite, ordinary. Her hair is long, gleaming, full and inviting; mine is short and a dull brown. Maybe our differences are a reflection of how different our parents really were.

The flash of a diamond ring catches my eye. "Did you get married again?"

"I'm engaged." She smiles, pleased I noticed. "You should come out to California and meet Trey."

"Maybe." I run a finger along the seam of my overalls.

"You really should get off the farm sometime, Dottie. See the world! Meet interesting people. Don't you want to travel? See things?"

I feel a tightening in my gut at her insinuation. She was always the impatient sort, not content to sit around and wait for crops to grow, for Christmas morning to dawn, for boys to call. Is that why I stayed in Kansas? Was I content? Or was I scared?

"I'm happy here."

She flops down on what used to be her bed, lying back, stretching her lithe body out like a sinewy rubber band. "I'd be bored out of my mind." She props her elbows on the bed, pushing up to look at me. "What do you *do* around here for fun?"

Feeling prickly and defensive, I snap, "Watch paint dry." Otto prances at my feet, and I pick him up and place him on the bed. "Pick fleas off the dog. You know, the usual."

Abby eyes Otto, then sits up, and waves at him. "Shoo!"

"He doesn't have fleas." I move Otto to my lap, then can't resist adding, "Just ticks."

She wraps her arms across her stomach as if to ward off some invisible critter. "Are you still teaching Sunday school?"

"Yes."

"And heading up the Easter egg hunt too, I suppose. How many committees are you on now?"

My defenses prickle. "Why?"

"Because you're not living your *own* life."

I laugh. "And whose life am I living? Groucho Marx's?"

"Mother's."

"Momma had a good life."

"Lonely, don't you think?"

"That wasn't her choice. What did you want her to do, abandon her marriage vows?"

Abby's pupils tighten. "Don't you want more in life, Dottie?" She watches me like I'm a strange plant from another world. "Don't you want to live a little? Experience things for yourself?"

"I like my life." My teeth click at my firm pronunciation. "Some people dream big dreams, Abby, like you. Others of us make do with what we have. But wishing on hay can't change your life any more than it can change mine."

"It's what you do with those dreams that matters. What do you dream of doing, Dottie?"

Suddenly the reason for her questions becomes clear. "Is this about selling the farm?"

She folds her hands together and places them on her slim thighs. "Momma never should have made those ridiculous stipulations in her will."

"It's been in our family for generations!"

"It's not about carrying on tradition, Dottie. Momma always wanted to control us. Control me. Probably because she couldn't control Daddy." Her features tighten, her skin stretching over her prominent cheekbones.

"Abby, if I could buy you out, I would. But I can't afford it." But someday I'll have enough—scrimp and save enough, squirrel enough away—to buy the farm lock, stock, and clapboard. Then it will be mine.

Silence beats between us, like a bell sounding the end of round one.

Then the hard line of her jaw softens. "Let's not talk about things we don't agree on."

My fragile hopes for this visit shatter and crash around me. "How long can you stay?"

"Don't worry." She stretches back again along the length of the bed. Her hair spreads out around her like a glossy pool. "I'm flying out tomorrow. I have to be in L.A. for a show. A *new* show."

I tuck a strand of hair behind my ear and ask the perfunctory question her statement demands. "What kind of a show?"

"Stage. I haven't been on the stage in a while."

Seems to me she's on stage performing every minute of her life. But what do I know?

"I've been in front of the cameras so much recently." She combs her manicured nails through her long hair. "An audience will be refreshing. Invigorating!" She rolls to her side, propping her hand against her head. "It's really a fantastic opportunity, a chance to really stretch my acting skills. At first I was hesitant. It's a challenging, complicated part. I've never played anything like this before. You should come out and see the show."

"Oh, uh . . ." I search for an answer, something that won't commit me to a trip to Los Angeles.

She shrugs a narrow shoulder as if maybe she doesn't care. But I know the look. *Her* look. She tugs off first one shoe, then the other, and tosses them behind her where they clunk on the wooden floor. "It's okay. You don't have to come. It doesn't matter anyway."

Why do we always end up hurting each other? It seems to be our cycle of life.

"You know," she says, "Momma made me go to all of your baseball games."

"Softball," I correct.

"Whatever." She waves her hand, the diamond flashing like a mirrored ball on a dance floor. "I remember that tournament when it snowed. You never had to sit through a recital in a snowstorm."

No, just loud music and knobby-kneed girls. But this time I keep my thoughts to myself. "I'm sorry, Abby. I'll try to come to a show. Okay?"

She's quiet for a long moment while I lose myself in a maze of regrets and if-only's. If only I could contain my temper. If only I could curb my tongue. If only we could find some common ground between us and not stray into old territory.

"Want me to help unpack?" I ask.

Beneath a curtain of hair, she looks at me. Vulnerability softens her gaze. It's a little-girl quality that reminds me of when she was small and helpless. "Dottie?" A catch in her voice tugs at me. "Have you ever . . . ?"

I brace myself for her next question: wanted to get married? wanted to leave the farm? wanted to make a wish and see it come to fruition?

"Have you ever thought of finding our father?"

A jolt pulses through me.

"Might be nice to . . ."

"What? Have a family reunion?" I hate the bitterness that pushes its way out of me like a wound oozing yellow pus. I thought that gash had healed over long ago with a thick, silvery scar. "He left, Abby," I say, repeating my mother's words. It was enough explanation for Momma, and it's enough for me.

Abby glances down at the bedspread, plucks at a loose thread in the dotted Swiss material, and rolls it between her long, delicate fingers. "Just to see how he is," she says.

I stare at my stubby hands. Dirt has made them dry and scratchy. My answer is simple, but the complications and contradictions lie deep within me. My gaze drifts toward the window, toward the lonely drive.

"He knows how to find us."

Chapter Two

I am awakened by a low guttural growl. My hands are clenched, my muscles tight, and I feel as if I've slept tense and frowning. I blink against the darkness, feeling a wave of panic like a sudden gust of hot air.

"What is it, boy?" I reach for the furry lump beside me. Otto's not in his usual place, curled at my hip. Instead he stands at the edge of the bed, body rigid. In the darkness he is not much more than a dark blob, but I reach out and his short, bristly fur tickles my palm. "You hear something?"

My ears strain against the quiet. I shift, and the bedsprings creak beneath me. Sitting upright, I push back the covers. Cool, damp spring air puckers my skin. Slowly my brain shifts around like a Rubik's Cube, locking pieces of an unfathomable puzzle into place.

Abby. She's home. In the guest room. "It's okay." I breathe deeper and pet Otto, smooth down his fur, while reassuring myself all is well. "Is she still on the phone?"

After Abby changed into ripped jeans (which differ from my torn overalls mainly in that she paid lots of money for the look, and admittedly they are sexier than mine) and a cropped T-shirt that revealed her pierced belly button, we ate tomato soup and a tossed salad. The conversation at dinner revolved around Abby, her life and adventures, and her upcoming wedding. It was like old times, sitting together at the wobbly wooden table in the kitchen. Except soup couldn't buffer the friction between us as Momma used to.

For a distraction I turned on the television. But this only pushed us further apart and exaggerated the differences in our lives. Every show featured actors she knew or had met, and each demanded a comment or two or three.

"Met him at a party. He's very short."

"That guy there. He's gay."

"She's had work done."

Not having much else to say, we turned in early. Abby called friends on her cell phone, and for a while I tried to read while lying in Momma's bed. I never intended to take over Momma's room after she passed on, but I missed her and stayed to feel closer to her. Not even a serial killer running rampant in the pages of a best seller could keep my attention from wandering to the room next door, where Abby chattered and laughed and moved about, opening drawers, shoving them closed.

A sudden clunking noise jars me now, calling forth images the book planted in my mind of nightly intruders, blood splatters, and dead bodies. Otto growls deep in his throat, and my pulse clicks into gear. I check the clock on the bedside table. It's a round, old-fashioned clock with glowing green numbers and tiny bells on top that jangle when I bother to set it. The hands point to the two and three. What could Abby be doing this late? Maybe she's on New York or L.A. time or some other zone that only actors get into.

Now fully awake, I crawl out of bed and set Otto on the floor at my feet. He sticks close as I pad into the hallway. Only the countryside can be this dark, with no city lights throwing off shadows or shades of gray. I push my hand outward to feel my way along doors and walls. I inch toward the guest room, pause, and listen. The door, which was shut earlier when Abby and I retired for the night, is now ajar.

"Abby?" I whisper into the dark.

She doesn't answer.

Otto brushes against my leg. The wooden floor chills my bare feet. I'm wearing only my button-down flannel pajamas, the drawstring pants loose and baggy, the hem dragging. Feeling vulnerable, I hike the pants up.

A scraping and shuffling noise makes my heart race at a fast clip. I turn around in the hallway, trying to figure out which direction the noise is coming from. The clicking of Otto's nails on the weathered hardwood floor alerts me to his scouting ahead. At the entrance to the den, I see a wedge of light coming from the cellar door in the floor.

Together Otto and I move into the den. This old farmhouse used to be one room with a kitchen and cellar. The one bath was added in the thirties, then later one bedroom. Our parents added another as their family grew, but it's still rather small, definitely humble. Reaching down, I pull the wooden handle upward in a strong, swift motion, but it still makes a groaning sound. Light bursts out of the hole in the floor.

Mustiness rises like memories that have long been buried. The cellar is where I placed Momma's clothes, keepsakes, and whatnots from her bedroom after she died. It's where we've always stored canned goods from the garden, toilet paper and paper towels I buy on sale, and the tax returns I file every year.

The sounds below the floorboards where I'm standing become more distinct. Is Abby down there? If so, why? When we were kids, she used to bribe me to go to the cellar in her place when Momma would ask her to fetch a can of green beans. If it's not her, then who? Or what? Maybe some critter got in and can't get out. But a frightened animal didn't turn on the cellar light.

An uneasy feeling settles over me. I tiptoe to the hat rack beside the back door and grab my umbrella for a weapon. Just in case. Then I ease first one foot then the other down the ladder. The scuffling noises grow louder. Still near the top of the ladder, I bend low toward the railing and peer down into the cellar.

Abby.

I release a pent-up breath and relax my grip on the umbrella. Part of me wants to throw it at her, scare her the way she's scared me.

Abby bends over a box, digging her hands into the contents. She's wearing a fancy nightgown, the slinky material hugging her curves. Her usually tidy hair is pulled up in a semblance of a ponytail, but the ends stick out in all directions like broom bristles gone amok.

She straightens, then shoves the box away and grabs another, yanking it off a stack and letting it fall to the concrete floor. Momma taught me to save everything, so there are old canning jars, mailing boxes, clothes I can't wear anymore, worn-out towels and linens. "You never know what you might need one day," she used to say. Some of her boxes I never went through as the pain of losing her was too great to relive with each document or saved letter. And I didn't want to pry into Momma's past without her consent. So I simply boxed and stored her things in the cellar.

Abby mumbles something to herself, then jabbers away like she's ten and playing Barbies again. She speaks so low I can't make out the words. Pausing, she leans over and looks at a stack of papers. A script? Is she working on lines? Then she arches her neck, clears her throat, and lets out a screeching cackle that makes the hair at the back of my neck stand on end. Otto, who stands behind me at the top of the stairs, starts barking.

Abby lurches sideways and looks up at us. Her hand clutches her chest, as if to still her heart. "Oh, good grief, Dottie! You scared me to death."

"I scared *you?*" I fist the umbrella against my palm. "What are you doing?"

"I was feeling sentimental. You know. Silly really. So I thought I'd look through some of Momma's things." Abby folds up one of Momma's sweaters. The same one she haphazardly tossed aside a moment ago. She runs her manicured hand down the length of the wool, a red fingernail poking through what appears to be a moth hole near the neckline. "You have all this to help you, Dottie, to feed your memories."

Feeling bold I step down from the ladder. Behind me Otto shifts from foot to foot, wanting to follow yet hesitant. "You got the piano. Remember? If you want something else, then all you have to do is ask."

She throws Momma's sweater at the box and misses. "I had to sell it."

My breath freezes in my chest. "What? Why?"

"Don't look at me like I just killed the dog. That piano was horribly out of tune. And so old it couldn't be fixed."

"It was Momma's."

"It's late." She pushes a box out of the way with her big toe, not bothering to clean up the mess she's made. Yawning, she steps to the foot of the ladder. "I have an early flight." She stands there, waiting for me to move out of her way.

DISCOMFITED, I REMAIN awake, curled into the sturdy chair that belonged to my father. Or so Momma told me. She never spoke ill of him, never said she missed him. It was as if their lives were two largely perpendicular lines, highways bisecting each other once or twice, then never crossing again. I'd hoped when she mentioned it was his chair that she might tell me more about their marriage, his leaving, but she'd kept her feelings to herself as she always had.

I cup my hands over the chair's padded arms, rub my fingers against the rough brown material Momma had used to reupholster it when they first married. Otto nestles beside me with a snort.

"It's okay." I slide my hand along his narrow body, unsure if I'm trying to convince him or me. Questions and concerns boil inside my mind, and I stir them around until they're a froth of uncertainty.

Before the usual teenage arguments over space and control, there had been times of sisterly laughter: giggles on rainy mornings, tickling fingers under the covers when Abby climbed into my bed, afraid after watching a scary movie. I cherish those memories, tuck them around me like a warm quilt on nights when I feel lonely.

"How'd you get so brave?" she once asked me.

I shrugged. I wasn't brave. I had my own fears. They just didn't include witches, Godzilla, or Roddy McDowell dressed like an ape. "It's just make-believe."

I couldn't understand her fear and she couldn't understand mine.

There's a chill in the air, and I pull a blanket Momma knitted long ago from the basket by the hearth. Under its beige and brown weight, I feel her comforting presence. Her sense of purpose and determination are woven into every stitch.

I MUST HAVE dozed because I wake with a start, my head bobbing. Blinking, confused, I straighten, feel my muscles stiffen. My neck aches from sleeping scrunched in the chair. Weak morning light sneaks through the slit in the front window curtains. The place Otto occupied is now cold and empty.

"Here, boy." I snap my fingers for him to come.

There is no answer. Where is he? I push to my feet, feel my joints groan. I pat my leg and call louder, "Come here, boy."

He doesn't.

Confused, I shuffle to the kitchen to check the time. It's early still, but the sun should be offering more light. A peek out the window above the sink reveals distended clouds threatening overhead. We need the rain.

Shouldn't Abby be heading to the airport?

"Abby?" The door to the guest bedroom is wide open, the bed empty, covers strewn haphazardly. Her suitcase is gone. The bathroom is a flood of damp blue towels on the floor. A heavy weariness settles over my chest and I turn away.

A tiny scratching sound draws me back to the guest room. I stare at the closed closet door. A whimper tugs at me, then a muffled bark. I wrench open the humidity-swollen door. Otto rushes out, noses my leg, then sniffs around the room. He barks once, then sits and looks at me, his soft brown eyes concerned.

"What were you doing in there?"

I sit down next to him and rub his velvety ears. Panting beside me, his sides heaving, his pink tongue hanging out the side of his mouth, he resembles an old man with graying beard and mustache. I pick him up and cuddle him against my chest.

Daddy never said good-bye either. I simply woke one morning, padded into the kitchen to the smell of bacon frying, and looked toward his empty chair. "Where's Daddy?"

Momma's brows pinched together and her eyes welled. "He's gone."

I thought she meant he'd gone to work early. But that night when I stared out the front window, watching for his truck, Momma said, "He's not coming back, Dottie."

I suspect my sister won't be back either. At least not for a while.

I push up from the floor, then reach for a forgotten blue towel and begin to fold it. Wishing on haystacks doesn't accomplish anything.

THE SKY IS thick and gray this morning, much like my mood. Livid clouds churn and boil, bumping and bulging along the horizon. I go about my chores, feeding the chickens and hogs. Otto scarfs down his food while I pour out Wheaties for myself. I dress in a plain pair of navy slacks that I keep on hand for church committee meetings and add a simple pullover blue-checked top.

The morning chill gives way to the warm, damp blanket

of an impending thundershower, and droplets of moisture fill the air, leaving the windows dotted and the grass wet.

"Don't worry," I reassure Otto as he trots behind me from room to bathroom. Over the past couple of years, he's grown accustomed to my being home most of the time. I retired early to tend to Momma when she needed full-time care. I always assumed I'd go back to teaching, but Principal Buchanan filled my position before Momma died and I was available once more. And frankly, I didn't miss teaching as much as I thought I would.

Otto's brown eyes anxiously watch me put on the nicest shoes I own, which tells him when I'm about to leave. "This is important." I give him one more pat on the head. "I'll be back soon."

As I descend the back steps toward my waiting truck, I hear him whimper through the locked door. Guilt makes me hesitate, but a quick glance at the darkening sky pushes me on. Rain is almost a certainty. Maybe worse. I need to hurry so I can be home before the storm hits.

It's only ten minutes to town, and I pass a dozen small farms with fields cleared for planting. Maize is a small town, even for Kansas. Folks I've known all my life come and go into the Food Mart and bank along Main Street. But the town appears deserted this morning. The buildings look like they were up-to-date in the 1950s and haven't been renovated or repaired since. I pull into an open parking space in front of Craig Hanson's office, turn off the ignition, and step on the emergency brake. A burst of wind tugs the truck's door from my grasp as I open it. Rain spits a few drops against my face and arms.

Ducking my head, I make a run for it before the cloud overhead lets loose. I jump through a hedge that separates the parking row and the storefront sidewalk. "Attorney at Law" is etched on the door's glass window. A "We're Open" sign lies crookedly against the pane. It flops about as I open and shut the door, having to push hard against the relentless wind.

"Well, look who blew in!" Molly Quinton sits behind her computer terminal. Curly gray hair surrounds her kind face like smoke rings. She broke the habit years ago, but her voice still has a husky quality to it. "How you doing, Dottie?"

"Oh, fine. How are you? Mark's leg better?"

"He gets the cast off Wednesday." Molly's lined forehead compresses like a folded fan. "Something wrong? I've been checking the weather."

"Is Craig available?"

"Course. Go right on in."

I slip inside Craig's office. A mini TV on the corner of his desk blares, ". . . *moving eastward at a fast clip . . .*"

Craig closes a book and slides it into a drawer. His socked feet are propped on the corner of his desk. "What are you doing out in this weather?"

"Taking a leisurely stroll. Can we talk?"

"Have a seat."

We went through school together. Craig asked me to marry him in first grade and told me his girl troubles in middle school. I fell in love with him during our senior year, but it was a secret affair on my part. He never knew how I felt.

Craig followed in his father's footsteps to an Ivy League school and got a law degree, whereas I stayed, attended the community college nearby, then Wichita State. He came home with a wife and baby in tow and set up practice in the same office with his daddy who has since gone on to his great reward. I taught his oldest children when they reached eighth grade but retired before his youngest two made it that far.

With an economy of movement, Craig leans over and turns down the volume on the TV but does not turn it off. The meteorologist's voice becomes a mumble. I catch a glimpse of angry reds moving across the projected map.

"What's going on?" He studies me with a steady, amused gaze. "Let me guess."

"Are you clairvoyant all of a sudden?" It's our usual routine, except I don't feel like kidding around this morning.

He holds up his hand, closes his eyes as if he's Carnac the Magnificent answering questions from unopened envelopes. He twitches his mouth from one side to the other then opens one eye to stare at me. "Give me a minute now."

"You can't make me smile," I warn.

"Oh, not trying to do that." He snaps his fingers. "You've seen Abby. Right?"

I sink down onto the chair behind me. "Word travels fast."

"She blew through town yesterday, turning heads, stirring up gossip. You know the bit." He lifts his bad leg off the desk, easing it carefully to the floor. He was injured in a car wreck our senior year—a car wreck everyone blamed on Abby. It left him with a decided limp.

"Did she come by to see you?"

"That's not her style." He leans back in his chair, his fingers steepled. "So what's wrong? She say something to upset you?"

"You know, the usual." I push up from the chair, turn away, and try to tuck my feelings inside my sleeve the way my father used to hide handkerchiefs or coins for his magic tricks.

I study the pictures of Craig's family framed and perched on the shelves that house row after row of law books. His kids are well behaved, well-adjusted, and all-around good kids. They're a happy family, gregarious and friendly.

The TV cuts out and static crackles through the room.

"Cable." He swats the TV with his hand. A few seconds later the weatherman emerges from a gray screen of squiggly lines to talk about wind shear.

I finger a gold-framed photograph. "This a new one?"

"You know Lindsey. Always wanting pictures of the kids and family. I expect we'll come home from Disneyland with pictures of Mickey and Minnie and all of us in those stupid mouse ears."

I grin, picturing Craig covering his receding hairline with the black cap, mouse ears sticking out like satellite dishes. "When are you going?"

"Sometime in July. You should come with us."

"I'm sure Lindsey would love that."

"She wouldn't care."

His words pull the truth out like a dandelion weed, the root dangling, dripping bits of truth. When Abby blows into town, the women of Maize lock their doors and hold tight to their men. But no one fears me. No one sees me as a threat to their marriage. Not in a long, long time. Maybe not ever. Momma would say that's a reflection of my good character.

"It'd be good for you to travel some," Craig says, echoing Abby's words and rankling me. "Get away from here occasionally."

There was a time when local folks set me up with every Tom, Dick, or Hayseed who came into town for a family visit. I had a ton of first-and-only dates. I can't say I was very interested or encouraging. Maybe I still had my eye on the driveway . . . waiting. Or maybe I figured they'd all just walk right out of my life the way my father had. Whatever. It was a relief when my friends quit pestering me with prospective suitors.

"Your farm is safe, Dottie." Craig interrupts my thoughts, reading my underlining concerns. Of course, this isn't the first time I've come to him needing reassurance on this point.

I draw a slow breath and release it, release the tension I've been hoarding the way Momma collected plastic containers. "You can see in that crystal ball of yours?"

"I wrote Ruby's will. Abby cannot sell the farm out from under you. You both own it, fifty-fifty. And because of the stipulations your mother set forth, you must both consent fully in order to sell. God willing, nothing will happen to—"

"What do you mean, 'God willing'?"

"Any will can be broken. There's no fool-proof, iron-clad will." He taps a folder with his index finger. "But this is as close as anyone could get."

"You're a marvel. Or so they say."

"Indubitably." He winks.

"Conceited, aren't you?"

"Confident."

The TV stutters again, then the talking resumes. It's a station out of Wichita. The traffic reporter gives the latest on potential street flooding from the approaching thunderstorm. Whatever hits Wichita usually reaches us first.

In a quieter, confidential tone, I say, "She was looking for something. Searching, you know?"

"Aren't we all?" His smile crinkles into a frown along his forehead. "For money?"

"I don't think so. Not in the cellar. Drugs?"

"From you?" He laughs. "Did they run out in L.A.?"

"Maybe she thinks I still have Momma's painkillers."

He shrugs. "Maybe something else of value."

"She's dreaming then." I give a half laugh. "Momma never had anything of value."

His gaze is steady and makes me uncomfortable. He presses his thumbs together. "Look, I did hear this bit of gossip. Take it for what it's worth. Abby was in the bank yesterday trying to get a loan."

"So that's it." I cross my arms over my chest where a deep ache throbs. "She must have been looking for something to sell. She sold the piano. What's next? Why did Momma write her will the way she did? It just doesn't make sense."

"She wanted you to have the farm. She knew you loved it. But she couldn't leave Abby out in the cold. She always hoped Abby would come home one day. She hoped you two would eventually get along."

"Me, too." I look down at my hands, the worn silver key ring wrapped around my pointer finger. "Maybe we're too much like our parents. Opposites. Momma always said Abby was just like our father."

"A dreamer with big ideas."

"Foolish ideas." I tap my keys against my thigh. "You know, I really have tried. Before Momma died, I called Abby regularly with updates. When she came home for the funeral, I wanted us to reconcile. Even this time I was determined to make it work. But for some reason we always end up acting like we're ten and twelve again. Bickering. Snapping at each other."

"Family relationships can be the hardest. But for some reason the good Lord puts these people in our lives when we never would have chosen them as friends. Iron against iron."

"Sharpening us? So we can kill each other? Sometimes I wonder what it would have been like, how different it might have been if Momma had remarried. Do you ever wonder, what if things had turned out differently?"

"What if I didn't have this limp? What if I'd chosen another profession? What if I hadn't joined my father's

practice?" His shoulders slant at a stiff angle. "My relationship with my father was like yours and Abby's—I wanted to
set a different course."

"What else would you have done?"

He shrugs awkwardly. "You'll laugh."

"Maybe. But then I'll get you to laugh about it too."

"Fair enough. I've always wanted to write a book." He
laughs before I can. Except I don't feel like laughing at his
admission. "I know. I know. Everybody wants to write a
book."

"Write what? About law?"

"Fiction."

"You want to be the next John Grisham?"

"More like Tolkien."

This surprises me, but it also makes sense. I've seen his
home, with stacks of books in every room. He keeps a novel
in his bottom left drawer for when work is slow.

"Well, you still could. What's stopping you?"

"Paying bills." He chuckles and rubs his thumbnail along
his jaw. "Just an old daydream. Don't you ever—?" Abruptly,
he leans forward, turns the volume knob up on the TV.

"... on the leading edge of the storm and producing tornadic
conditions. This is one big storm brewing, folks." The forecaster's
tone is grim. "A super cell. And we're starting to see rotation."

Otto! He'll be cowering and quivering beneath the bed,
his anxious brown eyes alert and watching for me. But before
I can leap for the door, the civil defense sirens start to wail.

Molly jerks the office door open, her eyes wide, her features stretched. "It's a twister! Coming this way!"

"Take cover." Craig stands, leaning against the desk to
gain his balance.

"No." I move toward the door. "I have to get home."

Chapter Three

The wind whips through Maize. Flags salute. A light pole at the end of the street bobs and weaves like it's had a night out on the town. Tin cans rattle and roll from an overturned dumpster. A lawn chair clatters down the middle of Main Street, end over end. Rain lashes down, horizontal at times, swelling and cascading in waves. I squint up at the black clouds boiling over. Lightning zips in long, jagged streaks. Thunder follows right on its heels.

By the time I'm inside the truck, my clothes are soaked. Water drips from my bangs. The ignition catches quickly and wipers slap at the rain, but it's a losing battle. Suddenly there's a hammering sound, like someone is pummeling my truck with a baseball bat. Quarter-sized chunks bounce like Ping-Pong balls off the hood.

The storm is gaining strength. I jerk the gearshift into reverse, back into the street, and push through sheets of rain toward the farm. I can't see more than ten feet in front of the bumper. The town's lone traffic light swings precariously overhead and casts an eerie yellow glow against the gloom. Blackened buildings line the way, mere silhouettes. Electricity must be on the fritz. Hail crunches under the tires as I turn at the edge of town onto a one-lane highway that will take me straight to the farm. The wheels skid, making the back end of the truck whip right, then left. I jerk the steering wheel, keeping my foot off the brake, and manage to right the truck.

As quickly as the hail began, it stops. The civil defense sirens still wail, pull my nerves taut. I flip on the radio for news, a voice of reason and calm in the chaos around me. The news is anything but.

"A tornado has been spotted thirty miles west of Wichita. There's significant rotation . . ."

I tighten my hold on the steering wheel, lean forward, push the truck as fast as I dare. I grew up in Tornado Alley. I know what to do. Take shelter. And I will—just as soon as I get to the farm. I have to get the animals secure in the barn. Have to get Otto. He's all alone. The radio announces the position of the tornado—northwest of my location and moving due east and south. Coming right at us.

I punch the gas pedal and a roar of water sprays from beneath the truck. I worry about the chickens loose in the barnyard, the pigs grunting, butting up against the fence, bumping into each other, huddling together, squealing. And Otto. Is he scratching at the door to get out? Whining? Barking? Cowering?

A black lump in the road startles me. Two eyes. A wide nose. A cow. I stomp the brake and blast the horn. The truck whips around in a circle. I lose sight of the frightened animal and come to a jerking halt half on, half off the road. The rear bumper tilts down into a ditch.

My breath comes in hard gasps. Where did the cow go? I look out the back window, but she's disappeared. Wind buffets the truck. I press the gas, but the truck only makes a grinding sound. In the side mirror I can see mud shooting from the back tires. I jerk open the cab door and the wind slams it wide, nearly taking it off its hinges. Rain pelts me in the face. I try to get my bearings, searching for anything recognizable. On the road, a few feet away, a mailbox rolls over, the wind tossing it about like a handkerchief. On its side is painted my family name—Meyers.

Okay. I'm close. I can make it. Even on foot.

Fighting every inch of the way, fists clenched, eyes straining, I trudge through mud that seeps into my shoes and sucks at my two-inch heels. My ankle bobbles and I step on the side of my foot. Wincing, I kick off the shoe, all the while moving toward the house. Even though I can't see it, it must be there. Rain plasters my hair to my head, stinging my cheeks, slashing my eyes. I'm leaning so far forward that if the wind were to stop suddenly, I would fall flat on my face.

I find the driveway almost immediately, and it guides me right up to the house. The picket fence has taken a beating. Slats tilt like teeth needing braces. Many are missing altogether. I push and shove, then kick at the gate. Old habits die hard, and I turn to close it. The wind jerks the gate out of my hands and slams it closed with a decisive clink. I turn back into the wind, glance toward the barn obscured by rain and darkness. I need to secure the animals, but a vortex has formed not a hundred yards away, a pale gray beast devouring the farmland and stalking toward the house.

I creep in what feels like slow motion toward the porch.

A post offers refuge and I cling to it, catch my breath. The overhanging roof tries to shelter me, but the slanting rain stings my exposed skin. I fumble with the keys, unlock the bolt, and fall into the house.

"Otto!" My voice sounds hoarse. "Where are you, boy?"

The wind whistles, moans, slaps at the house. The shutters tremble. There's a *whoosh*, *pop*, *whoosh*, *pop* as something slides and smacks the roof. A rumbling fills the air. It sounds like I'm in a tin can and being shaken like a marble.

"Otto!" I charge through the rooms, search his hiding places. Behind the recliner. Under the kitchen table. Finally, dropping to my knees, I find him huddled in a tiny ball under the bed. He's shaking so badly his teeth chatter. His little body spasms as fear rocks through him. "Come here. Hurry, Otto!"

But he won't budge. His heavy brows hide his eyes in dark shadows. I stretch my arm out, my fingers barely grazing his side. The bed is too low for me to slide under, so I try again, stretching my arm as far as I can. The bed frame cuts into my shoulder. Finally I curl my fingers around his front leg and tug him toward me. He pulls back, fighting me.

Behind me, a window shatters. I duck and shield my head. Glass flies and an unseen hand flies through the room, knocking over pictures, tables, chairs. With a final tug I pull Otto from beneath the bed, press him against my chest, and start to rise.

Thunk! The sound explodes in my head.

Black clouds snuff out my vision, and I feel myself falling, falling, falling.

IT'S A SWIRLING world, everything spinning out of control around me. It feels as if the house itself has been picked up and is being spun like a top. But I remain still. I can't seem to raise a hand or lift a finger.

Scratching, wavering sounds twitch around me. I can't grab hold of or understand the words, if they are such.

It's as if I'm in the eye of chaos and everything else orbits around me. I watch it all as if on a giant movie screen. My truck skids past, its bumper crunched, the side caved in, the yellow paint caked with dirt. Otto runs in circles, racing around, barking. I call after him, but he doesn't listen, doesn't mind. Then there's Momma.

"Momma!" I cry out.

She simply waves and goes on, busy as if on an important errand. Swinging on her arm is a basket of Easter eggs, a reminder of things I have yet to do for the hunt on the town square. Then Abby blows past in a bright red convertible, her long hair trailing behind. She cackles at the wind. Craig hobbles past me too. Neither seems to notice me. And I am left behind. Alone.

Then it all starts again, everyone coming around for another lap. When I try to call out, no one hears. They're busy doing their own thing. It's as if my life has stopped and their lives have gone on. I feel tired just watching them. Their motion exhausts me.

I'm so very, very tired.

Still there is no rest, no comfort, no peace.

Chapter Four

P opcorn. The smell of buttery popcorn peels back layer after layer of darkness, like shucking corn one section at a time. The odor is wispy like corn silk, difficult to grasp or make sense of. But I follow the scent, sniffing, feeling a deep emptiness in the pit of my stomach.

There's movement. A grayness. But a heavy weight presses me down, pulls me back. I'm certain that even one eyelash would be too heavy to lift, so I burrow back into sleep.

SWEET, TENDER VOICES—the voices of children— penetrate the cloud that enfolds me within its dark crevices. The voices seem far away, just out of reach. For a moment they grow stronger, as though marching toward me.

The words punch out, *"My God . . . big, strong, mighty!"* It's a song I recognize from teaching Sunday school. *"There's nothing my God cannot do"*—the voices become shrill on the final notes—*"for you!"*

My skin contracts. My ears vibrate. I try to pull inward once more, but the safe cocoon has disappeared. My eyelids flutter and light explodes through the darkness. Colors bloom around me, revealing surreal shades and textures.

Is this heaven?

Somewhere over the final rainbow?

A bridge to Ever After?

"Hey!" a rough-and-tumble voice blasts in my ear. A hand grasps me with a firm, steady grip. "You awake for real now?" It's a grating voice, deep and gravelly, which makes the face of the tiny woman more startling.

I blink, squint at her animated features. For a moment her face looks pink, too pink, as if rouge were applied with a heavy hand to her rounded cheeks. Red lipstick is slashed across thin lips, missing the lip line and bleeding outward in tiny dashes. The light in the room reflects off tiny blonde hairs along the woman's lip line. But her short-cropped hair has been dyed a color that borders on maroon.

She can't be more than four feet tall.

I shrink back from her.

"You're awake!" She states the obvious, then *humphs*, shaking her head, her mouth turning down at the corners.

I close my eyes and see stars twinkle across my eyelids. Prying them open again, I look around the room awash with colors vibrating and shimmering. It's as if I've entered a new world. Green plants with spikey and rubbery leaves surround me. A few are accented with flowers of all shapes, sizes, and

colors. Their brilliant hues of red, yellow, and orange capti-
vate me as if they're lit from within.

I open my mouth but can't think of how to answer, what
to say. Is she even speaking to me? But with her face so close
to mine, she couldn't be speaking to anyone else. She stares at
me. And then it's as if a switch clicks in my brain. I remember
who I am, as if I'm only a dream I forgot.

"Where?" my voice croaks. My throat feels dry, caked in
sand. My eyes ache and water from the harsh light.

"They say you're from Kansas."

I nod, or think I'm nodding. Maybe I'm only blinking.

"Well, you ain't there no more."

My brain feels sluggish, like it needs a good jolt of coffee.

"Me, I'm from all over. But don't know where exactly.
Traveled all my life." She leans forward and whispers, "Carnie."
Her stale, caffeinated breath puffs against my face—cigarettes
mixed with peppermint.

Words fail me, as if I'm digging through a bag searching
for some lost item yet can't even remember what I was looking for.

"Worked carnivals all my life. And circuses. Born in a
circus. My ma didn't remember which state I was born in."
She slaps her leg and laughs. "Heck, being the fat lady, she
could've been in two states at once." She throws back her
head and laughs so loud my head begins to throb. Finally she
sobers, leans close again, and studies my face.

I try to push up but am too weak, like my limbs weigh
more than they should. There's a pinch in my arm, my side.
Plastic straws . . . no, tubes . . . wind around and connect to
me. There's a murmuring sound. Musical notes. The sound
draws my attention to the corner of the room. A box . . .
a television . . . is mounted high on a ledge. There's a face

I recognize but cannot name. She's a girl. Bouncy. She smiles and sings about summertime.

"Better just lie there till Gloria comes."

My throat aches with effort. I look around at the unfamiliar yet cheerful room. I don't recognize the bright curtains, a mixture of blues, greens, and reds in a sort of swirling pattern that makes my head dizzy if I stare at it too long.

"Where am I?"

"Depends on who you ask." She laughs, a caustic tittering that grates on my nerves like a saw over metal.

"I don't under—"

"Oh, don't matter. You're in the Santa Barbara Retirement Center."

I push up on my elbow to get a better look around, and the room starts to spin again. I flop back onto my pillow, which is full and puffy like a giant marshmallow. "Tired."

"Don't you worry, hon. Thing is, it's a multiple living complex. Everything from the comatose to the just-need-help-with-medication."

What kind of medication is *she* on?

"The ads say 'Rainbow's End.'" She stretches her arm wide like a rainbow arcing through the sky. "Has a nice ring to it. Gives it a positive spin. 'There's no place like *our* home.' Get it? *Our* home." She winks. "Well, that's what the ads say anyway. Course, we know where this road ends. Well, not for *you*. You're young. But the rest of us are just waiting . . ."

I blink again, rub my hand against the rough sheets, and realize I'm wearing some sort of a gown. A papery thin gown. "How . . . ?" I can't seem to locate the words. Or maybe I'm simply too tired to finish. "How long . . . ?"

"How long have you been here? A week or so. Don't worry, you didn't miss much. Not much goes on in this place. Except for maybe a dance every now and then. Do you dance?"

I shake my head. It's easier than speaking.

The tiny woman huffs out a breath. "What? Guess you'll have to learn how with that purty pair of shoes sittin' there waiting for your tootsies." She waves toward a table by my side.

Scrunched up between two potted plants is a pair of shoes. A glittering red pair that I've never seen before. Or have I? I *have* seen them somewhere. My gaze drifts toward the television.

The woman beside me places a hand on my arm. Her skin is sweaty and coarse. "You can bet you'll have old men flirting with—"

"Maybelle, what are you doing in here?" A woman in a pale blue polyester uniform has entered the room.

"She's awake!" The odd woman points at me with a fat, stubby finger so close to my nose that it makes my eyes cross.

"I see that." The woman with sky-blue eyes and a crown of yellow curls smiles at me. "Hello."

I stare at her, my eyelids suddenly heavy as thick curtains. All I want to do is sleep. And so I do.

I'm not sure if I just doze or sleep for a long time, but when I open my eyes again, the same woman is there, the one with yellow hair and a bright, toothy smile. The other woman, the small, garish clown, is gone.

"This is good news!" She takes my hand, places a finger over my pulse point. Her hands are slim, soft, gentle. "That Maybelle, she's a character. She wasn't bothering you, was she? She wanted to come in here the first day you arrived. We didn't think it would hurt if she talked to you. And we thought it might give a break to some of the other patients who listen to her all the time." The woman bends closer and whispers. "Don't get me wrong. She's very nice, but she does talk a lot. You've had lots of visitors from the center—some curious, some wanting to pray for you."

I feel as if I'm pulling myself up out of a deep well. Part of me wants to just let go, fall back into darkness, and sleep some more. Another part of me scrambles, trying to latch onto something solid, a word or phrase.

"Do you remember your name?"

"Dottie." I touch my throat. "Hurts."

Sympathy makes her eyes darken. "It says 'Dorothy' on your chart, but I'll change it if you like 'Dottie' better. You haven't used your vocal chords in a while. It'll take a little time. How about an ice chip?"

I nod.

"Good. I'll be right back." She touches my arm as if to reassure me. "Don't go anywhere now."

My eyes droop closed, but when I open them again, she's back pressing a plastic spoon with ice chips to the seam of my lips, which feel dry and cracked. I open my mouth. The pleasure of cold, wet ice on my tongue makes my nerves tingle all over.

"Glen?"

She tilts her head as if trying to figure out what I want. "Oh, Gloria. I'm Gloria. And I'm here to take care of you."

"How long . . . ?" I can't seem to finish a sentence or thought. They're in my head, but getting them out takes more effort than I can muster.

"How long have you been here? A week."

I rub my temple, trying to remember. A flash of rain,

lightning, hail. The wind roaring. The window broke. "Storm?"

"No, sugar. It's been three months since that storm. You've been in a coma. At first the doctors thought you might come out of it pretty quick. But then you didn't. You were hit in the head by flying debris. That storm made national news."

"Otto!" the name explodes out of me. My throat burns.

The woman's kind blue eyes soften. "Who?"

"My dog. He . . ." My throat tightens. I can't speak the unthinkable.

She pats my arm and squeezes my hand. "We can ask your sister. Don't worry. We'll find out—"

"Abby?"

"That's right. You're doing excellent remembering. A very good sign. The doctors didn't think you'd have any permanent damage, but then you didn't wake up when they thought you should have. Your sister moved you here. She comes . . . or calls." Gloria takes a remote control from the side table. "*In the Good Old Summertime,*" she says, then turns off the television.

"Here?"

"California. It was too far for her to travel back and forth to Kansas. We're just a bit north of Los Angeles. When you're feeling better, you can go outside and look around. It's really a beautiful area. I'll call your sister right after I alert your doctor. She'll want to know that you're awake."

I clutch the nurse's hand. That tiny effort zaps my strength. "Home. Help me?"

Gloria sits down on the bed next to me and cups my hand in hers. "Don't you worry about a thing. You just concentrate on getting well."

I lean back into the pillow. I want to sink back into darkness but can't block out the truth. The house. Farm. The picket fence shredded by the wind. The roar pounding in my ears, the wind beating the shutters. I remember soft fur, a quivering body, my sweet little companion. Where is he? Dead? Lost? I close my eyes, too tired to think anymore. I curl inward. A song floats around my head, the notes just out of reach, the words forming rabbits that morph into an image of Otto sitting on the porch, waiting to be let inside.

THE DIRECTOR OF the facility has come to welcome me. "We didn't know if we'd have room for you until—"

"Until that ol' bat who lived in your room croaked," Maybelle interjects. She apparently follows the nurses around, entering whatever rooms she wishes. The brutal truth of nursing homes, I'm told, is that someone has to die to make room for the next resident. Die or get well enough to go home. Most don't go home. And I'm not sure what's left of mine.

"Well, anyway." The director coughs, her cheeks bulging and turning red. "We're glad you're here."

My mind drifts along with my gaze toward the window and the light. Colors play about like dust motes. Beneath the window, that pair of sparkly shoes waits patiently, as if encouraging me to get up and get moving.

A day or two later—I'm unsure of how many, as I sleep often—the feeding tube is removed. I overhear doctors saying to each other, "It's a miracle."

A miracle I'm here at all. A miracle I woke up. But do miracles really happen today, in Kansas? Or California? It feels more like a punishment to be here, alone, without Otto.

Chapter Five

I 'm unsure what day it is. I've lost track of time. Mornings and nights, afternoons and evenings are switched around like mismatched pieces of a jigsaw puzzle. My thoughts are often fuzzy around the edges. I've been moved into a new room since I don't require constant care.

I've become the novelty of the facility. A charity case actually. A number of the residents bring bits and pieces of clothing, a book or magazine. An older gentleman gives me the apple from his lunch tray every afternoon.

"Can't eat these," Harold tells me, his dentures shifting in his mouth.

I don't have the heart to tell him I'm only allowed applesauce at the moment. So I line the apples in the bottom drawer next to my bed, their deep-red skin shiny and inviting.

A hodgepodge collection of elasticized waistbands, flannel shirts, sweats, and orthopedic shoes gathers in my new closet. At least I don't have to wear a hospital gown any longer. A group of women who shop weekly together at a local mall collected a donation and bought me some underwear, workout bras, and a nightgown. "We weren't sure of your size, dear." The woman tried not to look at my chest.

"This is fine. Great. Thanks."

"And here are some socks with little rubber pads on the foot so you don't slip or fall."

Moved by their kindness, I'm reminded of my friends and neighbors back in Kansas who would have brought me these things if I were still there. It's then I wonder if any other farms or homes were damaged in the storm. But there's no one to ask, no one with the answers.

Gloria isn't my nurse anymore, but she comes to see me before and after her shift. She's not one to sit still, reminding me of Momma. Gloria tends my plants, snipping brown leaves and wilted blossoms. She's so young and yet purposeful in everything she does. Watching her makes me wonder if I've wasted my years. Life, I realize, is short.

"Why do you work here?" I ask. "With all these old people."

She straightens the covers at the end of my bed. "Oh, goodness, I don't know. I love what I do. I like helping people." She cocks her head to the side. "Maybe because I was raised by my grandparents. Maybe it's my way of giving back to them. Sometimes I just think it's what I was made to do. It's my purpose. Does that make sense?"

I remember Granny brushing my hair, tying it back with a ribbon which usually slipped out before the day was through. She had such capable hands, nimble fingers. When she spotted a rip in my jeans, she'd find a cheerful patch and whip-stitch around it in less than a minute. She hated the T-shirts I preferred and once stitched scratchy lace around the neck and sleeves of my favorite one.

Gloria turns on the television and finds a movie playing. "Have you seen this one?"

I stare at the screen, recognizing faces but unable to recall any names.

"You'll like it. Can't go wrong with Gene Kelly and Cyd Charisse. Have you seen *Brigadoon*? They wake up from a long sleep. Every hundred years."

"Sounds like my own life."

But the movie can't hold my attention, which acts like a kite on a string, hooking right, dipping low, soaring among the clouds, crashing into a tree of confusion. Yet it stirs up glimpses of times past—Granny sitting next to me on the sofa on a Sunday afternoon, an old movie playing on our bunny-eared television. "Look at the stitching on that bodice," I remember her saying. "That took some work, I'm telling you."

"Oops!" Gloria gasps. "Too much water." She tosses something onto the bed to save it from a dousing. The base of the potted plant overflows. She grabs paper towels near the sink and starts sopping up the mess.

My hand reaches for the shoe lying on my bed, the red hue vibrant against the white sheets. I touch the little round sequels . . . no, sequins. Granny made our Christmas stockings with bright-colored beads and sequins sewn on to spell our names. Abby liked to pretend they were her name in lights. I cup my palm around the short heel of the shoe. "Where did these come from?"

"A visitor. Did they get wet?"

"No. They're fine. But who—?"

"A gentleman, I believe. Signed in at the front desk, I'm sure. I can check for you."

I nod and balance the shoe on my palm. "These remind me of . . ." I can't locate the right words.

"The ruby slippers," she prompts.

"That's it."

She smiles. "I thought maybe they might mean something to you. Kind of an odd gift." She walks over and touches the red sequins.

"Momma," I manage. "No, my grandmother. Granny loved the movie." I look to Gloria for help.

"*The Wizard of Oz.*"

I nod. "She helped with it."

Gloria sits beside me on the bed, looking at me curiously.

I rub my forehead. "Maybe I'm remembering it all wrong."

Momma was prone to quote from the movie. "Your father's following his yellow-brick road" is how she explained our father's absence. "Abby is seeking her somewhere over the rainbow" described Abby's acting career. When we'd head off to school or church or the doctor, she'd sometimes warble, off-key, *"We're off to see the wizard!"* When I was sick and in bed, Momma would dab my forehead with a cool cloth and say, "There's no place like home, is there?"

"No place like home," I repeat now, giving the shoes to Gloria.

She smiles. "Movies are such a part of our lives, aren't they?"

"Frankly, my dear . . ." My smile feels a bit hollow at the moment.

She laughs. "You're really doing so well. You'll be out

of this place in no time." She gives my arm a gentle squeeze, then carefully places the shoes back on the table with all the other gifts, cards, and plants. "They're a nice imitation. Don't you think?"

"DUNCAN MEYERS," GLORIA tells me later that week.

I'm in the middle of eating one of the many small meals I'm allowed throughout the day. Small, mushy, and pretty much tasteless. At the mention of my father's name, my insides turn to mush.

"Do you know him?" she asks. "He has your same last name."

I can't speak for the tightness in my throat.

She rushes forward. "Are you okay? Choking?"

I manage to push down the lump of scrambled eggs. "He's my father."

"Oh! Of course. I wish he'd told us you were related. I remember he was very quiet." She touches a couple of envelopes on my side table. "Mail today?"

I nod, turn my head to the side, and stare out the window at the late-evening sun. It's a wide, flat orange circle.

"You okay?" she asks.

When I blink, the room around me turns psychotic . . . psychedelic . . . the colors in the room merging, everything haloed by that orange glow. "Sure."

I've waited thirty years for my father to come home, and when he does—well, not home, but here to see me—I'm not even awake.

"Did the physical therapist see you today?"

"Yes," I answer automatically.

"And the speech therapist?"

"Sure." I stare at the shoes that seem to glitter from across the room. "I have to go."

"What's that?" Gloria studies me. "The restroom, you mean?"

I shake my head. "I've wasted so much time."

My recovery becomes more purposed. I begin pushing harder, forcing myself further with each exercise. I concentrate during stretching exercises, my muscles straining, my limbs shaking and quivering, and I stare at those shoes, focusing, focusing.

When weariness overwhelms me, I think of Otto, what I must do, and I grow stronger. I force myself to breathe, in and out, in and out. A song floats out of the mist of my brain and wraps around me. The crazy sounds warp and fuse. One day, I remember Momma playing that album late at night after Abby and I went to bed. The cover was black with a prism of light. The haunting sounds wrap around me, and I focus on what I must do to get out of here.

Chapter Six

"She's progressing well." Gloria is speaking to someone in the hallway outside my door.

Within arm's reach is the walker I've begun to use. The flashy . . . fleshy part of my palms hurt from leaning almost my full weight on the handles. I stare out at the parking lot dotted with palm trees, and a yellow-brick walkway crossing the street beyond. The light plays tricks on my eyes.

"Can I go in?" A familiar voice turns my head.

"Craig?" I try to rise too quickly, and my hand slips on the arm of the chair.

A sharp bark makes my heart lurch. A dark streak scampers across the floor, tiny nails scraping and clicking against the linoleum. Suddenly Otto is in my lap, licking my face. Silky fur fills my hands, and I stroke the quivering body over and over, hugging him close. His feet press into my legs and stomach.

With a chuckle, Craig hobbles into the room, carrying a couple of boxes. "I thought you two would like to see each other."

"You," I cough to clear the emotion clogging my throat, "brought him from Kansas?"

"All the way. He's been staying with us. The kids kept him entertained. It didn't seem necessary to move him here while you were still in a coma. And Abby didn't . . ." He shrugs. "She was busy with a show, getting ready to go on tour, so she couldn't care for him the way we could. When we heard you'd woken up, I checked with the facility to be sure you could have four-legged visitors."

"I was so worried! No one told me. I thought . . . I thought . . ." Hot tears fill my eyes. I bury my face in the wiry fur.

"Your sister didn't tell you?"

"I haven't seen her."

Craig frowns and leans a hip on the end of my bed. "We found him at your side after the storm. The kids hate to see him go. They've grown very attached, so I guess I'm going to have to provide a substitute when I get home."

"It'll be good for them to have a pet."

He's grinning at me in a crazy fashion.

"What?"

"It's just so good to see you. You look great. You do." His voice turns husky and he coughs into his fisted hand. "We were worried about you."

"I'm sorry." I open my arms wide, welcoming a hug.

He smells of sunshine and, surprisingly, sugar. I want to hold on to him, a piece of home. Otto squirms between us, and I pat Craig on the back. When he backs away, I catch a glimmer of emotion in his eyes. Feeling awkward at the attention, I scramble for something to say. "Did Lindsey come?"

"She's with the kids at the hotel. It's a couple of hours south of here. We're taking them to Disneyland this week. Want to go? I'll get you some mouse ears."

I laugh, stroking the soft fur along Otto's back. He nuzzles my arm and licks my hand where tape once kept my IV attached.

"I brought you something. I hope you can eat it." He picks up a bakery box and sets it on the end of my bed. "If not, then I will." He winks.

"No you won't. I'm tired of mushy food."

"Maybe you should check with your doctor first." He peels back a sticker and lifts the lid.

Inside are a dozen peaks, like little mountains of snowy frosting. "Mugcakes!"

"Here," he says, "have a cupcake."

We share a red velvet cupcake, the cake so moist it slides right down my throat. It tastes like heaven. Otto gives me *the look*, and I let him lick the cream-cheese frosting off my fingers. As the minutes grow quiet between Craig and I, comforts of home give me courage to ask. "The farm is gone then?"

He turns and brings the other cardboard box and places it in my lap. Otto snuggles against my side, licking his paw. "This is all we could salvage."

Unable to speak, I stare at the small container. My home, memories, and life compressed to the size of a shoebox.

As I slide my finger along the pressed cardboard edge, Craig tells me of my friends and neighbors and the damage caused by the storm. My house was the only one demolished, as if the tornado had made a straight trajectory for it.

"It's a miracle," he says, "you two weren't killed."

My throat tightens.

"I should have stopped you that day from going back to the farm."

I attempt a laugh, but it comes out garbled and I end up coughing. "Don't do that to yourself. Don't feel guilty."

He gives a self-conscious shrug. "That little fellow there, he was found right next to you, refusing to leave."

I rub the tips of Otto's ears as a thank-you for his faithfulness.

"The house," Craig continues, "was a total loss. Randy took what furniture might be salvageable and is trying to fix it up in his spare time. The basement was flooded, everything ruined from mold and exposure. Folks from the church rounded up what we could find of your stock—a few chickens and pigs—and found them homes. The money collected is in that box. It will help make ends meet for a while." His mouth compresses into a pencil-thin line. The creases forming along his cheek tell me he'd like to withhold the next part, like a confession.

"It's okay," I say. "You can tell me."

I flash back to a time when our roles were reversed. I was eighteen and sat beside Craig on his hospital bed, his leg in a contraption of white bandages, metal bolts, and rods.

"It's over, isn't it?"

"What?" I asked, purposefully evasive. At the time I wasn't sure if he meant dating my sister or his boyhood dream of the big leagues.

"My baseball career."

I met his gaze, even though every ounce of me wanted to turn away. Shouldn't his parents or the doctors answer that question? They could throw big Latin words at him to soften the blunt reality. But he and I had always told each other the truth.

Your history paper sucked.

You played lousy. The team deserved to lose.

I love you, but not like that. Like a friend.

The pain and difficulty of speaking the truth couldn't make me break our unspoken pact. "There are worse things," I said, trying to encourage him. "At least your brains are intact."

"Yeah, but I know what I can't have. There's not much comfort in that."

I reached over and clasped his hand. He transmitted his pain, that deep sorrow in his heart, into my hand. I'm the one who cried, not him.

But today is different. Today, tears form in his eyes, held back by sheer will. "I did my best, Dottie." His voice crackles with the emotion I feel. "Abby was determined to get power of attorney. She was your nearest kin. There wasn't much I could do." He looks down at his thumb, picks at a hangnail. "But already I'm working to get it reversed, now that you're awake and alert and doing well. I'm gathering paperwork for the judge."

"I don't know how I can pay you for—"

He waves away my comment. "Don't think about it."

Needing to withdraw and regroup, I dab my eyes on the soft sleeve of the faded flannel shirt someone donated. Craig hands me a tissue, then touches my shoulder. My throat tightens. "So she sold the farm?"

His mouth thins, his hand tightens on my shoulder, grows weighty. "It's as good as sold. Goes on the auction block in a couple of weeks."

I feel as if I'm trapped in a room with no windows or door, searching for a way out. It's the same feeling I had when the doctors finally told me, "There's nothing else we can do for your mother." I wasn't raised by a wimp. My mother was strong. She taught me to be strong and resilient, and I'm going to fight for what is mine. "How do I stop the auction?"

Regret darkens his eyes. "I don't know that you can, Dottie. Abby already signed the paperwork. Even reversing her power of attorney doesn't change that."

"There's got to be a way."

"How much do you have in savings?"

I lean forward. "Why?"

"You could bid on your own property."

"I don't have enough for that. Or is there half a million in that box there?"

"Afraid not."

I lean back, my arms around Otto. "Even without the house or barns, the land is worth a few hundred thousand. Who'd even give me a loan right now?" It's as if the breath has been pulled from my very fiber. I stare out the curtained window. A slight breeze ruffles the giant leaves of a palm. The green edges are frayed, battered, torn. "There's nothing left."

Craig gentles his grasp on my shoulder, then pulls away as if he doesn't know what to do with my pain, as if it's too much for him to absorb. "Friends. You'll always have friends there. And memories." He reaches forward and pets the furry lump on my lap. "And don't forget Otto here."

A smile comes easily. I am grateful to have Otto back. But my smile fades. His brown eyes watch me anxiously as if he senses my panic, my fear. "What can I do then?"

Craig folds his arms over his chest. "First, you're going to get well. Keep making improvements. You're making extraordinary progress. Then you'll find new dreams. A new life."

"You make it sound easy. The farm is all I ever wanted." That and . . .

"There's more to life than land and crops, Dottie. So much more." At least when Craig lost his dreams of the major leagues, he was young enough to adjust. He had his whole life before him. I've wasted so much time.

"My father was here." I watch him carefully for his reaction, which is swift.

His eyes widen and his mouth gapes open for half a second. "What? When?"

"Before I woke up. I didn't see him. But now I know he's alive."

"I tried to find him, Dottie. When Abby was pushing for control. But the trail went cold in Seattle."

"But he came here. To see me."

"How do you know?"

"He left me those shoes." I point to the imitation ruby slippers. "Crazy, huh? You know, my grandmother worked on that movie." I shrug. "It's kind of weird, I know. But he signed his name at the front desk. He was here." I lean back in my chair, my hand idly rubbing Otto's neck. "I'm going to find him."

Craig pushes up from his seat on the edge of the bed and walks over to the window where the sunlight reflects off the sequins. "Could these be real?"

"Oh, I don't think so. I've been thinking about it a lot, and I think they were meant as a message. I think he was telling me to come see him. And I'm going to."

"WANT TO LOOK through your box?" Gloria asks, touching the package Craig brought.

I shake my head. "Not now." I can't imagine looking through what remains—what little there is—of my life, my heritage. No matter what's inside the box, it won't be enough. It will just remind me of all that was lost. And I have to focus on the future, on what might be waiting for me.

Then I remember about the money collected from the sale of livestock. "Is there a safe where I can keep some cash?"

"Sure."

I ask her to take the cash from the box, which is a bigger stack than I imagined, and put it in the director's safe. Gloria stores the box in the drawer beside my bed with my apple collection.

"These look good," Gloria says, peeking at the cupcakes.

"Help yourself."

She closes the lid. "No, you need them. Hey, I've heard of this place." She tilts the box so I can read the label. "Supposed to be excellent."

"Auntie Em's Kitchen. My friend brought them. They're good." But the odd name has my gaze shifting toward the ruby-red shoes and the music that swirls through my head like hypnotic lights. Then Craig's query about the shoes comes back to me. *Could these be real?*

"Gloria?" I call to her before she walks out of the room with the stack of cash. "Would you mind putting those shoes in the safe too?"

"Sure." She scoops them up. "They are pretty. Wish they were real. I remember reading about them. . . . You know, a pair of ruby slippers sold for over a half million dollars."

"You're kidding?"

"Nope." She hooks the heels on her arm and heads toward the door. "Too much sunlight can't be good for them. Don't worry. They'll be safe."

Pushing to my feet, I walk around my room, concentrating on each step. In my head, I hear the *cha-ching* of change being made and a song lopes into my consciousness. It's an odd song about money and makes my head bob in rhythm. It reminds me of Momma.

"Knock, knock." My doctor is a short, balding man with a friendly smile and reading glasses propped on top of his head for easy access. He walks in carrying my thick folder. "How are you feeling today?"

I laugh. "Good. I was just thinking about a song . . . something I haven't heard in years. Is that—" I hesitate. "Is that normal?"

"A head injury can cause some temporary rewiring of the synapses. You see, the neuropeptides break their connection within the dedrites . . ." He slides the folder onto the table where I eat my meals and studies me. "Think of your brain like a snow globe." He shapes his hands like he's holding a small ball. "When you shake it, everything gets stirred up in there—names, faces, experiences, even obsolete data you probably think you've forgotten, like the telephone number you had as a child. So old memories come to the surface, while recent memories may get lost in the shuffle. Sometimes it's harder to remember something current than something from your childhood. It'll take some time, but the brain is pretty adaptable. It'll sort things out eventually."

"And . . ." I hesitate to ask the question.

"What?" He has such kind eyes.

"Well, it feels like my life . . ." I can't find the right words. "A moving . . . movie . . . has taken a prominent role."

He slides his glasses on and opens my folder, scanning a page, flipping pages. "Sometimes with a traumatic injury like yours the brain will attempt to reboot itself, to make sense of its surroundings by randomly associating new stimuli with a familiar place or event with which you have strong emotional ties. What kind of movie?"

"A children's movie."

"Long as it's not *The Terminator* or *The Shining*, right?" He grins.

"Or *Some Flew Over the Kookaburra's Nest.*"

His grin broadens. "Nothing to worry about. I'm guessing this movie had some significance in your past."

"Granny used to talk about it a lot, about the different people she met while working in Hollywood. We watched it every year."

"Makes perfect sense. Again, it's nothing to worry about. You're progressing well. Still seeing strange colors?"

I nod.

"Your retinal tests came back just fine. Like I said, it's going to take some time for things to settle down."

I stare out the window at the brilliant blue sky. "When can I leave?"

"This isn't a prison." He clips a pen to his coat pocket. "If you want to get out and experience the beautiful weather or go shopping, the facility offers lots of opportunities. Your only restriction is how you feel."

I SENSE SOMEONE staring at me, and I wake with a jolt. My hand automatically reaches for Otto. He's laying beside me, his ears pricked upward, twitching. For a moment I'm not sure if I'm awake or just dreaming. My eyelids are heavy and my body relaxes until a shadow near the bed shifts.

"Is someone there?" I've become accustomed to nurses

and doctors coming in my room at strange hours. Or not so strange. I sleep at odd times.

"Do you have them?" an exotic voice says. It's a woman's voice, the consonants clipped and precise, the vowels slightly warped.

"What?"

"The shoes."

"What are you talking about?"

"The ruby slippers."

I rub at my eyes, try to see the woman more clearly, but she stands in the shadows, several feet from the bed in the corner of the room. "No, I—"

"You be careful then. Very careful."

I struggle with the sheets and blanket, pushing them off me, and slide my legs to the side of the bed. I reach for the lamp. The light flickers and glares, pooling an orangey light around my bed and chasing away the grayness. I turn toward the shadowy woman. "What are you—"

She's not there. I plant my feet on the floor, take a couple of hesitant steps, my hand pressing into the mattress to steady me. Was I dreaming?

I realize the door to my room is open. I close it, lean against it, and breathe slow and deep.

Chapter Seven

The drawer where I keep my collection of apples is open. I ate one before I turned out the light, but I didn't forget and leave the drawer open. Or did I? The doctor said my short-term memory would take time to recover. A closer look reveals the shoebox lid is ajar.

It's all that's left of my home, a few mementos, bits of scrap paper found after the storm. Gently I place it on the bed and sit down beside it. Otto walks around on the covers, watches me with weary eyes, his eyebrows heavy with concern.

I pick up the stack of papers and photographs from inside. There's nothing of value here. Nothing that anyone else would want. A rusty screw rolls along the length of the box. Along the bottom are bits and pieces—a silver dollar, a pair of sunglasses with one lens missing, a bent fork, a yellowed die, a crusty ribbon from a high school football game. Nothing of significance and yet all more precious to me since this is all that remains.

Picking up a dull penny, I rub the pad of my thumb over the engraved face and date, close my eyes. Bits and pieces of memories roll through my mind until I crumple my features in an effort to block out the images. When I open my eyes, the penny is hidden within my tight fist.

I recognize Momma's careful handwriting on a torn envelope. Whatever was once inside is missing now. My fingers glide over her lettering, the smeared ink. The address means nothing. I skim over the name, which I don't recognize. Finally, I set the envelope aside.

One by one, I look through a handful of black-and-white photographs. Some are yellowed from age, others splotched and dotted with water damage. There's a color picture of Abby and me in our pajamas on Christmas morning, our hair in sponge curlers, eyes bright with excitement. Behind us the Christmas tree leans precariously toward the window. We helped Momma pick it out at Ernie's tree farm. The trunk was so crooked, we finally hammered a nail in the wall and attached a string to the top of the tree.

There's a black-and-white of Momma in her teens holding a baby pig. I flip the picture over and on the back is the date—May 1965. Looking back at the picture, I study her smile, her smooth complexion, capable hands that hadn't yet been worn down by hard work. Her long skirt hides her polio-withered leg. She didn't know what lay ahead for her, the hardships of the future.

The next picture stumps me. At first the man is a stranger to me, but then I recognize him. It's the eyes, his smile, which is slightly slanted to the left. A young version of my father. *What does he look like now?* If only I'd been awake when he came to see me. If only . . .

My chest tightens. When I was four, I called him Daddy. Abby was a couple of years younger than me, young enough not to remember. I stare at his smile, recognize the cowlick in his forehead as my own. Abby has his chin, his straight teeth. He was an undeniably handsome man. For a time I imagined he was a prince or a knight who would ride in and save me from a spelling test I wasn't prepared for, or to declare me a princess and therefore worthy of some boy's attention, or to rescue me from Tommy Parker who pressured me in the back of his father's Buick.

But wishing never worked out so well. My father never rode in on a steed or even in a dilapidated clunker.

Other times I imagined he was a tattooed biker, sitting in prison, or a snarling monster like Hannibal Lecter, trying to convince myself that it was a good thing he'd left. *We* didn't want *him*, not the other way around. But the truth, I've always known, lay somewhere in between.

In this picture, the wind ruffles his sandy hair. His shirt is open at the collar, revealing a hint of a white undershirt. His sleeves are rolled up, showing muscular forearms. He's leaning back against a fence, his elbows propped on the top rung, his hands dangling. I can't remember his hand smoothing my hair, holding mine, or teaching me how to tie my shoes. I do remember the warmth of his touch against my ear, then quick as a flash he'd show me a coin, usually a penny, sometimes a quarter, that he'd pulled from behind my ear. My childish heart longs to lean into that hand, to know him. My adult, analytical brain wonders what he's like. Who he voted for in the last election. Does he save money like me? Or squander it like Abby? Does he like football? Baseball? Women? Does he have a girlfriend? Another wife? Other children? The questions pile up like the coins I collected at his expense.

Beside him in the picture is a woman I don't recognize. She wears her hair pulled back in a pony tail. Her face is young and fresh, scrubbed and buffed with an inner glow. She has a hand on my father's shoulder, as if she leans on him more than he leans on her. Or maybe she's trying to take hold of him in some way. The resemblance between them is clear. They share the same cowlick, the same nose.

The writing on the back of the photograph isn't Momma's. The ink is waterlogged, forming a purple halo around each line and stroke. It reads, *Liz visits on her way to California.* The woman must be my father's older sister. From some forgotten drawer in my brain, I pull an old memory of my father telling me about Aunt Liz. "She knows what she wants, she sure does. All of us Meyers do." Abby sure knew what she wanted. So what's wrong with me?

But I *did* have a dream. A dream I was scared to believe in. I wasted so many years waiting for him, looking down that empty driveway. Since the tornado, I've learned that life is unpredictable and often shorter than we expect. No more waiting. If I want something, I have to go after it.

When I was young, I told a friend, "My daddy's dead." Momma overheard and corrected me. "Dottie, that is not true." But I wanted it to be true. Because that was easier to accept, a handy explanation for why he never came home.

Abby concocted her own tale, telling a friend, "Our daddy bumped his head and forgot where he belongs. It's called ambinesia."

"Amnesia," I corrected, but I liked her idea better. A live father could find his way home one day.

But Momma heard about our stories. "Girls," she said, "you can't lock up a bird and expect him to like it. Love means letting go. If he comes back of his own accord, then he might just decide to stay."

I pick up the envelope with Momma's writing and read the address again. San Francisco. Then the name, *Mrs. Elizabeth Turney*. Elizabeth? Could that be Aunt Liz's full name? Her married name?

A strange emotion flows through my veins. It feels like anticipation . . . almost excitement over the possibility. The hope buried inside me begins to burns brighter. Maybe she knows where my father lives.

WITH DETERMINATION, I take one step after another. Sunshine pours in through windows, making me squint and turning the tiled floor a daffodil yellow. I've set aside the walker and now use the wooden support railing that runs along every wall when I need it. I push myself harder, trying to keep up with Otto. He scurries around my legs and often races ahead of me, nudging a greeting to those he meets, barking at others. I've lost him for the moment.

"Good morning, Dottie." Harold plays dominoes at a square table.

"Who's winning?" I ask.

Four sets of dentures smile at me. "I am!" they each say.

"Have you seen—"

"That way." Carl Rogers—or is it Roper?—tilts his head toward the side indicating the direction Otto took.

"Thanks." I turn down a hallway.

"Dottie!" Marge Shepherd calls. A smiling woman in a

blonde wig, she's recovering from chemotherapy. "I always wanted to be a blonde," she told me when we first met. She sits with a group of knitters. Their needles *click* and *clack* with urgency. "How are you?"

"Good, thanks." I have one of Marge's creations, a bright-red lap blanket, on the foot of my bed. "Have you seen—"

"Otto came by and gave all of us some sugar." Patty Simmons adjusts her reading glasses. "You'll be moving as fast as him soon."

"You won't be with us long." Bernice Young waggles her double chin. "Sure hope you come back to visit."

"I will." Then I spot Otto sitting at a side entrance, his barely-there tail twitching in anticipation.

I push open the door that leads to the courtyard and Otto bolts forward. He races between the shuffling feet of a group of women who are on their way to the shuttle bus for an excursion to a nearby mall. It's a warm summer day, a California day, with blue skies and warm breezes. Along the path delicate pink flowers are blooming. The courtyard is lush and green and reminds me of the fields back home.

"You should go shopping with us, Dottie!" someone calls out.

I sit on the nearest bench to catch my breath. "Next time."

The sunshine feels good on my upturned face. When Otto finally plops down in the grass, panting beside me, I'm reminded that he needs water. I push to my feet and begin the long trek back to my room. The runway . . . hallway . . . is empty as everyone has gathered in the lobby to hear a singing group. The children, seven of them, sing and dance on a makeshift stage, sectioned off by potted plants. The residents clap their hands in rhythm (and not), nodding their heads, smiling.

Now where did Otto go? I glance around my feet. A UPS delivery guy turns down a hallway near the main desk. Behind him, a flash of a tiny gray tail. I follow at a much slower pace, pausing to listen for Otto's nails against linoleum.

Soon, my heart pounding from exertion, I approach a tiny alcove. I pause at the doorway and lean against the frame, somewhat disoriented, as if I've been playing pin-the-tail-on-the-donkey and my mask was whisked off suddenly. The hallways and rooms all look so similar. Then I catch a whiff of roasted corn. It's dark inside the room, but as my eyes adjust I notice a jumble of books crammed into shelves. A sign reads, *Take your chance . . .* no, *choice . . . but please return.*

"Otto!" I whisper, hoping he'll hear me and come of his own accord. With a huff, I shove my too-long bangs away from my forehead and peek behind a sturdy reading chair. Something crunches beneath my tennis shoe. I squint down at a smattering of popcorn.

"Who are you looking for?" A splintered voice comes out of the gray shadows and startles me.

I whirl around and see in the murky light a figure, tall and lanky, standing on a stepladder. Her arms are long and as skinny as twigs. She wears a wide grin beneath a mop of straw-like hair that sticks out in all directions.

"My dog. He went this way, I think. But I'm not sure."

"Like most folks these days. Everybody wants to go their own way." Her funny expression makes me want to laugh.

"I'm Dottie."

"I'm a bit confused myself." She offers a hand for me to shake, squeezing the tips of my fingers rather than my whole hand. "Sophia. How do?"

"Fine, thank you."

"You can't be *too* fine or you wouldn't be here. And I'm certainly not fine. I'm, well . . ." She turns slightly away from me. She's wearing a long blue chambray shirt belted around a full crinkled skirt that's elevated a few inches in the back. Following the slant of the flowing material, I notice the real problem. The gauzy skirt is pinched in the ladder joint and she's stuck.

"Can I help you?"

"I don't know." She twists, trying to get a better view of her predicament.

"Should I call an attendant?"

"Oh, no. I'll just get in trouble again."

"Again?"

"You don't want to know." She grabs a crinkly sack of popcorn off the shelf, pops a couple of kernels in her mouth and offers the bag to me. "Hungry?"

"No thanks. Were you looking for a book?" I edge around the ladder and tug on the material.

She holds up a gray lightbulb. "Trying to be helpful."

I reach out, and she places the burned-out bulb in the palm of my hand. I set it on a lower shelf and flip on the light switch by the door. Light scatters the dark. The colors pop out at me as if they're playing peek-a-boo. Sophia blinks down at me.

"Let's see what we can do about this. I don't want to rip your skirt."

"I'm not the brightest bulb in the drawer . . . but if we could close the ladder it might release me."

"You'll have to step down first." I take her hand.

She takes a hesitant step downward, pointing the toe of her flat shoes as she does. Her skirt rises higher in the back. She wobbles. Her eyes grow wide.

"I won't look. I promise."

"Believe you me, there are plenty of widowers in here who would."

Laughing, I help her down the last two steps. She remains on tiptoe. "Hold on now," I place her hand on my shoulder, "while I try to close the ladder." The material pops loose, and Sophia tumbles forward. I shriek a warning and grab for her but miss. She lands with a *whoosh* in an old upright chair. Popcorn flies out of the bag.

I let go of the ladder, which bangs against a bookshelf, and rush to her, crunching bits of popcorn into the carpet. "Are you okay?"

"Oh, sure." The corners of her eyes tilt downward. Her wide mouth twists. She kicks her legs out in front of her and rolls her ankles. "Boy, it feels good to be free."

"How long have you been up there?"

"I'm not sure. The lights were out and no one came in for a long time." She waves a hand. "No nevermind now."

"You could have hurt yourself."

"Oh, I'm fine." Sophia grins, then looks down at herself. "Oops!" Her breasts appear to be lopsided. One of them now rests at her waist. She grabs the lump, shifts it into place, and laughs. "My stuffing leaks out sometimes." Seeing my confusion, she adds, "I had surgery. You know, breast cancer. Complete mastectomy. Sometimes my manufactured parts go awry."

"Oh, I'm sorry." I avert my gaze. "I—"

She adjusts her clothes, pulling and shifting material this way and that, then pats her hips and arms. "Still, I'm pretty agile, if I do say so. For my age."

I don't ask her what age that might be. Momma raised me to be polite. But Sophia doesn't look nearly as old as some of the folks in this facility.

Her gaze roams over me as if searching for a badge or some reason for my existence. "You work here?"

"No. I'm . . . well, I was searching for my dog."

"You one of those people who bring their animals for us to pet?"

"No, I live here."

The clicking of tiny nails against linoleum makes me turn around. Otto rounds the corner and instantly heads for the scattered popcorn, licking at the carpet, sniffing around for more bits. I scoop him up into my arms and introduce him to Sophia.

"I wasn't much help to you, was I?" Sophia offers Otto a fluffy kernel off the palm of her hand.

"I wouldn't say that. The smell of cracked corn—" I pause, shake my head. "That was wrong. Um . . . popcorn. It lured Otto to us. So you were a huge help."

"I'd like to believe that. It's so hard to feel useful in this place. No one seems to need me anymore."

"That's not true! You changed the lightbulb. Maybe you could help me keep an eye on Otto. He runs off all the time. I spend most of my time walking around looking for him. Of course, the walking is good for me."

"An optimist, are you? I like that." She rubs Otto's dark furry head. "He's a curious little wanderer, is he?"

"More like trouble."

"But you love him very much."

"Most definitely."

"That's good. That's important. My daddy always said, 'Everyone needs someone to love.'"

But did he mean only a dog? The fact that my sole companion is Otto makes for a sad commentary on my life. Not that I've thought much about that over the years. It's just how things worked out. I wonder if Sophia has someone, or if she's alone. Like me.

She peers closer at me, wrinkling the skin between her eyebrows. "You're awfully young for a place like this. Or do you have a wizard of a plastic surgeon?"

I laugh. "I was in a coma. Now I'm recovering."

Her eyes widen. "Oh, of course! I visited you. You look different with your eyes open, minus all the tubes and such."

"You visited me?"

"Prayed for you." She pats my arm. "Worked, didn't it? Look at you now!"

Prayers to me are like wishing on haystacks. "Well, I don't know about—"

"Sure it did. Don't get all practical on me now. We see what we want in this life. Don't get me wrong, I'm not taking credit. I'm not smart enough to do something wonderful like that. But even someone like me can believe."

"Is that all it takes?"

"To move a mountain." She pops more popcorn into her mouth and chews. "You walk all the way from the Blue Building?"

"I'm not there anymore. They've moved me since I'm more motivational." I frown.

She laughs. "You are that! A miracle for sure." She hooks her arm through mine. "But I think you meant 'mobile.' Come on, I'll walk you back. Where are we?"

"You don't know?"

"Tell you the truth, I get lost in this place all the time. Plays with my sense of direction, which is much better out of doors." She looks at the room number on the plaque outside the door then peeks back inside as if she forgot something.

She scratches her head, a frown deepening the wrinkles lining her forehead. "Sometimes my son thinks I've lost my brain." She leans close. "He might be right."

"Lost it?" A smile tugs at my lips. "Then we make the perfect pair. Where could it have gone?"

She chuckles and pats my arm, then rubs Otto's head. "I like the way you think."

Chapter Eight

"Someone's looking for you, Dottie," Chuck Wyler says as he joins a group of senior residents watching *Antiques Roadshow*. They're planning a trip to Seattle with all their personal heirlooms in tow for an upcoming show.

"Thanks, Chuck." I concentrate on Wii bowling, which has become a popular sport at the facility. To me, it's a way to work on regaining my balance and coordination. I left Otto in my room because my pooch has a tendency to get under my feet and trip me. Sophia and Maybelle sit on a nearby sofa sharing a coconut cupcake.

I click the button on the Wii remote, step forward, pull my arm back as if I'm holding a bouncing—no, bowling— ball and let it go. The virtual pink ball rolls in slow motion down the alley on the screen but hooks left and winds up in the gutter.

"You're twisting your arm," Maybelle advises from her armchair view. "Give it some power, girl! And keep your wrist straight."

I retrace my motions. This time, I throw the "ball" over my head and make all the Miis behind me jump and spin.

"Try again." Maybelle leans forward, her elbows on her dimpled thighs, watching my every action with the scrutiny of an Olympic coach. "Go faster."

"You have to go slow," Sophia contradicts.

I step toward the TV, release the virtual ball, and watch it roll toward the pins at a pokey pace. It's as if time slows as the ball has little momentum. But then it strikes the first pin. The rest topple, bumping and knocking into each other until not one is left standing.

"Whoo-hoo!" Maybelle raises her arms in triumph.

Sophia claps.

Someone from the *Antiques Roadshow* crew says, "Keep it down."

I punch the air, turning and freezing with my arm raised high at the sight of a strange man watching us. Watching me. Slowly, I retract my arm.

The man wears a navy suit. Suddenly self-conscious, I tug at the hem of my shirt. Sophia and Maybelle compliment my spare, and I clear my throat to get their attention.

"Excuse me," the man says, his tone clipped, "I'm looking for a Miss Dorothy Meyers."

My eyebrows arch. My friends look at me. He's about my age, but I don't recognize him. And apparently, he doesn't know me either. I give a slight wave of my hand, like I'm in school again. "That's me."

"Could I have a word with you in private, miss?" He has a crisp New England accent.

I hesitate. "What about?"

"Official business, ma'am." He pulls a black wallet from his breast pocket, flips it out, then back, and slides it back into his pocket. "FBI."

"Oooh! You're in trouble." Maybelle's heavily made-up eyes are big and round. Her faded lipstick-stained lips pinch together.

The man does look official, with a government haircut and plain suit. He's relatively nondescript as if he could be anyone, fit into any crowd. Except for the blue suit, which doesn't fit in here at the extended-care facility. Scrubs, warm-ups, or pajamas are the usual attire. Only preachers and funeral directors wear suits here.

Feeling my stomach contract, I motion to the doorway that leads to the hall. "We could go down to my room."

"That'll be fine, ma'am."

Maybelle starts to rise.

"It's okay." I motion her back.

We pass Frank Porter sitting in the hallway in his wheelchair. He saves French fries from his lunch for Otto. "I hear your dog whining, Dottie. Aren't you going to let him out?"

"Later," I say, aware of the FBI man behind me.

Opening the door, I nudge Otto back with my foot, then decide it might be better to hold him. He rubs the top of his head against my chin. But his body stiffens when he sees the FBI agenda—um, agent—behind me. "Shh, it's okay. No barking."

The agent closes the door, cutting me off from the rest of the facility. My nerves jangle a warning, but I silence them. This is probably about the tornado. Or maybe the upcoming auction. "What can I do for you?"

"Do you know Abigail Meyers Edgerton?"

I sit in the chair by the window, not offering the only one I have to my guest who is not really a guest. "Of course. She's my sister."

He nods and jots something down in a palm-size notebook he's pulled from his jacket pocket. "And do you know her current location?"

"Not really. No."

"Her residence?"

"L.A."

"Address?"

It surprises me that I don't know. I never memorized her address but had it written down in my address book at home. Which was probably lost in the storm. "I lost all my records in the storm. The facility here may have that information, Mr. . . ."

He gives a slight nod. "I see. And—"

"What's wrong?"

"We are seeking Ms. Edgerton—or does she go by Meyers?—for questioning. When was the last time you saw her?"

"I'm not sure. She visited me here while I was in a coma, I believe." Suddenly I wonder if that's the reason I haven't seen her. Does she know our father has been here? Is she trying to find him too? I rub my temple, wish my brain was working at full capacity.

The man scribbles something in his notebook. He walks along the length of my bed, his brown shoes scuffing the linoleum as he comes to a halt. He stares out the window for a moment and crosses his arms over his barrel-sized chest, brushing a waxy leaf on the potted plant beside him. "You seem like the type who wants to cooperate." He turns and settles his gaze on me. His eyes, narrowly set in a square face, are the color of toasted wheat. "It's about the shoes, ma'am."

"Shoes?" I swallow hard, give my head a shake as if I've misheard.

"The ruby slippers. Do you know where they are?"

My skin contracts and heat rushes to the surface. "I . . . uh . . ." My hand cups my forehead.

"Do you know why your sister might have an interest in the shoes?"

I can only stare at this man. Words fail me.

"The shoes, Miss Meyers, are considered stolen property."

"Stolen property?" I repeat the words as if trying to decipher their meaning.

"Crossed state lines. A pair was stolen from the Judy Garland Museum in Grand Rapids."

None of this makes sense. Words and phrases twist around in my head and hog-tie my tongue.

"Ma'am?"

I blink.

"Are you okay?"

I shake my head. Or do I nod? My ears vibrate with the pounding of my pulse.

He waits a minute or two, I'm not sure how long. Finally, he scribbles something on a piece of notebook paper, rips it from the spiral, and hands it to me. "This is serious business, Miss Meyers. If you learn of anything, don't hesitate to call. Day or night."

"WHAT DID THAT man want?" Maybelle has appeared in my doorway.

I feel numb, unsure how long I've been sitting and staring out the window.

"Are you okay?" Sophia follows Maybelle.

"What did the FBI want with you?" Maybelle gives a half hop and settles on top of my bed like we're about to have a slumber party. "You kill somebody?"

Sophia sits on the footstool next to me. "You're cold." I glance down and see she's holding my hand between her long tapered fingers.

"Should we call the nurse?" Maybelle's dyed eyebrows slant into a frown.

Sophia chafes my hands gently. "Just frazzled, I'd say. Did that man say something to upset you, Dottie?"

I blink as if coming out of a stupor. "He wanted to know about the ruby slippers."

Sophia's features crumple into confusion.

"The ruby slippers from *The Wizard of Oz*?" Maybelle's eyebrows shoot upward. "Those shoes—"

"I have them." Panic takes hold of me, and I glance toward the door "Shut it, will you?"

Sophia does, coming back to my side. "I'm not sure I'm following you."

I motion for my friends to move closer and whisper, "I have a pair of ruby slippers. Someone left them here while I was in a coma. I think it was my father." Pushing up from the chair, I pace the room. "I have to get out of here. I have to find out what's going on."

THE CURSOR BLINKS at me, waiting, expectant. The computer in the recreation room is available to any resident. It takes my fingers a while to remember how to type. I punch in

75

my father's name: Duncan Ernest Meyers. When that doesn't yield any clear results, I remove the middle name and try again. There are a few hits, and I check each one, but none match. I narrow the search to Seattle, but still I come up with nothing.

Then I attempt to find Elizabeth Turney. With Otto sitting in my lap, I Google my aunt and find seventeen women listed by that name. I study birth dates and narrow down the year of her birth and approximate age to rule out all but one.

It's a quick click to her obituary.

Something inside me compresses.

Born in 1942 in Kansas, this Elizabeth Turney would have been slightly older than my father. Her maiden name of Meyers is listed, as are her closest relations: her husband of thirty-eight years, Tim Turney, and one brother, though his name is not mentioned.

I click on a link and study a photo gallery of Elizabeth Turney, which I then compare to the picture in my possession. I'm positive it's the same woman. Whoever she is, she knew my parents at some point. Maybe her husband did too. It's the only lead I have.

Tim Turney lives in San Francisco. His phone number is unlisted, but I jot down his address and now have a destination in mind.

I WALK BACK to my room, Otto prancing at my feet, circling me, darting in and out of rooms. There's a commotion of voices up ahead, and Otto races ahead of me.

Maybelle barrels out of my room, her usually garish face pale, arms waving.

"What's wrong?" I ask.

"She's here! She's back. And she's mad!"

"Who?"

"Don't go in there!"

Has Maybelle mixed up her medication? Otto's barks are louder, more insistent. Breathing hard, I stumble into my room.

"Can you get that yapping dog to shut up?" Abby's appearance startles me. Her hair, now red, is curly and teased about her head. She wears expensive, silver-studded jeans and a simple, white, too-tight T-shirt and pointy-toed heels.

"Nice to see you too, Abs. I'm doing fine, thanks."

"You certainly look better than the last time I saw you. You looked like a corpse!" She shivers then plops onto the end of the bed and crosses her long legs. "When are you getting out of here?"

It's then I notice the closet door is open. When I left, it was closed. I think. But I can't be sure. "What are you doing here, Abby?"

"I came to check on you. After all, you're my ward."

"Call off the sale of the farm, Abby."

"Dottie, much as I'd like to, I can't. I already signed the papers agreeing to the sale. I know you don't like it, but there are medical expenses. While you've been lounging around here, I've been stressed and working, trying to pay all the bills. Just to get the farm cleared of debris took quite a bit."

I cross my arms over my chest. "You couldn't be too concerned with how I'm doing. You haven't been to see me once."

"That's not true. I was here when you arrived. Since then, the nurses have kept me informed. I've been busy with this show. Earning a living. It's been such a success that we're taking it on the road. We leave at the end of this week."

Which is my goal too. But I don't bother to tell her that.

"Craig is stirring up all sorts of trouble." Her frown deepens. Maybe it's the lighting or my imagination, but there's a tint of green to her skin.

"It's his job."

She flicks her raging red hair over her shoulder. "I don't have a problem with that. I don't want to tell you what to do. Now that you're all right, you can make your own decisions. I did what I had to do. Of course, I wanted to protect you. Take care of you. You *are* my sister."

I stare at her, unblinking, unmoved by her feigned devotion.

Her eyes soften at the edges. "I care about you, Dottie. I—"

"Uh-huh." Why don't I believe that? "What do you want, Abby?"

"Nothing."

Moving toward my bed, I run a hand down the side, taking great care with each step. Abby swivels around to face me. From this angle I can see into the closet, how the clothes have been pushed to the side. Someone has been rifling through my things. Pulling open the drawer in the bedside table, I grab the box Craig brought me. "Is this what you want? It's all that was left after the storm."

Her eyes brighten, and she reaches for the box.

I yank it back and tuck it under my arm.

Her hand swipes the empty space between us, her long nails like talons.

My suspicions are confirmed. Behind her, Craig stands in the doorway, waiting, watching. He said he'd come by to see me before returning to Kansas. His face is sunburned, as is his scalp, which shows through his thinning hair. A stuffed animal dangles from his hand, hanging loose at his side.

Fortified now, I glare at my sister. "What do you want, Abby? You were searching for something when you came to the farm last time. And now here today. In fact, some guy from the FBI was here and wanted to talk to you."

She blanches, her skin stretching over her cheekbones. "The FBI? What did he say?" She glances over her shoulder toward the door. "What did he want? Did he mention," she takes a step toward me and lowers her voice, "the shoes?" Her eyes round and she points a finger at me. "He did! What did he say?"

"That they're stolen property."

"He was bluffing. You can't trust—"

"What is this about?"

She turns away from me. "Momma's ruby slippers. Well, they were originally Granny's. She worked on the movie. Maybe you've forgotten with that head thing of yours."

"I remember." But did I forget Momma's telling me about a pair of ruby slippers? I don't think so.

Craig steps into the room. His usual affable expression has given way to a look almost as menacing as Abby's. "Abby," he says in his best authoritative manner, "what's going on here?"

"Oh, great. Are you going to slap me with a lawsuit or something?"

"What's going on here?" Gloria soars into the room. Her face is flushed, her blue eyes bright, as if she's been running. "Maybelle said—"

"I'm checking on my sister." Abby places her hands on her slim hips. "Seeing if you're taking care of her or if—"

Gloria laughs. "You have no power here. Dottie's attorney just submitted papers giving her back all of her rights."

Otto punctuates her words with his own bark, then a low menacing growl.

Abby grabs the red lap blanket off the end of the bed and throws it on top of Otto. The blanket covers him completely. Under the knitted yarn, his body makes a little wiggling, squirming lump.

I jump up too fast, feel a wave of dizziness. My knees weaken and I sit down hard on the bed.

"Go away." Gloria steps between Otto and Abby. "I won't allow you to upset my pa—"

"Very well." She glares at me, her green eyes flashing. "But I'll be back."

Otto barks again, the sound muffled by the blanket.

Abby turns on her heel, swooshing her long hair over her shoulder, and is gone before I can catch my breath.

Gloria whisks the blanket off Otto, folds it, and sets it on a shelf in the closet. "She's gone now," she tells Otto. "You're safe."

"Abby does like to make an entrance." I stare at the empty space my sister occupied. "And exit."

"All she needed was fire and smoke." Craig puts an arm around my shoulder. "You okay?"

I nod.

"Did she look green to you?"

I attempt a smile.

He hands me the stuffed animal from Disneyland. It's a purplish monkey with a long, curling tail and a funny-shaped hat on its head. "The kids picked it out. It's from a movie, I think."

"It's Abu." Gloria takes hold of my wrist and checks my pulse. "From *Aladdin*."

Craig limps over to the chair by the window and sits, the cushions making a puffing sound as air *whooshes* out of the cracks in the plastic edging. "So what's this about a pair of shoes?"

"Slippers, actually. The ruby slippers from *The Wizard of Oz*." I rub Otto's soft chin.

"I looked them up on the Internet." Gloria rearranges the plants and cards on my bedside table. "No one knows where all the shoes are."

"There's more than one pair?" I'm not sure if my brain is on the fritz again or if this conversation is just so fantastical, so bizarre, I can't fully grasp it.

"No one knows how many pairs of ruby slippers were made," Gloria continues. "Apparently, when movies are filmed, they usually make several identical costumes for the lead actor. You never know when there might be a rip in the material or if there's a scene where they get wet and several shots are required. The same goes for shoes. Especially when the actor or actress is dancing. Why, Cyd Charisse could go through many pairs from rehearsal to filming each dance scene."

"What else did you learn about the slippers?"

Gloria tosses away an empty water cup. "One pair was made exclusively for the close-up at the end of the movie when Dorothy clicks her heels and says—"

"There's no place like home." The words come out before I contemplate them. My throat tightens as I remember the front porch where Momma and I would sip coffee in the morning, watching the bird feeder where flocks stopped on their way south. Longing swells inside me. Maybe, just maybe, I can find my father and save the farm too. I could rebuild the house.

"How much could a pair of shoes like that be worth?" Craig asks, meeting my gaze and seeming to understand exactly what I'm contemplating.

"They're part of our culture." Gloria hands me a cup of water. "One of a kind."

"Or five of a kind." Craig winks.

"There's a pair in the Smithsonian," Gloria continues. "A couple of folks own pairs privately. Another pair was stolen from the Judy Garland Museum. One woman won a pair in a contest in 1939."

So the agent *was* after the shoes. But if Abby stole them, why would she be looking for them now? Or did my father—?

"The last time a pair was auctioned off," Gloria breaks into my thoughts, "the shoes were sold for more than $600,000."

My back straightens. "Say that again."

Craig meets my gaze. "Six hundred thousand possibilities."

"But wouldn't another pair just make them worth less?"

"Not necessarily. It would depend on many factors, like the condition they're in. Or whether they were actually worn by Judy Garland."

My heart starts pounding with anticipation. "Would my shoes realistically sell for that much money?"

Gloria picks a brown leaf off a plant sent to me by my church back in Maize. "Probably more."

"Inflation," Craig says.

"So that's what Abby's been after this whole time."

"What a woman won't do to find the perfect pair of shoes, huh?" Craig grins then grows serious. "The auction is in eight days. Not much time."

Chapter Nine

Craig says good-bye and promises to do all he can to stall the auction. I locate Sophia. "I need to talk to you." I think about the FBI agent who visited me, and that strange woman in the night. Not to mention my sister. "And I don't want anyone to overhear us."

Sophia hooks her arm through mine. "Let's walk down to the wharf. It's not too far."

Otto and Maybelle join us, and we walk along a red-brick street, crossing over to a sculpture of three dolphins leaping from a fountain surrounded by tall palm trees. The rush of water soothes my frazzled nerves as I tell my story.

"Why would she tell Abby about the ruby slippers and not me?" I ask the most perplexing question, the one that haunts and hurts me the most.

"Maybe because Abby was—is—an actress," Sophia suggests. "Mothers try to find common ground with their children. You shared the farm with your mother. I went to football and baseball games and rock-and-roll concerts with my son."

"My mother drank," Maybelle says as she lights up a cigarette.

I put an arm around her and stare at the dolphins arcing through the air. The sun glints off the blotched blue coating, making them shimmer with different rainbow hues. My mind drifts back to my childhood, before DVDs and videos, back when *The Wizard of Oz* was televised once a year. Abby and I would settle on the sofa with a knitted blanket and a bowl of Jiffy Pop popcorn between us. She hid under the blanket when the ugly green witch appeared, and I laughed at her. Momma would usually be in the kitchen cleaning up after dinner, folding clothes, darning socks. She was never idle, never one to just sit and watch a movie straight through.

Granny, before she passed on, would tell us stories of working in Hollywood. Demanding directors, insecure actresses, flamboyant and brilliant designers. She could look at a film and know exactly who the designer was: Adrian, Edith Head, Walter Plunkett. When Abby would pepper her with questions, she'd wave a hand and say, "That was a lifetime ago."

"The farm auction is set for Tuesday, one week from tomorrow," I say as we step onto the planks of Stearns Wharf. "But I can't just sell the shoes. I have to know where they came from, why my father gave them to me. If he . . ."

"Stole them?" Maybelle says what I can't.

"If I do sell them, then I might be able to save the farm."

"Your sister would get what she wants," Sophia adds.

"Money," Maybelle blows out a stream of smoke.

Sophia coughs and waves away the smoke. "And you'd

have your life back." She points to some wooden benches. "Do you need to rest?"

"I'm fine." Then I remember my friends are older than me. "Do you?"

Maybelle is the only one huffing, her short legs having to take two steps to our one, but she puffs her cigarette and keeps chugging forward.

I stare out at the ocean that stretches for miles in either direction, the blue hues shifting and changing. "It's going to take a miracle."

"Miracles happen." Sophia smiles, the wind making her hair stand out in all directions. "After all, you're alive and well."

Miracles. Wishes on haystacks. She might as well have said the wizard who lives in the Emerald City will help you. Which almost makes me laugh, considering all that's happening in my life.

It's not that I don't believe in God. I was raised in the church. I attended every Sunday, or at least I did before the tornado. Services take place here at the facility with local preachers from different denominations coming in on a rotating basis, but I haven't bothered. I showed up for church all those years, but God didn't show up for me when I needed him most. Does God really care what I do? Where I go? That I've lost everything?

I was raised believing God was all-knowing and all-powerful, able to see everything I did wrong, able to squash me like a pesky fly. Momma was accepting of God's will, as she called it. Or was it simple resignation?

Crippled from a bout of polio as a child, Momma never seemed to doubt God. Her faith, even when polio came back in a different form and stole the strength from her muscles, never wavered. What did she know or learn that I haven't yet?

I remember some verse my pastor used in a sermon or two, something about running and not growing tired, soaring like an Easter . . . eagle. Am I the one who's crippled? Spiritually, that is? If so, then maybe that's why I can't muster enough faith to believe in miracles.

Maybe God is simply absent from my life the way my father has been all these years. Perhaps my future is entirely up to me. But I wouldn't mind a little help from the Almighty if he's paying attention. So I toss up a prayer.

"I could use a little help down here."

THE BEACH IS crowded with older couples and young families. Children shriek at the chilled water, splashing and running. Otto noses around, sniffing and searching. Running a few feet ahead of me, he scampers back when the cold surf touches his paws. Sophia walks along beside me, quiet in her own thoughts, her sandals dangling from her fingertips. Maybelle marches off to find some refreshments.

Using a Popsicle stick, a sticky Coke can, and my cupped hands, I sit on the beach scooping and patting a rather lopsided California coastal map in the sand. Otto sits beside me, his tongue lolling out of his mouth, slobber dripping off the end of his tongue.

Sophia pushes her sunglasses to the top of her head. Sunlight turns her hair golden. "A Wii just isn't the same, is it? All that virtual stuff, it can't measure up to reality. It's fun to play around with and it does get you moving, but it doesn't compare to playing volleyball on the beach in the warm sun with the sand between your toes."

I smile at her. "Or the salty taste."

"Standing about in your house slippers can't slough

the dead skin off your heels either." She brushes sand from the bottoms of her feet.

"Neither can walking in someone else's shoes."

She tilts her head, studying me with an open curiosity.

"My sister said that's what I've been doing. Or was doing . . . before the tornado." I trail my finger through the sand, drawing a line and turning it into my name. "Most of the time, I guess, I was just trying to make a living, get by on what we had. Help Momma.

"There was always something to do. Days were long. During the school year, when I was teaching, I'd get up at 4:00 a.m. to feed the stock, do a little work in the fields. Then I'd shower and get to work. Some of my students worked for us during the summer." I shrug. "I thought it was a good life. It was hard, but I liked it." I scoop up a handful of warm sand and let the grains trickle down between my fingers. "What's wrong with that?"

"Nothing, Dottie. If you want the farm, then you have to fight for it."

"Here ya go." Maybelle plops down beside me, shoving a bare foot right through Oregon on my map. She passes each of us a sweaty Coke can, then places a cup of water in front of Otto who laps it up.

"Which means going to Seattle." I jab the Popsicle stick into the top of my map like a flag. "That's where Craig thinks my father might be living."

"You know," Maybelle pulls a squished box of popcorn out from under her arm and shoves it toward Sophia, "that junk show so many folks are going to—"

"*Antiques Roadshow.*" Sophia opens the red-and-white striped box, her face lighting up.

"It's gonna be in Seattle."

"Maybe I could go with the tour from the facility."

"That would work," Maybelle says. "They're leaving Wednesday. Might still be room in the van."

"But then I wouldn't be able to stop in San Francisco." I draw two lines in the sand resembling the Golden Gate Bridge. "And I need to do that."

"I can take you!" Sophia offers the box of popcorn for us to sample.

Maybelle scowls. "How?"

"My car. I can take you wherever you need to go." There's a tremor of need in Sophia's voice. "It'll be an adventure. We can take our time or go as fast as we need to."

"You could take a train or a bus," Maybelle suggests.

Sophia frowns. "Have you tried to sleep on a train?"

"As a matter fact, I have." Maybelle slurps her Coke, making kissing sounds with her thin lips. "I was in the circus. Remember?"

Sophia shakes her head. "Besides she'll need a car to get around in Seattle."

"You can't drive."

"Can too. I have a license, issued by the State of California. And I'll have you know, I've never had a wreck or received a ticket in my life."

"What'd you do? Keep the car parked in the garage the whole time?"

"Phooey!" Sophia bats her hands at Maybelle.

I try to interrupt. "Look—"

"Why do you even have a car?" Maybelle is like a bulldog with a bone. "Not much point where we live."

"I like knowing I can come and go as I please." Sophia gives Otto a bite of popcorn. "Besides, my son gave it to me. He lives in Oregon now."

"Seems like a foolish thing to do." Maybelle scratches her head and a tuft of steel gray roots stand, topped by a maroon red. "Can you even read a map?"

"Of course! See here—Santa Barbara," she points to my rough outline, "San Francisco. We can take the Pacific Coast Highway or get there faster on the Ventura Freeway. No problem."

"This ain't a good idea," Maybelle grumbles.

"You should come with us," I say, sensing she might be feeling left out.

She purses her lips and shakes her head. "Nope. Not me. I done traveled all my life. Not anymore."

"If we push hard," Sophia draws her finger up the sandy coastline, "I think we can make it to Seattle by Thursday. That's plenty of time to find your father. And we can take the shoes to the *Antiques Roadshow* over the weekend. Might stir interest for a quick sale. Then, *voila!*"

"Save the farm." I nudge Sophia's finger back toward Oregon. "Which gives us time to see your son on the way."

"Oh, I'll have plenty of time for that later."

"Sophia," I say, "if there's one thing I've learned through my ordeal, it's that there's no guarantee there will be a tomorrow or a next week."

Her mouth tightens. "You're right. Every day is a gift."

"My ma always said, 'Maybelle, eat your fill today 'cause there might not be any vittles tomorrow.' Kinda the same thing, don't ya think?"

I smile.

"Mothers never stop worrying about their little chicks." Sophia wraps an arm around Maybelle's shoulders.

"Not my ma. She kicked me out when I was sixteen."

"I'm sorry," I say. I may not have had a father, but I had a mother who loved me and took care of me.

"Ah, don't matter," Maybelle huffs. "Learned to get by on my own. That's all any of us has. Right?"

"We have God," Sophia says.

It sounds like a glib answer, but I suspect with her it's not.

"Easy for you to say," Maybelle grumbles and jabs a stick at the sand.

"No, it's not. I learned the hard way. Like everybody else." Sophia's eyes cloud with dark emotions as she looks at me.

"I hope I'm doing the right thing." I admit my doubts.

"My daddy always said, 'The truth shall set you free.' And whatever you find on this trip, I think it might just set you free."

"From what?"

"Whatever you're holding onto. Or whatever has a hold of you."

What truth could there be in a pair of old slippers? My father wasn't nearly as forthcoming with advice as Sophia's. I don't remember anything profound he ever told me. I do remember he liked to play with cards, asking me to guess which card he placed in his pocket, telling me to pick one out of the deck and then telling me what it was. He also could hide a penny in his hands and pull the coin out of my ear. At one time, I thought he was magical. But with one decision—*poof!*—he disappeared from my life, and the magic vanished forever.

I don't expect miracles or magic to come from this trip. I'll be satisfied with the truth.

Chapter Ten

ell, so long. Let me know what happens."
Maybelle hugs us good-bye and heads back
inside to the cafeteria for breakfast.

I carry the suitcase Sophia loaned me. It looks as if it's been around the world seven times on every major and minor airline. Tucked safely inside are the ruby red slippers.

"Come on, let's hit the road." Dragging her suitcase, Sophia leads me along the damp sidewalk. It must have rained last night as the grass shimmers with moisture. She steps off the curb and stops at a black Jeep Wrangler. It's an older model but in good condition. The top has faded from black to gray.

"This is your car?"

"My son's. He's very generous. He might be reckless, but he has a good heart. He wanted to get me some fancy convertible. 'You'll be stylin',' he said. But this was good enough for me. And it's fun to drive."

Sophia gives a little hop to clamber into the driver's seat. I settle beside her in the passenger seat. There's a rip in the plastic cushion, and the jagged edge rubs against my hip. Otto settles on my lap, his paws digging into my knees as he peers over the dash and out the dusty windshield.

"Don't take offense," Sophia says, taking the wheel and keying the ignition, "but somewhere along this journey we're going to have to do some shopping."

"Shopping?" I notice the Jeep's engine resists but finally catches.

"Don't get me wrong, Dottie. You're a pretty girl. Very pretty."

Not an adjective I would have used. I touch the untucked hem of the blue-and-white-striped shirt I inherited from someone at the facility. "What? You don't think I look California chic?"

"If you're going to meet your father, then you need to look your best."

That puts a lump right in my throat.

"Don't worry—my treat." She releases the clutch, and the Jeep lurches forward. She grins, and for a moment I can see what she must have been like at twenty—wild and full of life. "Hang on to your hat."

I'm not wearing one, but that seems beside the point. We're off, bumping along the red-bricked road, on an adventure I'm not sure I'm ready for. But I'm convinced that if I don't take this journey, I'll never find the answers I need.

BEFORE WE REACH the highway, Sophia is balancing a bag of peanuts in her lap while shifting gears and steering. She looks as nimble as a juggler. A peanut sticks to her lip then falls onto her lap. Otto jumps across the stick shift before I can say, "No!"

Panicking, I check to make sure the Jeep doesn't veer out of its lane or slam into the back of another unsuspecting car. When I'm assured all is well and that Sophia has everything under control, I add, "Sorry."

"He's just a hungry boy. Aren't you, Otto?"

He licks his chops and waits anxiously for the next peanut to drop. I pull him back into my lap with one hand under his belly. He carefully watches Sophia, his eyebrows twitching.

I wonder if she was the type of woman to drive, drink coffee, and apply mascara all at the same time. Which makes me wonder what she did for a living before retiring, before moving into the facility.

"Did you ever work?" I pull a dog treat Gloria bought for Otto out of my bag and give it to him.

"Oh, sure. Had to. I was a single mom, just like yours. Let's see, what all did I do? I was a secretary, but not very good. A clown. I did get a few laughs. I was an extra in the movies. You name it, I've done it."

"Really?" Granny sought her fortune in Hollywood and found her life on a small Kansas farm. My sister had big dreams that led her to Hollywood. "Did you want to be an actress?"

"Oh, goodness no. I fell into it. Helped pay the bills."

"What movies?"

"Did you ever see *Maverick*? The TV show? You might be too young. Oh my goodness, James Garner was so handsome.

Let's see, what else? I was in *Cleopatra*, with Elizabeth Taylor. Scenes with the masses, just another face in the crowd." She glances in the rearview mirror, tilts it toward her, then back. "Not too bad a face. Anyway, and yes, Liz Taylor was just as beautiful in person, if not more so. And kind. Let's see," she sips her Coke while shifting gears with her right hand as the Jeep enters the freeway ramp. "I was in that movie with Debbie Reynolds."

"*Singin' in the Rain?*"

"No, the Wild West one."

I shrug.

"I can't remember the name. It'll come to me some-time. Middle of the night probably. But I wasn't just an extra. I became a gofer. I'd get the stars coffee or little things they needed. Anything from maxi pads to scarves and hair spray. Doris Day needed throat lozenges one day when I was on the set for . . . oh, what was the name of that movie? I've forgot-ten more than most people—"

A sports car whips in front of the Jeep, nearly taking the bumper with it. Sophia blasts the horn. Traffic on the Ventura Freeway resembles salmon swimming upstream. So many cars and trucks are jam-packed together moving as one along the curves of the highway. My nerves are as snarled as the traffic.

"Are you okay?" Sophia glances toward me, then back at the road.

I give a curt nod.

"Are you a control freak?" Her curled lip makes me laugh.

"Not anymore," I laugh nervously. "But I probably used to be. I've never been one to sit idly by while someone else does the work."

"You're the take-charge type. Taking care of the farm, your mother. Never afraid, just charge!"

I know that in at least one area of my life, I've let fear rule me. Now I'm being forced to face that fear head-on.

"Don't worry," she says. "I know what I'm doing." She steers with the inside of her wrist. "I even drove a taxi for a while. A friend owned a limo service, and I filled in occasionally for sick drivers."

"You sure have lived a varied life." Mine must seem boring.

"Well, you do what you have to do to make ends meet."

"I've only been a teacher. I've been about as adventurous as a turtle my entire life." What was I waiting for? My father to return home? The truth yanks off my shell, and I cringe against the light of it.

"Running a farm sounds very adventurous, what with weather and livestock. I bet lots of things have happened to you. Why, just being a teacher . . . well, there's just nothing more interesting than kids—what they say, what they do. Besides, there's something to be said for stability. But I've always been drawn to adventure." Sophia takes a quick breath. "My daddy is that way. Encouraging me to take chances, try new things."

"Your father is still alive?"

"Oh, sure."

"Where is he?"

"Around." She glances over her shoulder before switching lanes.

"What about your son's father? Did he leave you?"

"We were never married." Her answer doesn't seem loaded with baggage of regret, uncertainty, or bitterness. "I suppose I should regret that now. Regret doing things I had no business doing. But that's how we learn. And empathize with others. If we never made mistakes, we wouldn't need God, right? Besides, good can come from mistakes. All things work together for good. That's what my daddy always says."

My throat constricts. I know firsthand the destruction that can result from being left behind. Maybe leaving, forging ahead, unaware of what you leave in your wake, is the way to go. Being left behind sucks. Is that why Abby seems determined to always leave first?

"I ended up with a son to raise on my own, and that was hard. But I don't regret having him. Not for one minute. Thing is, with a husband, he would have carried half the blame."

"Blame?"

"For all the things I did wrong as a parent."

"Why do you think you did anything wrong?"

"All parents make mistakes, whether they admit it or not. I sure did. So many . . ." Her brow furrows. She shakes her head, mumbles something under her breath. "I'm sure my son could chronicle a thousand things I did wrong."

"I don't blame my mother for anything."

"Blame your father, do you?"

"No. Maybe. I don't know. I haven't thought about it much."

"One or the other usually gets the blame."

I run my finger along the armrest between the seats. "Your son must not blame you for much or he wouldn't have given you a car."

"Conscious or subconscious, it's there." She waves her hand, rolling her thin, bony wrist. "Not much I can do about it now. But I do wish . . ."

"Wish what?"

"I do wish I could be of help to Leo. Must be the plight

of most parents. So many times we want to help but can't for various and sundry reasons. Wonder if that's how my daddy felt all those times I was too stubborn to turn to him for help."

Is that what I've been, too stubborn to try to find my father? Stubborn in wanting him to come home of his own accord? Was that Momma's problem? Stubbornness and pride? Running my hands down Otto's back, I remember what it was like to lie in the hospital bed, not knowing if he lived or not. I couldn't do anything to help him, and it was the most awful feeling in the world. I ache for Sophia and the anguish she feels for her son. One thing that trapped feeling taught me—life is too short to be stubborn or proud. It's why I'm on this journey north.

"How would you help him?" I ask.

She tightens her grip on the steering wheel. Her swollen, freckled knuckles whiten with the pressure. "I would tell him—" She shakes her head, flips on the blinker, and switches lanes to move around a dilapidated truck carrying yard equipment. Three exhausted, sun-bronzed faces stare blankly at us from the bed of the truck as we pass. "No, I wouldn't. You can't tell some people anything. Sometimes folks just gotta learn things for themselves. If he asks, of course, I'll speak the truth."

Cars pass us with drivers chatting on their cell phones. So many people, yet so few connections made with those around them. I think of my relationship with Abby, how I want us to get along but how we always seem to bring out the worst in each other, like we're stuck in a junior-high time warp. What keeps us apart? Different interests? Or is it something deeper? Pride? Hurt? Selfishness?

"Look there!" Sophia points to a billboard.

I recognize the iconic figures of Dorothy, the Kansas farm girl, and her three friends skipping along a yellow-brick roadway. The caption reads, "Let the joyous news be spread!" Dates for a children's theatrical production are listed below.

I could certainly use a little joyous news right now.

Chapter Eleven

The blue sky seems endless, with only a few clouds on the horizon to the west of us. The Jeep stalls on the highway when we're sitting in traffic. "Sitting" being the operative word.

"What do we do?" I sit upright, glancing behind me at the long line of cars, some of which are beginning to lay on their horns in an angry cacophony.

"We're fine." Sophia shifts to neutral.

Ahead, another endlessly long line creeps forward, leaving a gap between our bumper and a micro convertible. A Yukon squeezes between us. Otto barks at a poodle in the next minivan.

Sophia turns the key and restarts the Jeep. "See, no worries!"

The Jeep jerks, surges forward. Sophia brakes and accelerates ad nauseam. I eat a couple of bites of a snack cracker we bought at a convenience store in an effort to settle my stomach. The anticipation and nervousness of the day wanes, giving way to exhaustion. I lean my head back and my eyes droop. Soon my head is bobbing.

I jerk awake.

Sophia glances over at me. "Did you have a good nap?"

I blink, shift in my seat. "Sorry." Otto jumps into my lap from the bed he apparently made on the floor at my feet. Panting, he walks around on the tops of my legs in circles, his little paws digging into my thighs. The air conditioner blasts cool air on my face, and I turn the vent toward Otto's limp pink tongue. "I shouldn't have slept."

"Why not? You were tired."

"Sometimes I just feel exhausted."

"Of course you do. Your body has been through a lot in the past few months. Don't you worry about a thing. I like driving."

It's an odd area we're in—a contrast in sights with forests on one side, ocean on the other. White-capped waves roll toward shore, breaking onto rocks. The sandy beach is dotted with beachcombers lying on pink, green, and yellow towels. An occasional umbrella pops open. Along the walkway paralleling the beach, tanned and scantily clad bodies jog, walk, and Rollerblade.

"Keep watching. You might see dolphins. Further north there are seals. I thought since we were so close you should see this little stretch of coastline. I know we're in a hurry, but—"

"Don't apologize. It's breathtaking." A hum of excitement vibrates through me. I feel like a kid again. "Where are we?"

"Carmel-by-the-Sea. Are you hungry?"

I touch my stomach, feel an emptiness deep inside. "I could be."

"Good! There's a fabulous little restaurant right on the water. Great seafood." She glances at the dashboard. "We made such great time that this might be a good place to do our shopping."

We meander along the coast, passing golf courses that bump up against the ocean. Jagged, rocky cliffs jut outward, accentuated by the fluidity of the surf. So far the trip has been a feast for my starved eyes. I've always loved how the waving Kansas cornfields resembled an emerald green sea that turned to a golden hue in the fall. But nothing has prepared me for the endless blue ocean, the sight of which quenches a thirst deep in my soul.

Back home, a few gentle hills rolled across the Kansas plains, but most of it was as flat as Momma's Bisquick pancakes. The land was solid, safe, comfortable. The contours of the California coast make the road twist and turn ahead of us. At first the peaks and ledges, cliffs and drop-offs unnerve me. But as the day progresses I begin to look forward to finding out what's beyond the next bend.

We pull over at an overlook to catch a glimpse of gray seals as they languish on the rocks along the beach as if they have nothing better to do but lie around, lifting their head occasionally to bark. Otto answers back. Brown pelicans pick their way along the shore as baby seals play in the surf, their parents looking on sleepily as the sun warms their skin. Their sleek, rounded bodies are like dark moonstones set in golden sand.

"This is nothing like Kansas," I whisper. For the first time since I was transported out of my comfortable existence, I'm actually glad to be here.

Not far off shore, a large shape breaks the water, making an enormous splash. "That was no seal."

"Whales!" Sophia clutches my arm excitedly. "It's been years since I spotted one."

"What kind was it?" I wonder aloud.

"This time of year probably a humpback. Maybe even a blue whale."

"How do you know that?"

She shrugs and smiles. "I'm full of useless information, when I can remember it!"

A few minutes later, we park near the seaside restaurant, gleaming with bleached woodwork. We leave Otto in the car, with the windows cracked. "Should we take," Sophia tilts her head to the side, "the shoes?"

"Might not be a bad idea. Just in case they are . . . well, you know."

With the shoes tucked safely inside Sophia's giant handbag, we walk into the restaurant. In the foyer, a wall-size aquarium holds bright, colorful fish that flick their fantails and stare with dark, unconcerned eyes. We settle into our seats on a patio overlooking the water. A canvas overhang keeps direct sunlight off us. A slight breeze off the ocean stirs the air with whispers of relief.

"This is my treat. Unless Clint shows up. Then I just might let him pick up the tab."

"Clint?"

She rolls her eyes. "Don't you have movies in Kansas? Clint Eastwood!"

"You know him?"

"He might not remember me. But then again, he might." She waves her hand at the menu. "Just pick something yummy. I might have to sample."

I half expect to see a famous face sitting at a table nearby, but I'm not sure I'd recognize a star if one orbited our table. I feel overdressed in my T-shirt and jeans in the sense that I have more clothes covering my body than anyone else sitting at the linen-covered tables. But Sophia's right, I do need new clothes. Something that matches at least. But I don't want her funding this trip. I still have money from the sale of my animals.

I lean forward, my elbows on the small round table between us. "You're on a fixed income."

"The eternal realist," she says. "Don't worry about me. I'm good and fixed."

"How?" I stare at her. She's dressed casually. Her clothes are on the nice side but not fancy. She doesn't shop like some of the wealthy widows who live at the facility. But the fact that she lives there says something about her. It's not the Ritz, but it is upscale. "Did catering to stars give you enough to retire on? Or was it driving taxis? Do you even get social security?"

She touches my hand. "My father has provided very well for me."

I feel a pinprick of jealousy. "Did he leave you a lot of money?" I ask, more to make my point than to pry. But didn't she say he was alive?

Momma was always adamant that we never accept charity. I suppose it was her mid-western attitude that makes me, even now, not want to be indebted to anyone. Abby used to like to play up our situation—Momma being a single mother; she had a knack for giving listeners a weepy look that had them handing her five dollars or bringing over supper or even wrapping up extra presents at Christmas that Momma always made us return.

"We can make it on our own," she often scolded when we complained. I used to think she was embarrassed by our circumstances, but as I grew older I realized pride ran deep inside her.

A few minutes later our lunch arrives. A basket of assorted breads is placed between us. As we let our meals of almond-crusted mahi mahi and salmon with a mango relish cool, I try to explain my difficulty in accepting help and how Momma wouldn't let us accept charity.

"So it's not you," I finish. "It's my stubborn mid-western pride."

Sophia smiles tenderly. "Maybe this is a lesson you need to learn. It's okay to accept the love of others. Especially when you're always quick to help others yourself." She rolls her silverware out of a linen napkin and sets the pieces at the edge of her plate. "When I was pregnant with my son, I was put on bed rest. Now there is nothing that will make you more dependent on others than having to stay in bed all the day long." She takes a bite of her fish. "Mmm, very good." With her fork, she points at mine. "How is it?"

"Delicious." The mango gives it a tangy sweet flavor.

"I'm sure you've felt some of that over the past few weeks."

"Momma, too, during her last few years."

She reaches for the bread and offers some to me. "Of course. I was single and unable to work. I didn't even have insurance. But I was so proud. Proud I'd made it by myself for so many years. But suddenly it wasn't just me I had to think about. I had a baby. Another person was depending on me, and that was very humbling."

I take one of the wheat rolls and a chilled pat of butter from a little dish. "What did you do?"

"A few neighbors and friends brought me food and such, but as time dragged on, they disappeared. Then some folks from a church I attended a few times chipped in and helped pay for my medical expenses and doctor bills. Basically, they loved me when I wasn't lovable at all. They'd come sit with me during the day or at night and just talk. At first, I wasn't happy about that. I thought they were going to lecture me, point out the error of my ways. Believe me, I knew all the mistakes I'd made. But they didn't do that. They just brought me food, books, and magazines. They even helped me pay my rent. All without making any judgmental comments about how I'd gotten myself into the situation."

I remember how our church in Maize offered to help Momma, but she declined, saying there were needier folks. After a while, they quit offering.

"Back then," Sophia butters her roll, "in the early '70s, single mothers were looked down upon. It must have been hard on your mother too. Divorced women were stigmatized." She sits up suddenly, places her hands on her hips. "Why is it men's reputations remain intact if they get some girl pregnant or go off and leave their families? It's the women who take the hit, and we're the ones who stick around and clean up the mess." She draws a quick breath, then shrugs. "Sorry. Personal soapbox."

"You're right. My mother stayed. She did the hard work. Maybe that's why I never wanted to get married. Never wanted to end up a single mom, struggling the way she did."

"Not all men run off," she says. "Some are loyal and honorable."

I shrug off the notion and turn the conversation away from me. "I remember some women at our church told Momma it was her fault for letting her husband run off."

"Oh, that gets my hog! What was she supposed to do, goat-tie him?"

I smile softly at her mix-up of words. "Momma used to say, trapping a bird only gives you a trapped bird. Nothing more, nothing less."

"Great wisdom your Momma had."

Or was it a good excuse not to risk her heart again by asking my father to return? I remember Momma's determined gait, halting sometimes, lopsided and cumbersome, but steady and resolute. I've tried to emulate her, keeping my chin up, no matter what. But was it only an empty façade? "So what happened with your situation, Sophia?"

"Oh, I had a beautiful baby boy. As you'll see. A bit wild and boisterous, but aren't most? Named him Leo." She whispers, "Wanted him to make better decisions than I did, be smarter than me. So I named him after the smartest person I could think of."

"DaVinci?"

"Exactly!" She laughs. "He turned out to be a free spirit just like the original. Smarter than I ever was." Her pensive smile tells me how proud she is of her son, yet there's an edge of worry. "I made some wonderful friends back then. Many have now gone on, but," she pauses, sips her water, "that's what happens when you get old."

"You don't have to be old to lose someone you love."

Her eyes soften. "You are so right. It's painful, isn't it?"

My chest tightens, and I shift in my seat, take another bite of salmon, glance around at the other tables.

"I didn't mean to upset you, Dottie."

"You didn't. I'm fine. Really." I sniff back emotions I thought I'd moved beyond. "Sometimes I think I'm past all that. Then it sneaks up on me. Or maybe it's the head injury that stirs it all up again." I clear my throat, wave the focus away from me. "So everything turned out okay with your situation."

She watches me for a moment. "I insisted I repay all those kind folks from the church for their generosity. They argued with me, but I insisted. They told me how wonderful it made each of them feel to be able to give, how they had learned the value of hands-on ministry, instead of just writing a check. In the end, they agreed to let me pay them back. I worked hard. It took three years to save enough money. Then when I presented them with the last check, they gave me a gift in return: They had saved my checks and invested the money for me. They gave it all back to help me raise my son." Tears glisten in her blue eyes. "If I had known at the start how much those folks were going to do for me, I would have balked. Pride is such a huge obstacle."

I nod, remembering Momma's irritability as she had to lean more and more on me to run the farm. "I suppose I am prideful." I draw the tines of my fork through the saffron rice. "It took a lot of work—the farm, caring for Momma, teaching. Even now, I wish I could do this trip alone. Not that I'm not enjoying your company. I am. And I am grateful—to you, to Maybelle, to Craig. I just . . ."

Sophia leans forward and reaches a hand across the table. "It's not easy to accept help from others. I'm not pointing out your shortcomings; I have enough trouble seeing my own. I'm simply telling you what I went through. If we could do everything for ourselves, we wouldn't need each other now, would we? And what kind of a world would this be?" She pulls back, dabs her mouth with her napkin, and grins. "Now, let's go shopping."

"I CAN'T AFFORD to buy a hankie in this town!"

She laughs. "I know a specialty shop that makes poor folks' dreams come true."

Pressure builds in my chest, behind my eyes. A hard lump wells up in my throat. I mull over all she has said. When I can speak without my voice wavering, I whisper, "Thank you."

She loops her arm through mine as we walk two blocks over from the oceanfront drive. "Don't forget you're helping me too."

We enter the Rainbow Resale shop. A *ding-dong* sounds as the glass door closes behind us.

"Did you see that sign?" Sophia asks. When I shake my head, she pulls open the door again and shows me the poster taped to the glass. Another advertisement for the *Wizard of Oz* stage show. In this one a young actress stares off at a rainbow, with the caption, *A place where there isn't any trouble.*

"I don't think that place exists," I say.

We go back into the store where row after row of clothes racks are crowded into a small space. It's a sea of cottons and polyesters, linens and sequins. Everything is organized according to color, making a rainbow throughout the store.

"I'll be right there!" a woman calls from somewhere toward the back of the store.

"This is not your ordinary resale shop," Sophia whispers. "The women who empty out their closets and donate already have their pot of gold. I mean, they live in Carmel! So these aren't your everyday, run-of-the-mill clothes." She holds up the shimmery sleeve of a pale yellow blouse. "Designers. Custom-made. Quality."

This is probably not the store for me then. I take a step back, thinking it might be best to just keep my mismatched clothes for now. Many of the clothes look like ball gowns and prom dresses. Maybe they're red-carpet designs. Definitely not my style. If I have a style.

"I'm not very good at shopping."

"Oh, I'll help." Sophia gives me a quick once-over. "You've got a great figure. It'll be fun shopping for you." She pats her backside. "You don't have any major flaws that need hiding."

"I'm really not the fancy type." I reach toward a sequined dress the color of lemon drops but don't touch.

"Simple is pretty too. And you are that." She flaps a pant leg at me. "This pair of khakis probably cost a hundred."

"Dollars?"

"Well, not pesos! The lady that bought these retail probably only wore them once. And now they're affordable."

A row of emerald-green dresses parts, and a diminutive woman with a pair of purple glasses lying crooked across her nose steps through. At first I thought she was bending down, but now I realize she's just bent and would barely surpass Maybelle in height. "Hello there! I'm Violet." Her face creases into a wide, beaming smile. She tugs off her glasses and they dangle from a chain around her neck. "How can I help you?"

It takes only a few minutes for the saleslady and Sophia to round up some pants and tops for me to try on, pulling from every shade of this rainbow room. Thankfully there's not a sequin or prom dress in the bundle. The striped curtain covering the dressing room doesn't quite meet both sides of the doorway as I pull on a pair of khakis and a plain blue button-down. There's no mirror in the tiny room, so I have to step outside the cubicle to solicit Sophia's and Violet's approval.

"What do you think?"

"Perfect." Sophia grins. "You look fabulous! And look what I found." She shoves a leather jacket at me. Fringe dangles from the arms and across the shoulders. It's not anything I would have picked because it's not practical, but I like the buttery softness. "Try this on with those jeans."

It fits. But Sophia won't let me look at the price tag. She unpins the safety pin hooked to the lining and hands it to Violet. "She needs this. We're on our way to San Francisco, and it can get cold at night."

"We won't be there long. A raincoat might be more practical for Seattle."

"We'll look at those too."

Back in the dressing room, I start to unbutton the blue shirt but only make it as far as the second button before I lean against the wall, suddenly exhausted. I stare at the four walls. The paint is old and scarred. Hanging on the metal hook is a sleeveless, peach-colored blouse. Plain and simple, that's me. Definitely not something Abby would wear to meet our father. What about me? Will a leather jacket bolster my courage? Make me look special? Should I try to dress up? I don't want to pretend to be something I'm not.

This evening we'll arrive in San Francisco. The map to my uncle's home is in the car with Otto. My insides rumble with uncertainty. Will he know who I am? Will he even care? Is he sophisticated? An urbanite? Will he think I'm just a country bumpkin? I touch my now-long hair that I've pulled back into a ponytail. I should have had it cut at the facility.

"Hey," Sophia calls from the other side of the woefully inadequate curtain, "you okay in there?"

"Sure," I manage, my throat tense. Hurriedly I change into the next outfit then step out.

"Oh, yes!" The saleslady claps her hands. "Perfect fit. You could be a model."

I stare at her, wondering what her commission is on sales.

"Are you okay?" Sophia asks, following me into the dressing room.

"Sure."

"You don't look okay."

"I'm getting tired. Long day."

She watches me carefully.

I focus on hanging up the first blouse and pants I tried on. Unsure which of my many anxieties to share, I start with the one that burbles to the top of the list. "What if this man, my uncle, doesn't know who I am? What if—"

"Why, then you'll tell him. Besides how would he not know who you are?"

"What if my father never told his sister about us? What if they didn't want to know us? What if they—"

"Too many 'what ifs'! Here, try this on for size. What if your aunt and uncle wanted to know you all these years? What if they've missed being a part of your life? What if your uncle hugs you and weeps with joy?"

"That's too optimistic. Too unrealistic." The room feels as if it's shrinking. Sweat pops out on my forehead.

"Why? What's wrong with optimism? My daddy says to believe. Not 'hope for the best, plan for the worst.'"

"That's the farmer's mentality in Kansas—hope for rain, prepare for drought." It's logical, rational, reasonable. "Maybe your father is used to getting what he wants."

"Believe!" Sophia glides out of the dressing room, straightening the curtain behind her.

I lean against the dressing room wall. Bits of stray thread and lost buttons lie on the carpet at my feet. *Believe.*

I've never thought of myself as a pessimist. I always considered myself a plain, ordinary realist. Abby was the optimist, and her hopes had often been crushed. Only a few months ago, she stood in front of a mirror telling me how hard it was to get a job in Hollywood. Her pot of gold at the end of the rainbow had left her feeling empty and unwanted.

It always seemed foolish to me to open myself up to disappointment. I wanted to be strong like Momma. Not vulnerable like Abby. But was that simply pride? Was Momma too proud to risk being hurt? Is Abby the brave one?

It was Abby who every holiday asked, "Will Daddy come home?" Later she tempered the question to, "Do you think Daddy will call?" Then finally, "Does Daddy think about us?" Her optimism seemed foolish and reckless.

But now it makes my heartbeat quicken. He *did* think of me! After all, he came to visit while I was in the coma. Hope pushes to the surface, like a tiny seedling desperate for sunlight.

A scratching on the curtain reminds me that I need to get moving. I change into the next outfit that Sophia and Violet have selected for me. The jeans are a bit baggy.

"Those can't be a size six," Violet *tsks*. She puts on her reading glasses and checks the inside label, pulling the material away from my skin. "Oh, I know who brought those in. I better not say! I bet she changed the label to make us think she wears a smaller size!" She swivels around and hollers, "Marla! Marla!"

A teen with a tattoo that covers one exposed shoulder appears from the back. She's chewing something and swallows quickly. "Yeah?"

"Will you find another pair like this? Make sure it's a size six." Off Marla voyages into the sea of colors. "A new blouse came in the store the other day," Violet says more to herself than us. "Now where did I put that?"

"So what do you think?" Sophia asks when we're alone.

"Believing hurts."

She smiles. "If you have faith the size of a tiny seed, anything is possible, farmer girl. Why limit yourself? Why limit life?" She leans close enough for me to smell her face powder. "Why limit God?"

Is that what I've been doing? Limiting God?

After we pick out several matching slacks and shirts, we check out. This time, I insist on using the money from the sale of livestock. But Sophia insists on buying me the leather jacket. "Just because." We thank Violet for all of her help and head toward the door. It's time to get back on the road.

"If we hurry," Sophia says, brushing past Marla who is rehanging some of the clothes I tried on, "we can be in San Francisco by dinner."

"Hey!" Marla points at Sophia's bag. "What are you doing there?"

The heel of a ruby slipper is hooked around the strap.

"Are you stealing those shoes?"

Chapter Twelve

n o," I say, smiling to alleviate her suspicions. "These are my shoes. Sophia was carrying them for me."

But this girl looks like she's seen it all. And she's not believing us.

Violet hurries over, her eyes large behind her glasses. "What's happened? What's wrong?"

"They were trying to steal those shoes."

"No, really." I pull a shoe out of Sophia's purse. "It's mine."

Violet snorts. "Said you weren't the fancy type."

Sophia meets my worried gaze.

Violet takes the ruby-red slipper from my hands. She turns it over, studying the label inside.

I hold my breath, wondering if we can make a quick escape. If Violet realizes these shoes are *the* ruby slippers, then she could accuse us of stealing them and claim them for herself.

"Not a designer," she huffs.

Marla shrugs and wanders off without an apology.

"I'd remember a pair of shoes like that if I had any in my store." Violet hands the shoe back to me.

Shoving the shoe back into Sophia's cavernous purse as far into the bottom as I can push it, we make a quick exit.

THE STEEP HILLS that make up the city of San Francisco frighten me. I am, after all, accustomed to the flat plains of Kansas. Sensing my fear, Otto burrows under my arm. My pulse raises each time the Jeep noses down a hill. The drive is daunting and exhilarating. It feels like I'm going to fall right out of the windshield and over the front bumper. I try to hold back a gasp and clutch the dashboard as we crest another rise. My foot stamps on the floorboard as if there's a brake pedal on the passenger side. Suddenly I can relate to all those parents of students I taught over the years. They often complained of teen drivers and feeling out of control. I always tried to empathize but couldn't until this moment.

"Look over there," Sophia points. "Do you see that white pointy building? It's the Sentinel. Next to it is the TransAmerica building." But before I can turn to catch a glimpse, she's already pointing out some other sight.

She weaves around the city, giving me tiny glimpses of this diverse area. We pass Spanish missions and gaudy tattoo parlors. Chinatown is alive with colors that make me dizzy. What amazes me is how much greenery is wedged into tiny spaces. If there's an empty space or even a crack in the sidewalk, plants sprout and bloom. The variety of foliage surprises me, too, as I spot trees of all kinds including palms. Hydrangeas and chrysanthemums bloom in an assortment of dazzling colors. Each time we reach the top of a hill, the views are spectacular, revealing glimpses of the calm bay, an array of boats, and more sights to be explored.

"Just not enough time," Sophia grumbles.

We pass yellow cable cars and bicyclists who pedal effortlessly uphill. I feel as if I've entered a foreign country or landed on a strange planet, some fantasy place I never dreamed of.

Sophia brakes, rolling down her window, and a gust of air blows into the Jeep. She catches the attention of two men who are holding hands. One walks up to the Jeep. A diamond earring glitters in his earlobe. He has a bright, welcoming smile. She asks for assistance, and he politely points us in the right direction.

After several dizzying turns, she pulls to a stop at the crest of a hill. "Can you make out that street sign?"

I squint but shriek as the Jeep rolls backward. Half turning in my seat, I brace a hand against the back of Sophia's and stare in horror as we roll back down the sharp incline.

"It's okay. It's okay!" She readjusts the gearshift, brakes, then pulls the emergency brake. We come to a jarring halt midway to the bottom.

"Want me to get out and push?" It's not the real reason I want to eject myself.

"We're fine." She restarts the Jeep. "Did you read the name of that cross street?"

"Coventry, I think." A thick ball of uncertainty wedges in my throat. The steep hills and the tall houses loom around me, making me feel claustrophobic, as if I'm shrinking by the minute and everything around me is growing in enormity, including my fears.

"How come you're never afraid?" Abby's words haunt me. Maybe because I always stayed in my comfort zone.

"We're almost there." Sophia pulls me back to the present and the panicky feeling of falling. The wind buffets the Jeep's plastic windows. When she gets the vehicle moving in the right direction, she doesn't pause or hesitate but gives it a burst of gas to get us over the top. The light is still red as she turns the corner, causing a burly fellow in a delivery truck to honk at us.

"Didn't want to take a chance of stalling out again," she explains.

Panting, Otto looks at me, and I realize I've been squeezing him.

A few minutes later, we locate a parking place along the curb. Sophia backs the Jeep into the space with more skill than a professional driver. "Right there," she says. "Your uncle's house is right there."

It's a pale-blue three-story sandwiched between a yellow and pink model. Looking back the way we came, the streets resemble giant oceanic waves whose undulations mirror my insides at the moment.

Sophia touches my hand. "Come on. I'll be right beside you."

Doubts pound against my thoughts and jumble my emotions. What if my uncle doesn't know where my father is? But what if he doesn't even know about me? Or worse, doesn't care?

"What's the worst that could happen?" Sophia vocalizes my fears. She opens the driver's door and steps out on the sidewalk as if there is no other option. But there is. We could leave. We could turn around and head back to Santa Barbara. My new comfort zone.

No, I have to do this.

When we stand on the front stoop, she reaches over and clasps my hand. "Believe."

I draw a rough breath and try to imagine what my uncle-by-marriage might be like. Tall or short? Kind? With a sharp edge?

"If you don't ring the bell," Sophia says, "we'll have to stand here all night until someone comes out for the morning paper."

But all I can do is stare at the frosted-glass door.

Sophia rings the bell for me. I can hear it echo through the hallways inside the house. A garbage truck rumbles past behind us. Footsteps on concrete draw my attention to a jogger. Then a car horn blares down the street. Otto barks a retort.

"No one's home." I turn back to Sophia, tug on her arm. "Maybe we should—"

"What are you going to do? You need this man to help you find your father."

She's right. But it doesn't make it any easier to wait, to wonder, to worry. What if he doesn't have the answers I need?

Sophia puts an arm around my shoulders and leans toward the etched glass. It's then a tall, shadowy figure moves slowly toward the door, as if walking down a long hallway. The lock jiggles, and the door creaks open.

An elderly gentleman, erect and handsome in spite of the years etched in his face, gives us a quizzical look. His silver hair is well kept and clipped short. He's dressed in a starched gray shirt and suit pants. Belt and tie are in place, as if he's ready to go to the office or just arrived home. "Can I help you?"

Sophia looks expectantly toward me, but words fail to emerge.

"We were hoping you might know of someone named . . ." She waits for me to fill in the name of my father, but his name sticks in my throat.

Hesitantly, I speak up. "Tim Turney?"

"Well, you sure do know how to brighten up a gloomy day," he says, glancing beyond us at the clouds floating in from the ocean. "What can I do for you two ladies?"

His expression is open, expectant, as if we might be there with the Publisher's Clearing House prize. Do I jump right in? The hopefulness in his gaze stops me. "I'm Dottie Meyers."

I study his face and search for recognition in his misty gray eyes. There seems to be a glimmer of something. Maybe it's just my imagination, my own hope reflecting off him. I watch for any hesitation, recoil, or disappointment.

"My father and mother are Duncan and—"

"Ruby. Of course." He studies me just as thoroughly, then gives a slight nod as if answering a silent question to himself. "I'm sorry. You've stunned me." He jerks to the right, freezes, turns back to us. "I, uh . . . oh my!"

"Maybe you should sit down," Sophia suggests, reaching toward him.

"Yes." His knees dip, but Sophia boosts him upward.

"Here," she moves him into his house, "let me help you. Dottie . . ."

The sound of my name galvanizes me. I take my uncle's other arm and steer him back into his house. Gleaming hardwoods stretch out before us as we walk down a narrow hallway. My uncle's footsteps are more of a shuffling, scuffing, halting cadence, his movements jerky and rigid. Black-framed pictures feature younger versions of Tim and Elizabeth posing in front of famous destination spots—the Eiffel Tower, Westminster Abbey, a Lenin monument, the Sphinx. It's a gallery of a life well spent.

We pass steep stairs on the right and a kitchen on the left. I catch a quick glimpse of clean black granite counters and a lone white plate holding the crust of a piece of toast. A hint of ginger lingers in the air.

Hearing Otto's nails clicking against the hardwoods, I ask, "Is it all right for my dog to come in?"

"Of course. What's the name?"

"Otto. He's a little spoiled in that he goes everywhere with me."

"We should all be so spoiled." He gestures stiffly toward a little sitting room nestled among broad windows, which open to a small courtyard filled with lush foliage and vibrant purple and pink flowers. The decorations in the room are sparse, the colors subdued variations of beige and brown. More pictures cover the walls. In here, the photographs are black-and-whites. They're close-ups of objects, like a solitary chair, a pile of leaves, an ordinary coffee cup held by a pair of elderly hands. The pictures don't seem to be about the object as much as the light slanting through the frame.

"Why, yes," Tim says as we position him in front of a chair. He sinks down onto the cushion but his gaze remains on me. "I see a little of Ruby in you. She had those same dark-brown eyes. Naturally pretty, without all the fluff and fuss." A wistful smile plays about his tight mouth. "How is she?"

"Momma?" Pretty isn't the first word that comes to mind when I think of Ruby Meyers. Practical. Capable. Reserved. These words describe me too. Obviously, this man knows Momma, but he doesn't seem to know she's gone. Remembering that his wife died two years ago, I hate breaking the sorrowful news to him as he seems eager for some word. But I notice his smile is congealing. Swallowing my reservations, I say, "Momma passed on last year."

Only his eyes move as he looks toward Sophia. A muscle near his temple twitches. Moisture builds in the corner of his eyes, turning them the color of warm flannel. "I lost my Elizabeth not long ago." He rubs his jaw and tugs on his ear lobe. "Been two years now. Two years." He pulls out a handkerchief and wipes underneath his nose. "That always takes me by surprise."

I step back, not knowing if I should take a seat or reach out to him.

"Oh, Ruby." His voice roughens. He stares off toward a window at the sky beyond as if looking back through the years. "And I never knew. Never knew. But you lost your mother." He reaches forward and clasps my hand. His hands are cool but gentle. "I'm so sorry, dear. So very sorry." He blinks and looks back at me and Sophia as if seeing us for the first time. "Look at me, not much of a host." He pushes to his feet, his hands braced on the chair's arms. "Have a seat. Please. Elizabeth would say I'm the worst sort of host."

"We showed up completely unannounced." I make the excuse for our bad manners. When I was a girl, I loved it when someone pulled up the drive unexpected, even though it sent Momma rushing around fussing, making sure the house was straightened. But I enjoyed the sudden surprise, the distraction from the ordinary, the fact that someone was interested in me.

"I'm glad you did stop by. Glad you did. Can I get you anything to drink?"

"I'm fine." I sit in what looks to be a stiff, upright chair, but the cushions feel worn and settled. I indicate with my palm down that Otto should stay on the floor.

"I'd love some water," Sophia says.

"Would you like tea?"

"Don't go to any trouble. Water's fine."

He turns and retreats to the kitchen. His steps are hesitant, his motions stiff.

"See!" Sophia says. "He knew you. Isn't that wonderful?"

He does seem glad to see me. And he seems to have fond memories of Momma. But why did my aunt and uncle never visit or contact us? Why didn't they write or call?

While we wait for Tim to return, I peruse the bookshelves. All of the books are hardcover, their dust jackets removed. The covers vary from forest green to emerald red. Titles are etched along the spines in silver and gold. Tiny framed photographs dot the shelves. I lean close to view one of a diminished cathedral. It's deceptively small, reduced in size, but it must hold some significance. I want to know about my family, my aunt and uncle, if they had children, if I have cousins. I want to study a picture of my aunt, search her face for any traces of my father. Then I remember how Tim compared me to my mother, not my father. I feel a cloud of regret that I didn't search for my aunt long before now.

The questions I want to ask about why they never came to see us turn into pointed questions at myself. Why didn't I seek them out? Why didn't I try to find them? Did staying in my comfort zone prevent me from experiencing joyous events beyond my imagination?

"That's your Aunt Elizabeth," Tim says behind me as I examine a tiny black-and-white photo of the woman I've come to recognize. She had luminous eyes that seemed to take in every sight. She was thin, almost waiflike, with a wisp of a nose. I reach out to help my uncle as he carries in a tray with three glasses of water. There's no ice, but the water is cool when I lift it to my lips.

"She was beautiful." I'm drawn back to the delicate frame on the shelf. "I found a picture of her among Momma's things. She was with my father."

"Oh, Duncan. Elizabeth adored her younger brother. Everyone did, I suppose. Everyone."

My heart starts to pound. I feel Sophia's gaze heavily upon me. "Did?" I repeat his word. Past tense. "But—"

Tim's brow folds downward. "Oh, no. I shouldn't have frightened you, my dear. He's alive and kicking. Far as I know. Just not a part of my life much, so I tend to think of him in the past tense." He rubs the back of his neck, turning stiffly to the right and left. "Fact is, I think of most people in the past. These days I don't get around much. Live in the past more than the present, I suppose. Live in these old photographs."

He's still standing, waiting as a gentleman for me to find a seat. So I settle myself back in the surprisingly comfortable chair. Otto puts a paw on my leg, signaling he wants to sit in my lap. I give a sharp shake of my head then rub his ears.

"Elizabeth would have hated all of these pictures of her about. She didn't even like to have her picture taken. She preferred to be behind the camera. Always was that way. After . . ." He gestures toward one, then reaches out, touches the corner of the frame lovingly. "I had the few pictures of her framed. I miss her face."

Nothing else is said for a moment. Somewhere in the distance I hear the slow perpetual ticking of a clock.

"They looked alike." My voice is too loud in the quiet of the room.

Tim slants a quizzical gaze at me.

"Elizabeth and my father," I explain.

"Not in stature. She was slight. He was burly." He blinks. "Is burly. But you could see the resemblance in their eyes. No mistaking those eyes."

"And cowlick."

A smile plays about his mouth. "They shared many of the same traits. The Meyers legacy, I always called it."

Hearing of family traits acts like a waterfall on my senses, chilling me with regrets and yet drawing me ever closer. "What do you mean?"

"Oh, they could charm the soul right out of a saint. And the one being charmed never quite knew. Or if they did, didn't care." His fingers fold over the curved arm of the chair.

"And she charmed you." It's a statement, not a question, as I can see it in his gaze and gestures.

"To the core of my heart." He looks down at the floor for a moment before speaking again. "Ruby suffered the same fate."

This surprises me. At first it doesn't seem to fit Momma, but as I contemplate the way she lived her life, I begin to wonder. She rarely mentioned my father, but maybe that was a coping skill. She never did find love again. Maybe no one else measured up to my father.

"Do you know where my father is?" I ask.

He seems surprised by the question. "Where he's been for the past thirty or so years." His gaze narrows. "Don't you know, my dear?"

I shake my head, feel my throat compress. "Seattle?"

The corners of Tim's mouth pull downward. He leans forward, places his hand on mine. His skin is smooth but paper thin, cool to the touch as if life has started to drain out of him.

"We hadn't had contact with Duncan for years and years. But he came to Elizabeth's funeral. From what I understand, he's very powerful. The people he told me he'd met . . . heady to think of the influence he must have. Very powerful."

Otto curls into a lump on the floor, finally settling down.

"Powerful?" I ask.

"Oh, yes. Don't you know? Maybe it's hard for children to see their parents as the world sees them."

I'm confused and surprised by his statement.

"Surprised me when he came to the funeral. I hadn't contacted him. Not that he wasn't welcome. I just wasn't thinking clearly . . . I think he read the obituary in the paper. I'm not exactly sure."

He leans back, pulls a handkerchief from his pocket, and dabs his eyes, then rubs the thin white material beneath his nose and sniffs. "My days are filled with things I should have done or meant to do. I suppose I put contacting Duncan out of my mind as I was missing Elizabeth. He must be suffering something awful with Ruby gone too. Was it sudden?" Before I can answer, he continues. "Elizabeth went fast. A heart attack. She passed out and never woke. A blessing, I suppose. I didn't want her to suffer, but I would have liked to have told her . . ." He shakes his head. "I'm sorry. Sometimes I go on and on. I don't mean to."

"It's okay," Sophia says.

"My father left when I was four and never came back." I wish I could erase the hard edge from my tone.

Tim flinches as if suddenly wounded. "W-what? H-how could that be?"

"I haven't seen my father in thirty years. I don't even know if he knows Momma died. Or cares. He didn't come to her funeral." Bitterness saturates my words. I want to ask why he went to his sister's funeral and not his wife's.

"But he came to see you," Sophia says.

I take comfort in that reminder.

Tim leans back as if all the air has escaped him. "I just can't believe that. He said . . ." He shakes his head as if trying to rearrange his understanding. "I can't believe that."

My heart skips a beat, imagining my father speaking of us, talking as if he knew us. "What did he say?"

"I asked about Ruby and you two girls." He rubs the handkerchief over his face again. "You're not girls anymore. But I guess you're locked in my mind as a certain age. He said you were all fine. But how could he know that if . . ."

Anger pulses through me. "He couldn't."

"I-I'm so sorry, my dear."

"I asked Momma if she wanted me to contact him before she passed, but she didn't want some contrived family reunion. She said he knew where we were. And so I never let him know about Momma. He never came." I don't know why I'm telling him this. I try to keep my voice dispassionate, but my heart beats a different rhythm and pace.

Tim remains quiet as if absorbing all the information I've given him and reorienting himself to a new reality. Maybe I shouldn't have dumped so much on him. My tone was a bit jarring, my words sharp. I thought I'd given up on those feelings, dismissed them a long time ago.

Tim's gaze drifts toward a three-by-five-inch framed photo of Elizabeth, her smile wistful, incomplete. My heart aches for him.

"You knew Momma?" I ask.

Slowly he comes back to this moment from some recollection. "Knew her? Of course I did, my dear. Why," he chuckles,

"I was in love with her. For a while anyway. Until she ran off with Duncan. Took my heart with her. If I'd known he'd treat her the way he did, I would have stayed and fought for her. But I thought she'd made her choice." He shrugs his narrow shoulder. "He was younger than me. And I thought . . . well . . . maybe it turned out the way it was supposed to. I'll never know."

"Sounds like they both made their choices. Where is Duncan now?" Sophia asks.

"Seattle, as you said." He looks at me again, his eyes soft and tender. "He left me his card. I tucked it in my wallet at the funeral and haven't touched it since." He pushes forward in his chair and pulls a wallet out of his back pocket. With slow, fumbling fingers, he opens the fold and removes a slightly bent white card. "I don't know when he moved. But it was a different address than what we had. I don't know if he built a new place or what."

A surge of an emotion I would rather dismiss easily but seems to be ground deep into my bones rises up in me. I'm not sure this was a good idea coming to San Francisco, finding Tim. He seems kind, sweet, and maybe it was worth the emotional upheaval just to meet him, just to have some family connection. But to know my father is powerful, talks about me like he knows me, is not what I wanted to hear.

"So Seattle is where we're headed." Sophia's words are soft, barely uttered. "Are you okay, Dottie?"

The few feet between us seems like a great distance.

"She looks pale." Tim pushes up from his seat, stumbles on the rug, then gains his equilibrium. "Can I get her something?"

Otto jumps to his feet, taps his tiny paws on the floor, and looks at me anxiously.

"I'm okay." I don't want anyone fussing over me. "Really." I touch my forehead, feel my hand trembling. I reach down and soothe Otto's worried brow. "Maybe we should go."

"But you just got here," Tim protests.

"She needs to rest," Sophia says. "Dottie's still recovering."

"Recovering?" Tim asks.

"She was in an accident."

"A tornado." The syllables feel disjointed in my mouth as I piece all the parts of my story together.

"You poor dear," Tim says, hovering close.

"And we're on our way to find her father."

"He left me something while I was in a coma. A pair of slippers. I have to know why."

As if in slow motion, Tim sinks down into his chair again. "The slippers. I've seen them once. A long time ago."

Sophia pulls them out of her purse.

He reaches for them, cradles them in his hands. A smile plays at his mouth. "Ruby's slippers."

Chapter Thirteen

My uncle invites us to stay the night. Seeing that it's already too late to venture further up the coast, we accept his generous offer. He seems reluctant for us to leave anyway, as if he's lonely and in need of company.

Sophia and I manage to haul our luggage upstairs, with Otto racing ahead and behind and around our feet. On the third floor is a lovely guest bedroom with windows that overlook the city. As the sun dips toward the horizon, lights sprinkle on throughout the city like an ocean of fireflies.

"We must take Dottie to Fisherman's Wharf for dinner," Sophia insists.

It's chillier than I expected, and I'm grateful for the leather jacket. After a cable car ride to Pier 39, we stroll along the plank walkway. Sophia buys a sweatshirt with red-embroidered letters that spell "San Francisco" in the shape of the Golden Gate Bridge. The smells of the wharf are sharp and pungent, and chilly wind whips at my hair and the flags overhead. The pier is crowded with tourists and we shuffle along, moving slowly for Tim's sake, taking in the sights and sounds of the bay, where ships and sailboats are moored. Across the rippling water is Alcatraz. The freedom and fear, worry and exhilaration I am experiencing on this journey make me wonder if my quiet home in Kansas wasn't a prison that I had created for myself.

"I haven't been down here in years," Tim says. Pride deepens his voice as he points out different attractions.

We stop at the Bubba Gump Shrimp Company for a dinner of fried fish and shrimp. The batter is crisp, the fish fluffy white, the tartar sauce piquant yet sweet. Pelicans and seagulls perch along the wooden railings. There's a salty tang and bite in the air.

Tim and Sophia chat amiably, bonding over talk of vitamins, prescriptions, high blood pressure, and arthritis. They compare which medications worked for them and which didn't, the side effects that made some intolerable, and others they couldn't live without.

Later we sit on the wharf, watching sea lions lounging only a few yards away on miniature piers. Tourists snap pictures. A couple walks past holding hands, whispering to each other, pointing out sailboats and shops. A man on stilts wobbles past as he juggles brightly colored balls. His translucent stilts are lit from within, flashing different colors every few seconds.

Sophia buys a pretzel from a vendor and offers a bite to Tim. He tries pulling off a piece, but his fingers fumble and Sophia helps him. They share a chuckle at their awkwardness, then Sophia wipes a chunk of coarse salt off his upper lip.

I look away, feeling as if I'm intruding. Many times I've gone to dinner with Craig and his wife, Lindsey, with Abby and her many beaus, with friends and their significant others. I never felt lonely, never felt as if I was missing out on something. But tonight I do.

"You want some, Dottie?" Sophia asks.

"No, thanks. I'm full." But I feel empty inside.

The night is black, clouds blocking out the stars and the moon. Lights strung along the wharf reflect in the dark water like tiny jewels of sunken treasure bobbing to the surface.

"When I see your father again," Tim says, sitting between Sophia and me, "I might just punch him in the nose."

I laugh, then realize he's serious. His arthritic hands are curled into loose fists resting on his thighs. I cup a hand over his gently. "Thank you."

"For what? I didn't do anything to help you, my dear. Or Ruby. I should have helped. I should have tracked down that fool and made him go back to his family."

Sudden tears prickle my eyes like tiny needles. My cheeks feel cold in the ocean breeze. "Nobody ever even wanted to stand up for us before."

"Well, they should have. Ruby should have let us know. I could have done something, persuaded Duncan—"

"Momma didn't want him to feel forced to come home. She only wanted him if he wanted her."

He nods. "She was always proud. To a fault maybe. She always overdid, pushed herself. She wouldn't accept help or excuses. Even with that bad leg of hers. She wanted to be like everyone else."

"Pride's a cold bed to lie in," Sophia says, tearing off a piece of pretzel.

Is pride why my own bed is empty but for Otto? I ask, "Why didn't we have contact with you and Aunt Elizabeth?"

The creases around his mouth deepen. "It's my fault, my dear."

"Your fault?"

"I was in love with your mother when I left for California. Elizabeth moved out here not long after. I didn't know it until years later, but she apparently had a crush on me back in Kansas." In the yellow lights of the wharf, his ears redden. "Men can be stupid that way, not seeing what's right in front of them. Took me a while to get over Ruby. And then one day I took notice of Elizabeth, and that was that. It was as if she healed my wounded heart and stole it all at once. That sound crazy?"

"Not at all," Sophia says. "Love heals."

They don't seem to notice I'm silent on the subject of love and romance. I glance past the wooden railing at the sea lions, their bloated bodies content to lie where they are. Two rub noses. Another barks into the night. It's a forlorn and lonely sound that echoes deep in my soul.

"Elizabeth knew how I felt about Ruby," Tim continues. "Not that she was the jealous type. She never said anything. But I thought keeping our distance was a good idea. She seemed relieved not to be around your mother. I didn't want to stir up any strife or cause Elizabeth to be jealous or think my heart still pined for someone else. Now, though, I regret that choice."

"You didn't know." I wonder if I should tell him about the letter Elizabeth wrote Momma. Of course, all that was left was an empty envelope. I rub a hand along Tim's back. "You didn't know."

"That's true of many things in this life, my dear." He

curls his fingers over the bench seat. "Many times I wondered about my purpose in life. I couldn't imagine that being an accountant and financial adviser would change the world or make it a better place. Looking back, I know now my greatest purpose was loving Elizabeth. Might not seem big, but a life doesn't have to be magnificent to be important."

"Exactly." Sophia eyes a popcorn vendor nearby. "I've been around a lot of important people who seemed to be destined for great things. But I've always seen my own life as a series of small, purpose-filled moments."

"And there's satisfaction in that," Tim says.

"Which means your usefulness isn't over just because your wife is passed on," Sophia says.

Tears spring to Tim's eyes.

"It might be just beginning." Sophia turns to me. "For you too."

MAYBE IT'S THE long drive or simply the ocean air, but I sleep hard that night as if I haven't slept in a year. I wake to morning light streaming through thin white curtains in the guest bedroom. Sophia tiptoes about the room, murmuring to herself. As I sit up, I realize she's dressed in loose slacks and a long-sleeved yellow top, her suitcase packed and zipped.

"Good morning, sleepy head." She smiles.

"What time is it?"

"Almost time for breakfast. Tim is preparing French toast. He insisted. Then he'll give us directions and we'll be off."

I stare out the window at the awakening city, cars moving along the roller-coaster roadways, bumper to bumper. Somewhere out there is my purpose.

After taking Otto for a quick walk, I shower and dress. Tim serves us a hearty breakfast of French toast topped with maple syrup and fresh fruit on the side. Then we pack our things and maneuver the luggage back down the stairs without bumping a wall. We stand at the doorway, delaying the inevitable good-byes. I've come to like my uncle immensely. I sense his equal reluctance to see us go. Remembering the look in his eyes when we first arrived and asked for him by name, as if he'd won some prize, I make a rash decision.

"I know this is short notice, but would you like to go with us?"

A peculiar expression crosses his features. He steps forward and embraces me, holding me against his chest for a long moment. It's then I hear a distant whir and realize it's the microwave in the kitchen. Soon there's the pop, pop, pop of kernels and the buttery smell fills the hallway. "I was hoping you'd ask." He steps back and releases me. "Your popcorn is almost ready."

"You won't miss work, will you?"

"Retired last year."

"Excellent!" Sophia kisses him on the cheek.

"I'm not sure I'll be of any use to you on this trip, but I would like the chance to help you, Dottie. If I'd only known . . ." he seems stumped by his own helplessness. His features contract. "I would have tried to knock some sense into Duncan, or at the least turned him out at Elizabeth's funeral."

"It's okay." I place a hand on his arm.

"I feel responsible." He talks as if his honor has been tarnished.

"But it wasn't your responsibility. You couldn't have done anything."

"Two more stubborn people, Ruby and Duncan, you'll never know. Still . . ."

His words stick inside me like a piece of old chewing gum on the bottom of my shoe. Is that what people will remember me for? My stubbornness? *You remember Dottie Meyers, don't you? She wouldn't give up on that old farm, would she? Held on till the bitter end.*

"Maybe Miss Sophia is right," Tim says. "Maybe I still have some purpose left."

I recognize a deep determination in this man I've quickly come to respect and admire. "Okay, then, you better get packed."

"Already am, my dear. Already am." He glances over at the closet door beneath the stairs where a simple black suitcase waits.

Chapter Fourteen

I settle into the backseat with Otto since Tim seems too brittle to climb in the back. Soon we are off and out of the city and back on the Pacific Coast Highway, heading north.

There's no toll for crossing the Golden Gate Bridge moving out of the city. With Sophia driving, I sit back and absorb the scenery. The warm glow of the morning sun glints on the crossbeams, creating a golden halo for the bridge. I've never seen it in person before, only in pictures or on the news. It stretches out ahead of us, the traffic heavy on the other side with inbound commuters.

"This is the jumpers bridge," Sophia tells me, raising her voice over the road noise. "I saw a special on it. People still come here to jump. I'm not sure I understand that."

"Life gets to be too much of a burden." Tim peers out the side window. "Sad, isn't it?"

"Especially when this looks like such a hopeful place." I look up at clouds tinged with gold around the edges, the blue sky streaked with sunlight.

"You're right." Sophia runs her fingers through her straw-colored hair. "There's so much in life to be hopeful about."

But I don't feel all that hopeful these days. "What if someone lost all they had?"

Tim turns to look at me, but he stops part way, unable to meet my gaze fully. "I have. And more."

I regret reminding him of his wife's death. I know the pain of mourning for Momma. The grief never seems to end, and I imagine it's only worse with the loss of a spouse.

"That's how I found my Elizabeth."

"*Found* her?" Sophia takes her eyes off the road for only a moment. She grips the steering wheel with both hands.

"I had to have surgery. Elizabeth had moved out here not long after I did. We saw each other occasionally. We were friendly but nothing more. Selfishly, I admit, I used her to find out what her brother, Duncan, and Ruby were up to. She's the one who told me they'd been married." He remains silent for a moment as if caught in his own memories.

"What did you lose?" Sophia prompts.

"I went with friends to a beach down south, and when I dove into the water, I hit something. Fractured my neck. Couldn't even feel my toes or walk for a while. They put in a steel rod. I'm good as new now. Maybe better. Definitely better. Because I ended up with Elizabeth. She liked to say I was her Man of Steel." He raises an arm like a body builder showing off his bicep.

His accident changed the course of his life for the better. Maybe good can come out of bad, as Sophia says. If the tornado hadn't wiped out my farm, I wouldn't be on my way to find my father. And I never would have met Sophia and Tim. If I don't watch out, I'll end up an optimist like Sophia. I'm beginning to think it's contagious.

"After Elizabeth passed away," Tim turns back to face the windshield, "I didn't think I'd go on after that."

I follow his gaze, watch tourists walking across the bridge, many stopping to look over the edge.

"Can't say I ever thought of jumping off a bridge." Tim's voice quavers. "But if my heart had stopped from grief, I wouldn't have been disappointed to see my life end."

"And now?" Sophia asks.

"Now, my dear, I miss Elizabeth as much as I ever did. But some of the darkness has lifted. I can't say there's a rainbow on this side of grief, but I manage to get through each day. Maybe the silver lining for me is meeting you two."

"Being useful," Sophia says, "that's the ticket. Or it has been for me. I need to feel useful. I've known friends who received a diagnosis of cancer, like I did, who curled up in an emotional ball and just waited to die. The doctors didn't give me much hope either. My cancer was pretty far advanced. They did the mastectomy as a last-ditch effort. But I'm still here. For some reason God isn't through with me yet. The doctors said I was a miracle. They said that! I believe in miracles. This was surely God at work."

"But you had to believe," Tim says.

"You're right. That is what it takes—believing. Don't know how long I'll be around, but for today I'm here. If I can be helpful to someone, it keeps my spirits lifted."

"You've been a big help to me." I reach forward and touch her shoulder.

Sophia grins in answer, meeting my eyes in the rearview

mirror. "You're helping me too. Giving this old woman some-thing to do. And, Tim, you're being a big help to us both."

"That must be why I feel so good today." He looks back, his face solemn, but a twinkle sparks in his eye.

The ocean gives way to hills and cooler weather. We pass around the popcorn bag, and I feed a kernel to Otto. His little body keeps my lap warm, as the cooler air seeps right through the plastic top of the Jeep. The highway seems to hover along the bluffs overlooking the ocean. We skim past craft shops, bakeries, and bed-and-breakfasts. The weathered shingles of the shops match the gray sky and make the day seem colder.

"Did you ever watch *Murder, She Wrote?*" Sophia asks.

"Uh, sure. Wasn't it about a writer who solves crimes or something?"

"Angela Lansbury." Tim gives a sigh. "She was a looker in her day."

"And sweet as can be."

"You knew her?" I stroke Otto's fur.

"Way before she became Jessica Fletcher." Sophia waves her hand at white-picket fences we pass along the way. "Mendocino is where they filmed the TV show."

"We could sure use her to solve the mystery of these blasted shoes." I twist and fidget in my seat to find a more comfortable position. My eyelids grow heavy again as we move into heavier tree-lined areas. Using Abu, the odd monkey Craig gave me, as a pillow for my head, I doze in the back seat with Otto curled against me.

WHEN I BLINK myself awake, it's darker. How long did I sleep? Is it about to storm? I lean forward to peer out the windshield. On either side of us are gigantic redwoods. I feel like we've driven onto the set of *Honey, I Shrunk the Kids*. Giant ferns populate the forest around us.

Tim notices me when my hand accidentally brushes his shoulder. "You're awake."

Sophia flips on the Jeep's headlights to illuminate the narrow road ahead. Darkness folds in around us, though it's just past noon.

"This is what they call the old-growth forest." Tim takes on the role of tour guide again. "Many of these trees are hundreds of years old. Some over a thousand. Makes even me look young."

I stare out the window at the magnificent craggy trunks that seem to reach all the way to heaven. I keep one hand on Otto and peer out into the shadows. "It's kind of creepy in here."

"Oh, nothing to be afraid of." Tim swivels in his seat as best he can to look back at me. "Elizabeth used to come up here for her photography. I've always found the forest endlessly fascinating. There's something magical about being in one, especially one this size. Makes me feel small and yet a part of it all."

"No lions or tigers or bears?" Sophia grins.

"Maybe bears. There are quite a few black bears roaming around. I've seen a few myself. And an occasional elk. We saw an Olympic elk, I believe it was, just grazing out in the meadow." Tim laughs. "Mountain lions wouldn't be unheard of."

"Terrific," I mutter to myself and hold Otto a bit closer.

We find a stopping point and walk among the gigantic trees. I feel small. Sunlight rains down through the canopy of leaves in golden splashes of warmth.

"Makes you really think, doesn't it?" Sophia's voice has a hushed quality as if muffled by a mound of leaves.

The twittering of birds sounds like an ancient hymn among the enormous trees. A blue jay swoops down to the forest floor and hops on skinny legs. A low guttural growl comes from Otto, and I grab him before he takes off after the bird. "Think about what?"

"How much there is to know, and how little we do know about things. There was a time when I thought I knew everything. I don't know if everyone experiences that or not. Maybe it's a teenage thing. But the older I get—"

"The more I don't know," Tim finishes her statement.

"Exactly!"

They share a smile between them. I'm at least thirty years their junior, but I feel the same. I'm not sure I ever felt like I knew all there was to know. There was always so much I didn't understand. Maybe that's why I liked math. There was always a formula to help me find the answer. But the answers to my life have always been shrouded in mystery.

"There's always more for us to learn."

"It's like the seasons. Just when we think winter will never end, when life seems barren and hopeless, spring always arrives, offering rebirth and brave new possibilities, and we push on through what we once thought was dead. At any stage of life," she smiles, "we can blossom."

"I like the way you think." Tim takes her arm in his. He leads her toward a giant redwood. The two of them walk slowly, shaking their heads in wonder. Sophia laughs, the sound lifting off the ground and toward the treetops like a bird in flight. Tim smiles at her. "See this spruce? It's a Sitka spruce. Helps protect the redwoods from the ocean's salty spray."

"So many reflections of life here. You see these giants and you can't imagine they need protection from anything. Do you know what my daddy says?"

"No." Something cold and ugly wells up inside me. No one protected me from the cruelty of life. Momma tried, but she couldn't. Maybe no one can. Suddenly I feel exposed to the elements, vulnerable and scared. "And no offense, Sophia, but I don't want to know."

Her eyes widen. Tim turns in my direction.

Instantly I regret my words. I don't even know why I'm suddenly angry. "I'm sorry."

I've killed the moment as thoroughly as if I chopped down one of these historic trees. Solemnly we all turn back toward the Jeep and quietly climb inside. I feel chilled down to my very core. Regret wraps around me like a heavy blanket but offers no warmth.

"I'm sorry, Sophia. I shouldn't have snapped at you. I don't even know why I did. I just . . . well, I don't know why, but whenever you talk about your father, it makes me angry."

"It's okay." She turns the key in the ignition. "It's my fault. I should have been more sensitive. I'm a stupid old fool."

"No, you're not. It's my fault. I hate the bitterness and anger still inside me. I resent not having any words of wisdom from my own father. He wasn't there for me, for my mother. He didn't leave us any pithy sayings. He never—" My voice breaks and I stop talking before I embarrass myself further. "And he waltzed back into my life while I was unconscious and left me a pair of shoes with no explanation."

The Jeep isn't moving. I look up and find Sophia watching me in the rearview mirror. Tim sits quietly, his hands clasped in his lap, still as one of the petrified trees.

"I should have been more sensitive to your feelings." Sophia's voice and intonation are soft and feathery. "I'm sorry, Dottie. My father wasn't there for me either."

My gaze locks with hers in the elongated mirror. "But you're always quoting things he told you. Are you just—"

"Not my *real* father." She shakes her head, clenches her hands on the steering wheel. "No, my father died in the war. Somewhere in Africa. When I was a little girl, I'd imagine things that he might tell me. Sometimes I thought I could hear him calling my name, but it was just the wind. For a long time I drifted in life, afraid to love, afraid to depend on a man. Oh, I knew it wasn't my father's fault that he didn't return. But I had learned that no man was dependable the way I needed him to be. And that's probably the truth of it. Maybe that's the truth I needed to learn. That truth is what ultimately led me to God. When I speak of my father, my daddy, I'm speaking of God. He adopted me, became my real father. He *is* my father. In heaven maybe, but as real as real can be."

"I would have rather had a flesh-and-blood father." Bitterness runs through my heart as thick and red as my own blood.

"That's how my son felt too." Sorrow deepens her voice. "So I quit talking about God so much, so I wouldn't offend. I still lean on his wisdom though." She sighs. "I don't think that's right either. It's a hard balance. And now I've hurt you."

"No," I say, my voice breaking. "It's okay." I reach forward as she reaches back and we clasp hands, lock eyes.

"Should we be going?" Tim asks, his voice gentle as a summer rain.

A SONG SPINS through my head, blocking out my thoughts. Sometimes it feels like it's driving me, pushing me. The words are odd and slip away from me.

Sophia didn't actually lie to me. Maybe we all live with the reality we need to get through each day.

Can a person believe, truly feel like God is their real father? Frankly, it sounds like something a pink-haired tel-evangelist might say. The words ring false from overdone lips, but from Sophia? She's not some whacko on TV. My anger, I realize, isn't aimed at her. God, perhaps. My father, most definitely.

My feelings about my father, how he abandoned me, deserted our family, have been projected onto God. To me, God has always been cold and uncaring, just like my father. To me, he has always seemed far away, just like my father. Always silent. But was he really? Did God send the tornado? If so, why?

I've always believed in God, never doubted his power to create something as magnificent as these trees or as tranquil as a prairie stretching out for miles and miles. Just like I never questioned whether Duncan Meyers was my real father. But I questioned my father's love. If he loved my mother, Abby, and me, then how could he leave? How could he just walk away, never contact us? If he loved us, why didn't he reach out to us? His reluctance was proof enough for me.

But he has reached out now. Which leaves me confused. Why? What does he want? Maybe answers aren't easy or simple.

And so, maybe I've also believed God didn't really love me. All this time I thought I prayed but maybe I never really did. Compared to Momma, my problems didn't amount to much. Momma always put on a brave face, pretended not to need her husband or anyone else. Have I pretended not to need anyone all these years? Including God? Maybe I thought I had things under control. Or was my unbelief a way of not being hurt? Of holding back my love, scared I'd be rejected. If I didn't ask anything of God, then I couldn't expect anything in return. And I couldn't be hurt. Again.

I remember my father holding out a copper coin to me when I was young. It was a shiny, newly minted coin. Then, with a flick of his wrist, the coin disappeared. He showed me the palm of his hand. Empty. I grabbed his hand, looked between his fingers, up his sleeve, then dropped down on my hands and knees and searched the floor.

"Better check my elbow too."

I did, raising his arm high, then digging into his shirt pocket.

"Oh, ho! Look what we have here!"

The warmth of his hand brushed my ear. There was a flash, a glint of light. He held the coin out to me once more.

I grabbed first my ear then lunged for the coin.

He laughed and tickled me.

It became *our* trick, each night when he came home. We'd reenact the same routine night after night. Until suddenly he didn't come home anymore. I still had the coins, and for a while, I'd dig them out of my drawer and rub my fingers over the shiny pieces. When I was ten, I went out to the cornfield and heaved the coins as far as I could. I never went looking for them, just as I swore I'd never go looking for him either. But things change.

With the same frustration, I toss away the haunting questions as I lean back in the Jeep. I stare out the window at a slice of blue sky beyond the canopy of the redwoods. I don't have to see the sun to know it's there. My experience tells me it is. The problem is, my experience, or lack thereof, leaves a gaping hole in my heart.

"DO YOU THINK we should call Duncan before we arrive?" Tim asks.

"Better to surprise him, don't you think?" Sophia offers.

"Don't give him time to escape." I strap the seat belt across my lap and settle Otto on the seat beside me. Anxious about how my father will respond to my visit, and how I'll feel seeing him, I remember the promise I made to Sophia. I especially want her to see her son to make up for my bad behavior earlier. "We need to take a slight detour. Remember?"

"We don't have time for—"

"This is something you have to do," I say. "There's no guarantee that we have tomorrow. You don't want to live with regrets." Maybe that's what I'm feeling—regret that I didn't push Momma to bring Daddy home. It's too late for some things, but not for Sophia and her son. Not for me. Maybe not for my father. Or so I hope. "Please, Sophia. Let's go see your son."

Chapter Fifteen

I t's a log cabin deep in the woods. The road leading to it is a dirt path, with grass sprouting between the tire tracks. A bicycle leans against a stack of chopped wood. A barbecue grill holds water, probably from the last rain. The cabin is rustic. No luxuries. No real amenities. No satellite systems or antenna. No curtains in the windows. Still, it looks clean. The crisp scent of pine perfumes the chilly air. I reach over the backseat and grab my leather jacket from atop the luggage.

"Are we in California or Oregon?" Tim asks.

"Oregon." Sophia parks the Jeep beside the cabin and opens her door. "Aren't you coming?"

"Is it okay?" I ask.

"Of course."

It's too quiet in these woods. Except for the song of a distant bird, the crunch of pine needles beneath our feet, it's still and hushed. Sophia knocks on the door of the cabin. She waits, giving her son enough time to circle the small interior several times. With a determined slant of her jaw, she stands erect, unmoving.

"Maybe he's not home." Tim lifts an old ax by the well-worn handle and swings it around to land with a decided *thunk* on the wood stump.

Sophia stares resolutely at the door for another minute. She shifts from one foot to the other, raising her shoulders, pressing her arm against her side in a self-conscious move. With a heavy sigh, her mouth sags with disappointment, and she turns away. "Let's go."

"We should wait." I'm not sure why I say this, but it seems the right thing to do. "We've come this far."

"We still have a long way to go." Sophia walks away from the cabin, circles a ring of rocks that are charred on the inside as if the site's been used for campfires. I notice a rope strung from one tree to another, like a laundry line. The simple cabin makes my home in Kansas seem luxurious. We settle into makeshift chairs. Tim and Sophia share a stump. Otto and I make ourselves comfortable on the carpet of soft pine needles. I turn my wrist as if to check my watch but stop myself. We are in a hurry, but I want to do this for Sophia. I want to give her the time she needs. Yet I feel a growing sense of urgency with each passing second as some annoying song circles through my head.

"It's really quiet here." Tim looks at me, his eyes imploring as if he wants to magically conjure up Sophia's son so she won't be disappointed.

"Leo likes it that way. Always has. He never cared for the city."

A distant hoot straightens my spine. "Could be wild animals out this way."

A growl of what sounds like a chain saw ricochets off the tree limbs above. It grinds and reverberates through the woods. Sophia stands first, looking anxiously about, her expression a mixture of excitement and confusion. Tim pushes to a standing position, his brow compressed into worry lines. I pull Otto onto my lap.

A four-wheeler bursts out of the forest and charges forward. The man astride has a mane of shaggy blond hair and a raggedy beard. Sophia gives a mild shriek. Her face breaks into a wide Carol Channing grin. Otto leaps down, runs off a few feet and stands his ground, barking for all he's worth. The four-wheeler eats up the distance between us. Otto yelps, tucks his tail, and scurries behind me. I scramble to my feet. Tim pulls Sophia out of harm's way as she waves. The four-wheeler barrels over the ashes of the forgotten campfire remains. Wheels roll past me in a blur of colors and sounds. The man skids to a stop, throws the four-wheeler into reverse, and zips around to face us, his whooping and hollering competing with the *vroom* of his vehicle.

He revs the engine then charges straight for Sophia. She's practically hopping up and down with excitement. Tim steps in front of her, his arms stretched out wide. Fearing the crazed driver will run them over, I grab a thick stick off the ground and hurl it at the man, thumping him on his head. He turns, his face a snarling growl. He leaps off the four-wheeler and practically hurtles himself at me. I raise my arm as if to thwack him good if he dares touch me.

He stops, glares down at me, then tips back his head and roars with laughter. I blink at him dumbfounded. Then he turns away from me and scoops Sophia into his arms, spins her around, and releases her breathless. She readjusts herself, as one breast has sagged downward.

Otto ventures forth then and yaps at this beast of a man. The man stalks forward, making a grab for Otto. But Otto isn't playing this game. He turns tail and runs a few steps away, then stops and barks from a safer distance.

"What do you think you're doing?" I demand.

He straightens, bracing his hands on his narrow hips.

"This is Leo," Sophia steps forward. "Son—"

"What are you doing here?" His eyes narrow.

"Your mother," I glance toward Sophia, "she wanted—"

"It's the Jeep," she stammers. "It's stalling out on us."

Leo props a fist on his back hip. He wears jeans and a thin white T-shirt stretched over sinewy muscles that spring and bound with stealth-like grace though he's standing still. "You drove all the way from Santa Barbara for me to take a look at the Jeep?"

"We're on our way to Seattle. Can you look at it for us, son?"

He rubs his hands on the back of his jeans. "I'll get my tools."

The man turns and walks around the back side of the cabin as the rest of us release pent-up breaths. Tim and I look at each other. I'm not sure what's going through his mind, but I know what I'm thinking. *Let's get out of here.*

I press a hand to my chest to still the thudding of my heart. "What on earth just happened?"

"Is he crazy?" Tim's gray eyes narrow on Sophia.

"Oh, no." She laughs. "He's always been a bit wild. He's had some rough times lately. Doesn't like anyone to check up on him. What boy wants his mother stopping by unannounced?

Why I didn't even think he might have been," she hesitates and glances at the cabin, "entertaining."

"Terrific." I regret suggesting our visit now.

"I thought it best if we act like we need him rather than . . . well . . . Is that all right?"

"Works for me." Hopefully, we can see this through quickly. Maybe he'll fix the Jeep, then we'll get out of here lickety-split.

The crunch of footsteps precedes Leo's reappearance, and our brief conversation comes to a halt. He holds a rusted metal box. His walk is more of a stalking motion—unhurried yet purposeful. His worn jeans are frayed around the pockets and at the ends. He wears tan hiking boots. Sophia follows after him toward the Jeep.

Tim and I linger together. He hooks his arm through mine. "He's a strange one."

"Seriously."

"Do you think he was just joking earlier?"

I shrug. I've seen crazy behavior by teenagers in my classes, but this man is no teen. Makes me wonder if he's on drugs. Or if he needs some kind of medication. Or is this, for him, normal behavior?

"He seems untamed." Tim's voice is low enough for only me to hear. He sticks close beside me, as does Otto.

"Wild," I agree.

Together we edge closer to the Jeep.

Leo rubs the back of his neck and squats down beside the Jeep and peers at its belly.

"Could it be the starter?" Sophia looks at her son as if he holds all the answers.

"Or bad gas." He straightens.

When I taught school, I always tried to get students with bad attitudes to talk to me. It was better than hostile silence and it often released their anger.

"Sophia said you gave her the Jeep."

His glaring eyes unnerve me. They seem to size me up and dismiss me at the same time. "Are you saying this is my fault?"

"No! I meant—"

"She gave me a car once."

"What mother wouldn't do that?" Sophia reaches a hand toward him but pulls it back before touching his shoulder.

"A son giving his mother a car, that's a generous thing to do. A generous thing." Tim is either oblivious to the tension or trying to move the conversation along to, "Thanks, it was nice meeting you."

Leo shrugs, apparently uncomfortable in the role of nice guy, and digs into his tool box. "I didn't need it." He pulls out a wrench and jabs it at something under the hood.

"I'm pretty good with tractors," I offer, lame as it sounds, and peer under the hood. When it came to the farm equipment, my engine repair technique generally involved banging something hard and metallic against it. I admit, this didn't always work.

He glances up, stares at me unblinkingly, then goes back to work.

"Dottie lives on a farm," Sophia explains. "Or she did."

"Did you look at the spark plugs?" I ask.

"Did you?" he counters.

So much for helping. I turn away.

"Start it, will you?"

"Sure." I take the key from Sophia and slide into the driver's seat. "You know you could really use some—"

"Shh!" His sharp glance at me makes me swallow my words.

Leo cocks his head to the side, listening. He stalks to my side of the Jeep. Now what? He whips his arm out and thrusts it into the Jeep, brushing my leg with his forearm. Reaching past me, he cuts the engine. Before I can protest, he pulls away and returns to the front of the Jeep, wrestling with something under the hood. I get out of the Jeep, stand near Sophia and Tim, turning to look at his lonely cabin.

What would drive a man to live out here by himself? He's not that old. Not old enough to retire anyway. Maybe my age, maybe a bit more. So what gives? A felony? Bad personality?

A rustling behind me scatters my thoughts. I jerk around. This man is unpredictable, unnerving. No telling what he might do. Now he's lying beneath the Jeep, banging on something underneath. His long legs stretch outward, his work boots scarred, muddy, and askew. His shirt has ridden upward, giving a glimpse of a tan, hairy torso. I look away, uninterested.

"Start it up again," he calls out.

Sophia, Tim, and I look from one to the other.

"Hey, farm girl!" his voice is sharp, like incisors.

My eyes narrow. "My name is Dottie."

"Start it up, will ya?"

With a hefty sigh, reminding me of Abby as a resentful teen, I trudge back to the Jeep and turn the key, start the engine, then vacate the driver's seat so I don't get in his way again.

But a sudden yelp sends a jolt down my spine. Leo hollers, his legs kicking out crazily.

Panicked, I race for the Jeep, fumble with the key to turn it off. In the silence afterward, I meet Sophia's wide, shocked eyes. I jump from the Jeep, coming around the wide-open door, my heart pounding. "Is he okay?"

Leo rolls out from beneath the Jeep, his shoulders shaking, his torso contracting. Laughter rumbles out of him. Laughter.

For the second time I want to kick him.

Sophia chuckles along with her son, pats him briefly on the back as if to reassure herself. "Leo always was a prankster."

I want to tell her she failed miserably as a mother. He's like one of the junior high kids I used to teach trapped in a thirty-something body. A nice body. But still . . . I'm ready to get out of here. "Is it fixed?"

He jumps to his feet, agile as a large, overgrown cat, with a spring in his step that is both surprising and alarming. "Ready as it'll ever be."

"Good," I say, "then we can go."

I can't avoid the hurt look in Sophia's eyes as she watches her son. I recognize the longing and need that I once had looking down that long lonely drive as I waited for my father to come home.

"Where are you headed?" He starts gathering up his tools.

"Seattle," Sophia answers.

Wasn't he listening earlier?

"Sophia," I say, "if you want to stay here . . ."

"I won't abandon you." Her ferocity matches her son's.

Leo props a fist on his hip and looks right at me with an unnerving stare. "What's in Seattle?"

"We're going to find Dottie's father," Tim explains.

Uncomfortable beneath the weight of Leo's stare, I bend down and pet Otto, pick him up, and cuddle him against my chest.

"I can't guarantee this Jeep will get you there."

"We'll be okay." I'm not sure I believe my own bravado.

"Hold on then." He gathers up his tools and jogs off toward the cabin.

"What's he doing now?" Trepidation makes Tim's voice quaver.

"I don't know." Sophia watches for him, her gaze anxious, hands twisting.

I know what it's like to say good-bye and I don't want her to have to. Guilt presses in on me. "Look, Sophia," I manage, not believing what I'm about to say, "if you'd like to invite him along, so you can spend more time with him, then it's okay with me."

"Really?" She hugs me quick and hard.

I have a feeling I will regret this. After I settle Otto into the back of the Jeep, I suggest to Tim that he climb in the back too. "It'll give Sophia and her son a chance to visit."

"Hold on!" Leo calls. He tosses a bag in my direction.

I catch it against my chest. It's a small gym bag, light enough to only carry a change of clothes and a toothbrush. Otto barks again. I have the urge to tell Otto to sic 'im, but I wouldn't put my little dog in that kind of danger. If only Otto were a Great Dane.

"You riding in the back with me?" Leo's gaze slides over me.

"No, I was going to let you ride up front."

"Don't worry, farm girl. I don't bite. Want a boost?"

"No, thanks." Clamping my mouth shut, I climb into the Jeep and pull Otto onto my lap.

Leo moves with the ease of a mountain lion, leaping into the backseat. He pulls Abu out from under him. I reach for the monkey, but Leo angles him just out of reach. "This your security blanket?"

"A gift."

"From a lover?"

I feel my cheeks burn.

He grins and tosses Abu to me. "Much Abu about nothing, eh?"

Chapter Sixteen

e drive up the coast and further into Oregon. With every minute, my irritation tightens into knots along my spine. Every time Leo looks over at me or moves, bumping into my arm or leg or hip, I jerk away. I can't help it. He just rubs me the wrong way.

At another little town we drive through, Sophia pulls into a parking lot outside an appliance store.

"What are we doing?" Tim lifts his head as if he nodded off a ways back.

"I need a microwave." She waves a plastic-covered packet of popcorn then grabs an extra out of her bag. She's out of the Jeep in half a second, sliding the packets into her skirt pockets.

While avoiding Leo, looking anywhere but in his direction, I notice another *Wizard of Oz* advertisement posted in the window of a novelty shop. The picture is of the famous director in charge of the production and says, "Pay no attention to that man behind the curtain."

"You a fan?" Leo leans close, following my gaze with his golden eyes.

"No, not really." Not anymore. I'm getting annoyed by the way Oz keeps intruding in my life.

Two minutes and forty-five seconds later, Sophia walks out, her arms carrying two bags of popped corn. Behind her, a couple of surprised faces watch from inside the giant-paned glass window that advertises a twenty-percent-off sale.

"You borrowed their microwave oven?" I ask.

"They weren't using them. I bet it'll lead to a sale."

"How do you figure that, my dear?" Tim takes one of the bags from her and pulls apart the top, hissing at the heat, then handing it back to Leo and me.

Leo scoops out a handful and says as he chews, "The smell." He offers me the bag, but I decline. He takes another handful but pauses before shoving it in his mouth. "The smell entices customers." He raises his eyebrows with what I'm guessing is some kind of message. A piece of popcorn pops out of his mouth as he talks and sticks to his untamed beard. "Haven't you ever heard of baking bread when you're trying to sell your house? It makes the house smell homey—like the buyer has come home. Same as wearing cologne on a date." He leans close and sniffs, then makes an approving (or so I think) growling sound in his throat. "It's all marketing."

He could use a little PR work. But I have a feeling he never has to advertise for dates. I imagine plenty of women are enticed by him.

"Chocolate chip cookies work too," Sophia adds. "I did that once."

The buttery odor fills the inside of the Jeep and makes

my mouth water, but I'm not tempted to share with Leo. Out of principle. If I take even one bite, then it would prove Leo's theory of marketing, and I don't want to agree with anything he says.

Otto doesn't have the same qualms. Where once my little dog was afraid of this mangy-looking man, Otto is now his new best friend. Traitor that he is, he stands half on my lap, half on Leo's thickly muscled, jean-clad thigh, his little tail wagging as the man tosses him one kernel after another and laughs at his ability to catch each morsel.

"Watch it there, buddy." Leo pushes Otto's nose out of his lap as my dog searches for a lost kernel. "So what's the big deal about finding your father?"

I shrug. "No special reason."

"He owe you money or something?"

"No."

"He abuse you?"

Shocked, I stare back at him. I don't have an answer for that.

He grins. "Gotcha!"

"What?"

"You're a prickly pear, aren't you?"

"No, I'm not. I simply—"

"What?" He twists to face me, propping his thigh on the seat between us. His shin presses into my hip and thigh. He stretches one arm across the back of the seat, making me feel trapped. "What's wrong? You mad I came on this trip?"

I inch as far away from him as my seat belt will allow. "I actually invited you. Didn't your mother tell you?"

"You did? I thought it was my idea. Great minds think alike." He leans close, so close I can see the tiny pores in his skin, the red-gold hair sprouting from his chin. He smells of the outdoors, sweaty and piney with just a hint of cologne. Just the right touch for enticing, I imagine. "Hey, it's no big deal. This is the West Coast—anything and everything is accepted. If you don't like men—"

"I wouldn't use the plural of that word."

He laughs in a loud, obnoxious way that some women might call full and vibrant.

Tim and Sophia turn their heads toward us then back toward the roadway. I catch a glimpse of Sophia's satisfied smile. Does she think we're getting along back here? With a huff, I cross my arms over my chest and decide to make the best of it. Maybe I can feign sleep.

But Leo nudges my shoulder. "You remind me of a school teacher I had once."

"What did you do? Put gum in her chair? Burn her desk? Pull a knife on her?"

For a long moment he doesn't answer. He studies me as if I'm under a microscope. Resisting the urge to flinch or look away, I glare right back. Intelligence sparkles in his eyes. His mouth tugs sideways. He's enjoying this too much.

"So . . ." I prompt, uncomfortable with his scrutiny. "Did you get kicked out of her class?"

"Nope." His mouth tugs to one side in a self-satisfied grin. "Top student. Highest grade in the class."

Why do I doubt that?

"I kissed her."

I shouldn't be surprised, but I am.

"Not sure that had anything to do with my grade though. But I think she'd have given me an *A* for the kiss."

His confidence grates on me. He acts just like the irritating fourteen-year-olds I used to teach. They weren't all irritating, but some knew, or thought they knew, how to push my buttons. I showed them, and I can show this one too.

"You don't believe me?" he asks.

"I didn't say that."

"You didn't have to. It's the look."

"Then look the other way."

He chuckles, then leans forward between his mother and Tim, bracing his hands on the back of the front seats. "Go that way, Mom."

"To the right?"

"Yeah. You've never been up this way. Want to show you something." He flops back in his seat, draping his long arm along the back of the seat. "You don't mind, do you, Dottie?"

"Mind what?"

"Taking a detour. This is your trip after all."

"We are in a bit of a hurry." Now I feel like a bona fide teen. Worse, I can feel the heat of his arm against my shoulders.

He leans toward me, his breath stirring loose tendrils of my hair. "You don't mind me calling you, Dottie, do you? Or would you prefer Farm Girl? I could call you *Miss* Dottie, if you like that better."

"Dottie is fine." I grind my teeth.

"You don't like *Miss*? It's more proper."

"It makes me sound old."

"How old are you, Dottie?" His repetition of my name sets my teeth on edge.

"Thirty-four." I shake my head. I slept through my last birthday. "Thirty-five."

"At least you're not going backwards. That's not old. Well, not *too* old."

"Too old for what?" I cross my arms over my chest and look out the side window, the plastic buffeted by the wind. I wish we could suddenly, magically arrive in Seattle.

"Too old to have fun. You do have fun, don't you, Dottie?" He looks toward the front. "Hey, Mom, you still have fun, don't you?"

"What?"

"Believe me, my mom knows how to have fun. But Tim there, he might be too old for fun. Should I ask him?"

I elbow him in the side. "Leave them alone. Don't you have any manners?"

"I was raised in a barn," he raises his voice, "wasn't I, Mom? But you might like that, eh, Farm Girl?"

"What, dear?" Sophia asks.

"How old are *you*?" I decide to let my own manners fly out the window and put this man in his place.

"Thirty-five. That is, in two months I'll be thirty-five."

"And you don't have anything better to do with your life than to live in an out-of-the-way cabin in some God-forsaken woods?"

"Whoa! God-forsaken? I don't think so. God's there. Didn't you see him?"

"I don't know what you—"

"You missed him then. Too bad. But yeah," he arches his back and stretches. I ignore the way his muscles bunch and bulge beneath his T-shirt. "That's about all I have to do. What do you do, Dottie?"

"I'm retired." My lips press firmly together, and my knees do the same in a vain attempt to keep his leg from rubbing against mine.

"Retired? Really! You're awfully young to retire. Did you make your first million by thirty? What did you do?"

I don't want to answer, but I started this. I brace myself for his raucous laughter. "I was a teacher. So, no, I didn't make millions."

His silence causes me to turn my head. "I bet you were a good one."

Disarmed, I glance down at my hands holding Otto in place. "I don't know about that."

"Don't doubt your contributions. You did something important. Teaching kids . . . well, there's nothing more important or worthy than that. I had this teacher . . . really made an impact on me."

I prepare myself for some innuendo about the teacher he kissed, but it never comes. When I dare to glance at him, he's staring off, lost in his own thoughts. Finally the teacher part of me can't keep silent. I have a compulsion to help, to spur him on toward some kind of productive life, if for no other reason than to help Sophia with her unruly son. "Don't you want to contribute?"

"How do you know I'm not?" He leans forward, bracing his forearms on his knees, and stares out the front windshield. "It's right up here, Mom. You're going to turn left." Tilting his head, he looks back at me. "I ran a computer company for a while. Sold it. Didn't know what else I wanted to do. So I bought a cabin. Now I have time to figure out what's important."

"Have you figured it out yet?"

He leans back, resting his hands behind his head, arching his broad chest outward. His sheer masculinity makes me uncomfortable. Perhaps because he seems so comfortable in his own skin. "Maybe." His golden-brown eyes have flecks of green in them. He studies me, examines every inch of me. My skin tingles as if he's touched me. "Have you?"

"I haven't a clue."

I can see admiration spark in his eyes. "Most people are afraid to admit that." He claps his hand on my leg and squeezes my thigh. "I like you, Dottie. I really do."

It's in that moment I realize I'm seriously attracted to this man, and the thought shocks me more than when he barreled out of the woods and into my life.

IT TAKES A few minutes for Tim to climb out of the passenger seat. When Sophia succeeds first, Leo reaches over me and jerks her seat upward. He climbs over me to get out first. Bracing one hand against the back of the driver's pushed-forward seat and the other along the door frame, I start to exit the Jeep. But Leo turns abruptly, blocking my exit. If he'll just get out my way, then I can jump down or crawl my undignified way out of this awkward position.

Instead, he reaches in, loops his arms around my waist, and hauls me out. My chest collides with his. My face is too close to his hairy, smiling one. I push against his broad shoulders, but he doesn't release me until he's good and ready, which then makes me stumble backward. By that time, he's reaching in for Otto and placing him on the ground between us.

"This is a family farm that goes back four generations," Leo explains. "Friends of mine own it."

We leave the Jeep in what is little more than a cleared field and walk. My uncle and I team up, our footsteps less certain, more unhurried, while Sophia and Leo walk ahead of us. At times, Leo loops an arm around his mother's shoulders. She smiles up at him, beaming with undiluted happiness. There's something sweet about it, and yet it's an odd relationship I can't quite figure out.

Tim's breath is almost as short as mine.

"Would you like to sit down and rest?"

"I'm okay. Slow but okay." He nods toward the couple ahead of us. "Sophia reminds me of your mother. I like her."

"Really?" The two women seem light-years apart. Sophia has a modern air, whereas my mother was old-fashioned, set in her ways.

"Oh, sure. There's a spark of something that's indistinguishable and yet undeniable too."

I glance over at him, see the admiration in his eyes, then look toward Sophia who swings her skirt with her hands. There's a bit of a little girl in her walk. A bit of tomboy too. "What was my mother like when she was young?"

"Oh, charming. Full of life. Lots of fun. She wasn't frivolous though. She'd had her share of suffering."

"Momma never talked about hard times. But she wasn't false sunshine either. Resolute."

"She was that. But you know about her leg."

"Polio crippled it, made it not grow as large as her other one."

"She was sick for an entire year. Horrible stuff. All parents used to worry their kids would get polio. And there wasn't anything to prevent it back then. It killed many, crippled more. For a long time it made Ruby shy. Embarrassed her. When the other kids were running and carrying on, she couldn't keep up. She hated that. She didn't want to be left behind. She didn't want to stand out that way, and she didn't want special attention paid to her because of it."

"Momma didn't want charity."

"She didn't like weakness. Except . . ."

"Except?"

"She had a sentimental weakness for those shoes."

"I think my grandmother must have gotten them when she worked in Hollywood."

"Could have. All I really know is your grandmother gave them to Ruby when she was recovering from polio."

A pressure tightens about my chest. I never really thought of what Momma went through as she had to relearn how to walk. But now I do, having had to push myself over the last month. I realize I've slowed my steps and rush forward a couple of steps to catch up with him.

"She didn't want Ruby to waste her life, just waste away. The shoes encouraged her to get up, to walk and push for her dreams."

His words rattle around in my brain. Is that what I've been doing all these years? Wasting my life? Waiting for my father to come home? Unwilling to trust men who might leave me as my father did? Was that the message my father was trying to send me with the shoes?

"I always wondered what happened to those shoes." Tim stops beside a wooden bench. "I understand your Momma wore them on her wedding day." The trees offer a cool respite as we sit in the shadows. "Got her dream, I guess."

"Only for a short time." Maybe that's why Momma never mentioned them again. "Do you think they're the real ruby slippers? Not just some imitation?"

"I'm no expert." He rubs his jaw. "I suppose your grandmother was gifted enough with a needle to make her own. Wasn't she originally from California?"

"She was. She met my grandfather after the war and moved to Kansas to his family farm. He died not long after Momma was born."

"Your grandmother earned money by making dresses for folks. I believe she made several for my mother over the years."

"I wonder why she never went back to California?"

He draws a slow breath. "Ah, not an easy thing to do, pack up and leave."

"She used to talk about the great designers, the actors and actresses she met. I was still young when she died, but I remember. And Abby . . . well, I always thought her stories of Hollywood fed Abby's dreams. Momma thought so too. But why, if those shoes meant so much to her, didn't she tell me about them?"

"Maybe Ruby's dreams died when your father left. Maybe she quit believing." He indicates we should walk on, and we do in relative silence, only the scuff of a shoe, the crunch of gravel, the rasp of my breath accompanies us. Then he asks, "Are you thinking Duncan stole them from her? Maybe hoped to sell them, use the money?"

A cold knot settles in my stomach. Could guilt have made him bring the shoes to me? If so, then maybe he won't be happy to see me.

We reach the top of a summit where Sophia and Leo are waiting for us. I feel light-headed from the exercise.

"Look out there." Leo throws his arm wide.

I step toward a railing and look out over a red waving sea, a field of ruby red. "What is it?"

"Cranberries," Leo says. "It's a cranberry farm."

Water covers the fields, making the berries undulate. "Why is it flooded?"

"They're being harvested. The fields are flooded, and the berries float to the surface."

"They're beautiful," Sophia exclaims. "Can we go down there?"

"Sure. They sell dried cranberries as well as other baked goods." Leo turns away from the railing. "Dottie, you okay?"

I don't feel okay. I break out in a sudden sweat. Then the ground rushes up to meet me. The edges of my vision go dark.

"SHE'S COMING 'ROUND."

I feel like I'm climbing a rope out of a dark pit, one hand over the next.

"Dottie!" Sophia calls to me from somewhere far away.

Something rock solid and warm cradles me. I want to sink into the warmth and sleep. It's the same feeling I had coming out of the coma, which frightens me. I struggle to push away from the darkness. I open my eyes to the concerned faces of my friends.

"What happened?" Sophia asks.

"I'm okay." I struggle to get up. Leo holds me, his arms banded around me. "Really."

"Did you eat today?" Sophia asks.

"She wasn't hungry at breakfast." Tim bends over me. His sharp features are soft with worry.

"She didn't eat any popcorn." Leo's voice, so close, so low and rumbling, makes me look up. I realize I'm in his arms. He brushes dirt from my face, his fingers gentle, making my nerves buck. "Just rest easy a moment," he says.

It's that same exhausted feeling that seems to sneak up on me and overwhelm me at times. Suddenly all I want to do is sleep.

"Oh, dear!" Tim says, his voice far away. "She's passing out again! Should we take her to a doctor?"

"She's just tired," Sophia says.

I manage a nod. "I just need to rest. I'm okay."

My eyelids feel heavy. A warmth surrounds me.

"We're not too far from the Jeep," a deep voice resonates through me.

Remembering the walk to this spot, I think it's a long ways.

"She's been pushing too hard," Sophia says. "Her doctor told her to rest."

"Her doctor?" Leo asks. "What's wrong with her?"

Sophia explains my circumstances, how we met in the facility.

I don't hear Leo's response, but I'm listening for it, waiting . . .

Then I relax into a deep sleep.

Chapter Seventeen

"We'd best stop for the night." Sophia's voice penetrates my fog.

I force open my eyes, then shutter them as intense sunlight slashes through the side window. The Jeep sways beneath me. Otto is curled against my tummy. I feel warm and comfortable and want to go right back to sleep. I'm lying on my side, my head resting on . . . my hand rubs against roughened material. Jeans. A leg!

I jerk upright, knock into something hard.

Someone behind me grunts. Leo rubs his chin. "You okay?"

"Oh, good, she's awake," Tim says. "My dear, we were so worried about you."

I probe the new tender spot on the back of my head and reluctantly meet Leo's penetrating gaze. "Are you?"

"I've had worse." He works his jaw from one side to the other.

I reach out to touch his jaw but pull back. "I'm sorry."

Suddenly I'm embarrassed that I needed rescuing. I've always been the capable one, the one Momma leaned on, the one others depended on.

"You okay?" he asks.

"Yeah. Thanks," I manage, not knowing what else to say. "For . . . helping."

"My pleasure." His tone makes me feel even more uncomfortable. My nerve endings vibrate. I meet his smiling gaze and quickly look away. "You a Pink Floyd fan?"

"What?"

"Pink Floyd, the rock band. You a fan?"

My brow scrunches into a frown. "Why?"

"You were humming one of their songs."

"I was?" Heat rises to the surface of my skin again.

"Sounded like Pink Floyd anyway."

Suddenly, it all makes sense. "The songs that have been spinning around my head for weeks. They're from a Pink Floyd album. *Dark . . . dark . . .*"

"*Dark Side of the Moon?*" he asks.

I remember Momma playing it late at night. The songs would often put me to sleep.

Sophia shifts around in the driver's seat, leaning forward, peering out the windshield. "Any ideas on where we should stay?"

"Let's go on." I readjust Otto onto my lap, avoiding Leo's steady gaze. "It can't be that much further." I want to be there. Yesterday.

"There's a hotel not far." Leo stretches his arm along the back of the seat, skimming my shoulders, bumping my pony-tail. "Not fancy, but clean."

"Sounds perfect," his mother says. "My treat."

"I called it first." Leo opens the bag of popcorn he folded up earlier and searches for a few more edible kernels. He offers them to me.

My stomach rumbles and I take the few bits, my finger-tips grazing his warm palm. I avoid his gaze that makes me feel vulnerable.

"Dried cranberries?" Leo hands me a bag of dark-red, shriveled-looking raisins. "They're good." Before I can thank him again, he lurches forward, leaning between the two front seats. "I'll take care of the motel. Does everyone want their own room? Or do we want to bunk up?" He grins back at me, laughs at my shocked expression. "Don't worry, we'll let Mom and Tim stay together. And you and I—"

My jaw drops lower.

"Gotcha again!" He tips his head back and roars with laughter.

He faces the front again, his broad shoulders too wide for the space between the front seats, and directs his mother to a motel advertising free wireless connections and cheap rates.

We sort out the luggage, Leo taking the majority of it. He opens one door and deposits my suitcase along with Sophia's.

"Next time." He winks at me.

I'm pretty sure he's not serious. He couldn't be inter-ested in me. But a part of me warms to the thought. Closing the door on his smug face, I refuse to admit my heart is racing. My irritation reassures me. What woman wouldn't be annoyed by that man?

"We'll be right next door." His voice is muffled by the closed door, but I detect a lilt of humor.

With a huff, I turn from the door, crossing my arms over my chest.

A glimmer of a tear touches Sophia's eye. She reaches forward and touches my arm. "Thank you."

"For what?"

"For insisting we visit my son." She taps her heart, resting her hand there. "And then inviting him along . . . nothing could make me happier."

I brush off smudges of dirt from my pants and check the mirror. What a mess! I decide to change clothes before we go to dinner. Not to look nice. Just to be clean and decent.

AT DINNER LEO gives me a long, slow once-over with those insolent eyes, noting my new apricot shirt and white slacks. My insides feel like they're glowing. I regret not staying in the other outfit. I sit on the opposite side of the table from Leo, creating something of a buffer zone. But those eyes keep looking right at me. Leo breaks all the rules of propriety. Didn't Sophia ever tell him not to stare? Not to kiss his teacher? Not to talk politics?

"He was more crooked even than Nixon!" Leo declares and reaches for the rolls. "He doesn't have a prayer to win the election."

Thankfully we're the only diners remaining at the quaint seaside restaurant. I wish I'd stayed at the motel or in the Jeep with Otto. I'm exhausted and can barely hold my eyes open as I order soup.

"You need something more substantial," Leo says. "Meat. It'll build back your strength. Bring her a steak," he tells the waitress.

Who died and made him my boss? "But I don't—"

"Sure you do." He gives the waitress a nod to go ahead and jot down my order.

I glare at him but decide not to argue further. The waitress can bring me a steak, but I won't eat it. A decidedly childish decision. This man brings out the worst in me.

The steak arrives a few minutes after the shrimp bisque, which is light and delicate, and the sizzling smell mingles with the warm scent of Sophia's salmon and Tim's linguine. My stomach traitorously rumbles. Leo carves into his own medium-rare steak, gobbling it down like a starving animal.

"Aren't you going to eat?" Leo watches me as I spoon up the thick, rich soup I ordered on the side.

"I'm enjoying my soup, thank you."

"Oh, you two!" Sophia shakes her head. "Just admit you like each other."

I choke on the soup, and Tim pats me on the back. Leo grins at my discomfort.

Sophia turns her attention to her own meal, drawing a deep breath. "This salmon smells delicious. Anyone want to try it?"

Tim nods, and she cuts off a hunk of her salmon and places it on the edge of his plate.

Leo leans his elbows on the table, looking directly at me. "I'm just trying to help you. Don't read anything into it."

"Read what?" I give him a blank stare, trying for

innocence, and enjoy watching his face darken. I emulate a move Abby would make and bat my eyes. "That you care?"

He carves into his steak, starts to shove a bite into his mouth, but pauses. "Hey, not my concern at all. Next time you faint, I'll just leave you in the roadway for someone else to pick up and carry."

I decide I am way out of my league trying to tease or manipulate this man. I don't have Abby's skills. Looking toward the wide windows that stretch along the restaurant overlooking the Pacific Ocean, I can't see the waves, but I feel their turbulence churn inside me. I shove aside the bowl of bisque, rearrange the plates, and yank off a hunk of bread.

"Why are you on this journey?" Leo asks, chewing hard and fast.

"I told you." I grab the knife beside my plate and concentrate on cutting my own steak into bite-size pieces. "We're going to Seattle to find my father."

"Uh-huh." His brows tighten into a frown. He glances at Sophia and Tim. "What else?"

"Nothing."

Tim clears his throat. "Should we tell him?"

"It's Dottie's decision," Sophia says.

I keep cutting my steak, the little bites piling up. I don't want to discuss the ruby slippers. I don't want to discuss any part of this trip. I'm not sure whether Leo would laugh at the idea of selling the shoes to save the farm, but the slight possibility is enough to keep me from saying anything. But the silence at the table begins to make me anxious. "Why don't you tell us more about you, Leo? What are you doing living all alone out in the wilderness?"

"Enjoying life. That all right with you?"

I shrug and take a bite. The steak is juicy and tender. "If that's what you want."

"Who doesn't want to enjoy life?" Leo has already eaten half his steak.

I chew slowly, having learned to take food at a slower pace. "So that's what you want? To live alone? In the middle of nowhere?" As soon as the words are out of my mouth, I regret them. The same could be said about me. "Don't get me wrong. That's okay."

"I'm liking the idea of my cabin a lot better right now. Were you volunteering your company?"

"Oh, you two!" Sophia shakes her head.

"I'm not going to see my father for him to give me a handout, if that's what you think." Why did I say that? I scold myself to drop the subject.

Most of my life I felt I had some control. How hard I studied determined my grades. How hard I worked in the fields determined how the crops grew. But recent events have left me feeling out of control, as if I have no say in my future. Leo, for some reason, makes me feel as if I've lost control of my emotions too.

"I didn't say that."

"You did in the car."

"Okay, so why?" He crosses his arms over his chest and watches me. "Why are you going to find him? Does he owe you money?"

"No. I just . . ." I decide the blunt truth is the best way out of this adversarial conversation. "I've waited too long to see him. He left my mother when I was four years old."

Leo nods, as if understanding my need to know the man whose genes I carry. "Why now?"

"Is that what you're hoping for?" Tim gently implores. "To finally have a relationship with your father?"

I shrug, surprised at the emotions that churn up inside me, whipping up like a cyclone at the thought. "I can't deny I'd like that. But I don't expect it either. Still, maybe after all this time he's ready." Unless my father stole the shoes.

Sophia sips her tea and I imagine her quietly thinking, *Believe.*

"You're brave to go after what you want." Leo leans forward, resting his elbows on the table.

But I'm not sure I know what I'm ultimately after. My dad? The farm? The ruby slippers? Something that belonged to my mother? Or grandmother? Right now, I'd like to go home. "And what do I want?"

"Family." Leo's voice is as gentle as a caress.

Leo's answer rips the roof right off my heart, and I scramble to gather my flailing emotions about me. I feel raw, exposed. I stare at my plate and realize a hunk is missing from my steak. It's now a hard lump in my belly.

"There's a family for everyone," Sophia says. "Sometimes it doesn't meet society's expectations. But it can be just as satisfying, just as encouraging. Sometimes more so."

I nod. Could I be content with just this little group of friends for family? I believe I could. They have each given up their time and so much more to help me. And I want to help them. Isn't that what a family is?

"I am grateful for you." I put a hand on Sophia's back, my throat tightening. "And Tim. I never thought I'd have an uncle of my own." Much as I dislike admitting it, I'm grateful to Leo too. "Even you, Leo. You've all helped me so much." Pressure builds behind my eyes. "I'll always be grateful."

"There's a plan for everyone." Sophia touches the corner of her mouth with the linen napkin and smiles at me. "You're on your way to finding yours."

"But what if there isn't a plan, a rhyme or reason or sense to anything? Maybe life is just hard," I say. "Leo says he's enjoying life, but for me it's always been a struggle. That's my reality."

"Maybe this is all there is." Leo shoves a bite in his mouth and chews forcefully as if he's willing to be devil's advocate. Which suits him.

"That's not what I taught you." Sadness deepens Sophia's voice.

"Maybe what you taught me was all nonsense. God wasn't real to me the way he was to you, Mom."

"Now, now." Tim gives an uncomfortable cough.

"Because, son," she speaks in a quiet, yet authoritative way, "you were too busy with your own agenda. You wouldn't relinquish control."

These words take aim at my own heart.

"Not anymore. I've let everything go." Leo leans back, tipping his chair on its hind legs, his arms wide, seemingly defenseless. But I sense he has more layers, more protection.

"You said you found God in the wilderness," I interject, trying to ease the friction at the table.

"Not the way you imagine."

"How then?" I need to know, need to feel God is there, that I'm not all on my own.

"He's in creation. You can see it in nature. Unless you're determined not to. But does God care what I do?" Leo flops his chair forward. "God watches from a distance, if he watches at all. He doesn't have a plan, for my life or yours, Dottie. They don't teach that in Sunday school to little kids because it's a hard, cold reality. But as an adult, it's something we all have to face."

"Maybe you don't think he has a plan," Sophia's voice is wispy thin. "Or maybe you're afraid to hear what God might say or what he might ask you to do. Man was made in God's image, but man imposes his own weaknesses and failings on God, until God seems as powerless as we are."

Leo tosses his napkin on the table. "I didn't ask for you to show up on my doorstep. I didn't ask for your advice or your opinion about my life."

Before any of us can utter a word, he stalks out of the restaurant and into the night.

Chapter Eighteen

he wind off the ocean blusters and moans as I tread carefully along the rocky, uneven ground.

With the excuse that I needed to walk Otto, I left the table and released Otto from the Jeep. I feed him a few bites of my steak that I wrapped in a paper napkin, and he licks my hands clean. I then wipe off my hands on the back of my white slacks and immediately regret it. I'm used to overalls and hand-me-downs, not designer wear. Otto wanders a crooked path in front of me, drifting off to my left to sniff at some rock.

The lights from the restaurant give off a soft glow, and I spot the silhouette of Leo sitting on a ledge, his shoulders hunched as he looks out over the dark ocean. The night air is thick with clouds, the sky murky. The coolness puckers my skin.

Much as I try, I can't silence my shoes or pebbles beneath them. But Leo doesn't turn. I stop near him, but not too close. "Is this okay?" I ask.

He scoots over, making room for me, and places his hand on the rock as if inviting me to sit beside him. I inch closer and slide onto the cragged rock, leaving as much space between us as possible. His profile looks like a carving, chiseled and solid. The beard softens his hard edge. I wonder if his mother ever wanted him to be in the movies. He's handsome in a rugged, masculine, imperfect way.

Resting his arms on his knees, he glances at me. "How was dessert?"

"Tim ordered the apple pie, but I didn't try any."

"You should have."

In other words, I should have stayed in the restaurant, finished dinner, and left him alone. "Look, I know I need to gain weight." I touch my stomach which still feels heavy with the steak. "And I will, but not all in one night."

The side of his mouth pulls into a rueful smile. He reaches down and scratches Otto behind the ear. "Ever feel like you're fourteen again?"

"Occasionally." Lately, more and more. It certainly happens when I'm around Abby. And now this man. Does that mean when I care about someone, I regress in age? What on earth will happen when I meet my father? Will I become four years old again?

He rubs his hands together, the palms rasping against each other. "Never wanted to go back to those years. They were bad enough the first time around. Not worth revisiting."

"Pimples. Hormones. Insecurities. Who needs that, right?"

He turns and looks at me, his gaze intense as he studies my features as if searching for a small imperfection. "Yeah. Just when I think I've grown up, my mom comes along and proves I haven't."

"Sophia wants the best for you."

"Yeah, yeah. I know."

"She wants to see you happy."

"Who's to say I'm not? Don't you think it's arrogant to look at someone else's life and say they're unhappy in comparison to your own standards or expectations?"

I've had that most of my life. *If you could just find someone to marry, Dottie, then you wouldn't be alone.* I've heard it time and again. I understand how Leo feels more than I ever thought I would. "Maybe it's not your mom that you're reacting to."

"And what am I reacting to?"

"God." Before he can balk, I rush forward. "I say that because I've done the same thing. When people—your mom, to be exact—kept mentioning God, I overreacted. But it wasn't what she was saying so much as my feelings about God that had me reacting . . ." I rub my temple. "I'm not saying this very well."

"Yes, you are. I know what you're saying. Nonbelievers sometimes react violently to talk of God. And it's a spiritual issue."

"A spiritual battle." I feel a chill deep inside.

"You may be right. Mom and I have battled over spiritual issues before. She made it sound easy. And it wasn't easy."

"I don't think it was easy for her either." I think back on all she told me about her life. "Maybe we each have to come to the end of our rope before we're ready."

"Been there."

"Me too." I rub my palms against my white slacks. "I just think Sophia wants to make sure you're okay before . . ." I veer off course, deciding I shouldn't put words in Sophia's mouth, especially when she's not even here.

"Before what?"

Crossing my arms over my chest, I watch as Otto sniffs around, nose to the ground. He pauses, sniffs the air, barks, then sits nearby. I stare into the darkness, the shifting shadows that move and swell over the ocean, listen to the growling of the waves. "Before my mother passed away, she was worried about me, what would become of me, if I'd be all alone. You know the drill. It's what a mother does—worry about her little chicks. Right? Sophia's whole ordeal scared her. Made her face her own mortality. I mean, my situation certainly had me—"

"What are you talking about?"

"The tornado, even the coma, had me realize life isn't forever. We all know that at some level, but losing the farm made it very real for me."

"I meant my mom."

His abrupt words rattle me. "Her bout with cancer. It's one of those attention grabbers."

"My mother had cancer?"

I stare at his wide eyes, read fear in their depths. My heart quickens. "You didn't know?"

"No."

I dip my head into my hands, rub my temples. "I'm sorry. I just assumed you did. She's very open about it all." How long has it been since the two of them have spoken? "Why wouldn't she tell you?"

His mouth twists and he looks away. "Because I'm a jerk, that's why. Because I made it clear I needed my space. I didn't want to hear her platitudes of how God will help me through. I guess I had to experience that for myself. And I went off to lick my wounds."

"So she didn't want to burden you."

He shrugs a shoulder, presses his hands together, fingers splayed wide, and utters a harsh word aimed at himself.

"Hey, it's not your fault." I reach toward him before I can stop myself. His back is hard but warm to the touch. Tension coils in his muscles beneath his thin T-shirt. They flex beneath my palm. "She's fine. She's doing really well. I didn't mean she was about to die or anything. She's made a full recovery. But anytime someone faces a diagnosis like that, they're confronted with their mortality."

He's silent for a long time. I pull my hand away, but his warmth remains against my flesh. The steady breeze is soft against my face, the air cools my heated skin. I remember sitting on the front porch with Momma, watching the tops of the cornstalks undulating in a late-summer breeze, the stalks bending and waving as if some invisible guest wandered among them.

What was Leo's childhood like? Did he have an adversarial relationship with Sophia? Like Momma and Abby? Did he have moments of comfort and strength? Time to think and breathe? Crouched in the garden with Momma, I had plenty of opportunities to ask her questions, listen to her talk about the day, her thoughts and explanations. I pulled on her beliefs like a hand-me-down coat. I've lived my life as if they were my own. But were they?

"Why do we have to pull weeds?" I remember grumbling.

"If we didn't, the weeds would choke the good plants."

"Kill them?"

"That's right. Just as in life we have to weed things out

of our lives that choke our time, our attention, keep us from doing good things."

"Like homework?"

Momma paused in patting down the soil where she'd pulled a weed with a long root resembling a bleached carrot. "More like frivolous activities. Time wasters. Like tele—"

"Dancing," I spit out the word as I thought of Abby's dance classes that cost Momma extra money. Money we didn't have.

"Your sister loves her dance classes. And maybe she'll use them someday. I think of them as an investment in her future."

"I don't like dancing." I stood up and flapped my arms like Abby had in her last recital when she'd worn a butterfly costume. I jumped and leaped, swaying and twirling, in a caricature of my sister's abilities.

Momma laughed at my poor technique and went back to pulling weeds. "Just because it's not your cup of soup, doesn't mean it's not useful or worthwhile."

Breathless, I flopped down on the ground beside her, kicked my legs outward, rolling my foot first one way then the other. "Did you ever dance, Momma?"

"With this old leg?" She rubbed her knee, touched her thin calf, then pushed to a standing position. I watched her gather the discarded weeds carefully into an old milk pail. She limped off in the direction of the barn, and I jumped up to help carry her load.

Remembering Leo beside me, I realize I don't know his mother well. But aren't most mothers the same? Don't they want the best for their children? "Sophia," I say, "probably wanted to protect you. Mine did. She didn't tell me she was having symptoms. She probably would have hidden the diagnosis if she could have, if she hadn't needed my help, if she hadn't wanted to prepare me for her death. And that's what she did."

"When did your mom die?" Leo's voice sounds gruff, but I recognize it as his attempt to be gentle. And I realize how much the thought of almost losing his mother has hit him.

"A year ago. She was sick for ten years though. Polio returned slow but determined." This isn't usually a topic I discuss, especially with a stranger. Though I've known Leo less than a day, we're no longer strangers. Sophia's words give me strength. Helping another gives my pain meaning, gives me a sense of peace. "The last year Momma needed me home full time, so I quit teaching to be with her. She wanted me to hire a nurse, but I wanted to be there, to spend what little time she had left together."

"You're braver than I am."

"You never know how you'll react till you're in a situation. But you do what's necessary."

"You must have made your mother proud."

"Maybe. I don't know. I'm beginning to realize she wanted me to find my own life. Things she said toward the end . . . maybe she feared I was too dependent on her."

"She knew her happiness wasn't yours."

His words strike a resonant chord inside me. But I always thought I wanted to be there, to stay on the farm. Did Momma think I wanted—needed—something else? She was never the type to push. She was usually content to wait and watch. Patience, she said, was a virtue.

For a few moments Leo and I sit together, a foot apart, our gazes parallel, our thoughts adrift. The waves break and shatter against the rocks. I remember conversations I've had with Abby and Craig over the past few months. Travel, Abby encouraged. Family, Craig emphasized. Maybe my idea of happiness isn't theirs. Or maybe they were right. Maybe Abby knows me better than I know myself. Maybe I've been living Momma's life, not my own. Maybe I have let fear rule my life.

The emptiness and excuses coming from Leo are familiar because I've heard them from my own mouth. Looking at him now, I ask, "Are you happy?"

He shrugs, his eyes still trained on the ocean. "Are you?"

"No," I state the truth. "I lost my home. My farm. Everything." I reach down and touch Otto's wisp of a tail. "Almost everything."

"So if you really want a family, like Tim said, is that what the farm means to you?"

I draw in the cool air and release it with my reservations and fears. "I've always been a caretaker. Taking care of my mother. The farm. Otto. That's just what I did. I don't know what else to do." I press my thumbs together. "What am I supposed to do now? It seems so pointless."

"What if it is?"

"I don't know if I'm that cynical. Are you?"

"It's worth asking the questions. I had to explore those possibilities to figure out what I believe."

"My mother was content to care for the stock and grow corn and hay."

"But you weren't?"

Reluctantly, I nod. "I felt restless. But then again, I didn't want to leave the farm. I wanted to be there in case . . . I didn't want to be like my sister."

He rests the side of his head on his fisted hand. "What's she like?"

"Flighty."

"Is she happy?"

That stops me. "I don't know. Maybe. Maybe not. I'm not sure I know her well enough to know. She always seems to be striving, searching. I used to think she was reckless. But now I'm starting to think she's braver than I've ever been. Shouldn't I know more about my sister?"

"Maybe you're not supposed to know. Maybe it's none of your business."

"Maybe I've been as arrogant as everyone who's ever said to me, 'Dottie, you should find some nice man and fall in love.' Like that's as easy as going to the drugstore."

"Or the drive-thru. 'I'll take a side of fries and throw in the love of my life.'" He laughs, shaking his head as if he's heard the same thing. "So what would make you happy, Dottie? What do you want? To find a nice guy? Get married? Sail the South Pacific?"

"I never thought I'd see the Pacific Ocean! I don't really know. I'm going to find my father. After that . . ." I shrug. "One day at a time at this point." Will I save the farm? Sell the shoes? Run away and find a new life? "My sister—"

"The flighty one?"

"Yes. She's put the farm up for auction. Eight days . . . six days until that happens. Six. Then it won't be mine anymore. Not that there's much left after the tornado."

"So what's to go back to then?"

"My life. Memories."

"Why are you really going to find your father? To borrow money?" His voice holds no condemnation, just curiosity.

"He visited me while I was in a coma. He left me something. I don't know what it means. I don't know what he was trying to say, if he wanted me to find him. That's what I'm hoping." Hoping. It's a powerful emotion that sweeps over me like a blast of wind. I refrain from being too specific about what my father left. Not that I don't trust Leo, but saying it out loud just sounds so strange. I shrug. "I want to know more about this . . . heirloom. Was it Momma's? My grandmother's? I have nothing left belonging to them. Nothing. None of the quilts Granny made. None of the blankets Momma knitted. Bottom line, I waited all my life for my father to come, to reach out to me. Now that he has, I have to go to him."

"Makes sense."

"Honestly, I'm scared."

The surf murmurs against the shore. It comforts me and yet at the same time makes my life seem small, inconsequential, while my fears seem as vast as the ocean.

"Scared of what?"

"What if . . ." I take a steadying breath before I admit the truth. "What if he doesn't want to see me, talk to me?"

"But isn't that already true?" His words make me flinch. Yet those same words shine a light on that truth from a different angle. Not rose-colored as Sophia would view my situation, but not as harsh or brutal either as my own way of looking at my fear. "You're afraid of what's been true your whole life."

The painful truth silences any incongruity. "You're right. Ridiculous, huh?"

"Not at all." He reaches for my hand, turning toward me at the same time, and cups my face. His dark, deep-set eyes seem to see right into my soul. An uneasiness settles over me. I want to pull away, but I don't dare. "But I don't think that's your real fear."

A caustic laugh emerges from deep inside me. I tug my hand out of his grasp. "Oh, yeah? And what am I afraid of?"

"To be loved." This time, his words are harsh, revealing every shadowed and hidden crevice of my heart.

Much as I would like to deny it, I can't. I *am* afraid. My heart flutters even now in my chest, like the wings of a tiny bird unable to fly.

"It's okay, Dottie." His words are a low growl. "I'm afraid too."

I don't move toward him, but I don't move away either. Two frightened people, side by side, who are afraid to risk, afraid to love, afraid of being wounded, can't reach out to one another. "Maybe," I venture a hypothesis, "that's why we can't explore . . . experience God. We're afraid of him."

He gives a slight snort. "Afraid to be disappointed."

"Afraid to be rejected."

"It's not like my mom said. I'd do anything for someone, for God even, if I knew I wouldn't be a disappointment." He clasps his hands between his legs. His shoulders are rounded, his back bowed. "The truth is, I'd probably let God down. I'm a screwup."

His vulnerability has me reaching toward him. I place a hand on his shoulder. "I don't believe that."

"It's true. I—"

I wait for him to continue, but he shakes his head, his lips compressed. Heat rolls off him, emphasized more so by the coolness in the night air. Tension coils within his muscles. It's an odd feeling, being drawn to him and nervous at the same time. I want to know what he's thinking, what he's feeling. "What?"

He spits out a word I've heard teens utilize during tests or athletic events or simply walking down the middle school hallway. Usually I would dole out detentions or reprimand them. But this is a man, a man afraid and frustrated and needing release. Sometimes right and wrong isn't a list of dos and don'ts. Sometimes "right" is acceptance, openness, and love. I keep silent, waiting until he's ready to share more. He's taken a huge step this evening in sharing even this much. But why open up to me? Am I just a big-sister type, easy to talk to? Or am I the strong, steady friend, easy to shift burdens to my narrow-but-strong shoulders? Or is there something more between us? Something I can't fathom? Something I'm afraid to admit I might want?

Finally he releases a long breath. "I had a company. My own company. But I made some bad decisions. I trusted the wrong person. I let my need for . . . well, my emotions got in the way of business, clouded my judgment."

I wonder if some woman brought him down, like Delilah betrayed Samson. Strange emotions ripple through me, a mixture of wanting to shelter him and envy that some woman could have that effect on him. I've never felt this way. And it doesn't seem rational.

"Frankly," he interrupts my crazy thoughts, "I got greedy. Instead of looking at the situation objectively, I just jumped in. Because it's what I wanted. I wasn't thinking of the good of the company. I wasn't thinking of the hundred or so people who worked for me. It was all about me. And I lost it all."

I think about this journey I'm on. In some ways it's totally selfish of me, to keep the shoes from my sister, to consider stopping the auction. Am I the one being greedy? At what cost?

Leo looks away, coughs, then holds my gaze with his own. "I lost my company. Ended up with a package of stocks and bonds and cash. My so-called friend and mentor took it over." He looks down at his hands. "But I felt like a failure. Fact is, I did fail. And I didn't like who I'd become. Everything revolved around me—what I wanted, what I needed. So that's why I moved to the cabin. I had to figure out who I am, what I want."

My heart aches for him. I'm not sure this man who has run his own company has much in common with a simple Kansas farm girl, and yet there is a deep connection of hurts, dreams, and failures that somehow binds us together.

"I've been fighting my sister over selling the farm for a long time. I thought she was being selfish. But now I'm starting to think it was me. I don't know. I loved my life on the farm. Or maybe it's simply all I knew. Maybe I feared giving it up meant giving up the dream that my father would return. But . . ." I place my hands on my knees, rub my thighs as the coolness makes my skin numb. A chill passes through me. "I haven't been happy for a long time. I don't mean since the tornado. Way before that."

"You liked caring for someone. You enjoyed being loved in return."

"Yet it wasn't enough. I knew I was missing out on life. I'd see my friends marry, move away, start families. Their lives changed, mine didn't."

"Were you afraid no one would love you, accept you the way your mother did?"

"Probably." It's the first time I've ever admitted the truth even to myself. It's not necessarily pleasant, but it is freeing.

Looking deeply into my eyes, he leans toward me. For a moment I think he might kiss me. My heart hammers at the possibility.

Suddenly he grabs my elbow. He looks behind me, toward the parking lot.

"Otto!" I realize he isn't at my feet anymore. I hear the

padding of his paws and his panting before I see him trotting toward me. "Come here, boy."

"Shh." Leo squeezes my arm.

"What's wrong?" I start to turn, but his fingers tighten even more. He places a hand against my face.

My stomach flips. "What—"

"Don't move."

My heart thumps heavily.

"I've seen that car before."

Disappointment collides with confusion. "What car? Where?"

"We're being followed." His golden gaze drills into me. "Why?"

Chapter Nineteen

eo tugs me off the rock and up the embankment toward the restaurant. Fog has begun to roll in. The tiny lights that line the rim of the building's roof glow eerily. His hand on my arm is warm and firm. Even though he pulls me slightly off balance, he also manages to steady me. I feel awkward, like that little girl dancing in the garden, my footsteps heavy and clumsy as I dodge Otto who seems bent on getting between my feet.

I glance toward the parking area, search for signs of a suspicious car. Headlights flash in the distance like two halos, on then off. A gray darkness swallows the light. Wisps of cool air float about us, chilling me to the bone.

Leo bursts through the restaurant's doors, startling a waitress who drops a stack of menus. He motions to Tim and Sophia. "Let's go!" His voice rumbles through the establishment. "Check!"

"No dogs in here," someone calls.

I scoop Otto into my arms. "I'm sorry."

We gather our belongings, purses, jackets, boxes of left-over food. Tim fumbles with his wallet. Leo grows impatient waiting for the waitress. He stalks across the restaurant where the tired woman stands at a computer. He sets several bills on the desk. Then he's back, hurrying Tim along. Before we walk out the door, I peer out into the gray murkiness.

"Still there?" Leo asks.

"I don't know. I can't see anything."

"Who?" Sophia asks.

"What's going on?" Tim struggles with a sleeve of his jacket. Sophia helps him tug the material over his stooped shoulders.

Leo starts to open the door then stops. "Let's get back to the motel."

Sophia's face crinkles with worry. "Is Dottie in danger?"

Leo's face darkens. "I don't think she's told me everything about this trip. We have to talk."

"Back at the motel."

Otto gives one bark as if to emphasize the urgency to leave.

Leo nods grimly.

As I open the door, another of those *Wizard of Oz* advertisements grabs my attention. This time, the Wicked Witch of the West peers out, her face green, her eyes familiar. I gasp. "Oh my!"

"What is it?" Leo asks.

"Isn't that . . . ?" Sophia steps forward and peers closer.

I nod. "My sister."

"Abigail?" Tim asks.

"She likes to be called Abby," I tell him, noticing the dates for the show are this week. The caption on the poster reads, *"I'll get you, my pretty—and your little dog too!"*

"Well," Leo pulls the door open further so we can all leave the restaurant, "you did say she was flighty."

BACK AT THE motel, we search the parking lot for any sign of the car following us . . . me. Leo seems dubious at best about the shoes and that someone might be following me, looking for them. I explain all the strange happenings, my sister's odd behavior concerning them. Casually, he puts an arm around my shoulders. He provides a shelter I want to lean into but resist. I've been strong on my own for so long. And before that, I was strong for my mother and sister. Old habits are hard to break.

"Don't worry," he says, his breath bathing my ear. "I'm right next door. If you need me—"

"We'll be fine." I slide the key into the door.

With a backward glance toward Sophia and me, he moves toward his and Tim's room.

I hold the door for Otto and Sophia who move ahead of me into the room. She flips on the light and makes a strangled sound that jolts my heart just as Otto begins barking.

"What is it?" I peer around her, which takes effort as she's much taller than I am. But nothing seems different to me. Our luggage remains on opposite sides of the room, just as we left it. The monkey Craig gave me sits on the bed, staring blankly ahead, its arms and legs splayed. "Did you see a mouse?" I imagine a furry creature scurrying for cover when the light surged, and a shiver ripples down my spine.

She shakes her head. "We've been robbed!"

Her announcement hits me like a rock falling out of the clear blue sky. "The shoes!" I jerk open the closet door, see the open shoebox, the crumpled yellow tissue paper. "They're gone!"

"I have the shoes." Sophia clutches her large purse to her chest. "They're in my bag."

I take a calming breath. The room looks as serene as when we left it.

Leo rushes into the doorway, his features hard and unrelenting as he pushes into the room. "What was taken?"

"Nothing. We weren't robbed." I watch Otto sniffing the carpet, running this way and that, circling around as if following a scented trail.

Tim peeks in the doorway, his knobby hands fisted. "Where are they?"

"Right here." I touch Sophia's bag, amused and moved by their gallant behavior. "We weren't robbed." I put an arm around Sophia who is trembling. "False alarm. We're all a little jumpy. Paranoid in the extreme."

"No." She edges into the room, stepping lightly as if she might disturb some evidence.

Are we looking at the same room? Everything looks normal. "Okay," I remain calm, trying to keep an open mind about this. "Tell me what you see that makes you think—"

"I left my suitcase closed, the tabs locked in place."

I stare at her battered suitcase which looks like it dates back to the 1930s. The lid is flat, the brass locks upright, unlatched.

"Are you sure, Sophia?" Tim's gaze skips around the room faster than he can move. "You didn't forget, my dear?"

"Mom forgets names and places but not how she arranges her things," Leo says, his voice deep and hushed. "She always arranges her suitcase just so in case the help decides to look through her things."

"Well, maybe that's all this is." I search for a plausible solution.

"This isn't the kind of place," Leo says, "where they turn down the covers and place chocolates on your pillow."

With a trembling hand, Sophia moves forward. She cautiously lifts the lid and nods as if answering her own question. "Yes. Most definitely. Someone has been looking through here." She points her finger at her pajamas scrunched to the side. "See this!"

I stare hard, trying to see fingerprints or explosives or something that seems out of the ordinary. But everything looks normal.

"I would never leave my panty hose dangling out of the pocket like that. And I keep my pajamas folded neatly."

Maybe Sophia simply forgot or was careless, but I don't want to tell her she's exaggerating. Then I remember Abby rifling through Momma's boxes, tossing clothes this way and that without regard to their care, but I bat the memory away. "What should we do?"

"Check your things. See if anything was taken," Leo says. "Maybe whoever broke in here was only searching."

"The ruby slippers are the only valuable we're carrying. Could someone know I have them?"

Sophia shrugs. "You know Maybelle. She blabs all the time."

"Or my sister. If she suspects—"

"Or your father," Tim adds.

I reach for Sophia's bag and slide my hand inside until it

bumps against a heel. I pull out a ruby slipper. It's reassuring to look at them, to know they're safe. They're my reason to find my father—my ticket, so to speak.

Leo stares at it silently for a long moment as if he can't quite believe what he's seeing. "What thief would be so neat? Maybe it's a woman. What guy would go to so much trouble for a pair of shoes?"

Sophia turns to me then. Anxiety creases the paper-thin skin at the corner of her eyes. "Leo could be right. It might be your sister. Could she be following us? Could she have broken in here and searched for the slippers?"

I sit on the edge of the bed, suddenly exhausted. "Abby?" Is my sister capable of something like that? "No. Absolutely not."

"That poster. We know she's somewhere nearby." A muscle tenses along Leo's neck and shoulder.

"But how would she know where I am?" I'm not ready to condemn my sister just yet. She wasn't as neat as whoever broke into this motel room.

"Why would she want these shoes so badly?" Leo asks. "Has to be more than a shoe fetish or sibling rivalry."

"They might be worth hundreds of thousands of dollars," Sophia explains.

Leo's gaze shifts between all three of us. "You're serious?"

"Very."

Otto starts barking. He stands outside the bathroom, his body rigid.

"Otto! Come here, boy."

But he stands firm.

"Wait." Leo puts a hand out to hold me back when I start to go to pick Otto up. He stealthily peers into the dark bathroom and shrugs. "Nothing there." He lifts Otto into his arms.

But something happened in this room while we were gone. I reach for my purse and pull a name and phone number out of my wallet. I pick up the phone.

"Wait!" Leo says.

"What?"

"Fingerprints."

I sigh. "I doubt she or he or they or whoever it was broke in here to make a phone call."

He nods agreement. "Are you calling the police?"

"That's a good idea, my dear." Tim's gray eyes pinch with worry.

"No. The FBI."

WE STEP AWAY from the "crime scene," which is starting to feel like a bad episode of *CSI*, and camp out in Leo and Tim's room while we wait for Agent Chesterfield, who surprised me when he said he was only an hour away. I doubt my ability to sleep with all the excitement and turmoil, but exhaustion must lurk inside me like a dormant virus, waiting for my immune system to dip low, then it springs forth and overwhelms me. I fall into a deep, hard sleep without dreams.

A hand on my shoulder gives me a gentle shake. I shift to my side, bury my face in the rough pillowcase.

"The FBI is here." Leo's gruff voice as much as his serious tone make my eyes blink wide open. "Heard a knock on your door."

The room is as black as the deepest part of the ocean. Leo takes my hand, his grasp firm, almost possessive. But it makes me feel safe. He leads me to the door. "Mom and Tim are sleeping." His whisper brushes my ear. His warm breath tickles the side of my neck, and a tiny shiver ripples along my skin. "Don't worry." His fingers tighten on mine. "I'll be with you."

Don't worry. The words seduce me. I want to cling to them, believe in them. I want to trust, but that's been a difficult concept all my life. I realize then it's not just God I have a hard time trusting but men too. It's why I was never satisfied with Craig's explanation of Momma's will, with his assurances that Abby couldn't sell the farm out from under me. Leo seems loyal and kind beneath all the gruffness, but I also know he's something of a loner. Will he walk away from me as easily as he walked away from a company, from civilization?

Otto's whimper makes me turn. "Okay. You can come."

Together the three of us slip out of the room. I feel like I'm back in college, sneaking into the house after a date with some guy that should have ended long before it did. I hold Otto against my shoulder as his little nose sniffs at the night air. Chilly with the coolness of the ocean, the air puckers my skin. The night isn't as dark as it is gray. The security lights in the parking lot skim along the edges of fog, making it hard to see more than a couple of feet. Otto utters a growl deep in his throat.

"Shh. It's okay." I pat his back. "Agent Chesterfield?" We follow along the balcony railing until we stand outside my room. Leo's hand is firm at my back, giving both comfort and concern. "Are you sure—?"

"Good evening." The deep, clipped tones jump out of the fog from behind us.

Otto's bark shatters the quiet, and the hair on the back of my neck stands on end. I place a hand on Otto, and he quiets down.

"What are you doing?" Leo growls.

"Keeping an eye out." The agent gives me a slight nod. "Ms. Meyers." He takes a step toward us. Curling steam floats out of the top of the Styrofoam coffee cup he holds. "So what happened?"

I explain how Leo recognized a car he'd seen several times that day.

Agent Chesterfield's gaze narrows on Leo. "Can you give me a description?"

"A dark-blue sedan. Maybe a Chrysler."

"Sure it's not black?"

"I'm sure." Leo's jaw is set in a hard line.

"Did you get a license number?"

"No."

"Could you tell how many people were in the car?"

"Tinted windows."

"One or two?" the agent asks.

"Windows?" I interject.

"People," Leo answers for the agent, his gaze aimed straight at Chesterfield, his shoulders square. "I don't know."

"Male or female?"

"I don't know that either."

"And you found your room ransacked?" the agent asks as if his coffee hasn't jolted him awake yet.

"Not exactly." I key the door and we enter. Leo flips on the light. Nothing has changed. It looks normal. "I think whoever broke in here was looking for the shoes."

Leo puts a hand on my arm.

"Why would they look here for the shoes?" The agent sets his coffee on the desk. "Do you have them?" He begins taking notes as he walks through the room. Behind the agent's back, Leo gives a slight shake of the head. A warning? Chesterfield draws a layout of the room on a little notepad, shoves the pencil through the spiral top, and reaches for the drawer.

"Shouldn't fingerprints be taken?" Leo's question stops the agent who pauses, his hand an inch from the knobby handle.

He coughs. "I'll have the office send someone over later." He gives me a pointed look. "So don't touch anything."

I hold up my hands like I'm under arrest.

Then the agent walks to the bathroom. A shaft of light surges. A moment later, he returns, hooking his thumb over his shoulder. "Did you see that?"

Heart thumping, I walk past him, my arms tight around Otto's warm, tense body. I turn into the bathroom and come to a complete stop as I stare at the mirror. Red lipstick letters sprawl across the mirror.

It reads, *I want those shoes!*

"DO YOU KNOW where the ruby slippers are?" Agent Chesterfield asks point blank.

"No." Leo answers for me. He stands with his arms crossed over his chest like a sentry.

A scowl pinches Chesterfield's features. "Are you being straight with me?"

Leo remains silent. I look from him to the agent, my nerves fraying. "Why would anyone think I have the shoes?"

"You tell me."

"My grandmother worked with Judy Garland."

"What else?"

"I don't know."

"Be careful, ma'am. Whoever stole those shoes committed a felony."

I swallow hard.

"You don't know who might be after those shoes," Chesterfield continues. "Or what they'll do to acquire them. When you're dealing with something as valuable as the ruby slippers . . ."

"Of course."

Agent Chesterfield says good night and disappears into the fog.

Leo takes me by the arm and steers me back toward his room. Once inside the complete darkness, he clicks the bolt and adds the chain. Then he leans his back against the wall, easing the curtain away from the window and squints out at the solid grayness. Unable to see much in the room beyond, I wait for my eyes to adjust. Across the room, Tim lets out a hefty snore. Closer, Sophia's snores are gentler.

"What's wrong?" I whisper, not wanting to wake either of them.

"We're leaving." His tone is sharp as a blade slicing through the quiet. "Now."

"What? But why?"

"That guy is no more an FBI agent than I am."

"But he said—"

"Doesn't make it so. Don't you see? He could be the one following you."

"But—"

"He could have broken into the room. How else do you explain that he was this far north of L.A.?"

"There could be a million reasons."

"Okay." He crosses his arms and waits.

But I have no suggestions. He's right, of course. I've been a naïve sucker.

"I'm an idiot."

He hooks a hand behind my neck and pulls me toward him until our foreheads are almost touching. Staring deeply into my eyes, he says, "Why didn't you tell him about your father?"

"I don't know."

"You could have told him you had the shoes. Why didn't you?"

"Because you—"

"No. You already had your doubts about him." As quickly as he pulled me to him, he releases me. "Mother, Tim, wake up!" Leo moves through the room, shaking beds, tossing a suitcase onto the end of one. "We need to get out of here."

Tim stirs, pushing up slowly, awkwardly. "What's happened?"

"Leo?" Sophia tosses back the covers. She sits up and readjusts her curves, pushing them into place. "Someone turn on the lights."

"No. No lights." Leo's movements are brusque.

My body begins to tremble with tiny aftershocks.

Moving through the room, gathering his things, Leo bumps into me. He braces my shoulders with his hands. "You okay?"

"This is all very strange."

"I know. Give me the shoes."

"Why?"

"I'll keep them safe." There's a hesitation in me, and Leo reads it. "You're going to have to trust me. Can you do that?"

I teeter on the brink of indecision for a moment, maybe two. I glance first in Tim's direction. He's slowly getting up from the bed. Sophia tucks the bedspread around the pillow. Leo waits for my answer. All my life Momma told me to obey the law, follow the rules. And I have. But what if this FBI agent is an imposter? What if he's after the shoes? I don't know whom to trust. Whom do I believe?

My friends watch me. *My friends.* Sophia pauses in helping Tim pull his shirt over an undershirt. But they've quit moving and wait for my answer. Suddenly I know what to say and whom to trust. It's not just my friends though. I toss a prayer heavenward because this is going to take a miracle to turn out all right.

Then I say, "Okay. Let's go."

Chapter Twenty

ale Earnhardt Jr. has nothing on Leo in the aggressive driving department. He takes a turn without slowing the Jeep or even signaling. A friend of mine, Ralph Perkins, taught driver's ed back in Kansas. The car his students drove had an extra brake pedal on the passenger side. Ralph said he'd only had to use it twice. I could use it now.

When Leo pumps the gas pedal and swerves the wheel, I slam my hand against the dashboard to brace myself. Otto leans his paws on the door, then the dash. I try to keep him from flying through the windshield. Leo weaves the Jeep in and out of early morning traffic, changing lanes as fast as Abby changes her mind.

We pass three billboards promoting my sister's stage show, her jaded face blown up ten times its normal size.

"Why my little party's just beginning!"

"I can cause accidents too!"

"What have you done with the ruby slippers?"

Her eyes glare at me from the billboards as if she's watching my every move, taking note of where we're going.

Could Sophia be right? Could Abby have broken into my motel room? Could she be that desperate? Does she know Chesterfield? Could he be one of her actor friends?

A FEW HOURS later we pass a large road sign that reads, *Welcome to Seattle, the Emerald City.*

Cloaked in clouds, the city rises out of the mist and gloominess as a sparkling diamond of hope. The wind buffets the Jeep, making the clouds shift and sway, slowly receding. The sun emerges, and I can see the Space Needle towering over other buildings, reaching heavenward. The skyline looks futuristic, like a city beamed down from some other planet. Of course, most any modern city would seem futuristic after living in Maize all your life. A flash of gold grabs my attention as we zip north.

"What was that?"

"The Needle?"

"No, close to it. Looked like . . . well, nothing I've ever seen before."

"The Blob," Leo says. "Some call it the hemorrhoids."

I wrinkle my nose. "But what is it?"

"Sort of a rock-and-roll museum on steroids."

The address Tim has provided for my father is north of the city.

"He's in the ritzy part." Leo turns the wheel confidently. "Your dad must have bucks. It's like Cinderella in reverse."

"What?"

"You've got the glass—or in this case, ruby—slippers and you're searching for your prince."

"My father is no prince."

"Isn't he what you've been searching for all your life?"

I never saw myself as an animated Disney cartoon, but then I never saw my life as a yellow-brick road either.

As I stare out the window at the BMWs and Jaguars mingling with Suburbans and hybrids, I contemplate the decisions I've made in my life. Were they all rooted in my father's leaving? My nerves twist and twitch at the thought. I lick my dry lips, hook a loose strand behind my ear.

At least I no longer look like a country bumpkin, thanks to Sophia. I'm wearing a long jean skirt and white blouse with dressy boots that match the leather jacket. It's a citified outfit and somehow boosts my confidence. If I'd arrived in my mismatched clothes, then I'd look as needy as I feel. Because I realize, as we wind our way through the streets of Seattle, that I *do* want a father. The father I never had. My expectations are too high. So once again, I mentally downshift to prepare myself for disappointment.

From the backseat Tim gives directions. He and Sophia have been whispering about something. We turn into a shopping center.

Surprised, I ask, "This is where my father lives?"

"No, my dear." Tim places a steady hand on my shoulder. "A girl doesn't meet her father for the first time every day. I thought you girls might enjoy a few hours at a spa."

Sophia claps her hands against her face. "Isn't that great, Dottie?"

Part of me wants to stall my imminent family reunion as long as possible, though part of me feels the need to hurry.

Time is running out on the farm; the auction is fast approaching. Putting off seeing my father till this afternoon won't make that much difference, will it?

The idea of getting my hair styled is appealing, but pampering is not something I'm suited for. All the attention makes me uncomfortable. I'm accustomed to doing, as Momma trained me, not having things done for me.

"What about Otto?" I ask, thinking of a good excuse for us to skip the spa. I cup my hands around his body, which wiggles, his nub of a tail twitching with excitement.

"There's a groomer next door," Tim points out.

"He'll *love* that," I say, my tone as sarcastic as any teen I've taught.

"Terrific!" Tim rubs Otto's head.

"He'll be as cute as a bug," Sophia says.

Reluctantly I get out of the Jeep. It appears to be a glamorous spa, not like Betty's Cut and Curl back home. "Maybe they're too busy."

"I made us all reservations, my dear." Tim waits patiently for Leo to fold the front seat forward. "Nothing like a good massage to work out the kinks after a long drive."

"Us?" Sophia asks.

"All of us!" Tim proclaims. "My treat."

"What do you mean? All of us?" With his mane of hair being blown by the wind, Leo looks wild and crazed, like a lion about to be placed in a cage. "I'm not—"

"You could use a shave and trim, my boy." Tim pats the younger man on the shoulder as Leo helps him out of the Jeep. "And a good steam bath will make us all feel human again."

OVER THE NEXT few hours, I see very little of my friends, except passing in the hall in big, fluffy robes as we shuffle from facials and salt glows to massages and pedicures. All the attention makes me squirm and my insides tighten as lotions and oils are rubbed into my skin and my muscles kneaded and plied. I close my eyes, try to force myself to relax.

I remember a time in the first grade. I had joined the Camp Fire Girls because I wanted to go camping. Instead, our troop held a father/daughter banquet. I didn't bother to tell Momma about it. Why hurt her more? I left the special invitation on the school bus. But our troop leader's husband called Momma and offered to take me. Momma scrimped and saved to buy me a special dress. She made me sleep on sponge curlers the night before. My hair kinked and curled in directions God never intended. I stared into the mirror at my ridiculous reflection and tried not to cry. Momma was so proud. All I could think about was how the lace socks made my ankles itch.

I felt that itch deep in my soul. I had been waiting for my father, watching the road for him. I wished for him, prayed for him to come home. And all those times the wrong car drove up our drive had convinced me that God didn't hear my prayers. Wishes didn't come true.

It's not the pampering and primping that makes me uncomfortable and tense today. It's the fact that I know what I want. I know why I've come to Seattle. It's not the farm. It's not the shoes. It's the man I've never known, the man hiding behind my little-girl memories: my father.

If ever I needed to believe in wishes and dreams, in prayers and miracles, it's now. So while the massage therapist tugs on my toes, I squeeze my eyes shut and pray like I've never prayed before.

God, I'm not good at this. I don't ask much. Sophia says to just believe. So I'm putting it all on the line here. I'm gonna believe you can make this work. I'm gonna believe I'll find my father. And that he'll want me. I'm gonna believe he didn't steal the shoes. You know what I want, probably better than I do. Because right now, I'm confused. The shoes. The farm. What am I going to do? What do you want me to do, God?

It's the first time I've ever asked God that question, and it's a bit unnerving to put all my hopes and dreams out there for God to destroy or to renew.

After I've been buffed and polished to a high sheen, I stare at the woman in the mirror, barely recognizing her. Maybe it's that my hair looks glossy and as bouncy as a shampoo ad on television. I've never seen my nails so smooth and clean. I asked for a simple look and ended up with what the woman called a French manicure. She went to a lot of trouble to make my nails look natural. Maybe it's not the new clothes or the new "do" or the massage. Maybe it's hope beginning to percolate inside me that makes me feel suddenly reborn.

As I push up from the stylist's chair, I find Sophia in the waiting room already. Her sandy-colored hair no longer looks dry as straw but is styled in a smooth blunt cut that accentuates her square jaw and big eyes.

"You're stunning." I hook a lock of hair behind my ear. I told the stylist to cut it short and leave the bangs long. A ponytail is no longer an option.

"You're beautiful, Dottie." She touches a lock of my brown hair, which the stylist had wanted to highlight with "shimmers of gold." I told her, "No, thanks," holding on firmly to the chair like I was sitting in a dentist's office.

Tim comes around the corner, moving more agile than we had seen him. He does a quickstep, as if he borrowed the move from Fred Astaire. "Whoa ho! Look at you two lovely ladies!" But he's staring straight at Sophia. Still, I give him a hug, my thanks caught in my throat. He pats my back. "My, my. I'm going to have to spring for a fancy dinner with you two looking so fine." Tears shimmer in his gray eyes like morning mist. "Now, wait till you see—"

Leo appears behind him. At least I think it's Leo. I recognize the T-shirt and faded jeans. But the rest is a shock to my system. His blond hair has been trimmed and frames his tanned face. His beard is shaved into a stylish goatee with mustache. He looks like a movie star or movie mogul. "Ready?" His tone is gruff. He pulls the Jeep's keys out of his jean pocket. "Let's go."

I get the sense he's embarrassed by all the fuss and attention. Women in the lobby turn his way, the staff fawns over him, and I find myself staring at him and breathing in the clean woodsy scent of him. We follow him to the Jeep. Leo isn't content waiting for the valet to bring the car; he seems anxious to get away from the spa.

While the rest pile into the Jeep, I pick up Otto from the groomer's. My scruffy dog now has tiny red bows on each ear. He looks like Ottila the Huntress, an old man in drag. He must not realize how ridiculous he looks or he wouldn't be wagging his bobbed tail as much as he is.

"That's the wrong dog," Leo says as I climb in the front passenger seat.

"Don't make fun of him."

"Don't worry, Otto ol' boy," Leo buckles his seat belt. "I'll find you a mud puddle or cow patty to roll in." He starts to key the ignition but pauses and looks at me. "You okay?"

"Yes. Sure." I stare down at my hands—manicured and polished, tense with awareness. "And you?"

"Ready to get out of here."

"Not your cup of tea?" I steal a glance in his direction.

His eyes are warm as melted honey. "You look good, farm girl."

"Oh, uh . . ." I fiddle with a red bow on Otto's ear but feel my body turn up the heat. "Thanks. So do you."

WE STAND OUTSIDE a wrought-iron gate with stone extensions. It's large enough, grand enough to be the entrance to Hearst Castle. Except this apparently leads to my father's house.

"Who *is* your father?" Leo asks.

"Duncan Meyers." The name has no other special meaning. Not to me anyway. Could all this belong to him? From the looks of it, he's made millions. Or billions. A man with this much money wouldn't steal a pair of shoes from a museum, would he? I look to my uncle. "What does my father do?"

Tim shrugs, looking equally impressed and surprised. "He was an engineer. That's about all I know. He wanted to make airplanes." He shakes his head. "Looks like he's done all right for himself though."

Slowly I back away from the gate. There go my theories for why my father never came home. No money? Wrong. Dead? Wrong again. The only remaining theory hurts too much to contemplate.

Leo puts a comforting arm around my waist. "You can do this."

Sophia sandwiches me in on the other side. "Give him a chance. Maybe it's what he's been waiting for."

I remind myself that he did come to see me at the facility. Sorting through the barbed thoughts that prick my heart is painful. My father is rich. With a capital R. I always had an image of him living in a hovel, too poor to afford a phone, much less a computer where he could search for me and Abby. But the truth is, nothing kept him from finding us. Nothing kept him from helping my mother, who lived hand to mouth her whole life. He didn't lose track of us. He couldn't *not* get to us. He simply *chose* not to. Until I was in a coma.

"Dottie?" Leo says. "What do you want to do?"

My friends crowd around me. Otto sits at my feet, his eyes searching for an answer. An electronic eye peers at us from the stone wall that surrounds my father's property. Someone is watching us. Suddenly I don't want my father to know I was ever here.

"I can't do this. I can't. We should go. Really. Now."

Sophia grabs my hand. "Dottie, you have to try at least. If you don't, then you'll always wonder 'what if.'"

"Believe," I whisper, the word not even audible but pounding in my chest. Tears scald my eyes. I squeeze them shut, draw a shuddering breath.

"That's right." Sophia squeezes my fingers. "Keep believing. We're here with you. We won't leave you."

"Want me to go punch Duncan in the nose?" Tim's features are so severe, so contrary to his usual look, that I laugh.

"No, I . . ." But I hesitate. Doubts swirl around me like a cyclone, blowing away my confidence, tossing my dreams recklessly aside.

"You have to face this." Leo's breath warms my cheek. "Remember, you're only afraid of what you already believe."

I pinch my lips together.

"You said I shouldn't run away from my problems," he says. "Fear can't run my life. Was that just advice for me? Or is that what you really believe? You can't run from your life either. You have to face your fears."

"No matter what?" My voice sounds as congested as my emotions feel.

"No matter what. You can do it."

I swallow hard and look at each of my friends. Love and trust fills their eyes, warms my heart. "With all of you," I place my shaky hand between us all, "I can."

Leo is the first to cover mine. Our gazes meet and meld with purpose.

Sophia places a hand on top of our joined ones. "*E pluribus utrum.*"

Tim lays his hand on our stack of hands. "I believe you mean *unum*, my dear." He smiles tenderly. "A perfect sentiment though. 'Out of many—'"

"Take your picture and move along," a guard says behind us.

We turn as one.

The guard wears a beige shirt and slacks, with a fancy insignia embroidered on the pocket. "Go ahead. Folks are always stopping, taking pictures. You can't see the house from here, but it's still impressive, isn't it?"

I glance back at the gate, look at the drive that winds along a manicured lawn. It disappears over a hill.

"We're here to see Mr. Meyers," Leo says.

The guard, who appears to put too much sugar in his coffee each day, lifts his eyebrows toward a receding hairline. "Really?" He reaches for a clip chart and flips pages back and forth then back again. "I don't see anyone on the list for today."

"The list?" I ask.

"Those approved for a visit."

Sophia takes a tiny step forward. "You just call up to the house and tell Mr. Meyers his daughter is here to see him."

He scratches his head. "Don't think he has a daughter."

"Much as you know!" Sophia snorts.

I give a slight shake of my head to warn her not to say too much. I don't want to draw attention to myself.

"Go on," Tim says. "You call him."

The guard hesitates then returns to the brick guard house. A minute later, he leans out of the doorway, phone in hand, "What'd you say your name is?"

"It doesn't matter. Really."

"Dottie," Sophia says.

Shaking my head, blinking away the stinging tears that threaten, I add, "Dorothy."

The guard repeats my name into the phone. A second later, the wide gate moves, sliding along a track.

"We can go in?" Tim asks.

"Just step up to the speaker there."

Together we move toward a little black box perched on a metal stand. Our shoes crunch gravel. We all stare at the speaker as if my father might pop out of the top.

Sophia gives me a soft push. "Go on. Speak to him."

Leo gives me a nod of encouragement.

"We're right here with you," Tim says.

"Hello?"

"You have to push the button," the guard prompts from his seat inside the little brick house. He reaches for a Styrofoam coffee cup.

I reach forward and press a round button. "Hello?"

A crackling noise emits from the box and I yank my hand back as if it's scalded. "Dorothy Meyers?" A deep male voice comes forth. "Is that you?"

"Uh, yes." I glance at my friends. "Are you . . . ?" Do I say "my father" or use his name? Momma never had rules for something like this.

"Is your sister there too?"

"Abby?" I glance behind me as if she might have suddenly appeared. "No." Leo presses the button for me. "No. She's not here."

"Bring her with you. Friday. Ten o'clock."

"Friday?"

"Friday!"

"But . . . we're here. Now. And . . ." I turn away from the speaker box. "Friday is two days away. Time is running out."

A crackling sound tells me that's the end of the conversation.

Sophia moves in close to me and puts an arm around my shoulder.

"Who does he think he is?" Leo kicks the pole and the speaker box wobbles.

"Hey," the guard shouts in a warning tone.

"He can't get away with this." Leo glares at the driveway leading over the hill toward my father's mansion. Without explanation, he begins to stalk up the drive.

Tim takes a step in the direction Leo went.

"Hey!" the guard hollers. "You can't go up there! Hey!" He starts running after Leo, but turns and comes back. "You have to get on the other side of the gate," he says to the rest of our party.

A minute later the heavy gate slides closed, locking us out. Sophia and Tim stand on either side of me, while the guard takes off running after Leo.

"What a terrible man!" Tim says. "Why, I never knew

Duncan to behave like this. He didn't even invite you inside."

A fresh breeze stirs the compressed air in my lungs. I breathe slowly and deeply. My legs won't take me any further, and I sit on the top stone step.

"I'm sorry." Sophia sits beside me. "Maybe we gave him a terrible surprise."

"Don't," I say. "Don't make excuses for him. I've made excuses my whole life. I imagined reasons he never came home. That he was too poor to buy a ticket. Or sick. Or even dead. I imagined he'd bumped his head and forgot about us. But the simple truth is that he didn't want us. I should have left well enough alone."

Tim shakes his head. "I'm sorry, Dottie, my dear. I'm so sorry for bringing you here."

"It's not your fault." I sniff back my regrets. At least now I know. "It's okay." But it may never be okay. I may never get over this pain that feels like a gigantic fist squeezing my heart.

"Come on," Sophia tugs on my arm.

"We have to wait for Leo to come back."

It's then that the reality of what has happened, my absolute worst nightmare, sinks deep into my soul: My father doesn't want me. He doesn't care about me. Maybe he only came to the facility to see Abby. Maybe he only cares about her.

Chapter Twenty-One

*L*eo paces like a tethered dog in front of the Jeep. He tried to get my father to come to the door, but under the threat of being arrested, he finally backed down and walked back to the gate.

"What are you so angry about?" Sophia asks her son while hanging onto my arm, keeping me close to make sure I'm all right.

He points toward the rise hiding the luxurious home he described to us. "He treated Dottie like she didn't matter. Like she was nothing!"

His words echo the pain inside me. But as I've always done, I tuck those feelings away in the dark, stuffy cellar of my soul.

"Yes." Sophia's tone is as soothing as chicken noodle soup, "but we all know better than that, don't we?"

"But—"

She raises a finger to interrupt his tirade. "Don't project your own injuries onto her." She gives Leo one of those looks that carry years of understanding between mother and son. "If you're angry at having no father, I can understand that. But don't make this situation worse than it is."

His face contorts until I expect steam to spew out of his ears. Then he whirls around and jumps into the driver's seat. He has the engine running before we can all pile inside.

No one says anything for a long time as we drive aimlessly around Seattle. The afternoon burns away the clouds and the sun shines bright, sparkling along the surface of Puget Sound like crystal shards scattered along the top. Store fronts are a blur as I stare out the window. Leo drives in a jerky, angry fashion. I simply hold onto Otto, rub a hand along his back in an effort to soothe and comfort myself. But there is no comfort for this kind of ache.

"You okay?" Leo glances at me for a moment then back at the traffic, which seems to have suddenly become tight-packed along the roadway. His hands clench around the steering wheel like he's strangling it.

"Of course she's not okay." Sophia pats me on the shoulder from the backseat. "She just met her father who was less than ideal. But she's going to be fine. We'll see to that."

"He has good qualities." Tim's voice is as gentle as the water appears out in the bay. "Or he used to. Maybe we caught him on a bad day, my dear."

"Maybe he's hurt that you haven't wanted to see him before now," Sophia suggests.

I spent most of my life imagining reasons why he didn't come home. I'm not about to start imagining reasons to empathize with him. A fragile piece of myself breaks apart inside, and a jagged piece comes hurtling out of me. "And how does he think *I* feel?"

Leo jerks the wheel to the right, pulling into a restaurant parking lot. "I'm hungry."

"I guess we could all use some food," Sophia agrees, waiting patiently for me to get out of the car. I help her step down, holding her hand, feeling her weight against me. Then she readjusts her clothing, making sure everything is evenly distributed. "Better?"

I nod.

Inside the restaurant, which houses old canoes from ancient civilizations, we're told it will be just a few minutes before they can seat us, so I excuse myself from the group and walk outside. I check on Otto, who is curled up in the front seat, his chin on his paws. The windows are rolled down partially to give him fresh air. The temperature seems to have dropped several degrees as the sun has begun its descent.

The anger I'm feeling is dark, almost sinister. Jealousy rolls through me in waves. My father doesn't want me. He wants Abby. He loves Abby, not me. Never me.

His stipulation for meeting face-to-face feels like a fresh slap of rejection. The same rejection I felt after he left, when I understood he wasn't coming back, when I realized we weren't like other families.

I remember him holding Abby in her little pink blanket, cuddling her, cooing over her. Tiny glimpses, snapshots of memory, are dim and fuzzy but bring my emotions into sharp clarity. Abby was the pretty one. The baby of the family. Cute and clean. Burbling and smiling. I was plain. Fussy even. Crying out when I banged my head or fell and scraped my hands. Pitching fits when I didn't get what I wanted.

Of course, I was only four years old. But the contrast has never left me.

Our brief exchange today smarts like a red wasp sting, throbbing and pulsing. Maybe I should just leave now. I could sell the ruby slippers and save the farm. Or I could keep the ruby slippers for myself. They are the only thing I have left of Momma and Granny. Abby can have our father, his estate, his money, his love, all of which seems worthless to me. I'll keep the memories of Momma. Her love, the memory of it, will have to be enough.

"Thanks, God," I whisper. "Not exactly what I was hoping for here."

Immediately I regret my words. Is it fair to blame God for someone else's actions? Doesn't he give us choices?

I return to the restaurant, weaving through mostly empty tables as it's earlier than the dinner hour, even for retired folks. Leo, Sophia, and Tim cease their talking as I approach. They watch me anxiously.

"How're you doing?" Leo asks.

I smile that he's saved me the seat beside him. "I'm okay. I've made a decision."

"You have?" Sophia asks. "What is it?"

"San Francisco is a nice place to settle." Tim pats the table, splaying his arthritic hands. "I'd like to have some family close by. You and I could—"

"Santa Barbara." Sophia's wide, luminous eyes glint with pleasure. "Now that would be a great place for you to—"

"Go where you want," Leo overrides them both. "Life's too short to be stuck in one place."

I laugh, feeling free of the emotions that seem to have mired me for so long. These people care about me. *Me!* "Thank you, all."

"For what?" Leo hands me a rolled napkin, heavy with silverware.

"For helping me. For caring about me." My throat clogs with emotions I didn't expect. "In a strange way, I think I've found a home with all of you. It's not a consolation prize. It's real and . . . I know that doesn't make much sense."

"Sure it does." Tim rubs the tips of his fingers along the veins in the wooden table. "Home isn't necessarily a place."

I touch my uncle's hand, then put my other arm along the back of Leo's chair, not quite daring to touch him. I meet Sophia's smile. "You've all helped me so much. Now," uncomfortable revealing so many emotions, I fumble with my napkin, uncurling it and laying it across my lap, "what I need to do is find my sister." I give my napkin one final, determined twist before releasing it and reaching for my glass of water. I take a sip, lick my lips of the cool water, then meet my friends' gazes. "She's on tour here in the Northwest. I'm going to take her to see our father, and we'll have a little family reunion. Then I'll decide what to do with Ruby's slippers."

WE DISCOVER ABBY'S troupe arrives in Seattle today. It's too late to find her tonight, so we settle into another hotel that allows dogs. I leave Sophia alone in the room while I take Otto for a walk. The wind picks up and is chilly, more like an early fall bite than late summer. Clouds have congregated overhead, blocking out the stars. Fog rolls inland.

I pull on my leather jacket and watch Otto wandering from tires to trees, fire hydrants to light poles, searching for the perfect spot to lift his leg.

"Want company?"

My insides twitch, unnerved that I didn't hear Leo

approach. Maybe I was too focused on the cold, my numb fingers, Otto taking forever to do his business. My little protector didn't utter so much as a growl. He's too busy sniffing and mapping out who's been there before him. Leo's eyes are warm, his smile disarming.

"Uh, sure." The fog alters my voice and seems to close in around us like a wispy curtain.

We both watch Otto, as that seems easier than staring at each other with nothing to say. One of Otto's red bows hangs loosely from his ear. I suspect he's been scratching at it.

Leo crosses his arms over his chest. Did he come out here just to stand? To guard me in case Chesterfield or my sister shows up?

"Did you see anyone following us?" I ask.

"No. But that doesn't mean they weren't."

"You still have the shoes?"

There's a flicker of understanding in Leo's eyes. He knows I don't completely trust him. "They're safe."

Silence settles between us, swelling and feeling more awkward by the second.

"Did you want something?" I ask.

"No."

More silence beats between us. I look skyward, but there's nothing to hold my attention, no first star to wish upon and get me out of this situation. I can't see the ocean or cars on the nearby street. The parking lot is dark and gray. The few security lights form hazy golden circles on the damp pavement, giving the place an otherworldly appearance.

"Hurry up, Otto. He's never in a hurry," I explain, wishing I had something witty to say. Abby would know what to say to a man, how to talk to him, questions to ask, how to act. How to flirt. It shocks me to realize I want to flirt with Leo.

I've always had male friends, Craig and Ben, other teachers and farmers, but I didn't flirt with them. Leo is different.

"You cold?" he asks.

I glance down at my arms crossed over my chest, my hands chafing the sleeves of my jacket, which is a nervous jitter more than an attempt to keep warm. "Not really."

He fingers the fringe that hangs from the underside of my sleeve. "You doing okay?"

"Fine. Tired." I remember Sophia chastising him for transporting his emotions to my situation. Maybe he wants to discuss his overreaction to my father's snub. We both grew up without a father. We have more in common than I imagined. "What about you?"

"Sure. Why wouldn't I be?"

"But you weren't today."

He jams his hands in his front jean pockets. "I tend to be overprotective. I didn't like the way your father was treating you."

Does that mean he sees me as weak? As someone who needs protection? Or—

"Sometimes," he says, "I don't think before I react. It's gotten me in trouble a few times."

"I can imagine."

"I got suspended in high school for punching out some guy."

Six months ago I wouldn't have smiled at that admission, but all that has happened to me seems to have mellowed my teacher's reactions. "What did he do?"

"Don't remember."

"I see. And do you remember why you kissed your teacher in school?" The question pops out of my mouth before I can contain it.

He smiles this time, a sly smile that makes something inside me flip over. "Yeah. You want to know about that, do you?"

"No, I just—"

"She wanted me to kiss her. She was young. Cute. It was her first year of teaching. It was my last year in high school." He shrugs. "I was eighteen. But don't worry. She didn't corrupt me." He steps closer, standing directly in front of me. He runs a finger along the ridge of my shoulder, tugging on my jacket's fringe. "What did you have in mind?"

His disarming grin sends a jolt straight through me. Instinctively I want to flee. But another part of me, the awakened part, wants me to stay right where I am, which flusters me more than his suggestive comment.

"I'm not a new teacher. I'm definitely not young. And I'm not interested in—"

"Be careful." He tilts his head, studying me. He leans close and whispers, "God's watching. You wouldn't lie to me now, would you?"

"You're awfully cocky."

"Yeah. I'm that. Do I scare you?"

"No." But I am afraid. Not of him. Of me. Of my feelings, my reactions to him.

"Then what are you afraid of?"

I swallow hard. "We're too much alike, you and me."

"You don't seem the cocky sort." Another smile tugs at the corner of his generous mouth.

"You stepped off the merry-go-round of life for a while." The words flow out of my mouth and at the same moment could be aimed right at me.

"I did."

"But would you do it again?"

"I hope not. I learned a lot and hopefully part of what I learned was how to structure my life so I don't have to take a time-out. What about you?"

"I've lived my life watching the merry-go-round go around and around without me. Just watching."

"Don't you think it's time you jumped on?"

I hesitate, not knowing what he wants, how to answer.

"You could put those fancy red shoes on and we could go dancing." A twinkle in his eye makes me wonder if he's joking. Or is he . . . flirting?

"I'm not the dancing type."

"Never know till you try."

I swallow my reservations. "Will that merry-go-round pass me by?"

"Time doesn't stand still. Didn't you say you learned that time is a gift?"

Rattled by his nearness, his words, I stare at the ground, searching my heart. The toe of his boot looks damp, the tan leather dark at the edges. I'm aware of his wide shoulders, of his breath stirring my hair, of my heart pounding.

"Have you ever been in love, Dottie?"

"Yes. No." I swallow hard, surprising myself, my thoughts drifting back to Craig. "I'm not sure. It didn't work out."

"You don't believe in love, do you?"

"Sure I do. I just . . . I'm not sure it ever works out."

"Maybe the kind of love you've experienced. But have you ever known an unselfish love?" His words bring pinpricks of tears to my eyes. I look away. He touches my chin, lifts it until my gaze meets his. "You're not too old to fall in love. To try again." He grabs my hand when I start to pull away. "I know you think you are. You like to pretend you're as old as Tim and my mom, but you're not. Heck, even they flirt with each other. You act like you don't need anyone, but we all need somebody."

"Did you learn that living in a cabin?"

"Yeah, I did." His hand cups my face, his thumb caressing my jaw, sending tingling sensations rippling throughout my body. "You have a lot of life left to live."

"So do you," I challenge him.

His eyes smolder with emotions I recognize. He pulls his hand away as if he was tempted but is now able to resist. "I'm damaged goods, Dottie. Not good for anyone. Just like your father."

I don't believe him. It's not a rational thought but gut instinct. Or a prompting of some kind. "I thought you believed in unconditional love."

"With God, maybe. Not so sure about people."

It's then I realize he's as scared of me as I am of him. Without thinking, without contemplating or calculating the risk, I rise up on my tiptoes and brush my lips against his. Some part of me wants to stir the passion that beats deep down inside this man. The edges of his whiskers tickle my mouth. Before I can pull away, he grabs me, his fingers pressing into my arms. He meets my startled gaze. Then he slants his mouth over mine and kisses me harder and longer than I've ever been kissed in my life.

The surprising thing is that I kiss him right back, for all I'm worth. Which doesn't seem like much, but combined with what Leo has to give . . . well, it begins to add up.

"Otto!" I break away, drawing in a gulp of air. I'm not sure how long we kissed. At once it seemed an eternity and yet too short. Which unnerves me.

Leo chuckles. "Not exactly what a guy wants to hear when he's kissing a woman."

"I'm sorry. But . . ." I scan the misty gray area. "Otto!"

A muffled bark answers me before I hear the click of his nails against concrete. He comes across the parking lot into view, one red bow bouncing along with him. I scoop him up into my arms, cradle him against my chest.

"So," Leo rubs his jaw thoughtfully, "are you sorry you thought of Otto? Or that you kissed me?"

I don't have an answer.

Chapter Twenty-Two

After Leo sees me to my room, I discover I'm all alone. Trying to escape my chaotic thoughts, and feeling a deep restlessness, I change into a donated pair of men's button-down PJs with drawstring pants in a pale-blue stripe then crawl between the stiff bed sheets. I lay in the dark, my eyes wide open. About midnight, Sophia slips into the room.

"Should I ask where you've been?" I smile into the darkness.

"Oh, you're awake! Tim and I went down to the pool."

"Oh, really."

"The whirlpool makes it nice and warm in there. Helps his arthritis."

"Uh-huh. I see."

"Really, we were just talking."

"He is nice."

I sense rather than see her smiling. "He is. But he's getting over his wife. So there wasn't any hanky-panky. He's lonely and needs a friend."

"You don't have to make excuses to me." I slide an arm under the pillow and roll to my side. "You're both adults."

"What about you? Where did you go?"

"I just walked Otto, then came back to the room."

She gathers up her toiletries and goes into the bathroom.

One late, late night, when I was in college, I heard Momma's voice coming out of the dark. "Where've you been?"

"I didn't want to wake you."

"If you'd been thinking about me, then you wouldn't have stayed out so late and worried me."

"I'm sorry, Momma." I sat on the footstool. "I should have called."

"Yes," she tapped my side with her blue slipper, "you should have. This is something I expect from your sister, from your . . ." She paused for a long, strained moment. I had a feeling she expected it from my father too but she never said those words. "But not from you."

"I said I'm sorry."

"I heard you."

Staring down at the floor, I clasped my hands between my knees, squeezed hard. "What was it like when you dated?"

"That was a long time ago."

"Did you," I paused, waiting for her to cut me off, but she remained silent, "do things that, well, maybe you shouldn't have? Stay out too late—"

"Are you in love with this boy?"

"No."

"Did you do something you're ashamed of? That you should tell me about?"

"Not really."

"Are you going out with him again?"

"Probably not." If he asked, I supposed I would. Just for something to do. But I doubted he'd call. I didn't encourage boys the way I saw other girls doing. I didn't flirt. I didn't say things I didn't mean. And I had a way of rejecting boys before they could reject me.

"Sometimes, Dottie, we do foolish things when we're in love. Sometimes in life we make bad decisions. But that doesn't excuse what we do. There are always consequences. Do you understand?"

"Do you regret that you got married?"

She placed her worn hands on her knees and pushed to her feet. "It's time for bed."

I never knew if she'd done foolish things with my father or if she regretted marrying him.

Sophia comes out of the bathroom, dressed in a lavender sleep shirt. She carefully puts her clothes back into her suitcase then turns off the light, and I hear her padding across the room. Gingerly, she settles on the edge of my bed. "Dottie?" she whispers loud enough to wake someone down the hall. "Are you asleep?"

"What is it?"

"I just wanted to say . . ." she locates my hand and places it between her two, "Leo isn't as gruff as he pretends. It's his defense mechanism. He really does care deeply."

"I know."

"Oh. Well, good." She pats my hand. "He's very nice too."

"I know."

"And handsome."

I smile but keep my feelings, and whatever is developing between Leo and me, to myself. I was never one to chat about boys with friends, my sister, or even Momma. Yet I have an itch to confide in Sophia.

She stands and goes to the other double bed. "Just giving you food for thought. Well, good night."

I toss and turn, my mind as jumbled as the bed covers. Unable to erase the memory of Leo's kiss, I relive it over and over in my mind. It feels like my body has finally awakened and doesn't want to waste time sleeping anymore.

With my eyes grainy from lack of sleep, I crawl out of bed as soon as I detect light coming through the separated curtains. Sophia lies on her side, sound asleep. Quietly I gather Otto and my jacket, pulling it over the baggy pajamas, and slide on my tennis shoes without tying the laces. Maybe the cool morning air will cool off my heated thoughts.

When we reach the parking lot, I spot Leo, leaning against the Jeep. I glance down at my striped pajamas and cringe. Maybe I can make a quick U-turn and go to the other side of the hotel without him noticing, but Otto sees his friend and takes off running. Too late.

With his shoulders hunched forward as if warding off the morning chill, Leo looks up. He grins at my slower approach. I shove a hand through my mashed hair. It's one thing to have kissed him last night, but it's quite another for him to see me all rumpled from lack of sleep early in the morning before my shower.

"Morning," he says.

"Hi." I fist my jacket closed.

"Just wake up?"

"Yeah."

He offers me a Styrofoam cup. "Coffee?"

"Sure." I take a sip, wondering if his lips have already touched the rim. "Thanks." My body warms from the inside out. "You didn't stay out here all night, did you?"

He shakes his head. "Just wanted to check on the Jeep. See if I saw any familiar cars, like the one that followed us."

"Did you?"

"Nothing unusual. Did you sleep okay?"

"I had a lot on my mind."

"Really?" He wraps a hand around the Styrofoam cup and leans forward to sip from the place my lips touched. "Were you thinking about me?"

Arching an eyebrow, I say, "I was trying to figure out the best way to find my sister. And what might happen when we go see my father tomorrow."

His gaze is steady, but the glimmer of humor dims. "And what did you figure out?"

I shrug, disappointed at myself for rebuffing him. I'm not good at this relationship game. "The only thing I know to do is go to the theater where her show is playing."

"Makes sense."

I want to restart the teasing, flirtatious banter, but I'm at a loss how to do that. I stick a lure into the water with, "Your mom was out late with Tim."

He remains quiet.

"She said it was innocent, but I think she likes him." When he doesn't respond, I give up. "Come on, Otto." But he seems content sniffing around, leaving his mark on every tire and potted plant. "He's not in a hurry."

"Are you?"

I shrug. "I guess not."

"I wanted to say something about last night."

A wedge of panic lodges in my throat. "Okay."

"I should have apologized to you."

An urge to duck and run overwhelms me, and if it weren't for Otto, I would. Before Leo can apologize for kissing me, I rearrange my features, attempt to appear calm and serene. "Oh?"

"I shouldn't have tried to force your dad to see you."

"My dad?"

"At his estate. I should have stayed with you. Helped you."

My panic dissolves into relief. He doesn't regret the kiss! And he doesn't seem to recognize my sudden, inexplicable joy. I try to contain the smile that wants to break out all over my face and concentrate on what he's saying.

"But . . . I . . ." He shrugs a broad shoulder, his muscles flexing and bunching. "I grew up without a father. Just like you. I don't know what it's like for a woman, but for a man—a boy—it's like a hole that needs filling. I searched for something to fill that emptiness in sports. I idolized my coaches. I was jealous of friends whose fathers stood on the sidelines hollering or those who volunteered to coach. But no one stepped in to offer me guidance." The lines around his mouth form deep grooves.

His hurts are so like my own. "I can understand that. My friend's dad coached our softball team. I didn't let on that it hurt, but it did. I felt that same emptiness. Especially one time when I had to go to some father/daughter dance. Momma made me go. But it wasn't the same going with someone else's dad."

He nods, his lips pressing flat, pinching dimples in the planes of his tan cheeks. "Your mom tried. So did mine. She did the best she could, but she's a woman. She didn't know how to be a man, what a man thinks, how he expresses his emotions, what he needs. She thought I could just turn to God, like he was a fairy godmother ready to grant my fondest desire."

"Doesn't work that way, does it? Fathers are important."

Leo steps toward Otto. "Come on, boy. Do your thing."

"It's hard to find the perfect spot."

"I guess." He smiles. "When I started working in the computer industry, I had a mentor. He gave me advice. Even helped finance the start of my own business. I made the mistake of letting him into that empty place. I started thinking of him as a father figure." He rolls his shoulders backwards. A blast of cold air makes his hair wave like the tops of the cornstalks back home. "And I got burned. It was business for him, pure and simple. He called the loan, which I couldn't pay. Took over my company, fired me. Fired me from my own company. It was a rude awakening."

I want to reach out and touch his arm. Leo seems so solid, so strong, that it's hard to imagine him wounded so deeply. But I should have known. The teens I worked with who were the most ornery were usually nursing some emotional injury.

He shrugs. The corners of his mouth pull in opposite directions. Uncertainty glimmers in his eyes. His pain pulsates within my own skin. "It is what it is. I should have known better than to put him in that position." The tautness in his voice pulls me toward him. "Or give him that kind of authority and control over me."

I place a hand on his arm. "I think I've always done the opposite. I've kept a distance from others so no one could hurt me the way my father did. Maybe that's a lesson for all of us—not to let anyone have that kind of control over our emotions. I put too many hopes and dreams, too many expectations on my father when I was a little girl. No one could live up to that. Especially an absent father. And my disappointment set me up for other disappointments."

"With men?"

"I was thinking more of God."

He nods. "He's not a genie in a bottle."

"That's the thing about wishes. People want something just plopped down in front of them, without being willing to provide any of the effort. Abby was like that. She always wished she'd make good grades, but she wasn't willing to put in the effort. Then she wished for a man, and two marriages and a fiancé later, I wonder if she's willing to work on a relationship. But that was never me. I was capable. I was strong." I smile. "Little but strong. And that kept me from depending on others. Even God. Until the tornado . . . and my coma."

"Then you had to depend on others. At least for a while."

"Now I hope I've achieved some balance. Or getting better."

"You know," he says, "a genie is supposed to grant you your wish, right? No questions asked. But God, I've learned, asks those pesky questions."

I never thought of God asking questions. Maybe I've been too focused on myself. "Like what?"

"Like whether what you want is good for you or not."

"So did you figure out what was good for you?"

"Yeah, my business wasn't good. I was a workaholic. And there's more to life than work." His gaze is potent.

"Being out of work," I say, "I'm not sure what else there is."

"You've found it, haven't you, Dottie?"

"What? What have I found? My father? Not the father I wanted."

"You've found freedom. Friends."

I study the ground. The grass looks like it's been dipped in sugar. Slowly I raise my gaze to meet his. "Definitely."

Chapter Twenty-Three

The phone is ringing when I get back to the motel room.

Sophia glances up from reading a book. "Took you a while. Everything okay?"

"The phone's ringing." I state the obvious as I move toward it. She doesn't seem inclined to answer.

"It's for you."

"Are you clairvoyant?"

"Some woman has called three times."

Picking up the phone, I give Sophia a quizzical look. "Hello?"

"Miss Dottie Meyers?" a male voice asks.

I mouth to Sophia, *It's a man.*

She shrugs and goes back to her reading.

"Yes," I say into the mouthpiece.

"I know you have those shoes. I want them. Now I'm willing to pay and pay well. But I won't be ripped off. I won't be cheated. I need to see them and make sure they're the real deal, not some dime-store copy. Did you get them from the museum? Don't get me wrong. I don't care where they came from. Long as they're authentic. But don't think about selling to someone else. You'll regret it."

"You're mistaken." I speak calmly, although my heart is pounding and my ears buzzing. "I don't have any shoes." I hang up.

Immediately the phone begins ringing again. I grab it, feeling more forceful, more irritated. "I told you—"

"Dorothy Meyers?" A feminine voice.

Startled, I stop my tirade. "Yes."

"I am calling to inquire about the ruby slippers." Her accent is exotic, like Persian perfume. "You must be careful with these shoes. They have great powers. If they are not cared for properly, who knows what damage they might cause."

A cold shiver runs down my spine. I recognize her voice. The one in my room back at the facility. "I know," she says, "how to handle them. They would be safe with me. You do not have to worry. Do you have an asking price? Because I am willing to go as high as I must."

I pull the phone away from my ear, stare at it as if what I'm hearing is unbelievable. Who are these people? Where did they get my number? My name? Are they all following me? Should we get a tailgate party going?

Slowly, feeling every ounce of energy drained out of me, I explain to the woman that I don't have any shoes. She blathers on about magical powers like I'm now living in a Harry Potter book. Politely, if not decisively, I hang up.

The phone continues to ring even after we ask the front desk not to allow any calls through. Finally we take it off the hook and place two pillows over it.

"This," I tell Sophia, "is getting weird."

She closes her book, and I realize it's the Bible. "What are you going to do?"

"I don't know." I rub Otto's ears, then start picking at the one remaining bow, tugging at it. It's held by the tiniest rubber band I've ever seen. "Any answers in that book of yours?" I realize my question sounds sarcastic, but I don't mean it that way.

She hands me the good book. "Every answer you'll ever need."

Before I can take it from her, she pulls back. "But I must warn you."

"What now?" *Your mission, should you choose to accept it . . .*

"The Word of God is powerful. Sharper than a two-edged sword. Search for the treasures between these covers," she tenderly caresses the leather cover, "but be warned." She gazes deeply into my eyes. "It can be dangerous."

She places the book into my hands. Her words sound a bit like the woman on the phone. I've grown up in the church, I learned the books of the Bible, Old Testament and New, in third grade. It's never seemed mystical or dangerous. "I don't think you have to worry, Sophia."

"It takes the Holy Spirit to discern these holy words, to make God's ways clear to us. If we rely on our hearts, we can easily be deceived."

I almost expect a blast of air as I turn open the front cover. But there is no gust, no trumpet sounding, nothing spooky or spectacular. On one of the first pages, I read that this Bible was given to Sophia by a church, maybe the one that ministered to her so long ago. Turning the fragile, ultra-thin pages, I flip past Genesis, Deuteronomy, Samuel, until I settle into Psalms. I skim along until one verse smacks me hard: *Your word is a lamp to my feet and a light to my path.* I hear Maybelle saying "ooh" in my head. I place Otto's red bow between the pages so I can find it again.

IT'S NOT HARD to find my sister, not with her gigantic green face posted all along the West Coast. We're not the first to find her either.

Parking outside the theater, Leo points toward a dark-blue sedan. The one that's been following us.

"I'm going to talk to whoever is in that car." Leo takes a step in that direction before I grab his arm.

"Don't." I've told him about the phone calls. "You don't know if they're crazy." I'm thinking of the woman who believes the shoes have special powers. "Or armed."

Leo gives me a look that says he's not afraid of any weapon or hidden agenda.

"Come on." I tug him toward the theater's box office.

"I'll stay and keep an eye on that car." Leo leans against the Jeep, arms crossed over his chest.

"I'll stay with him," Tim says, not looking half as tough as Leo.

"Me too." Sophia hesitates, her features crumpling into concern. "Unless you want me to come with you."

"I'll be fine." I'm not sure how my sister will respond to the news that I've found our father. She hinted a few months ago that she had an interest in finding him. Was it only because she wanted to find the slippers? Did she suspect that he had Momma's shoes? I'm not sure if she'll agree to go with me to see him. Or will she race to him? Their reunion could leave me out in the cold.

Pressing down the hurt stirred by this thought, I yank hard on the theater door, half expecting it to be locked. It's heavy, but it opens. A vast lobby opens to me. The chandeliers above are dark. The deep-red carpet muffles my footsteps. I approach a set of inner doors, remembering an old game show Momma sometimes watched when her leg was hurting and she needed rest. Monty Hall would swing an arm wide and say, "What's behind Door Number One?"

Behind the heavy carved door are row after row of darkened empty seats. The house lights are dimmed; just a few along the outside walls give off enough light to make the place eerie, like a Gothic tomb. But the stage down front is alive with activity. The footlights, alternating red and blue and green, shine brightly. A stagehand shoves a fake tree off to the left, behind a brown curtain. A flat drape of scenery flutters and makes a lemonade tidal wave out of the yellow brick road. Another backdrop descends, setting the stage for a Kansas wheat field, with stalks of corn painted in one corner. It reminds me of home, and longing swells inside my chest.

The door creaks behind me as it closes, and I slip into a seat in the back row. Even though no one is wearing makeup or costumes, I try to imagine what part each person is playing, easily picking out the Munchkins, who probably double as the flying monkeys. A pudgy man stands at the corner of the stage laughing, and I wonder if he's the wizard.

"Let's start with act two, scene three," someone calls from the dark seats in the middle section.

"Then you won't need me, right?"

I recognize my sister's voice from off stage.

Combing her long, wild tresses with her fingers, she ambles barefoot onto the stage and secures her hair with a ponytail holder. She steps over the footlights to the edge of the stage, shielding her eyes with her hand. "Lou, can I take a break?"

"Sure. Bring me some coffee when you come back."

"Will do!" Wearing jeans and a plain black scoop-neck T-shirt, she jumps down off the stage. She picks up a large purse and hooks it over her shoulder. She punches the bar across a doorway, and sunlight swallows her as she leaves the theater. I get up to follow.

"Who are you?" A deep voice startles me.

Pulled up short, I stare at a broad-shouldered man, with a shaved head and no sense of humor.

"What are you doing here?" he demands.

"Oh!" I scoot out into the aisle. "I'm early. Thought the show was this morning." I widen my eyes innocently but doubt I'm believable. "Guess I'll come back later."

The bouncer's brow pinches into a serious frown.

I exit the building as he watches to ensure I do leave.

It's an unusually sunny day in Seattle. The sky is a brilliant blue, and the grass and trees seem even greener. Pointing to the side of the building, I signal to Sophia, Tim, and Leo my next destination. They start toward me, crossing the parking lot. Sophia walks along a yellow line, like she's maneuvering a balance beam.

Keeping to the sidewalk, we walk around the perimeter of the building until we see Abby sitting with two men on concrete steps. One man has hair that stands on end. The other wears a T-shirt too small for his jumbo-sized belly. They look like Stan and Ollie. My sister laughs and talks, dramatizing some story with broad and exaggerated hand gestures. She doesn't care what the spotlight is, as long as she's at its center. As we approach, cigarette smoke irritates my eyes.

"Then we went out to—" Abby's gaze collides with mine. Slowly, she stands, placing a defiant hand on her hip. "Look who finally came to see me perform!" She glances at the men beside her. "My sister. What an unexpected pleasure."

"How are you, Abby?"

"If you'd given me some warning, I would have gotten you front-row seats." She takes a long, slow pull on her cigarette, smoke curling from her nostrils. "The show doesn't start till tomorrow night."

"I know." I step up onto the sidewalk. "I was hoping I could talk with you. Privately."

When one of her friends snubs out a cigarette under his tennis shoe, she puts a hand on his shoulder. "If your friends get to stay, then so do mine. I don't have anything to hide."

Is this how it will always be—animosity sparking between us like static electricity? We're a part of each other's lives, and yet we rub each other the wrong way every time we get near one another. Disappointment tugs at me.

"We haven't met. I'm Sophia. Do you have an extra?" Sophia walks up to Abby and indicates her cigarette.

The short, squat man pulls a pack from his hip pocket. He offers it to Tim and Leo, but they decline.

Sophia taps the end of her cigarette on the back of her hand and smiles. "It's been a long time." She leans over as the guy offers her a light. "Are you in the show?"

"The professor . . . wizard . . ." He thumbs the guy next to him. "He's in lighting."

Sophia blows out a long stream of smoke like one of those actresses from the forties when cigarettes were cool and came without health warnings. "I do love the theater. This is such a fabulous show." She begins chatting with the men, asking for their credits, their résumé of shows. She oohs and ahhs over every one. Tim and Leo move over toward Sophia, nodding and grinning at her stories, forming a hedge between us. They turn their backs on Abby and me to give us some semblance of privacy.

My sister takes a drag on her cigarette and blows a stream of smoke in my direction, tilting her head in a flamboyant and egotistical way. Even with all her acting skills, she can't carry off Sophia's elegance and sophistication. Abby merely looks like a rebellious teen, defiant and insolent. "So what do you want, sister dear?"

"I'm doing well, thanks. Look, I can walk and talk now."

"All at the same time? Do you want applause?"

"That's your department. I've left assisted living."

"That'll save a bundle each month. So what do you want? Money? Clothes?" Her gaze skims over the stylish used clothes I bought in Carmel. "A place to live?"

"Actually, I came to return the favor."

Her eyes widen. Her black lashes are spiky and thick with mascara. "What favor?"

"You took care of me when I couldn't. And even though you made decisions I never would have made, I still appreciate your help."

She looks startled, then her gaze narrows, her brow furrowing. "You're returning the favor? As in, you think I need your help?"

"A man came to see me recently."

"Well, good for you! It's about time."

"From the FBI. He wanted to know about you." I let that sink in fully while withholding my suspicions about the agent. "And the ruby slippers."

She glances over her shoulder at our friends. Then rising, she tilts her head to the side and takes a few steps away from the others. She waits for me to catch up before she asks, "What about the shoes?"

"Apparently a pair was stolen from some museum."

"Why should that concern me?"

I lift one eyebrow in retaliation. "You were looking for them."

"Now you think I did it? Great! My own sister—"

"*He* thinks you did it. The FBI suspects you. They're sitting outside this theater right now." Or at least someone is.

She glances over her shoulder. "I don't have anything to hide. So what do you want, sister dear? The shoes? Well, I don't have them. I never have."

"I do."

Her eyes widen. "How? Where?"

"They're safe." But I don't know for how long.

"Did your lawyer find them in the house rubble? Claim them as yours? If they were—"

"No. How did you even know about them?"

She shrugs and her gaze drifts off as if looking back toward the past. "Momma told me." Then it's like something clicks in her brain. "You've seen Dad then?"

"Not exactly. Not yet anyway."

"I figured if they weren't at the farm, then maybe he had them."

"What made you suddenly look for them after all these years?" I suspect she needed the money.

"I was at a dinner party and someone mentioned Judy Garland. I told them my grandmother worked with her during the making of *The Wizard of Oz*. We went around the table telling what we were most afraid of—the witch, the Munchkins, the flying monkeys." She laughs as if caught back up in the memory of that moment. "And then someone said they'd heard the ruby slippers had been stolen from some museum." She rolls her wrist. "I don't remember which one now. But it got me to thinking. And I wondered if those shoes Momma told me about were real. If she'd hidden them in the basement because she knew I was too scared to go down there."

"Why didn't you tell me that's what you wanted?"

"Because you wouldn't have let me have them. You would have wanted them for yourself. But honestly, what would you do with a pair of ruby slippers? Walk to the barn in them? I'm an actress. Theater . . . movies are my life. So it makes sense for me to have a piece of Hollywood history."

"You'd just sell them," I say.

"No, I wouldn't. Well, not right away. And before I had to bend over backward taking care of you, I had never thought of selling them. Now, I admit, it'd be nice to have the bucks, pay off all the hospital expenses that insurance didn't cover, the cost of moving you to the West Coast."

"I found him."

"Who?" Tiny flecks of gold brighten her green eyes.

"Our father."

She blinks slowly, staring at me for a solid minute. Her stance is defiant, but her features undergo a slow transformation. Her expressions have always been guarded, calculating. Now they seem slack for a moment, giving her a vulnerable look, like a little girl's. Her emotions are broadcast across her face. Not imagined or conjured-up emotions, but the real and raw type.

"Where?" She sounds breathless.

"Here in Seattle."

Her face blanches. Is it fear I see there? Shock? Or pain?

"He wants to see you."

She blinks slowly, as if she didn't hear me correctly. "What do you mean?"

"I went to see him." I skip the full description. "He asked for you. Asked me to bring you to see him."

It takes a moment for her to process my words, then her face crumples. Tears pour out of her eyes. She staggers away, one hand on my arm, clutching me, pulling me with her. She bends over and huge, wracking sobs assault her.

"Hey!" one of her friends says. "What'd you do?"

"Nothing."

Abby clutches her stomach with one hand as she tugs the sleeve of my shirt, her nails clawing at me, stretching the material. Her lit cigarette lies forgotten on the concrete. I step on it, crushing the last spark. "Abby?"

"Go away!" Her voice is broken by sobs. But she doesn't release me. She holds onto my sleeve, sucking in breath after breath. Suddenly she pushes away from me. She stands defiant, her crying contained. She glares at all of us defiantly, her eyes glittering in the midst of tears. "Leave!" She whirls away. She hugs herself, her hands balled into tight fists of self-control.

I look to her friends, to mine. They give us more distance, moving farther away. Sophia gives me an encouraging nod to go to my sister. Reluctantly I move toward Abby. I reach out to her, but my hand hesitates inches from her shoulder. I feel awkward and uncertain. Will she shrug me off? Will she reject me too? Finally I touch her, laying a hand flat on her back and noting the ravaging effects of tears on her makeup. Then she turns toward me, falls against me, her tears dampening my shirt. Her snuffles become a part of me. Her shaking rocks something loose inside me.

We cling to each other. I no longer can tell her sobs from mine, her tears from my own. I've never understood my sister until this moment. Maybe I didn't want to understand her. Maybe if I'd looked under the crusty exterior, I might have seen the hurt little girl who just wanted her daddy. The same little girl that I was. That I am.

After several minutes we stumble back toward the steps and Abby searches her bag for a tissue. We each try to blot away the running mascara, but we are forever changed. We look at each other, vulnerable yet still wary.

"I thought he didn't love me. But he wants to see me? He wants to see me!" Her voice rises higher than normal with a little-girl quality. "He really does?"

I swallow the hurt her question rouses in me. "Yes, Abby."

I resist warning her about our father. He might, after all, be different with her. She won't show up uninvited the way I did. I want him to be kind to her, to love her. Even if he can't love me. Why should both of us be wounded further?

Her watery eyes glow with hope. "What else did he say?"

"Nothing." At least that's not a lie.

She measures my answer as if unsure whether to believe me or not. Jealousy has always been a powerful force between us, but her mouth finally relaxes into a hesitant smile that wavers between fear and excitement. "Will you go with me?"

Her question surprises me. "If that's what you want."

She nods and reaches for my hand in a trusting way that opens my heart. "Have you always wanted to meet him too?"

"Yes. Of course."

"You always seemed so self-sufficient, Dottie. Like you didn't need anyone. Momma. Me. Daddy."

The way she can call him Daddy so easily unsettles me. Have I lost that childlike trust? Have I lost the ability to ever trust anyone? My gaze shifts toward Leo. His brow furrows with concern as he watches us.

"That's not true," I say. Pressure builds in my chest. "I needed . . ." My throat closes over the words.

"We needed each other, didn't we?"

I nod and squeeze her hand.

SO UNLIKE THE Abby I know, my sister doesn't even repair her makeup before returning to rehearsals. I agree to meet her for dinner that night. She seems distracted, confused, and more upset than I have ever seen her. When she arrives late, dressed in a lethal red dress that doesn't clash with her hair but somehow goes with the wild frenzy of curls, the skies turn stormy. Lightning flashes and an ominous shiver shoots down my spine. I introduce Abby to Sophia and Tim, who is her uncle.

"Our uncle!" Her green eyes widen and sparkle. She hugs Tim, resting her head momentarily on his shoulder. "It feels," she says, her voice bubbling with excitement, "like that moment at Christmas when you think you've unwrapped all the presents and lurking way under the tree is one last gift."

"Or finding one in the toe of your stocking," Sophia adds.

"Exactly!" She then turns her attention to Leo, who looks fairly respectable since the spa visit. He's wearing faded jeans and a polo. Abby's gaze heats up like Christmas lights left on too long. "And *who* are you?"

"This is my son, Leo." Sophia reaches out and touches his arm. Admiration and love is clear and shining in her brown eyes. I feel mine narrow with emotions I don't admire or want to admit.

"Were you going to keep him from me, sis?" Abby grins hungrily at Leo. "Oh, look!" She does a quick sidestep, hooking her arm through Leo's and cutting out every woman, rival, mother, or sister without hesitation or conscience and with the precision of a trained assassin. It's a move I've witnessed countless times but one I have yet to emulate. "Our table's ready." With that come-hither smile she's perfected over the years, she loops another arm through our uncle's, then escorts the two men to a table set in the far back corner near the kitchen. Abby's in her element now, sandwiched between two handsome men, albeit one elderly.

Sophia turns toward me, offers me her arm. As we fall in step behind the trio, she pats my arm. I try to ignore the way my stomach is twisting into a pretzel of a knot. I have no claim on either man. Tim is the type of man I wish my father had turned out to be. And Leo . . . my hand presses against my lips in a reflexive memory. Heat sears my cheeks. I clear my throat and look away.

What will it be like when I take her to meet our father tomorrow? The same? Worse?

Sophia and I sit beside each other, but I avoid her inquiring gaze. To see the confusion and pain in her eyes would require me to accept my own. This is my fate. My sister will charm my uncle—and tomorrow, our father—slicing me out of any relationship with the only men in my family. And Leo . . . will Abby hook him as she has so many others? I remember when she turned her attention on Craig our senior year in high school. He asked her to prom, of course. How could he resist? The pain I felt then returns now with all its razor-like sharpness. Maybe that's one reason I had a close relationship with Momma—Abby couldn't charm her. Momma loved us both, of course, but she and I understood one another.

"Abby," I say loudly enough to demand the attention of everyone at our table and possibly those surrounding us, "Sophia used to work in Hollywood."

"Really?" Abby gives her a closer look. "Behind the camera?"

"Some of both." Sophia unrolls the silverware from a paper napkin.

Abby doesn't usually pay attention to other women, unless they're competing for the same man. She gives Sophia a sidelong glance and casually tosses out the question, "What movies did you work on?"

When Sophia begins to list several well-known dramas, biblical epics, and westerns, Abby turns her shoulders more toward Sophia. "What parts did you play?"

"Any part I could get. A lot of shots in the crowd."

"Oh, sure. Anyone can get those."

"But not anyone does," Sophia counters.

Abby leans forward, arm on the table. "So did you know Eastwood?"

"We've met a few times," Sophia hedges.

"You said he'd remember you," I add to give her story more credence.

Sophia smiles secretly. "He might."

"I'd give anything to work for Clint. Do you know him well enough to call him?"

Now I understand why Sophia wanted to play coy. She knew what my sister wanted. I should have known too.

Sophia shakes her head. "I haven't been around the industry in a long time."

"What actors did you love?" I ask to change the subject.

"Oh, Greg Peck, of course. A gentleman if there ever was one. And Cary Grant. My absolute favorite was John."

"John Ford?"

"He was nice, sure. That is, if he liked *you*. But I meant Wayne."

"John Wayne?" Tim straightens. "You knew him?"

"Of course. Now *he* knew how to treat a woman."

"Yeah," Leo laughs, his gaze swerving toward me. A warmth spreads through my belly.

"Seems to me he liked to spank women a lot." I jump into the conversation like a novice swimmer in the deep end of the pool.

Three sets of eyes stare at me as if I've spoken heresy. But Leo grins.

"It's true," I argue, dog paddling for all I'm worth before I sink. My gaze shifts from Abby to Leo. He's watching me quietly, curiously. A bemused smile curls his lips. "*Th-the Quiet Man. Donovan's Reef.* And—" I snap my fingers once, twice. "Oh, that western." I look to Sophia for help. "What was it?"

"*True Grit?*" Leo rubs his jaw.

"No, no."

"You're thinking of the one with Maureen O'Hara," Sophia adds.

"Was she a redhead?" I ask.

"She was!" Sophia smiles.

"Must be something about redheads," Leo says dryly.

"McLintock!" Tim grins. "I loved westerns. Especially ones with the Duke. But Elizabeth didn't care for them too much. Maybe that's how it is between men and women."

Sophia pats his shoulder. "Some women like westerns."

Tim looks surprised. "That's nice to know."

"The old stars weren't really playing parts," Abby says with an air of authority. "They were playing themselves. The public didn't want to go see Henry Fonda play some down-and-out loser. They wanted to see Henry Fonda. Or Cary Grant. Or John Wayne. Or Clark Gable. It's the same now, although there aren't many big personalities anymore. Mel Gibson came close. Tom Cruise almost made it to that level."

"Jumping on couches was a little too big," Sophia says.

Laughter erupts at our table. I give a token chuckle, but as the conversation swirls around the movies and Sophia's and Abby's experiences, I grow quieter and quieter. I have nothing to add. Leo is caught up between them, laughing at their stories. A cloud of dread weighs heavily on me. Maybe it's watching the sister I know so well. As Abby becomes more animated, a part of me contracts and begins to fold up and disappear.

WATCHING MY SISTER at work, I have to admit she treats our uncle with a gentle kindness that surprises me. She offers him the salt and pepper, picks up his napkin when it falls off his lap, and touches his hand tenderly. I imagine her taking our father's arm tomorrow, smoothing a hand over his shoulder, asking if he feels all right, if he needs anything. It's the way I treated Momma.

When Abby laughs, she reaches out to Leo. She's always been very physical, very demonstrative. Halfway through our salads, I feel a prickling of irritation skitter along my spine watching her obvious flirtations.

I want Leo to push away her hand when it lingers on his arm, but he doesn't. Is he enjoying the attention? He smiles right back at her, open and carefree. But I remember that moment, the brief moment he and I shared. It seems like forever ago, the connection now broken, and Abby holds the virtual hammer.

"Pass the salt." My voice comes out louder than I intended.

My request forces Abby to release her clutches on Leo momentarily and reach for the saltshaker that's shaped like a lobster. "You should go light on the salt, Dottie. It's not good for you. Will make you bloat up."

"Thank you." I give an extra shake of the salt on my salad but regret it with my next bite. Still, I force myself to eat every last bite. I stab each lettuce leaf with the fork and jab it into my mouth.

"Pepper?" Leo hands the matching lobster pepper shaker to Abby. I watch their fingers brush.

"None for me, thanks." I grab my water, take a sip. Ice chunks bump my nose and water splashes my shirt. Lovely.

"Are you okay?" Sophia asks.

"Fine." I dab my face and shirt with my napkin, the ice water nothing compared to the cold hard lump in my belly.

"So tell me all about yourself." Abby turns her full attention to the most eligible bachelor at the table.

Leo ducks his head, and the tips of his ears redden. "Nothing much to tell."

"The strong silent type, huh?" Abby's mouth curves into a seductive smile. "I like that."

"How long have you been an actress?" he asks.

"Forever," I say.

Everyone at the table looks at me. Hurt registers in Abby's green eyes, and I regret my comment. I'm being ridiculous. I thought I understood myself, but lately I don't seem to know myself at all.

"Why don't you tell us all about your fiancé?" I suggest, trying to cover my rudeness.

"We broke up," Abby says, not looking too grief-stricken. More like she's on the prowl for a substitute. She slides back her chair and clutches her purse. "Think I'll go touch up my lipstick. Dottie," she gives me a tight smile that never reaches her eyes, "want to join me?"

"I don't wear lipstick."

"Which is exactly why you should come with me." She walks around the table and grabs my arm.

Chapter Twenty-Four

For this confrontation I would not have chosen a restroom. Especially one with curtains that barely cover the stalls. But Abby doesn't seem to care about the amenities or lack thereof. She concentrates on reapplying a heavy dose of gloss on her already glossy lips.

"Does anyone have TP out there?" a voice calls from one of the stalls.

"Not even paper towels," I say, looking around at the dingy tiled walls with specks of I-don't-know-what on them and the one empty stainless steel paper towel dispenser. "I can go—"

Abby grabs my arm, glares at me. "You're not going anywhere. Not till we talk this out." Then over her shoulder she hollers, "Don't you have tissues, lady?"

"Oh, maybe I do." There's a *thump*—perhaps elbow against wall, or maybe bag and floor—followed by rustling.

I ease my elbow away from Abby's grip. We look at each other for a moment, a standoff, and I remember the staring contests we had when we were in elementary school. I could usually make Abby laugh, but she doesn't seem to be in a good humor today.

For lack of something better to do, I turn on the faucet. Cold water shoots out of the roughened spout. Abby yanks her purse back. I punch the soap dispenser only to discover there isn't any. I reach past my sister, bumping her accidentally, but the other is empty as well.

"What do you think you're doing?" she asks.

"Trying to get soap."

"That's not what I meant. And you know it."

Looking around and realizing there isn't anything to dry my hands on, not even one of those loud blowers that might block out my sister's accusatory tone, I give my hands a shake.

Abby squeals. "Do you mind?'

"Are you scared of a little water?" I ask. "Afraid you're going to melt?"

For a long moment she's silent, as if searching for a clever comeback. Then she takes a threatening step toward me— threatening in the sense that anger burns in her eyes like I've never seen. "Listen to me, big sister. I know exactly what you're trying to do out there."

"Out where? In Seattle?"

"With that man. You've got the hots for him. And whereas I'm thrilled to see you actually interested in someone, let me give you a little advice." Her fingers pinch my arm, and I jerk away from her.

"You don't know what you're talking about. He's a friend! I just don't want you getting your claws into him, destroying him like you have every other man in your life."

Her features relax. She leans back, crossing her arms over (actually under) her enhanced chest. "So that's what this is about. It always comes back to Craig, doesn't it? And that night. You know, Dottie, it's been almost twenty years. Don't you think it's time you got over it? Got over Craig? He is, after all, married with a bazillion kids. *He* doesn't seem to be mad at me, so why should you be?"

"It's not about *that* night, Abby. It's about all the men whose lives you've turned upside down and inside out, if not physically then emotionally."

She laughs and the sound echoes off the beige tiles. Then a quiet descends. It's too quiet. Over Abby's shoulder I see a brown eye peeking out of the curtained stall.

"You think Craig would have ever made a living as a baseball player?" Abby asks. "No way! He's done just fine with that little office of his, settling wills and divorces and whatever else he does." Her eyes narrow. "Or is it that you think he would have been happier with a different wife? With you?"

I have no answer for her. Heat burns its way from my chest to my face. "Look, that lady is waiting for our fight to be over so she can get out of here." I motion toward the eye that suddenly disappears behind the curtain.

Abby waves her hand as if to shoo away a fly. "Pay no attention to her."

"It's okay," I say. "Really. Come on out."

There's a slight awkward pause, then the toilet flushes and the curtain jerks open. An elderly lady shuffles out, holding her purse over her stomach. She looks down at the floor as she passes us.

"There's no soap," I warn her.

But she doesn't stop. She jerks open the door and hustles out of the restroom as quickly as I'd like to.

"Admit it," Abby says. "You think I stole him from you, don't you? And now that hot guy out—"

"No, I don't think you stole Craig from me. But—"

"You were in love with him. Admit it!"

I swallow back all the words I've wanted to say all these years and replace them with, "I cared about him, of course. We were best friends. We still are friends. But you—"

"Do you want to know about that night?" she asks, looking smug and overconfident with her chin tilted at a jaunty angle. "You've wanted to blame me all these years. But the fact is, Craig was hot for me. He wanted me. He didn't want to go to the dance; he wanted to go find a motel. Does that shock you?"

Yes. But I don't admit it.

She laughs. "That's what you've wanted to believe, isn't it?"

Ashamed, I give a quick nod.

"Well, that's *not* what happened. Craig wanted to ask me about my plans for leaving our little farming community."

I feel a part of me go numb. I don't want to hear how Craig wanted to go away with her, wanted her.

"He wanted to leave Maize. To find a new, different kind of life."

"With you?"

"He didn't care about me any more than he cared about Maize. He admired me because I was forthright in my plans, my eagerness to move on."

"So why didn't *he* tell me this?"

"Because you were determined to stay right where you

were. You always liked the status quo. You clung to it. He didn't think you'd understand."

I probably wouldn't have understood. Even when Craig mentioned his desire to write, I didn't understand his need to stretch beyond our little world of corn and community.

"We actually went to the library that night of prom and looked at places we might go. We dreamed about our different futures. We wanted a different kind of life than our parents had. He felt hemmed in by his father's law practice, by his father's expectations." She shrugs as if to herself. "When we left the library . . . that's when we had the accident. Or maybe it was fate. Who knows? But everyone wanted to believe the worst. They wanted to believe we'd gone to that motel. But rumors never bothered me. Still, it's not a bum leg that's crippled Craig. It's fear. Same as you, Dottie."

My heart thumps hard against my breastbone. I can't find an answer, a comeback, anything to say.

"I was afraid too, Dottie. I'm not saying I never made mistakes."

This admission surprises me.

"When the tornado happened," she leans a hip on the counter, "I had to make some difficult decisions. There was a lot to do. I was at the hospital and at the farm. It wasn't easy. I had a lot of responsibilities. Things I wasn't used to doing. You were always the capable one, the one Momma leaned on. Suddenly I was in charge. And I was scared. Scared I'd screw it up. I wanted to do the right thing.

"But things were expensive, Dottie. I couldn't fly back and forth to Kansas to check on you, so I had you moved to California. Even though I wanted to save the farm for you, I couldn't. We have to sell. We need the money. Insurance covers only so much."

"I'm sorry, Abby. I didn't realize—"

"Listen, that's not what I'm getting at. What I'm trying to say—and I'm not doing a very good job of it—is I found out that I was more capable than I ever imagined. But the situation put pressure on my relationship with Trey. At first, I wanted to let him fix everything for me. But he didn't understand why I wanted to help you so much. He didn't like me being gone. It made me realize the sacrifices you made for so many years."

"Oh, Abby, I'm sorry about Trey. That you two broke up."

She shrugs. "It's good, I suppose. He was too self-absorbed. And I realized I wasn't really looking for a husband."

"You weren't?"

"No. I've been searching for my dad all these years. I hate to admit that. It sounds so childish. But that's why I went for older guys, for dominant, controlling men. Which is ultimately why all my relationships broke up. I wasn't a girl; I was a woman. And that's not what they wanted either."

"You've learned a lot through all these months."

"Isn't it about time?"

I step toward the door. "Thanks for tell—"

"Now it's your turn, Dottie. Is this how you're going to live the rest of your life? Afraid? Did you stay in that little rundown house hoping Daddy would come home one day? Is that what kept you there? Is that why you can't admit you loved Craig? That you love that guy out there?"

"I don't know. Okay? I don't. Maybe. Maybe you're right. Does that make you feel better?"

"Of course not. I want to see you happy, Dottie. I want to see you free from all of that. But you're clinging to it. You are. You're racing even now to try to buy back the farm at auction. But you want to know the truth? The truth is, that tornado was probably the best thing that's ever happened to you. It set you free from all of that. Daddy coming home or Craig turning to you isn't going to set you free. Maybe the truth finally will."

And the truth will set you free. A chill ripples over me and I wrap my arms across my stomach, trying to hold myself together when I feel like I'm coming apart at the seams.

"If that stud out there is really the guy you want," Abby wraps an arm around my waist, "then go for it, Dottie. You're lovable. And beautiful." She embraces me with both arms.

We cling to each other in that restroom, this time with nothing standing between us.

I LAY ON my side in the dark of the hotel room. Abby has called a dozen times since we left the restaurant with questions about our father. What does he look like? Where does he live? A house? Apartment? How do I explain his mansion of a house? Will Abby's eyes gleam with greed or resentment? How do I explain that he didn't even let me in? Will he invite us in this time? Or just Abby? What if he turns us both away?

A crazy mix of emotions swirls inside me. I want to protect Abby. It's an old instinct. And yet I fear her too. It's not her fault, this jealousy I feel. I want this to work out, more for her sake than mine.

"Does he have another family?" she asks.

My fingers curl around the end of the phone, gripping the plastic until all feeling is pressed away. I don't want to consider the possibility. What if he had more kids? What if we have half sisters and brothers? What if he doted on them the way he ignored us? The endless questions torture me.

Trying not to wake Sophia, who lies on her side sleeping in the other bed, I whisper, "I don't know."

"You didn't ask?"

"No." Fear measures my words.

"How long did you two talk? Tell me everything he said."

"It wasn't for long. You'll meet him tomorrow. Now go to sleep or you'll have bags under your eyes."

She sighs deeply on her end of the line. I can hear her shifting around, the rustle of sheets, the squeak of a headboard. "I can't sleep. I'm too excited."

It feels like we're little girls again, on Christmas Eve long ago, curled up in the same bed, our cold toes bumping against each other. For the first time in years I feel close to her, and I don't want to lose that. She needs me again. And I know now I need her too. "It'll be okay."

"Are you sure?" she asks, uncertainty in her voice.

"We have each other now, right?"

"Yes." A smile stretches out her answer.

"Try your best to sleep." My eyelids grow heavy. "Good night, Abby. I'll see you in the morning."

I hang up the phone. Guilt twists inside me. Maybe I should have told her more.

A banging on the hotel door jars me, and Otto starts barking. "Who could that be?"

Sophia rolls over. "Sounds like my son, but you better check first. What with all the strange calls we've had lately, you just never know."

Sure enough, when I open the door, the latch keeping anyone from pushing into the room, I see Leo standing there. "What's wrong?"

"Nothing. Otto need walking?"

I glance back at the bed where he's standing on the edge, wagging his tail. "I suppose."

"Come on then."

I slide on my shoes and tell Sophia, "I'll be quiet coming in."

"Have a good time." Her smile tells me she likes the idea of us walking together.

"I won't be gone long."

Together Leo and I walk around the periphery of the hotel while Otto explores every bush and tree. Leo is silent. I feel nervous, glancing over my shoulder when a car drives past. "So," I say, needing to fill the space between us with something other than my nerves, "how'd you like my sister?"

He chuckles, and I regret my choice of topic. I don't want to hear how pretty she is or how much fun. Not from Leo anyway. "She's a piece of work."

"What do you mean by that?"

"Well," he rubs his jaw with his thumb, "it's hard to see you two as sisters. Although there is a bit of rivalry there."

I bristle against his words. "What do you mean?"

His gaze remains on Otto, who zigs in and out of a line of bushes, but Leo's hand snags my elbow. He stops and turns me to face him. "Look, Dottie, I know what was going on, and I have to say, I'm flattered at the attention."

I'm grateful for the darkness as my face flares red hot. "You don't—"

"That's why I wanted to talk to you."

A weight of dread falls over me. I can hear blood pumping hot and furious through my veins, making my ears feel as if they're swelling. I cross my arms over my chest, preparing to hear the worst. But inside, in a tiny place in my head, I whisper a prayer. *Please, God, don't let him rebuff me.* Then I get the brilliant idea that I should do it first. Before he can. At least to save myself some humiliation. I laugh out loud, and it comes out coarse. "Oh, please. Don't worry. I'm not after you, Leo. Sure, we kissed. But—"

He pulls me against his chest. "But what?"

I swallow hard, find myself staring at his mouth, unable to drag my gaze away. "But . . ." My voice has shrunk. "I, uh . . ."

"Did you forget what it was like?"

"No."

"Good." Then he tilts his head and slants his mouth across mine. He's soft and insistent at the same time, demanding and giving. His strong arms envelope me with a warmth that melts my insides until they pool deep in my belly. Behind my eyelids, stars erupt along a background of night sky. When he pulls away, his mouth quirks into a cocky smile that this time sends pure pleasure through me. "Me either. And this time, you didn't think about anything else, not even Otto."

I mouth the name, as if trying to lock into place what he's talking about. My brain seems to be working in slow motion. Then memory snaps into place. "Otto. Where is—"

"Right there. Don't worry." He tightens his hold on me and whispers, "Don't be afraid." Then he steps away and bends down. "Come here, boy."

Otto comes to him immediately.

Inhaling deeply of the night air, I stare up at the darkness, feel Leo's shoulder brush my leg. For so long Otto was the only constant in my life. Since Momma's illness, changes have marked my days. Each one a new disaster. But what family hasn't been hit by a medical emergency or illness?

Fire, flood, tornado. There's often no one to blame. And until recently I've never been one to blame God. But I haven't been quick to credit him either.

This latest whirlwind turnaround of my relationship with Abby is a force of nature that has me wondering if it's a work of God. It certainly feels supernatural for Abby and me to talk and share heart to heart.

And Leo has pushed his way inside my heart in such a short period of time. It makes me realize how much I missed by staying on the farm all those years, afraid of venturing further than my own backyard, afraid of being wounded, afraid of so many things.

Less than a week ago I prayed for answers, for direction, for hope.

This time I offer up a silent *thank you*.

Chapter Twenty-Five

Back at our father's house the next day, Abby and I stand together as we once did on Easter Sundays of long ago, hair shining, faces scrubbed, anticipation churning. Abby is decked out today, hair swirling about her face, makeup carefully applied with a light but dramatic touch. She looks sure of herself, confident in black slacks and colorful jacket. She wears chunky jewelry around her neck and wrists. I wear one of the new-to-me outfits, the soft beige slacks pressed, the white blouse crisp with starch.

When I picked Abby up in the Jeep, leaving the rest of the Oz-or-bust gang at the hotel, Otto greeted her with a growl.

"Move over, you little beast." She waved a hand in his face.

I waited for Abby's usual greeting, "Is that what you're going to wear?" It's what she used to say in high school, putting me in my place, making me feel insecure. But today she gives me a bright smile. "You look nice, Dottie."

"Thanks. So do you."

"You think? I wasn't sure what to wear. I mean, what do you wear to meet your father for the first time? Pink?" A tiny wavering in the corner of her mouth revealed her insecurities. "So, you ready?"

"As ready as I'll ever be."

Now, idling outside the gate, it's my turn to say, "Are you ready?"

Abby is quiet for a long time as she stares at the colossal estate. "You're not serious, are you?" Her tone carries an accusation.

"You didn't tell me, Dottie."

"I didn't know how . . . what to say."

She gives me a nod, reaches for my hand, and squeezes my fingers. "Together, right?"

The guard checks his schedule and waves us through the wrought-iron gate. The winding road is paved smooth. Trees of all shapes and sizes seem to part before us, forming a canopy overhead. A jumbo weeping willow looks like a shaggy yellow dog. Ponderosa pines and big-leaf maples create a lush environment. Once away from the road, traffic noises recede and nature takes over. Myriad birds, thrushes and chickadees, with dark wings and golden bellies, flutter from tree branch to branch, chirping and making unusual calls that I never heard back in Kansas. Black squirrels scamper across a meticulously groomed lawn, chasing each other up the cragged trunk of an old walnut tree.

Last night's rain has left puddles at the side of the road. The grass is still damp.

We reach the top of the ridge, and I put a foot on the brake, gathering my nerve. The monstrosity of a house is a blend of modern and traditional, brick and stone, glass and marble. It is nothing I would have chosen. It's pompous in its self-importance, as if the designer went out of his (or her) way to waste money on unnecessary trappings like a Grecian fountain in the middle of a circular drive.

Slowly we descend the hill. Abby remains quiet. I steal a glance at her but can't read her expression. Shock? Anger? Excitement? Is she imagining what it would have been like to live here? When I park, we stand in the circular drive for a moment while Otto chases a lone squirrel. The heat of late summer presses in on me. Or maybe my nerves are cranking up my blood pressure. Butterflies morph into snarling tigers inside my stomach.

We head toward the wide double door that appears to be at least fourteen feet tall and made of solid, heavy wood. The panels gleam as if polished daily. The scent of rain is heavy in the air; I can hear drips fall off leaves nearby.

When we reach the stone steps, the door opens before we even ring the bell. A tall, stately man who looks unfazed by the enormous spectacle of his workplace is surprisingly casual in a simple black shirt and slacks. "Welcome, Ms. Meyers." His gaze shifts from Abby to me. He swings an arm wide to usher us inside. "Can I take your coats?"

Abby steps through the doorway first into a marble foyer that is as large as most houses in Kansas. She turns a circle, looking up at the domed ceiling. Around it little cherubs and fluffy white clouds float in a cerulean blue. "Oh, my!"

"Your coats?" the man prompts.

"Oh, no thanks." I hug the buttery soft leather, the fringe flapping at my arms. "I'll keep mine."

"As you wish." The man in black leads us to the other end of the great hall, to a simple, unassuming door. He knocks twice then turns the brass knob and lets the door open. "Mr. Meyers will see you now." Then he walks away, disappearing through yet another doorway.

The door yawns wide, and I stare at the opening. Inside, the room appears dark, shrouded in shadows and mystery. Abby looks at me, tears welling in her eyes. I offer a reassuring smile and enter first, Otto and Abby close at my heels.

The room seems small and cozy at first with its dark wood-paneled walls and hardwood floors that give it a womb-like quality. A rug covers most of the floor with deep shades of brown, highlighted with a pale, earthy blue. Near a wall of windows where thick, heavy curtains hang is a large bare desk that looks as if it's been swept clean. A massive leather chair sits behind the desk, turned away from us. My heart pounds as I wait for my father to swivel around and greet me for the first time in over thirty years. My limbs begin to quake.

Darkly stained wooden blinds cover the windows, but sunlight slants through them across the room, alternating shafts of light and shadow. The room takes on a different proportion, seeming to grow larger as my eyes adjust to the dimness. The ceiling is at least twenty feet high, if not more. Abby gives me a nudge with her elbow. My knees feel weak. Together we shuffle forward, standing before the imposing desk.

But the chair doesn't turn. My father doesn't speak.

What's he waiting for? For us to pass out? It's then I wonder if maybe he's watching us secretly from some hidden camera. A shiver ripples down my spine.

"Say something," Abby whispers.

"What?" I ask, my voice coming out hoarse. I clear my throat with a cough. "Um, hello. I brought her." My voice sounds tiny in the large room, engulfed by the enormity of the situation. "Here's Abigail . . . Abby."

She stands slightly behind me, like a little girl hiding behind her mother's skirts, so close that if I take a step back I'll crunch her toes in those pointy little shoes. I tighten my hold on my own emotions. Abby has never known our father, has even fewer memories than I do. She only knows the stories I told her when we were little, lying in the dark together. But I kept some all to myself, as if hoarding a favorite toy from her prying fingers. I can see the expectation in her, the hope, the fear. She wants our father to embrace her, to offer her the love she's always wanted. But I'm not sure he's that type of father.

"What's he doing?" Abby asks.

I shrug and turn to look at her, see her eyes fill with tears. A shadow behind her stirs. In the far corner, where two built-in bookshelves connect, a bulky shadow of a man looms.

Then a voice comes out of the darkness. "Hello."

"Are you my . . . Duncan Meyers?" I ask, feeling myself tremble.

"I am. Who are you?"

"D-Dorothy . . . most call me Dottie. And," I feel Abby clutching my arm as she turns, "this is Abby . . . Abigail. Are you—"

"Did you know I named you Abigail?"

Abby shakes her head.

"Ruby wanted to name you just plain ol' Gail. So we'd have Dorothy and Gail . . . you know, like the girl in *The Wizard of Oz*."

Abby nods as if she can't speak.

"I thought that was a bit much. Don't you?"

I don't know what to say. *Hello? How've you been for the past thirty years? Why didn't you care about my mother? My sister? Me?* But my voice fails right along with whatever confidence I once had, if any.

"Why did you come here?" he asks.

"I wanted to meet you. And you asked me to bring Abby, remember?"

"But why now?"

My throat burns. "You left the ruby slippers . . ."

"So that's it, eh?" He steps into the light, looking smaller than I imagined. His face is a road map of wrinkles, weathered and worn. What's left of his hair is gray and threadbare, his cowlick wiped away with age. His shoulders are stooped. He's not much taller than I am. I try to figure out how old he might be. He looks beaten and worn like a discarded paper sack. He can't be more than sixty or sixty-five. But maybe it's not age. Maybe it's something else. He moves slowly past us and settles behind the desk. "Please," he waves a hand toward two empty chairs facing him, "have a seat."

I glance at his bookshelves and desktop. There's not one picture displayed. Only row after row of books. No artwork brightens the walls. No knickknacks decorate or clutter the shelves. Nothing elaborates who this man is, what he likes, who or what he holds dear. I should have warned Abby, not tried to protect her. This will never be the kind of family either of us desires.

She clutches my hand. Her fingers are warm and smooth where mine are cold and callused from farm work. I'm not sure if Abby is trembling and I'm feeling the aftershocks or if it's me. The shaking rocks through me, unsettling my composure. I don't know how to think of this man or what to call him. Father? Dad? Mr. Meyers? So I don't call him anything. I simply sit in the leather seat across the desk from him. When I pat my thigh, Otto jumps into my lap.

Abby starts to sit next to me but instead walks around our father's desk. He looks up at her, leaning back into the comfort of the wide-backed chair. His mouth goes slack. She hesitates, then leans forward, arms outstretched, and embraces him. He remains seated as if not expecting her hug, as if he doesn't know what to make of it or do with it, as if maybe he's not accustomed to receiving them. His arm lifts as if to hug her back, but he never touches her. My arms close about Otto, his warm body comforting against me. After a long, agonizing moment, Abby pulls back.

"Remember this?" He holds out his hand. On his palm is a shiny quarter. Abby reaches for it, but he closes his palm. "I'm going to turn it into two coins."

She takes a half step back, watching him beneath heavy lids.

He folds his arm backward, his hand touching the back of his collar. He rubs his elbow with his other hand. "Abracadabra. One. Two . . ."

A flash of silver catches my attention. Then I hear the clink of a coin hitting the floor beneath his desk.

His features fold. He pushes back from his desk to retrieve the coin. "Let me try it again." His voice falters. "I practiced." He holds his hand out again. "I'm going to turn this coin into two."

Again he raises his arm, rubs his elbow while his fingers fumble beneath the back of his collar. Once more, the coin falls to the floor, rolls under the desk, and lands at my feet.

I slide the toe of my loafer over the coin and it snaps against the wood floor. I pick it up. It feels cool against my palm. "I remember."

"You do?" His voice lilts as if with hope.

I nod. "I remember the magic tricks you used to perform."

A wisp of a smile touches his thin lips. He looks to Abby, and my heart contracts. "What about you?"

"She was a baby," I explain.

Our father rubs his forehead as if trying to remember or correct his faulty recollection.

Abby backs away from him, returns to my side of the desk, and sits next to me. She avoids my gaze, but I can see the hurt, deep and gaping, in the way she sits, her shoulders slightly slumped when they're usually straight. She looks downward, the muscles along her jaw slacking. Her thumb rubs along her pointer finger. A tear splashes on the back of her hand.

Aching for both our lost dreams, I wish I'd prepared her for this disappointment. I touch her arm, smoothing my hand along the soft jean material of her jacket. She looks at me then, her green eyes clear and hard as glass.

"We're both here now," I address our father. "What did you want with us?"

"I wanted to see you." He shakes his head. His throat tightens and jerks. "You surprised me the other day when you arrived. I wasn't prepared . . . I didn't know . . ." He coughs, his jowls expanding. "You've grown up lovelier than I could have ever imagined."

His words surprise me. I suspect he's talking about Abby, not me. She's usually the recipient of such flattery and succumbs to its allure, but here and now the hardness of her expression remains.

"Why did you leave us?" Abby asks. Suddenly I like her brashness.

He stares at us a moment as if surprised we'd asked this question. "Ruby told me to."

"Momma?" I breathe.

He leans forward, his elbows resting on the edge of his desk. His shoulders seem narrower than I remember, as if they've been worn away by the hard knocks of life. "She never told you?"

I shake my head. "I didn't want to upset her. She didn't want to discuss it."

"Knowing her, Ruby didn't want to make me out to be the bad guy."

"She never said anything bad against you," Abby adds.

He folds his hands together. His knuckles are bumpy and large. His nails are trimmed neat and short. He wears a wedding ring, and my hope plummets like a coin off the top of a high-rise building. My fascination with him irritates me. I can't seem to stop staring, trying to take in every tiny detail.

"Oh, that's Ruby. She's not one to talk poorly about someone." He pats the desktop. "You see, girls, I had a dream."

My stomach tightens. A dream. Just like Craig. Just like Abby. Even Leo had a dream that died. What good did dreams do them?

"Ruby wanted me to pursue it. To come here and try my hand in the aerospace industry."

"You couldn't do that from our home?" I ask.

"Not back then. Boeing was building 747s, 707s . . . here on the West Coast. And I wanted to be a part of that. Ruby didn't. She said she'd reached her own dreams—living there on the farm, having little girls. She wanted me to go find my own dreams, follow my own yellow-brick road. She said I could always come back." He touches the ring on his left hand. "Said I was always welcome."

Abby crosses her arms over her chest. She seems to be withdrawing into her own protective shell. "Why didn't you come back then? You obviously reached your dreams. Did you forget about us?"

"It's a long road home." He remains silent for a moment, drawing first one breath then another. "At first the weeks went by slowly without you all. I called often. I loved my girls. My wife. But this was something I had to do. Or maybe it was something I rationalized. I don't know anymore."

I glance at Abby. She nods as if she understands, but I don't. Maybe it's because I've never felt driven by anything.

"But it wasn't always easy. I worked long hours. The phone calls and the letters grew more infrequent. I tried to get your mother to come out west. I was earning okay money then. We could have had a decent house, maybe even enough backyard for a garden. But she wanted to stay in Kansas. She said she didn't have to look further than her own back-yard for what she wanted. I assumed that meant me. Ah, well . . ."

He rubs the back of his neck. "She'd heard a lot about Hollywood and the glamorous people out here. I think she was scared. She felt safe in Kansas, surrounded by family and friends. She had insecurities, you might know, from her withered leg. Ruby didn't want me staying out of obligation. She was always afraid that I'd regret marrying her, thinking that she had held me back." He shifts in his chair, making its joints squeak and groan. "Looking back, I'd say she was afraid that I wanted someone else, that my ambition was just a symptom. She wanted me to have no regrets. She didn't want me to sacrifice anything for her. I don't know if she thought she didn't deserve it or . . ." He shrugs a shoulder. "I don't know."

Otto jumps down from my lap and disappears behind the desk. His nails click against the floor. I hear him sniffing around, his nose snuffling against the floor.

"The longer I stayed away," our father continues, he tugs at the wedding ring, "the more I wasn't needed by my wife, my girls. So I stayed here, retreated into my own world. Inside I felt like a fraud, going about my life, pursuing this dream which mattered less and less to me." He pushes the wedding ring securely onto his finger. "We're still married, your mother and I. Did you know that? We never divorced."

Abby leans forward, bracing an elbow against her knee. Her features soften. "You wanted what you couldn't have."

He gives her a long, slow glance. "No, I learned what was really important. Ruby learned that lesson before we met. She knew what mattered. But she'd managed to find her way home. But me, well . . ." He shrugs awkwardly. "So many years had passed. I didn't know how to get back. Have you heard the joke about old people saying they walked barefoot to school uphill both ways? Well, the journey here seemed like an uphill climb, but it was steeper trying to return home."

Suddenly his eyes widen, and he pushes his chair back. "Hello?" He scoops Otto into his arms. It's an awkward embrace. Otto utters a low growl. "What were you doing down there?"

"Here, boy." I snap my fingers.

Otto wags his tail, squirming and trying to get loose. My father gingerly puts him back on the floor.

"Wait." He snaps his fingers several times to get Otto's attention. He glances over at me. "What's his name?"

"Otto."

"Otto, my boy, I bet you smell what I keep in this drawer." He tugs open a heavy desk drawer and pulls out a candy dish filled with macadamia nuts. "Want one?" He holds a nut between thumb and forefinger.

Otto yaps.

Our father laughs. "Okay, little fellow." He drops the nut, and I don't have to see Otto to know that he instantly lunges for it. I can hear him chomping on the nut. My father gazes down affectionately. "Good, huh?"

He offers the nuts to Abby and me, but we both decline. He places the crystal dish back in the drawer and pushes it closed. Then he looks back at Abby and me, clasping his hands together on his desk. "So the polio finally got Ruby, did it?"

"Yes," I say.

"I read it in the paper. Still get the *Maize Weekly*. Helped me keep up with you girls. That's how I learned about the tornado and knew Dottie was in a coma."

"Why did you give me the shoes?" I ask.

"Those shoes. The ruby slippers. Your grandmother had them. Oh, how she loved them. Was very proud that Judy Garland had given them to her. She worked in Hollywood at one of the big movie lots in wardrobe."

"She was a seamstress," Abby says.

"Sure enough. Young and pretty herself, from what I understand. She worked on several films in the late thirties and up until 1945, when she married a captain just coming home from the war."

"She worked on *The Wizard of Oz*," Abby explains.

"Exactly." He folds his hands together. "That's where she met a young actress. A star in the making."

"Judy Garland," Abby adds.

"Being close to the same age, they became friends. Your grandmother was a motherly sort, and from what she said, Judy didn't have much of a relationship with her own mother. The two girls bonded. When the movie wrapped, Judy gave your grandmother the shoes."

"The ruby slippers."

He gazes out the windows as if lost in his own past. "She named your mother Ruby after those shoes she so adored. She loved to tell about that time in her life. Sometimes she'd get out those shoes to show them off. At first folks believed they were the real thing, but as years went by doubts crept in. I guess their lives were so far from Oz that they could no longer imagine her story was true. So your grandmother stopped talking about them, stopped showing them to people. And as memories will, they got pushed to the back of a closet as she became busy with the chore of living life.

"Then Ruby came down with polio. It was bad back in the fifties. Lots of folks died from it. She was only eight and in bed for months and months."

"Granny," I say, feeling my chest tighten, "read her the Oz books."

"While she was getting well. Then she gave your mother the ruby slippers."

I remember Momma asking me to read the books to her when she was bedridden at the end of her life. We didn't make it through the first one before she died.

For a moment my father doesn't speak, as if remembering a private moment of his own. "Those shoes meant a lot to Ruby. They gave her the will to recover, to learn to walk again after the polio." His blue eyes mist over. "She gave them to me before I left, said she wanted me to find *my* dreams. It's why I brought them to you." His blue eyes lock with mine.

Momma wore those shoes. She began life anew with those shoes, gaining confidence with each step. Pressure builds within my chest, and I fight back tears. My father wanted me to experience the same. And I have in a completely different way.

My father clears his throat. "Now, girls, those shoes are valuable. I'm not sure how much they're worth. But you should be careful with them."

"We're taking them to the *Antiques Roadshow*. To see if we can find out how much they're worth. If we sell them, then Dottie could buy back the farm."

But suddenly I don't want to sell the shoes that belonged to my mother. The shoes have brought my family back together.

A flicker of emotion crosses my father's wrinkled features. "I'm glad you girls came."

"Thank you," I manage, "for giving them to me." I realize my father wasn't there for me through most of my life, but in his way he tried when I needed him most. Tears pearl in my eyes like hot rocks.

Abby stands. "Good-bye." She pulls something from her pocket then, lays the blue printed tickets on his desk. "This is for you. For my show. If you want to come."

He gives a nod but doesn't say anything.

I think we've been quietly dismissed. With Abby beside me, we walk to the door. As we step out of the room and into the colossal foyer, I turn toward her and see tears running down her face.

"He doesn't know how to be a father, does he?" With an index finger, she tenderly pushes back a lock of hair stuck to my damp cheek.

"Maybe he knows better than we think." I link arms with her, and we walk toward the door. After about five steps I realize Otto isn't with us. I sigh. "Hold on. I've got to get Otto."

Hoping I can lure him out of the office without sticking my head back in the room, I tiptoe up to the door and whisper, "Otto!" But he doesn't come. I try snapping my fingers. No Otto. Irritated, I take another step closer. I hear a voice murmuring something. Craning my neck, I peer into the room.

My father sits on the floor, his back to me. Otto stands in front of my father, watching him with dark, serious eyes.

"Okay, my little friend, let's try this again. And now—" he raises his voice, as if making a proclamation—"a spectacular feat never before attempted by man or beast!" My father holds out a macadamia nut in his hand that Otto sniffs. Cupping it against his palm, my father bends his arm back, rubs his elbow and fumbles under the collar of his shirt for another. I can see a nut bulging out from under the stiff seam. But both nuts slip out and collide with the floor. Otto lunges forward and gobbles them down, then licks his hairy lips.

My father chuckles. "Better than a coin, eh?"

Again, painstakingly, he picks up two nuts, his fingers arthritic and fumbling. Once again he tries to do the trick. "I'm getting old, Otto. Old and useless. How about you?"

Before he can fail again, I move forward. "Here." I cover his hand with mine and help him pull a nut from his collar, then reveal two salty nuts to Otto.

While Otto chomps down on his treats, my father locks eyes with me. "You do remember."

"Yes."

He swallows hard, looks away from me. "I'm a fraud."

I kneel down beside him. "What do you mean?"

"I'm not a real father to you girls. I'm a lousy magician. And this isn't my house, Dottie."

I tilt my head then look around the room. "What are you talking about?"

"I work for the man who owns this house. I'm just an ordinary man. Nothing special. But I wanted you to think I hadn't wasted all those years. I wanted you to think I was extraordinary. But it just made me look worse. It looked like I never thought of you two girls, but that's untrue." His throat works up and down, then he sniffs. "Can you forgive me?"

Otto doesn't take his eyes off my father, waiting diligently for another treat.

"Of course." I reach forward, cup his forearm. "We've all tried to be what we're not at times."

Chapter Twenty-Six

As soon as I walk back into my hotel room, I flop onto the bed. Tears well up and pour out of me without my consent. My grief flows like a gusher.

Sophia sits down beside me on the bed and takes hold of my hand. She smooths the hair back from my damp face. She doesn't give me answers I don't want to hear or her father's sayings. She just offers comfort as if there are no words. Because there aren't any to justify my emotions or explain how I feel.

Finally I grab a tissue off the table and begin pacing through the room. "It's not the answer I was looking for. You know?" The words leap out of me. I sound like a rebellious teenager. Maybe I should have expressed more when I was that age rather than bottling it up inside me. "I wish I knew why all this happened!"

"I don't know."

"How can you be so calm? So centered? You haven't had a perfect life either."

"No one has. What's idyllic anyway? Some green pasture we can't possibly reach? Every pasture has potholes, ants, and cow patties. Everyone has to deal with problems. If we didn't have problems, we wouldn't ever grow or change."

"And you handle your problems by talking to God?"

"Yes."

Exhausted I sit back on the edge of the bed. "My father hoped those stupid shoes could help him reach his dreams."

She smooths a hand along my arm. "People put their faith in all kinds of things. Even themselves."

I take a shuddering breath. "That's what I did. I didn't trust anyone."

"Ruby's slippers have no power. I have no power. Neither do you, Dottie. We're just flesh and blood, and those shoes are leather and sequins. But God . . . you can trust him. He is mighty and powerful beyond our imagination. He'll never fail you."

I chew on that for a moment, push it around. If my life suddenly worked out, would I say God had answered my prayers? If none of it works out, will I say the opposite? But I'm not sure either is accurate. "Can I ask you something personal?"

"Of course."

"Does God ever answer when you talk to him?"

She gives a wistful smile. "You might think I'm crazy and have me locked up."

"What could be crazier than my life?"

She laughs. "True." She readjusts her skirt, leans back against the headboard. "Yes, of course, he talks to me. He tells me things, answers my questions. Sometimes it's like a quiet voice whispering deep in my soul. That's the Holy Spirit at work. Sometimes it's a word from the Bible. Sometimes a friend tells me something, or a song plays and the message is what I needed to hear. I sense it like a quickening in my spirit. I've learned through the years that the answers are there if I look for them."

"How do you know it's not just your imagination?" My own has run amok lately.

"I weigh it against God's Word. The Bible. If the message I'm hearing is contrary to the Ten Commandments or something Jesus said, then I toss it out."

Contemplating this, I pace the length of the bed and back. "I prayed. Did I tell you that?"

She shakes her head.

"I did. I prayed for a family. And look where that got me."

"Yes, look!" She leans forward, her eyes alight with excitement. "You're like a daughter to me. And you have a new uncle. And there's Leo too! Don't you see, Dottie? You *do* have a family. It may not be the family you imagined, but it's still a family. You have people who care about you, who love you. Your sister loves you too. And your father. He wouldn't have given you the shoes if he didn't. But we're all just human. Our love isn't perfect. Only God's is."

I trace the threads of the comforter with my thumb. "How did you get so wise?"

"The Word is powerful, remember?" She winks. "When I just started talking to God like he was a real person sitting beside me, my life changed. Tell him everything. He'll listen."

"What if I only have complaints?"

"You think he doesn't know them already?"

"Then why talk at all, if he knows everything anyway?"

"Because he wants a relationship with us. We aren't his robot slaves. He's not a wizard with a wand. He wants us to come to him as daughters of the king." She straightens, placing a hand against her chest. "He wants us to tell him everything—our troubles, our thoughts, our confusion, our joy."

"I think I know what I have to do tomorrow."

She smiles at me. "We'll be with you all the way."

WE STAND OUTSIDE the Seattle Convention Center together as a united group—Abby, Sophia, Tim, Leo, and me. Today is the day of truth. We'll learn if the ruby slippers are authentic or if they're a fraud, invented by my mother and her mother. But these shoes have value if only because they meant something to Momma and now to me.

Did they give my mother courage? Did they boost her confidence? Did they teach her to throw caution to the winds of life and dance? If so, then I want to keep them to remind me of how far I've come and where I still need to go.

But Abby may insist that we sell the shoes. She always needs the money. I do too, but it's not about money for me. This is about family. It's about finding a new life.

"Okay now," I say to the team huddled around me, "don't tell anyone why we're here. No one can know what we have." I tuck the box under my arm. "Not until we're on air and talking to the *Antiques Roadshow* host."

We all nod in agreement and walk together up the steps and into the building. First, we must pass through security. I hold the shoebox while Sophia hides Otto in her oversized purse. Tim sets off the security alarms. He explains he has a steel rod in his neck. They wand him, then pat him down thoroughly. Finally we make it into the convention center. Our tickets show our time of arrival. Someone points us in the direction of a long, long line.

People mill around, the crowd's thick. Lines for the concessions form as people get coffee, bagels, and donuts. Other lines snake around the hall with people who hold treasures of all shapes and sizes, from German beer steins to clown paintings. Otto sticks close to my heels as we weave in and out through the crowd.

"You can't have a dog in here." A woman's screechy voice stops me.

Leo steps forward, bumps my arm. "He's mine." He tilts his head at an awkward angle. His gaze is aimed between the woman and me, not settling on any specific thing. "My seeing-eye dog."

I cover a sudden urge to laugh. If Otto is a seeing eye dog, then I'm a cat.

"Oh. Well, uh . . ." Her brow folds into confusion lines. She focuses on the box I hold. "What brought you here today?" She looks like she rolled out of bed and drove straight to the convention center. Her hair is flat on one side of her head and sticks up in odd angles on the other.

"Family heirloom." I shift the box, tucking it under my other arm.

"What do you have?" Leo asks.

The woman grins broadly, revealing a gold eyetooth. "My father loved to collect things. All sorts of things. For a while he collected stamps. But we had a flood one year and it ruined every single one." She clicks her tongue. "Such a shame. Then he began to collect coins." She pats a leather binder. "For years I've wondered what to do with them. I was tempted for a while to just use the coins like regular money. But my grandson told me the coins might be worth much more than their marked value. Besides, some aren't regular coins at all." She opens the binder and flips through several plastic pages. "Look at this one!" She slips her hand inside the plastic sleeve and pulls out a grungy coin and rubs her thumb tenderly over it. "See it?"

I'm not sure what she wants me to see. I can't quite read the year. It's not a current American coin. I glance at Leo, but he's carefully staring off into nowhere. The woman looks to Leo too.

"Nope," he tells her. "And I don't think my dog can tell me either."

The woman's face reddens. "Oh, yes. Of course. Well, anyway . . ." She puts the coin away and closes the binder. "I thought I'd bring the collection here. I like to watch this show. Have for a long time. I should probably bring more of my parents' belongings that I have stored in the attic. But allergies keep me from going up there." She looks at Otto who is sitting calmly at Leo's feet.

"Well, good luck with that." Leo's hand links with my arm. He pushes us forward, leaving the woman in our wake.

We weave through the crowd and stop at the back of a line. I start avoiding anyone who looks at the box, turning away, not meeting their gaze. I hate to be rude, but so many people seem to be after these shoes. If I'm asked about them again, I decide to focus on whatever they have in their hands. A box of jewelry. A Civil War-era chair. A painting. Most people would rather talk about their antique, family history, or hopes for instant wealth.

The man who stands in front of us doesn't hold any obvious artifact.

I ask him, "Are you just observing? Or did you bring something?"

His eyes brighten. He reaches into his coat pocket. "Just a pair of spectacles."

"They look old," I observe, not knowing what else to say.

He begins to point out the details to me, how the glass was formed, the type of metal the wire frames are made with. My brain glazes over until I hear him mention Benjamin Franklin. "Excuse me?"

A man with a bullhorn announces, "Remember, you may only have two items per person. Two items!"

The man in front of me taps the wire frames. "I think these may have been his."

"Well, that would be significant, wouldn't it."

"How long does this usually take?" Abby shifts around, stretching, looking about, unable to stand still. This morning she has circles under her eyes. "I'm going to go check, see if there is a shorter line somewhere."

"Good luck with that," the man says. "I went to the show in San Diego last year. Took me all day."

"Don't worry." Leo nudges me with his broad shoulder.

"We'll make sure someone takes a look at these." Sophia taps the box.

"Dottie," Tim leans toward me, his voice hushed and urgent, "did you see who's here, my dear?"

I half expect him to say my father, but there's deep concern in his gray eyes. I glance around. Across the way, I spot Abby talking with the so-called FBI agent. "Oh, no. Now what?"

"Stay here." Leo stops me with a hand on my arm. "You don't want to lose your place in line. I'll see what they're talking about and—"

"What?" I catch him before he storms off, feel his bicep muscle bunch under my hand.

"Don't worry," he reassures me.

"But—"

His sudden frown makes my skin grow cold. "Where'd they go?"

There are so many people, it's easy to lose someone in the crowds. But usually it's not easy to miss my sister's red hair. Yet I don't see her anywhere. She's disappeared with Chesterfield.

"We'll split up and search for her," Sophia suggests.

"You stay here." Leo's gaze bores into me. "Stay in line. Keep those sh—" He stops himself. "Keep the box safe."

"We'll find your sister, my dear," Tim assures me, embracing my shoulders. I'm not sure if I'm more worried about Abby's safety or if she's bartering a deal without my consent.

My friends move away and into the crowd of people. I'm hemmed in on both sides by Benjamin Franklin's spectacles and a woman who talks incessantly about her Civil War musket. I want to ask if it's useable in case someone tries to steal the slippers right out of my hands.

"Excuse me."

I turn toward an elderly gentleman. He's tall and dignified in a dark-blue wool suit. "Are you Dorothy Meyers?"

Startled, I instinctively glance at his ear to see if there's a curlicuing wire coming out of it that would indicate he's with the FBI or Secret Service or some other government entity. "Why do you ask?"

"I've heard you have something," he leans toward me and whispers. "Something of value."

His gaze drops to my hands, and I tighten my grip on the shoebox.

"Are those them?" He mouths, *The shoes?*

"Who are you?"

"That's not important." He takes a step closer, and I smell mint on his breath. "But what *is* important is what I can do for *you*."

Every cell in my body tightens in response, pulling away, going into lockdown mode. I square my shoulders, lift my chin, and give him a half-lidded aloof glance, trying to appear cool and unaffected.

He leans so close this time, I detect a fleck of dandruff on the collar of his suit. "I'd like to make you an offer. A very generous one."

"Wait a minute!" An exotic woman with black hair and dark skin coloring intrudes on us. A diamond stud pierces her left nostril. She wears a long, flowing scarf around her neck. "How much has he offered?"

"Who are you?"

"You have to get in the back of the line!" The woman owning the musket edges her out with a blunt shoulder.

"Why are you making offers on something you haven't even seen?" I ask. "They may not be valuable at all."

"Don't think like that," Benjamin Franklin's heir says. "Gotta be positive!"

"You don't know their power," the exotic woman tells me.

"Really, please. I don't want to sell. I'm only here to find out . . ." I step out of line, clutching the box to me, and push through the crowd, determined to get out of this place, to get away from these people who only want the shoes. I hold the shoebox like it's a football and begin running. I don't know where I'm going. I just know I'm getting away from those who would take Momma's slippers. Otto is right at my heels.

Then I barrel right into Abby. She grunts with the force of our collision, the corner of the box jabbing her in the rib. Her features harden, and her mouth opens before she recognizes me. "Come on." She grabs my arm. "Where've you been? I've been searching all over for you."

"I was right where you left me. In that line." I glance behind me, but I seem to have lost my pursuers. "And all these people knew what I had in here. They all—"

"I know the producer," she says, ignoring my rambling. "He's going to put us on in five minutes."

"On what?"

"Television." She tugs me through the crowd.

I pull back.

"Don't worry," she says. "It's not live TV. It's all taped. They'll edit it."

"Abby." I square off with her. "You were talking to that man."

"What?" The noise of the crowd has grown too loud. People hustle past us, bumping against a shoulder, an elbow. Otto settles between my feet.

"That man! You were talking to him earlier."

She glances at her watch. "We're going to be late. We'll miss our opportunity." She grabs my arm again and jerks me forward. "Come on!"

We weave through the crowd, not breaking our connection, passing those walking in the same direction at a faster clip. Abby situates me in front of a table. Cameras surround us. Self-conscious, I brush the hair off my forehead. Just beyond the lights, I see Leo, Sophia, and Tim. They're smiling. I try to signal them to come join me.

An elderly gentleman steps up to the table.

"Hello!" Abby shakes hands with him. "Abby Meyers." Abby beams and tosses her hair off her shoulder. "I've been a fan of the *Roadshow* forever. I'm always amazed at the amount of history you guys know."

He gives her a tolerant smile. "So you think you have a pair of ruby slippers?"

I narrow my eyes at this man who seems doubtful and a tiny bit on the cynical side.

"I'm sure they're authentic!" Abby smiles for the camera. "They were given to my grandmother by Judy Garland herself." She turns to me then. "This is my sister, Dottie."

He holds out his hand, which I shake.

Otto races under the table.

"What was that?" he asks, taking a step back. "Was that a—"

"My dog. It's okay. Here, boy. Come here, Otto."

"Dogs aren't allowed in here." A man wearing jeans and a flannel shirt steps forward.

"He'll be quiet," Abby says, defending him.

I give her a smile of gratitude.

"As I was saying," she turns her attention to the little man who will judge our shoes, "our mother had these hidden for years and years. You see, she had polio when she was a little girl, and it damaged one of her legs. She walked with a limp."

"Abby," I put a hand on her arm, "tell him about our grandmother. She's the one who got them."

"Oh, you're right." She takes a calming breath, placing a hand over her heart. "I'm a bit flustered. Anyway, our grandmother worked in the wardrobe department at MGM. She and Judy Garland became friends during the shooting of *The Wizard of* Oz. When the movie wrapped, Judy gave them to her."

"Uh-huh." The man looks dubious at best. "Interesting story. You know there's not just one pair of shoes."

"Of course." Abby laughs, but her eyes shift toward me nervously.

"There's never just one dress or suit or pair of shoes for a Hollywood star, especially in a musical. Multiple costumes are made. In fact, all the studios kept their old costumes, reused them. But in the case of *The Wizard of Oz*, the costumes were so unique, so recognizable, they weren't reused, just pushed farther and farther into storage."

Her face relaxes into a smile. "Of course."

Sophia waves at me from the crowd. She's holding a bag of popcorn.

"For *The Wizard of Oz*," the host clears his throat, "one pair of shoes was used exclusively for the shot where Judy clicks her heels together. But other shoes were used and worn to a frazzle when Judy danced."

"Well, yes, but these," Abby pats the box, "have *J. G.* written on the soles."

The host's mouth quirks into a tight, disbelieving smile. "Yes, well, anyone could have placed that there."

"But—"

"Abby, wait."

The man raises a finger. "Don't forget that there were also shoes made that were not used in the film. Different styles. Debbie Reynolds owns a pair known as the Arabian ruby slippers, as they're in the style of an Arabian genie's. Of course, there was also a larger pair used by the witch—the one the house lands on. Let's take a look, shall we?"

I place the box on the table and pull off the lid. Then I notice the FBI agent and the exotic woman standing in the crowd, watching and waiting. A moment later the host cups one shoe in his hand, turns it over carefully, examining not only the sequins but also the heel and sole. "See this?" He points with his index finger at the stitching. "The original ruby slippers were handcrafted by the Innes Shoe Company. They used the actual foot of Judy Garland to fashion the shoes. A lot of stories have been told about these shoes. One is that Dorothy's dog, Toto, ate one of the slippers in her dressing room."

I glance under the table at Otto who's sitting quietly, his tongue hanging out one side of his mouth as he pants. I'll have to remember not to leave him alone with the shoes.

"One pair of shoes," the host says, "was given away in a contest to promote the movie back in 1940."

"Didn't the owner sell those shoes?" Abby asks.

"Indeed. But we'll get to that in a minute. Around 1960 some fake slippers were made and sold as the real deal. So that complicated matters in determining the authenticity of the actual ruby slippers used for the movie. Look inside," he turns the shoe over, his hand trembling slightly, "at this label. Every authentic pair of ruby slippers has either a white label with red-and-black lettering . . ."

I stare at the silver label in our pair of shoes. My emotions twist. Would it be better if our shoes were a fake? They'd still be important to me.

"Or," he continues, "an embossed stamp in either silver or gold."

"We have that!" Abby exclaims.

"Yes. But so did the fake pairs that were made because someone photographed one of the original pairs. Now the shoe manufacturer started with a basic pump that was then covered with red satin and lined with a creamy kid leather. Fish-scale sequins were used. They were unique to that time period. And you can tell by the thickness of the sequins. See! No dimple in the middle."

"Do ours have a dimple?" Abby leans closer.

"No dimple here." He smiles, this time pure pleasure lighting his eyes.

My mouth goes dry as we inch closer to a verdict. I feel my problems doubling. What will we do with these shoes? Split them? Abby taking one, me taking the other? It could be a showdown of western cinematic proportions.

"Each shoe," the host says, "was covered with anywhere from two to three thousand sequins. The shoes were dyed a deep crimson red. Since they used Technicolor film for this groundbreaking movie, the studio wanted to be sure the shoes didn't fade to orange on film."

He tenderly rubs his hand over the shoes. "Just imagine, Judy Garland might have worn these very shoes." He looks straight at a camera that seems to be moving closer to us.

I brace my hands on the table and force my gaze off the dark lens and onto the host's face which is tilted downward toward the shoes. "What's the answer?"

Leo, Sophia, and Tim edge toward us. I wave them over. Then we're all together, peering down at the shoes that brought us together. I can smell Sophia's buttery popcorn. She takes a couple of kernels and tosses them under the table for Otto.

The host carefully sets the shoe on the table like a gavel. "So you came to us today to determine if this pair of slippers is one of the original pairs worn by the late and great Judy Garland for *The Wizard of Oz?*"

"Absolutely. So what's the verdict?"

"What do you think so far?" he asks, like he's baiting a hook.

I get a sick feeling in the pit of my stomach. Could he be holding back a piece of the puzzle? Will he say our grandmother was a liar?

"From all you've said, I'd say these are definitely *the* ruby slippers." Abby positions herself for the camera, leaning toward the host, back arched, smile in place.

My heart hammers so hard in my chest I imagine my shirt buttons must be moving.

"Actually, one little thing tells me for sure whether these are the actual shoes used in the movie." He turns the shoes over again. "The television audience may not be able to see this, but there's a number here. A lot number." He picks up the other shoe. "These match."

"What does that mean?" Leo's breath bathes my hair. His hand settles on my waist as he peers down at the shoes.

"Many folks believe there were six or seven pairs of the ruby slippers made for the movie. Many of the pairs don't match, and experts think they were just tossed in a bin together. Your pair seems to be unique in that they do match. And they're the same size. Just five and a half."

"Judy Garland had small feet." Sophia stands beside me, her hand reassuringly at my back.

"So are you saying these *are the* ruby slippers?" I feel Otto next to my ankle. He leans into me, scratches his ear with his back foot.

"From your family story, which precedes the auction at the studios in the seventies, I'd say your grandmother must have been given, to the best of my judgment," the host grins for the camera, "the originals."

Abby whoops. I blink, not quite able to take it all in.

"So how much are they worth?" Abby takes the shoe from the host.

"There was an auction several years ago where a pair of ruby slippers was sold." The host talks right to the camera.

I stare at the shoes, imagining them on my mother's tiny feet. She was small but strong. Stronger than I had ever imagined.

"Christie's handled the auction," the host continues.

"They sold for over six hundred thousand," Abby adds, her eyes glittering with what I can only imagine is greed. She must have done her research.

"Yes," the host says.

Leo's hand on my shoulder presses gently, reassuringly into my flesh. His fingers graze my collarbone. "You okay?"

I swallow the emotions jamming my throat and nod.

"But I wouldn't put the price there. Because that was back in 2000." The host reaches for the other shoe which still rests in the box. "Inflation considered, along with the fact that these are a perfect match, I place their value at upwards of one million dollars. Maybe more."

Abby's eyes widen. She grabs my arm, shakes me. "Dottie! Can you believe it?"

WHEN THE CAMERA is off, we shake hands with the host, who gives us his card in case we want to be hooked up with an auction house. I pack the shoes back into the box and tuck them under my arm. Our little group exchanges hugs, first my uncle, then Sophia and finally Leo, holds my shoulders. "Pretty amazing, isn't it?"

"Overwhelming."

He wraps his arms around me, and for a moment I feel safe. It's been a long time since I've felt this way. And yet, there's something more—something that feels dangerous. Dangerous to my heart.

Pulling back enough to smile down at me, his gaze drops to my mouth and I feel my stomach tighten. He moves to kiss me.

But there's a tug at my arm. I jerk sideways. "The shoes!"

The FBI agent—or whoever he is—takes off through the crowd.

Leo springs into motion. He pushes and bounds his way through the parting crowd. Otto races ahead of me. His little body whips in and out of legs and feet, then through the doors and out of the convention center. Sophia and Tim follow behind me, with Abby screeching and hollering, "Stop him! Stop that man!"

"Where'd he go?" I burst through the doorway. If Chesterfield gets away with the shoes, then I'll have nothing left. As quickly as that thought enters my mind, I reject it. That's not true. Already I have gained so much.

Sophia catches up to me, out of breath. "Do you see him?"

Then I catch a glimpse of Leo's blond hair.

"Where's Otto?" I ask.

"Otto?" Tim reaches us, his tongue practically hanging out of his mouth as he draws quick breaths.

"Did he get away?" Abby arrives, standing beside me barefoot. She must have kicked off her high heels.

"I don't know yet."

We push out into the steamy sunshine. Otto's barking draws my attention. A tussle on the second tier of steps galvanizes me. I head down the stairs but turn midway and help Sophia and Tim, making sure they don't fall. When I turn around, Leo has Chesterfield on the ground. There's a flash of a fist, then a smack and grunting noise. A crowd has formed around them. A lady screams for police. Otto barks encouragement to Leo. The shoebox falls to the ground, kicked aside by scrambling feet. I rush forward, pulling off the top. Yellowed tissue paper falls out, but I can see the shoes safely inside.

"Leo!" I cry out. "I've got them." But he's too busy pummeling Chesterfield to notice.

Security arrives and pulls the two men apart. Chesterfield is arrested for trying to steal the ruby slippers. Leo stands nearby, arms crossed, his look fierce as Chesterfield is cuffed and escorted to a waiting police car. I can hear the squawk of a radio. People walk past and clap Leo on the back, calling him a hero.

My hero.

His face sweaty, he looks over at me and grins.

I notice a smear of what looks like blood across his cheek. His jaw is puffy. "Are you hurt?"

"Nah. You okay? The shoes?"

I nod. "Thank you."

"Never did like that guy."

"FBI, my elbow!" Sophia pulls a crumpled bag of popcorn out of her bag and bends down to give Otto a reward for his efforts.

Laughing, I hug them all. "Well, I guess now we can go home."

"But you don't have a home, my dear," Tim says.

"Yes, I do." It may not be a place, but I have one nevertheless, with friends and family that I love. For the first time in my life, I feel as if I truly belong, as if dreams can come true. "Where's Abby?"

She rushes up to us. "Way to go, Leo! You got the shoes, Dottie?" She puts a hand on the box I'm holding squarely. "Can you believe how much these babies are worth?"

"I've been approached by a couple of investors," Abby explains. "And let me tell you, they are eager to buy these. What do you want to do, Dottie?" She gives me the same little-girl look she always used when begging me to play. "Come on, Dottie!" she'd say, tugging on my arm. "Please!" Her adult voice cuts into my memories. "We could make a lot of money, more money than the farm sold for. It could be the start of a new life for you."

But it wouldn't give me what I've wanted all along—a family. Now I have Abby and my father. Maybe it's not how I imagined—the Beaver Cleaver model—but still, it's my family. Yet I don't want my sister hanging around if all she ultimately wants is to sell the shoes and cash in. I want Abby to share the love I have for her. Nothing else.

"Christie's or Sotheby's. Or some other auction house can handle the sale for you."

"You're sure?"

I cup the box between my two hands. "Do with the shoes what you want, Abby." I push the box toward her. "They're yours." Then I embrace her, a quick, tight hug into which I try to squeeze all my emotions. "I already have what I came for."

Epilogue

I smile as I park the Jeep outside the assisted-living facility. Sophia let me borrow her Jeep for the last couple of months while I got my life back on track. The money from the sale of the shoes afforded me a little house three blocks from the beach. I go there daily to hear the ocean, to talk to God, to listen to what he is trying to teach me. I don't hear whisperings in the wind or murmurings in the surf. But while I'm silent, words come to me—phrases I've heard in church, things I read in the Bible. It's the beginning of another long journey.

Tonight I'll return the keys to Sophia. I secured a job at a plant nursery in Santa Barbara. Digging in the dirt gives me pleasure. Occasionally in the evening I tutor students who live in my neighborhood, kids who need help with algebra and geometry, calculus and trigonometry. I like helping them, seeing them progress, grow like little seedlings.

I step out of the Jeep, rearrange the dress I bought for this special occasion. I'm not used to wearing hose or heels. "Don't laugh," I tell Otto as I place him on the ground and straighten his miniature bow tie that I found at a specialty pet shop. He runs across the grass and finds a spot to lift his leg. "Very gentlemanly."

I walk along the sidewalk, taking in the blooming hydrangeas, and he joins me. We enter the main building where the recreation center is. The televisions are turned off this evening. Music, provided by a three-piece band, fills the air with a jazzy beat.

From the far end of the room, I see my father. At first he doesn't see me. He's dressed in a tuxedo, the collar seeming to pinch him, making his face red. He moves slowly, picking up a folding chair, opening it, and placing it at the end of a row. Then he sees me, offers a slight wave.

I walk toward him, Otto at my heels.

"How are you?" The skin around his eyes droops with fatigue.

"Fine. You need help?" Not waiting for a reply, I grab another folded chair. The rubbery end of the leg catches in the folds of my dress.

"Oh, you'll rip it." He takes the chair from me, his hand brushing mine. "No need for you to work tonight." He opens the chair, the metal making a hollow sound, and sets it next to the other. "Is Abby coming?"

"She's on her way. Just running late."

"I have something for you."

Otto sits in proper begging form at my father's feet now. "Oh, you too, my friend." He reaches into his pants pocket and pulls out a dog treat shaped like a bone. "I read somewhere nuts might not be so good for you. So this will have to do."

Tears prickle my eyes at the thought of my father thinking in advance about Otto and his health. We're a long way from having a close relationship, but I figure we have years to work on it.

"You want it?" My father dangles the treat out in front of him.

Otto yaps.

"That's what I thought." He drops it, and Otto jumps to catch it. The treat is gone faster than one of my father's magic coins.

It's been months since I saw him in Seattle, but he's called me on the phone a few times. The first conversation was awkward, but I let go of my little-girl expectations. He'll never win Father of the Year, but if I accept him where he is, then maybe our relationship can grow. If I nourish it, feed it, give it plenty of sunshine.

He slides his hand inside his jacket and pulls out an eggshell-blue envelope. "Your mother wrote this years ago when she gave me the shoes. I . . ," he hesitates. Moisture gathers at the corners of his eyes and he sniffs. "Well, I thought you should have it."

I take the envelope, run my fingers over the outside, over the slight depression where in dark-blue ink she wrote, *Ruby's Slippers*. I recognize her schoolmarm penmanship but detect the slight tremor that worsened during her illness. "Oh, Momma."

"Aren't you going to open it?"

"Not now. Later. When I can savor it."

"I understand." He reaches out, hesitates, then places his warm hand on mine, cupping it protectively. "I miss her too."

"Are you sure you don't want to keep this?"

He gives a slight shake of his head. "You should have it. She explains where the shoes came from. Of course, you know all that now. But it's in her words."

I hold the envelope close, place it against my heart. Later tonight I'll share it with Abby. We can read it together and remember. "Thank you."

From across the room, Tim shuffles toward us, wringing his hands. "Is it about time?"

"You need a watch, my friend." My father places an arm around my uncle's narrow shoulders.

"My heart is tripping over itself with excitement. Think we could start early, my dear?"

"Brides are never ready early," I say. Not that I know that to be true. I'm just assuming. But I realize that his bride helped heal his heart.

"I feel like I'm twenty years old again." Tim taps his chest. "The old ticker still has it."

"We should all be so lucky." A wistful smile plays across my father's features.

"Dottie!" Gloria's voice rings out in the hall. She walks toward us. She's not in scrubs tonight but a shimmery yellow dress. "Look at you!" She beams. "You're gorgeous." She clasps my hands then hugs me close. "It's so good to see you. You seem to be doing well."

"I am. I've certainly learned a lot."

"Sometimes life is all the schooling we need." She smiles. "I'm sure you want to see Sophia, right? She's through that doorway." She places her hands on Tim's shoulders. "And you, mister, your guests will be arriving soon."

"I thought only the bride shouldn't be seen," Tim says.

"We don't want some other pretty lady to set her sights on you." Gloria gives us all a wink.

"I'll take care of him," my father says. Together the two men head off in the opposite direction of the bride's room.

I find Sophia dressed in a sparkly cream-colored, floor-length dress. Her eyes brighten as we enter the room.

"You wore it!" she exclaims. She touches the wide red ribbon at my waist. The dress isn't something I would choose. Not that I'd choose a dress in the first place. It's a slinky black material with tiny sparkles that catch the light.

"The bride always gets what she wants on her wedding day."

She grins. "And how is my groom?"

"He's looking for a way to escape," Maybelle pipes in. She's dressed in a multicolored sequin top and looks like a five-year-old's finger-painted work of art. I give her a hug. She's cynical as ever, but Sophia and I are working on her.

"Tim is just fine," Gloria assures us. "He's pacing outside."

"My father is watching after him." Sophia draws a slow breath and releases it. "I don't feel scattered at all. Maybe my old brain is making a comeback."

"Brains are overrated. It's the heart that counts."

Sophia smiles. "I'm so glad we're going to be related now. Do you think we can start the wedding early?"

I laugh and hug her close, breathe in her comforting scent of buttery popcorn and powdery tangerine. "That's what Tim said. But maybe we should wait for the guests to arrive."

The doors slap open. "Am I too late?"

"Right on time." I smile across the room at Abby. She looks like she's about to walk down the red carpet. Her apricot gown shimmers. Her hair is long and blonde now for some new show.

"Come on in." Sophia greets her with open arms.

"Where are the men going?" She hooks a thumb over her shoulder in the direction Tim and our father went. "Why, our little party is just beginning."

"It's a good thing you've got new lines to learn," I say as we embrace. She clings to me like the shimmery material that envelops her curves. "It's good to see you, sis." Then she pulls me aside and asks, "Dottie, why did you give me Momma's slippers?"

"Because I love you. I didn't want anything to ever come between us again."

"Do you have any regrets?"

I shake my head. "Not at all."

"It's taken me a while to absorb your gift, to process it. It was quite a sacrifice."

"It didn't feel that way to me. When I introduce you to my father, you'll understand."

She gives me a quizzical look. "Is that old head injury causing you problems? I've already met our father. Remember?"

My gaze meets Sophia's twinkling eyes momentarily. "Not our earthly father. This one speaks to us of his love, and he's powerful enough to act on it."

A couple of hands close over my shoulders, startling me. My heart gives a jolt in response. I turn to see Leo smiling at me. He gives me a quick hug, then his gaze skims over me, touching me intimately. "You look beautiful." His voice is a low rumble. "Like a dream."

He's wearing a black tuxedo that makes his shoulders look impossibly wide. His hair has grown since I last saw him, but it's still respectable. He's clean shaven, his skin tan. It's been a month since I've seen him. But we've spoken on the phone daily. He wanted to come see me several times, but

I put him off, needing time to sort through my feelings first.

"So do you," I stammer, then feel heat rise across my skin. My chest feels like it's on fire.

"I brought something for you."

"You did?" The fact that he thought of me, brought something for me, flusters me. What could it be? A corsage? A man has never given me flowers. Perhaps this will be the first time.

"That dress of yours needed something special."

Abby, Sophia, Maybelle, and Gloria have retreated to the far corner of the room. They stand in front of an oval mirror. Gloria places a little veil on top of Sophia's hair.

Leo picks up a box from a table nearby. It's a large blue box with a brown ribbon, too large for a corsage. Maybe it's a bouquet. Or an oversized mum like high school boys give their dates. He tugs off the top and pulls out one ruby slipper.

A gasp escapes me. "Where did you get these?"

"I bought them."

"You did?"

"I was just waiting for the right time to give them to you. When I thought you'd be ready to dance." Our eyes meet and a shimmer of heat passes between us.

"You know, someone thought these had special powers." My voice cracks.

"People will believe anything." He takes a step closer. "Come on, Cinderella, try them on."

His nearness is overwhelming. My lungs feel compressed. "What if they don't fit?"

"You think I'll go searching for another foot? Not when you've helped me find my courage."

Smiling, I sit in a nearby chair and slip off the shoes that I bought special for this occasion. Leo kneels in front of me, takes my foot in his hand, and rests it against his thigh. His hand cups my heel tenderly. Warmth spreads through me like a wildfire. He takes the shoe and slips it on my foot. It's snug, pinching my toes.

"Will you dance with me tonight?" He looks at me, his golden eyes shining with the same emotion that swells inside my chest. I sense what he's really asking.

I start to laugh, but the seriousness of his gaze holds me fast. "Would you mind if I wore my own shoes?"

The side of his mouth curls seductively. "You can go barefoot if you want."

That suits me better than any ruby slippers. This is the next turn in my yellow-brick road. And I'm ready to see what's beyond the bend.

"Then yes, I'd love to dance with you."

He takes me in his arms. I have to stand on tiptoe. But as he smiles down at me, I realize there really is no place like home. It's not a place with a picket fence of memories.

It's where love abounds.

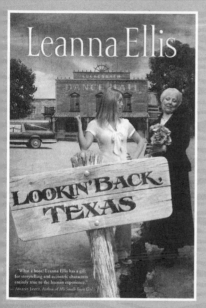
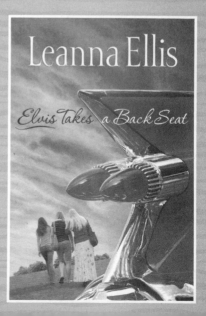

How to Become a Freelance editor

Start Your New Career in Less Than a Year

Dustin Schwanger

Contents

Introduction

❧

As I ran down the escalator, frantically trying to catch the almost-departing train, I could hear the whistle blow and I could see the train operator—and he could see me, too. Yet, the doors locked and the train left, another hour added to my hour-and-a-half commute. I sat alone, dejected—a little dramatic, but true. I missed my wife and baby boy. I had been away from home ten hours already at an "editing" job in which I compared foreign languages to English to make sure the bolding and the colors were correct. It was mind-numbing work.

At that point I had had the position for about six months. There was certainly a honeymoon period for the first month or so, but from then on I most definitely wanted to be divorced from it. Previous to that job, I worked as an editing intern for a publisher of religious books and journals. My intellect and creativity were stimulated continually. I also worked with my wife as an editor for the university's humanities publication center, again more opportunities to expand my knowledge and help craft important academic text and, most importantly to me, the chance to spend most of each day with my wife. On top of those positions, I was the editor in chief of a set of family-related publications. My staff of about thirty and I created an academic journal, a magazine, and a blog. But then I graduated. I had to grow up and face real life.

Sitting at the train station that day, I rejected the thought of "growing up." It was hard to imagine that I would be happy at any job that didn't stimulate me intellectually and enable me to use the entrepreneurial skills that I had gained from running my own publications. It was time for me to start pursuing my own editing career.

The next several months were extremely difficult but also rewarding. I learned how to build a website and built one for my business, I found freelance work, and I did all the other things needed to be done as not only an editor but also the owner of a business—all while holding down my full-time job and taking care of my family. The boat had to be close enough to the dock so that when I did decide to make the jump from a salaried position with benefits to an I-might-get-paid-sometime position without benefits, neither my little family nor I would drown.

Finally after about six months of working twelve to fourteen hours a day and with the encouragement of my good wife, I decided to make the jump to become a full-time freelance editor.

It hasn't been too long since I've made that jump—maybe four or five months. The transition has been quite a bit different than I thought it would be. But, it has also been just as rewarding as I thought. My focus going into this experience of being a freelance editor was on myself and my family and our needs, but as I have helped authors craft (and design) their words and have seen what that has meant to them, my focus has shifted outward. If you would like to be a truly great editor, as I hope to be, your focus must be not just on what you know or what you want but how you treat and interact with your authors. The purpose of this book is to prepare you for both aspects of a freelance editing career.

1

The Pros and Cons of Freelancing

When I sat at that train stop, I could only think of all the benefits of quitting my job and becoming a freelance editor. I could spend more time with my family, I could make my own schedule, I could work on the type of manuscripts that *I* wanted to, I could own my own business. It would be great, everything I've ever wanted. While I still wouldn't trade being a freelance editor for anything, most pros come with some cons, as well.

Working from Home

Family Time

Forbes listed ten great reasons for someone to work from home.[1] Among those were work/life balance, no commute, and more productivity. Those are, to me, three of the best aspects of working from home, but they still come with some caveats.

The most beneficial aspect for me has been my work/life balance. I get to see my wife, Caitlin, and one-year-old son, James, whenever I want. At this point I probably spend a little less time with them as I would if I were working a normal full-time job. But, I see them more often throughout the day. I get to play with my son in the morning when he's the happiest. I can watch him while Caitlin gets ready for the day or does other things that she needs or wants to do. We all have lunch together and take nice afternoon walks every day.

---

1. http://goo.gl/FhhEVl

And even though my work/life balance has been better since I've quit, there have been some things I've needed to adjust to. Because work is always at home, it is hard to know when to stop. I sometimes feel guilty for working, because I'm not spending time with my family, and sometimes I feel guilty spending time with my family, because I'm not working. We're trying to create a more concrete schedule for me, but that is a work in progress.

But this is the perspective of a full-time breadwinner. The draw of freelance editing for many, and maybe even you, is the chance to be a stay-at-home mom and contribute to the family's income. Freelance editing is a wonderful option for many moms. Caitlin, who is an editor, as well, works during James's naps and in the evenings when he's asleep. Her working part-time when James is asleep helps her avoid many of the work/life issues that I face working full-time from home.

No Commute

In an article written in the *American Journal of Preventative Medicine* entitled "Commuting Distance, Cardiorespiratory Fitness, and Metabolic Risk," the authors found that the amount of time commuted in a car was directly related to obesity and the health issues that accompany it.[2] Not having a commute doesn't automatically save you from those plights, but it does give you more time to exercise and less stress.

Your body isn't the only thing being stressed when you commute to work. Think about the miles you put on your car, the extra money you spend on gas (or bus fares), and all the extra time the car is in the shop from the wear and tear of commuting.

But, no commute means no coworkers. I really liked the people I worked with at my full-time job. I became good friends with a lot of them. That is one aspect of having a full-time job that I definitely miss. If you are a social butterfly (and I'm not one), you might need an office environment to help you get the socializing you need, and you do have an option of renting personal office space if it's too big of an issue. I have found that through face-to-face networking, I have really overcome the lack of social interaction I face working by myself. You will learn more about face-to-face networking in chapter 6.

---

2. http://goo.gl/Pty6AR

More Productivity

My most productive time is in the early morning; however, when I had a full-time job, that time was spent commuting. Now, I can get up a 4:30 a.m. and get a lot of my work done before there are very many distractions.

Distractions do come, however. Sometimes—actually, most of the time—James doesn't understand that Dad has to go to work. I shut my office (really my bedroom) door, and he pitter-patters over and starts pounding on and crying at the door, as he's doing this very second. Shopping and chores and other housework all have to get done, and it's so easy to get wrapped up in those tasks during the day instead of focusing on my work.

I Can Edit Anything

Sadly for me, my thought that "I can edit anything I want," turned into my telling others, "I can edit anything you want." That being said, though, I do have a lot of control over what I edit through the people with whom I network.

I dislike most fiction, so I don't go to fiction meetings and conferences. It's surely not what I want to edit. I mostly attend business and entrepreneurial meetings. From those I get books about business, finance, and marketing— drier books more to my liking. To edit the text you want to, just need to go to where those people are. If it's science fiction, go to science fiction conferences. If it's history, go to historical conventions. You must go out and mingle with potential clients.

Having Your Own Business

Looking at freelance editing from the outside, you might think that you will edit for forty hours a week. You may compare the $30 to $40 an hour that you see freelance editors getting to the $20 an hour you get and think it's a great way to double your income and have more time to do what you want. Don't worry—that's what I thought, too.

In his book *The E-Myth Revisited*, Michael Gerber says that within every small business owner—and you now own a small business—there are three people: the technician, the entrepreneur, and the manager. The dominant trait for most freelance editors is the technician, the person who can take mindless drivel and turn it into a work of art that rivals Shakespeare. That's mostly what I thought I'd be doing. Oh, I knew that I would have to make some business cards and even make a website and a blog, but with those, surely work would come looking for me.

Luckily for me, I quickly realized that that strategy for getting new clients wasn't going to work. And I was okay with that because I liked the idea of being the entrepreneur. The entrepreneur in us comes up with hundreds of ideas and new ways of doing things, most of which don't work. But the ideas that do work drive the success and innovation of little businesses like yours. To be a successful freelance editor, you have to be able to come up with unique ways of marketing yourself and building your business. That also takes time, quite a bit of time, especially in the beginning. That's why charging $40 an hour won't double your income. But, there's another person who demands your time: the manager.

The manager is the person in you that makes sure the red pens go into one cup and the blue pens go into another. He is also the person that does the accounting and tax work for your business. He writes contracts and sets up bank accounts. He does the stuff that is most easily and disastrously neglected. I personally struggle the most at being the manager. I love the thrill of editing and the challenge of growing my business. But accounting, taxes, and contracts are much harder for me to be motivated to control.

In order for your freelance editing business to thrive, you have to learn how to be all three people. Without the technician, your editing will be subpar. Without the entrepreneur, you won't have anything to edit. And, without the manager, the IRS will shut you down.

This may sound daunting, but you can get over these hurtles, especially because you'll know about them before you even begin your business. The entire second part of this book is dedicated to running and building your business.

A Few Other Thoughts

I've read quite a few blog posts that detail the benefits and drawbacks of being a freelance editor, and many suggest that you have your Visa or Mastercard ready for the times in which work or payments are slow. If you don't have enough money in the bank or from a spouse's income to cover a slow month or a slow *six* months, then you aren't ready to become a full-time freelance editor.

Jon Acuff, in his book *Quitter*, describes what will happen if you can't cover the monetary gap between your day job and your dream job:

The wife who never worried about money will have fiscal panic attacks. The husband who didn't tally how you spent your time will become an ever-present punch clock. Even the most easygoing person on the planet starts sweating when you play around with things like the mortgage. All in the name of your dream. Your dream? How do dreams pay the bills? Should you just dial up your utility providers and see if dreams are an acceptable form of payment? Is there a secret free food section you have access to when you're married to a dreamer? As it turns out, no.[3]

Visa and Mastercard aren't the "secret free food section." Before you quit your full-time job in search of your freelancing dream, have, at the very least, six months and bring in enough income per month to cover at least half of your monthly expenses. With these safety nets in place, you'll be able to work on increasing your clientele to meet the other half of your monthly expenses and have a cushion to fall back on when your income doesn't quite pay all the bills.

If you don't do this and *do* plan on living off of debt to get started, you'll probably fail. When you are pushed against the wall financially, you will not complete the long-term tasks that must be done to build your business a month from now or a year from now. Your only concern will be how you can get work *now*. And, when you are only thinking about the present, it is extremely difficult to get any editing work at all.

There are other benefits and drawbacks to being a freelance editor, and you can read more about those on the internet, but the things I've listed here seem to be some the most influential. None of the issues with being a freelance editor that I've faced would ever convince me to return to the traditional workplace. I love working from home. I love the freedom I have to work on and grow my business myself. I love freelance editing.

---

3. John Acuff, *Quitter.*

2

Training

❦

Become an Expert

It might seem really easy to become a freelance editor. You might like to read and you definitely know what bad writing is. But, bibliomania and a strong opinion don't make a good editor. You must become an expert.

Why Being an Expert Matters

Type "freelance editor" into Google, and click through page after page of freelance editors who have years of experience and a hefty list of past projects. You are in competition with not only these editors but also the tens of thousands of freelance editors who do not grace the halls of Google. If you're not an expert, you won't stand out from the crowd. If you're not an expert, you won't create thoughtful and helpful content on your blog that will enable you to build a platform and a business. You must become an expert.

What Does "Being an Expert" Mean?

Thankfully for you, I'm not suggesting that you have to stand out from the freelance editor who once was the managing editor of a major publisher. What you have to do is to be an expert editor *at your price point*. When you start looking for volunteer editing opportunities to sharpen your skills, you better be the best volunteer editor the author or company has ever seen. When you charge $5 or $10 or $40 an hour, you must exceed each client's expectations for the price he or she pays.

In his book *Platform*, Michael Hyatt says that exceeding a client's expectations creates a "wow" experience. When you create a wow experience for a client, he or she will begin to see you as someone to be trusted, an expert. As clients begin to see you as an expert, they will write glowing testimonials and refer people from their own network to you. Then, as you begin to have too many editing projects for your time, you will raise your rates and continue that process until you achieve a nice equilibrium—and most importantly you will continue to deliver wow experiences.

How to Create Wow

Your editing expertise is only one part of the process of creating a wow experience for your clients. How you interact with them, how quickly you respond to their emails, how you address their concerns all play into how authors view their experience with you. Why do many authors hate editors? A lot of the time authors will say that editors don't know how to edit. That opinion, however, is a symptom of editors' not understanding how to interact with authors. Interacting with authors in a way that creates good wow experiences is such an important issue that I will spend much of chapter 6 discussing it. Understanding how to create wow is the only way for you to become an expert and succeed at the business of editing. For now, though, we are back to the basics of editing.

Required Reading and Resources

Don't feel bad if you find yourself reading quickly through this section. What's most important for you isn't what I have to say about these books but that you actually buy and read them.

The Chicago Manual of Style, *16th edition*

If you could pick only one book to teach you how to be a copyeditor and to teach you the rules of the trade, this would be the book. The grammar, usage, and punctuation rules of the other style manuals are based off of Chicago style with modifications to fit their particular circumstances.

Chicago is quite the tome, weighing in at 1,026 pages, including the index. You *must* read it! I told you there was going to be some work involved in becoming a freelance editor, didn't I? But, thankfully for you, I don't think you need to study every single point. You can skim chapters 1 through 4. They discuss the editing process, printing, copyright issues—

things that you should be aware of but not necessarily have memorized. You should more slowly skim chapter 5 on grammar. I don't find myself going to chapter 5 very much as I'm editing, except to look at its usage guide (5.220) and its list of words with prepositions construed with them (5.191), both great resources.

Chapters 6 through 13 should be read carefully and memorized as much as possible. These chapters discuss topics from punctuation to capitalization to the treatment of numbers. It will be difficult to memorize every rule in these 344 pages, so at the very least you must know what rules are discussed. For example, you will remember reading that Chicago prefers either quotation marks or italics for words used as words. Because you remember reading that, you can look up the rule again and see that italics are preferred. If you don't know what's discussed in Chicago, you'll never know when to look something up.

Finally, chapters 14 and 15, which discuss citation styles, and chapter 16, which discusses indexing, can be skimmed.

Chicago comes in two formats, print and digital. I have used both, and both have their advantages. The search bar on the online version is very useful, but I still prefer to have the print version because I like being able to flip through it to find what I need, and I usually can remember where particular rules are on a page, which makes finding them fairly efficient. For new editors, I would suggest starting with the print version.

Publication Manual of the American Psychological Association, *6th edition (APA Style)*

Thankfully, you will not have to be as thorough in your understanding of the APA stylebook. This is the style that is used for many of the social and hard sciences. A few of the main differences from Chicago style are the treatment of tables and numbers and the style of citations. Many of the other rules are the same. Because you won't know what to look up unless you know what's in the style, you should skim the entire manual. At 272 pages, it is much less unwieldy.

MLA Handbook for Writers of Research Papers, *7th edition*

Like APA, MLA is much like Chicago. MLA style is most commonly used within the liberal arts and humanities, and you probably used this style in your English papers in high school. When you edit an article or book in MLA style, the main difference you'll be concerned about is the citation style. But, like APA, you should skim the entire manual, just so you know what's in there.

The Associated Press Stylebook 2013

This may not be required reading for everyone, but if you plan on going into news or magazine editing, you will want to be intimately familiar with AP style. AP produces a new stylebook each year, so you will need to stay on your toes!

Merriam-Webster's Collegiate Dictionary, *11th edition.*

The dictionary on your computer will not fulfill your needs as an editor. *Merriam-Webster's Collegiate Dictionary* should really be the only dictionary you use. You will use a dictionary much more than you anticipate. You will need to check spelling; proper word breaks; open, closed, or hyphenated compounds; capitalization; and the list goes on. The great thing about *Merriam-Webster*'s is that you don't have to own a print copy. Merriam-websters.com has all the up-to-date information you need.

Index to English, *8th edition, or* Merriam-Webster's Dictionary of English Usage

I love *Index to English.* It is a great, short, and sometimes funny guide to English usage. You should certainly read every word of it. *Merriam-Webster's Dictionary of English Usage*, on the other hand, is a dictionary. If you used to read the dictionary for fun in high school, as my wife did, this might be a captivating read. It covers the history of each controversial usage question and provides several examples of how a word has been used in the past and the current consensus on how a word should be used now. *Merriam-Webster's* doesn't get points for concision, but it's a good reference. Most of what I need on a daily basis can be found in *Index to English.*

The Copyeditor's Handbook: A Guide for Book Publishing and Corporate Communications, *3rd edition*

Whereas the *Chicago Manual of Style* is written in a drier, more factual style, Amy Einsohn's *Copyedior's Handbook* is written in a nice conversational tone. You should definitely read the entire book. In addition to discussing and giving great commentary on many principles and rules that Chicago covers, Einsohn includes editing exercises with answer keys. These exercises will be essential to your growth as an editor. As in many disciplines, learning how to be an editor comes more by doing than by reading.

The Copyeditor's Guide to Substance & Style, *3rd edition*

As in the *Copyeditors Handbook*, this book provides many wonderful exercises with keys. These are the exercises that I completed as I learned how to become an editor.

Other Resources

Editors on Editing

I hesitated to include this in my list of resources. I thought that the reading was pretty boring. But, that could be because it was for a college class during a time in which I wasn't planning on being an editor. *Editors on Editing* is a compilation of articles by seasoned editors on topics ranging from why editors are necessary to editing books for different markets to the current state of publishing. Check out the preview on Amazon, and if any of the articles interest you, pick up at least the Kindle version.

The Non-Designer's Design & Type Books

While this combined-volume book doesn't have to do specifically with editing, editors really should understand what makes a good design and what makes an appropriate typeface. There's a good chance, at least in the beginning, that you'll be editing text from advertisements, websites, blogs—and not books. If you can not only fix the grammatical and spelling mistakes in an author's text but also comment thoughtfully on the state of the design, your real and perceived value will increase and you will create repeat clients and referrals. Just read quickly through the book—it's an easy read, anyway—and try to familiarize yourself with the design and type principles.

The All New Print Production Handbook

If you want to go further into the publishing world than just editing, you ought to know the basics of printing. This is a great book to skim to understand the state and process of modern printing.

For more books on the business side of editing, see the resource·page for this book.[4]

Editing Courses

Before you start taking any classes, besides the lynda.com classes (more below) you should have read over chapters 6 through 13 in the *Chicago Manual of Style*. I did that before I ever took an editing class, and it made a big difference. While many of the students in my classes were staring at the professor in a dazed stupor as he discussed all the rules for a single comma, I was at least familiar with what he was talking about. That familiarity accelerated my learning enormously.

University and College Certifications

My training in editing was in a formal school setting. My school, Brigham Young University, offers a minor in editing comprising seven classes covering grammar, usage, editing, design, and publishing. It is the best minor the university offers, in my opinion. The faculty and the classes are wonderful, and it's hard to find another set of so few classes that completely prepare you for a career. If you happen to attend BYU, then definitely enroll in the editing minor.

I doubt, however, that many in my readership are prospective BYU students. If you are in college or are planning on attending, see if your school offers courses in editing or publishing. If the cost isn't too high and if you have enough time, the classes should be worthwhile.

But, university courses aren't at all necessary for you to be a successful freelance editor. If you're not in school right now, going back to get a certificate in editing or publishing will cost you thousands of dollars and won't help you much in the long run compared to learning through other noncertificate courses.

Editorial Freelancers Association Classes

The Editorial Freelancers Association (EFA) is the primary trade organization for editors. It has a job board, group insurance rates, and many other resources, including editing and publishing classes. This is where I would look to take classes if I needed them. The prices seem to be reason-

---

4. www.querypublishing.us/resource-page.html

able, and most importantly, the editors are seasoned and respected, unlike what you might find through other sources.

Here is a list of the EFA's current classes:

- Copyediting II—Section A
- Copyediting II and III—Section A Combo
- Copyediting II—Section B
- Copyediting II and III—Section B Combo
- Copyediting III—Section A
- Intro to Editing for the Children's Book Market
- Self-Publishing for Editors
- Self-Publishing for Editors and EBook Formatting for Beginners Combo
- Copyediting III—Section B
- Secrets of LinkedIn: Inside Tips That Work (Webinar)
- Save Yourself Aggravation, Overwork, and Underpayment: Define That Project Before You Start!
- EBook Formatting for Beginners
- Developmental Editing for College Textbook Publishers
- Developmental Editing of Fiction
- The ABCs of PDFs: Working with Adobe Acrobat Pro X/XI
- Word 2010 for PC: An Intro to Macros
- Combo: Word 2010 for PC Macros and the ABCs of PDFs
- The Basics of InDesign for Writers and Editors (Webinar)
- Fiction Editing and the Author-Editor Relationship: Two Sides of the Same Coin
- E-Editing I: PDF Markup
- E-Editing I and II Combo
- E-Editing II: Editing in Word
- Successful Self-Publishing From Both Sides

There are lots of good- and useful-looking classes in that list, classes I'd take if I had the time. The important classes for a new freelancer would be the Copyediting I, II, and III classes. Before taking any of the other classes, especially ones that aren't specifically about editing, I would check on lynda.com (I'll talk about this next) to see if a similar course is offered there.

The prices for the EFA's classes range from $39 to $238, although most of their copyediting classes are about $149 for members and $174 for nonmembers. The $25 nonmember fee seems standard throughout. The membership dues are $145 per year, so if you don't plan on taking any more than five classes, joining wouldn't save you any money.

As a note, there are other benefits of joining the EFA—the job board, group health insurance, conferences—but I haven't seen enough benefit to renew next year. I thought that the most beneficial aspect would be the job board, but there are so many other editors clamoring after the same jobs that it makes it hard to get anything from it. I'd just use the EFA for the classes.

Expand Your Skills

In the beginning, at least, there is a very good chance that you'll not be a freelance editor for Penguin or HarperCollins or any other publisher for that matter. Although publishers depend heavily on freelance editing, many are downsizing their pools of freelancers. This makes new positions very competitive.

The clients that you'll most likely have as you begin are individual authors who are planning to submit their manuscripts to traditional publishers or who are planning to self-publish. Your clients may also include companies that would rather freelance their editing out than hire a full- or part-time editor, given the expense of hiring new employees.

But, while there is a lot of work from these nonpublisher sources, the catch is that these companies are looking for people who can not only edit their books but design and index them, not only edit their advertisements but design them, and not only edit the web content but manipulate the HTML and CSS. There is work for freelancers who are just editors, but your market will grow exponentially as you incorporate other skills into your knowledge base.

Lynda.com

Don't feel discouraged that you don't know how to design an ad or book in InDesign or how to create a website in Dreamweaver or Muse. You can quickly learn these skills with practice and some online help.

Lynda.com is where I learned just about all the skills, aside from editing and indexing, that I needed to build and run Query Publishing. The services I provide include editing, indexing, print and digital book and magazine design, web design, interactive ebook design, and some others. Can you see how learning all these skills really opens up my market? My company can be a one-stop shop that provides everything authors need to publish their books or for a company that doesn't want to hire a communications and design department. That has very big appeal.

At $25 a month, the cost is much more manageable than the EFA classes. There is also a $37.50 a month price point that includes exercise files, so you can follow along with the instructor. I had this plan for a while, but I didn't find it very useful. Whenever I would watch a course, I had my own project that I'd be working on, and I could use what I learned directly on my project and not on the exercise file. The only benefit I saw in the exercise files was when there would be a script or some other download included in the files. But, usually those scripts are also freely available online from other sources.

I suggest lynda.com to everyone who has the faintest motivation to work for themselves in editing or any field related to words. No matter how difficult the freelance market may be, there are always opportunities for those who go out of their way to learn multiple skills to better help their clients.

* * * * * * *

You have a lot to learn as you begin your training to become a freelance editor. You are going to learn more rules about punctuation and numbers and capitalization than you ever thought existed. You're going to get confused. You're probably going to get discouraged. I know I did. I never had so many problems with punctuation as I did when I was first learning how to be an editor. I had so many rules in my head that I didn't know how to write anymore. Just work through it. It will take you some time to learn and feel comfortable editing. As I'll discuss in the next chapter, the best way to learn to edit, or do anything else, is to actually do it.

3

Getting Initial Experience

✺

Workbooks

Before you begin editing for clients, or even volunteer as an editor for friends and family, you should spend a lot of time completing editing exercises that have answer keys. If you start editing for others too soon, you will find lots of good changes to make, but there will also be many errors you miss simply because you didn't know the rules existed. Having an answer key will compel you to spend more time in Chicago figuring out the rules behind all the edits that you missed.

Here are a few books that contain exercises with keys:

- *The Copyeditor's Guide to Substance & Style* by EEI Press—This is, by far, the best of the three as far as practice exercises go.
- *The Copyeditor's Handbook: A Guide for Book Publishing and Corporate Communications* by Amy Einsohn
- *The Prentice Hall Editing Workbook* by Julie Lumpkins

Spend several weeks in these books. Do every exercise. Doing these exercises will not only help you learn how to edit and how to make all the editing marks but it will also build your confidence. You will begin to feel like a real editor. You will feel that you will be a blessing to your friend's manuscript and not a liability. This confidence will launch you into the next step.

Family and Friends

The next step of your editing career is to edit for friends and family for free. Tell everyone that you are a freelance editor and that you want to edit their writing to help them and to sharpen your skills. You know people who are looking for jobs; edit their résumés and cover letters. You may know someone who has written a book; edit it. You know people who have businesses; offer to edit and design advertisements for them. There is an endless supply of real-world editing and design experience just waiting for you.

Whenever you do work for someone who doesn't have your last name, get reviews. When you do good free work for family and friends, they will be more than happy to write you glowing testimonials. If, by this point, you don't have an editing website, which I wouldn't expect you to have, keep these testimonials in a Word document. When you are ready to build your website or design a flyer, you will have several wonderful testimonials that will establish your credibility in the eyes of your prospective clients.

It's important for you to have endorsements in places other than your website. You should have a professional LinkedIn account and other business accounts with services such as Google Places, Manta, and others that I'll discuss later. When you receive testimonials, send your clients a few links to your Google Places or Manta page and ask them to write their review there, as well. This will help you gain the trust of prospective clients and get more exposure online.

Organizations

When you are starting to feel more confident in your editing abilities, it's time to start volunteering for businesses. This will give you more varied and more professional experience. Additionally, having real companies listed on your résumé as editing clients will increase your credibility. Do not feel obligated to say that you are a volunteer editor on your résumé. If someone asks you, you can tell them; otherwise, there is no reason to bring it up.

To start editing for businesses, pick five or so companies that you'd be interested in editing for, and find the person that you think would be responsible for hiring editors. It could be the manager of the content department or the head HR person or even the owner of the company, depending on how big it is. You'll have to do some snooping around on the companies' websites and LinkedIn to figure it out. Also, you'll want to target smaller, local companies. It would be hard to get the attention of Apple or Boeing, for example, even if *you* offered to pay *them*.

Once you find the people responsible for hiring and their business addresses, send them a short introduction letter stating who you are and that you'd like to volunteer to edit for their company. Tell them that within the next few days they'll receive your résumé and cover letter. Print this on nice paper and sign the bottom.

Next, mail your résumé and a relatively short cover letter detailing how exactly you can help their company. It would be good to do some research about the company, so you can provide specific examples. Tell them that you want to volunteer for them for a specific amount of time—three months, six months, or however long you want. In the cover letter, tell them to expect a call from you on a specific day that gives you enough time to get the letter there. Tell them that this call is just to set up an appointment to talk later. Make sure you write this date in your planner; you don't want to miss it.

When the fateful day arrives when you actually have to call these people, don't be too nervous. If you've followed these steps, they should be very excited to speak with you. You will most likely have to ask the secretary to connect you to the person that you want to talk to. She'll ask if that person is expecting your call. Always say yes. You've sent that person a letter telling them exactly what day you would call, so your call should honestly be expected.

When you're on the phone with each of these people, make sure you're standing and smiling while talking to them. This will change the way you sound and help you have more confidence. When you are connected, introduce yourself and say that you were the person who sent the letters about volunteer editing. Tell them that you'd like to make an appointment at a more convenient time for you to discuss how you can help the company. Most of the time they'll just want to talk to you right then, so be prepared to have the "interview" during the phone call.

When you do have the interview, make sure you come prepared just as if it were a real job interview. Research the company. Have questions prepared for the interview. When you are discussing what you hope to accomplish through editing for the company, make sure you give no indication that you are just hoping for a job. Always say that you have been editing for individual authors and now would like to have more experience with corporate editing.

As I said before, give each company a specified duration of time for which you'd like to edit, maybe ten or twenty hours a week for three or six months. This is very important. If you let your companies think that your commitment is open-ended, then at some point you will have to "quit," and no matter how cordial the quitting is, it's always a negative experience. The biggest reason that you want to give a definite time period is that there is a chance that you'd like to be moved into a paid position. If you tell them that you will edit for free indefinitely, then you will. But if you edit for them for six months and do everything you possibly can to make yourself indispensable, then there is a good chance that they will want to hire you as a full- or part-time freelance editor when the time is up.

Edit for as many companies as you can. This will give you great, varied experience and help you expand your network. It will also give you more chances to be brought on as a paid freelancer. If you are a stay-at-home mom, don't take more than you have time for. Ten hours a week while the baby naps might be all you can do, and that's just fine.

I will repeat much of this section in chapter 4 on working with publishers. In that section, I will include sample introduction and cover letters. This process is adapted from Dan Miller's *48 Days to the Work You Love*, a book you should definitely read.

Elance and oDesk

I've been debating with myself on whether to include Elance and oDesk in this chapter. As you can see, I have decided to include these services but with the sole purpose of dissuading you from using them.

Elance and oDesk and other sites like them allow people who need editing or design help to post a job and have editors and designers bid on the projects. From what I've seen, the bidding makes the final price a race to the bottom. But, at this point, getting money isn't really your concern, so what's wrong with it? Nothing, except it's just not worth your time. Your time is much better spent with family and friends who will be eager to give you great testimonials and with companies that might hire you after three to six months of volunteer work.

****

From the time you pick up this book to the time you reach the end of your six or so months of volunteering for companies should take you about a year. Beginning a freelance editing career from scratch is certainly not a quick way to get money, but it is much cheaper and faster (and I think more useful) than going back to school. After this year of training and experience, you should be ready to earnestly begin seeking regular, paying clients, both authors and companies. The rest of this book will teach you how to get clients, how to interact with those clients, and how to run and operate your business.

4

Finding Work with Publishers

෪

The primary focus of this book is how to build your own business and find your own individual or corporate clients. This is what I have the most experience with and what I am the strongest in. I haven't had much experience with editing for publishers, but I will give you some pros and cons about editing for publishers and the best way to at least get their attention.

Benefits of Working with Publishers

Less Marketing

The biggest benefit of having publishers as clients is that they will be the ultimate repeat customers. The problem that most freelancers face is that one month they have no work and all the time in the world to market. The next month they have a ton of projects and no time to market, which means that they will have no work again the following month. It's a pretty vicious cycle. But, when you work with a publisher, you don't have to do any more marketing unless you are trying to find other publishers. In theory, at least, this should produce a more even work flow. But keep in mind that in the freelance business, it's often either feast or famine.

Fewer Business Worries

This is very similar to the previous point. In general, you will have to worry much less about the business aspects of freelance editing if you focus on editing for publishers. Websites, flyers, blog posts, and major networking are all much less necessary.

Good Books

When you look for publishers whose editing lists you'd like to join, look for publishers that print books that you're interested in. One of the greatest benefits of being an editor is the chance to read interesting content all day. You can almost guarantee that benefit by choosing publishers whose content fits your interests.

Drawbacks of Working with Publishers

Competition

Many publishers are shortening their lists of freelance editors. This not only decreases the number of publishers who are looking for or at least open to hiring new freelance editors but it also increases the number of well-qualified freelance editors available to take the open positions.

Pay

Pay is based on the time spent with a project and not the results provided. Being paid per hour will not reward you for becoming more proficient at your task. As you gain more experience, you will become a faster editor. This is great when you work with individual clients. Those clients are paying for a beautifully edited manuscript, regardless of the time it took to edit it. When you work with publishers, on the other hand, you are penalized for your increase in speed. It's a disincentive to doing a more efficient job.

Not Having Your Own Business

Personally, I love running my own business. That was one of the aspects of freelance editing that most appealed to me. If you are entrepreneurial, you won't want to work with publishers. Spending all your time editing for publishers is the same as having a remote job.

Fewer Relationships

I love getting to know and building relationships with my clients. It's great to work with clients and see their joy as I turn their unedited manuscript into a polished, well-designed book. You just don't get that when working for publishers.

Overall I prefer to not freelance for publishers. But, it might be a great fit for you. Below is the best process I've seen for at least getting publishers to take you seriously and send you an editing test.

How to Work with Publishers

This process is almost exactly the same as what I shared on how to start volunteering for companies. But, just in case you started reading here, I have included the process again.

Picking the Right Publishers

In the benefits section above, I said that you will want to pick publishers whose content is interesting to you. Not only will this make your editing work more enjoyable but it will also allow you to talk knowledgeably and passionately to the editor you contact.

There are a couple of great ways to pick which publishers to edit for. One way is to look at some of your favorite books and see which publishers produced them. When you look through the books, find small- or medium-sized publishers, or at least not huge publishers like Penguin or Routledge. It will be much harder to break through the bureaucracy and fight off the competition with the big publishers. Make a list of the publishers that you're interested in, and start finding the people to contact (more about that below).

Another way to find publishers is to use the *Writer's Market*, either in print or online. I think that the online version is better because it's cheaper—$5.99 for a month—and more importantly because you can search for keywords. For example, I studied classics in college, and if I wanted to find all the publishers that produce works in that field, I'd just enter *classics* into the search bar and it would give me that information. (You can also see if a copy of the book is available at your library or if they provide a free subscription online. Many libraries offer services like this.)

Another great thing about the *Writer's Market* is that it gives you the address and contact information of each publisher. Many times it will give you the name of the acquisitions editor since the service is primarily focused toward writers. You'll have to do your own snooping to find the managing editor or someone that you think would hire freelance editors.

I'll talk about that in the next section. You will want to find about fifteen to twenty publishers for your first round of inquiries.

Finding the Right People

Once you've picked your publishers, you now have to figure out whom in the organization to contact. Many small- to medium-sized publishers will have their staff listed on their websites. If this is the case, my first pick would be the managing editor and then the editor in chief. You don't really want to pick anyone lower than that unless the website explicitly says that they hire freelance editors. It's better to send your letters to someone who has delegated the hiring of freelancers to someone else than someone who will have no idea why you are contacting them.

But, you'll probably find that about half of the publishers you choose won't have their staff listed. That's just fine. The best way to find the right person then is to look through LinkedIn. Search in the "People" section of LinkedIn, and in the "Current Employer" box, type in the name of the publisher. That will list all the people who are employees of the company and on LinkedIn. Most people, especially in leadership, are on LinkedIn, so you should have great luck with this. There is one problem that you might run into, though. You might find the managing editor of the publisher, but you might need to get LinkedIn Pro to see the full name. There is an easy way to get around this. If you have this issue, just go to Google and type in the name of the publisher, the position that you found ("managing editor"), and "LinkedIn." The first result should be that person's LinkedIn page with his or her full name.

Introduction Letter

Once you've found all the right people and have gathered their contact information, you are ready to send introduction letters. In the letters, state who you are, say that you'd like to freelance edit for their company, and give a couple of sentences explaining your background. Close the letter by telling them that they will receive your cover letter and résumé within the next few days.

Here is an example of what I'd do for an introduction letter. Feel free to pattern yours after mine.

Dustin Schwanger
000 Birch St.
Sandusky, OH 44870

Mary Smith
Paulist Press
680 Macarthur Boulevard
Mahwah, NJ 07030

Dear Ms. Smith,

My name is Dustin Schwanger. I am a freelance editor and indexer focusing on classical and Christian publishing. I've worked as a salaried and freelance editor and am transitioning to freelancing full-time.

My background in classics and early Christian history and my experience in academic editing and publishing uniquely qualify me to work with Paulist Press as a freelance editor and indexer.

Within the next week you will receive my résumé and cover letter, and we can start to explore how my experience may best help Paulist Press.

Sincerely,

Dustin J. Schwanger

Notice that I say who I am, what my experience is, and what my next move will be. Everything is short and simple. Notice also the space between *sincerely* and my name. That space is for me to neatly sign the letter once it's printed. Print this letter, and everything else that you will send through the mail, on high-quality résumé paper. This will make you look much more professional. Also use your printer to print the sending and return addresses on the envelopes. That will also add a professional touch.

Résumé and Cover Letter

Next, mail your résumé and a relatively short cover letter detailing how exactly you can help the company. There are lots of different ways to write cover letters. You might have a better way of doing it than I do, but from what I've done and researched, this seems best to me: I usually spend, at most, one paragraph on my skill set. Prospective employers can easily see my skills in my résumé, so reviewing them in the cover letter isn't that effective. I just spend a few sentences showing in more detail how my skills fit their needs. Then I spend one to two paragraphs discussing personal qualities. These are the most important paragraphs in the cover letter. Many people will have the same or better skills than you, but if you can differentiate yourself when it comes to personal qualities, that will have a major impact on the reader.

On the next page is a sample of what I would write for a cover letter. Again, feel free to pattern yours after mine.

Notice that whenever I mention something my reader can easily see in my résumé, I show what quality that represents. Also, notice that I didn't say, "I look forward to hearing from you," which so untactfully graces too many cover letters. When you say that or something similar, you lose control of the hiring process. I let my reader know that *I* will contact *them*. That will almost guarantee that I will either be given an editing test or be told definitely that I can't help that publisher. Again, sign the letter and send the cover letter and résumé on very nice résumé paper.

Dustin Schwanger
000 Birch St.
Sandusky, OH 44870

Mary Smith
Paulist Press
680 Macarthur Boulevard
Mahwah, NJ 07030

Dear Ms. Smith,

With this letter, I wish to express my strong desire to become a freelance editor for Paulist Press. The combination of my education in classics and early Christian history and of my training and leadership in publishing make me a perfect fit for your press.

My collegiate education was in classics with an emphasis is early Christian history. In addition to the history and languages I studied in that discipline, I learned what great research looks like. I quickly put that knowledge to editorial use at the Neal A. Maxwell Institute for Religious Scholarship where I focused on nonfiction texts for both scholars and general readers.

In addition to the mechanics of editing, I understand how to be an outstanding freelance editor because I know how to lead a team of editors. As the managing editor of Query Publishing, I lead a small staff of freelance editors, and as the editor in chief at Stance for the Family, I led a team of up to thirty editors and writers. When I edit for others, I understand the quality of editing that is expected because I expect the same from my staff.

One of my great passions is Christian publishing. That is why I'm reaching out to you to pursue an opportunity to edit for your press. I would like to speak with you about the ways in which I can help you. Please expect my call on Tuesday, February 18, to schedule a convenient time for us to talk. Thank you very much for your time.

Sincerely,

Dustin Schwanger

Making the Call

When the fateful day arrives that you actually have to call this person, don't be too nervous. If you've followed these steps, he or she should be happy to speak with you. Most would-be freelancers just send a thousand résumés through email and expect to be hired. You have differentiated yourself. Your prospect will at least respect you for that. You will most likely have to ask the secretaries to connect you to the people that you want to talk to. The secretaries will ask you if they are expecting your call. Always say yes. You've sent each person a letter telling him or her exactly what day you would call, so your call should honestly be expected.

When you're on the phone with each of these people, make sure you're standing and smiling while talking to him or her. This will change the way you sound and help you have more confidence. When you are put through, introduce yourself and say that you were the person who sent the letters about freelance editing. Tell your prospect that you'd like to make an appointment at a more convenient time to discuss how you can help the company. Most of the time he or she will just want to talk to you right then, so be prepared to have the "interview."

When you talk to these editors, make sure you have done some research. It's best to have read some of what each press publishes and to be prepared to discuss it on the phone. At least have some titles that interest you or that you plan to read. Your chat with most of the editors will be fairly short. Most publishers that are open to hiring new freelancers will send you an editing test. If they do agree to send you an editing test, make sure to ask them how heavily they would like it edited, whether you should stick to black-and-white errors, and whether you should rephrase sentences that are unclear. Also ask them if there is a house style guide you should follow. You can ask if there will be a time limit and if you can use outside materials as you edit. Usually editors will answer all these questions in the process of explaining the test, but don't start taking the test until all of these questions are answered.

Taking the Test

This is the part of the process with which I can help you the least. Your success on the editing test comes down to your previous preparation and experience. I do have some suggestions, though, that may help you as you complete the test.

Most tests are timed. For the timed tests, it's more important that you are correct than fast. You need to take the time to look things up, but once you look something up, make the decision on what to do quickly. Don't fret over a choice; you'll waste a lot of time that way. You might think about creating a style sheet to keep track of decisions you've already made to save time and improve your consistency—just don't spend too much time on it.

I'd also read the manuscript out loud as you edit it, if I were you. Many times tests will leave out prepositions and other words that your mind can easily replace if you're reading silently.

After the Test

After you send back the test, you'll want to write a thank-you note to each of the editors. Thank them for their taking the time to talk to you and to review your test. Tell them that you'll call back on a specific date to discuss the results and the next steps. I wouldn't call any sooner than a week after you have sent in the test. You don't want to rush them.

The next step will usually be the editors telling you whether or not they want to hire you. Hopefully, if you have followed all these steps, they will want to hire you. But, if they say that you've done poorly on the test, be gracious and ask what you could have improved on and whether they would be open to you taking a different editing test in six months or so. If you know you want to work for these publishers and you are in the financial position to do so, ask them if you can volunteer for six months. This will give them time to see your editing improve and shine, especially in a situation that isn't as stressful and tricky as an editing test.

* * * * * * *

What I described above is the best way that I have seen to get the attention of publishers and, hopefully, to be employed by them. Sending the multiple letters and initiating the phone conversations, allows you to have top-of-mind positioning and will separate you from the crowd. Especially as a relatively new editor, you will have to do as many things as possible to differentiate yourself.

The rest of this book focuses on what I see as the most fertile fields of freelance editing and how to start, run, and build your editing business.

5

Your Marketing Toolkit

❦

Welcome to your new career: sales. If all you want to do is to just edit and not worry about the business side of working for yourself, then the last chapter on working with publishers is definitely for you. Otherwise, as I said in chapter 1, you have to be three people as a freelance editor: a technician, an entrepreneur, and a manager. The first part of this book covered the steps you need to become an editing technician. The rest of this book will discuss the entrepreneurial and managerial aspects of running your own editing business.

I came into freelance editing thinking that I was primarily going to be a technician. I thought I'd spend thirty-seven or so hours editing and a couple hours writing blog posts and a few minutes dealing with accounting and taxes each week. I thought that if I did that, work would just find me. I was wrong. I had to become a salesman.

This chapter will give you the ideas and tools you need to build a foundation for your editing sales career. These ideas and tools are necessary as a complement to your other sales and marketing adventures, like networking, but they won't necessarily bring in customers the way I thought they would.

Branding: Yourself or the Company

If you search for "freelance editing" in Google, you will mostly see freelance editors who have named their company after themselves. They are the brand. If you send your manuscripts to them, they will edit it themselves.

On the other hand, editing businesses like mine have the company as the brand, and I am just the owner of the company.

Either choice is fine; it just depends on what you want out of the business. If you are planning on editing everything yourself and just love the editing process, having your name as the name of the company is great. You can get a url like *dustinschwangerediting.com* or something like that. The benefit of this approach is that it's more personable. Your prospective clients are hiring a real person whose picture they can see, not some company, to edit their manuscript.

The downside to branding yourself is that you will always be the one who edits the manuscripts that are sent in. No matter how successful and popular your service gets, you will have placed a limit on your income. Your income will be limited to how much time you personally have to edit. And, that isn't necessarily a bad thing. Maybe you don't like the business side of editing very much and would rather spend your time editing and not having to worry about hiring and leading your own freelancers. Maybe this is simply a part-time endeavor to contribute to the family's income. There are many reasons why it's okay not to be concerned about the time and income limitations of having your own name as the brand of your editing business.

However, the vision I have for my little company is much grander than I could ever accomplish if I were the brand. While I still do quite a bit of the editing and design work for my business, I also have freelancers to whom I give excess work. As business increases, more of the editing and design work will be shifted to the freelancers and my time will be spent more on the strategic side of growing and running the company. If I were continually bogged down with editing work, I would have little time to grow the business. Ultimately I want my company to be a real business in that it still makes money when I take a day off. Most freelance editors are simply self-employed: when they don't work, they don't get paid.

Both choices are great. As I said, it just depends on your personality and what you want out of your business. The rest of the suggestions in this book will work for you whether you brand yourself or the company.

Have a Great Logo

You have to have a great logo, something that will draw prospective clients in and something that will help you to be memorable. If you are good with design, you can create a logo yourself. I didn't have the time or the drive to create my own logo, so I used a designer on Fiverr.com to design it for me. I added all the add-ons, so it cost me about $50 total to have a great-looking logo. That's a lot cheaper than hiring a graphic designer from somewhere else.

Business Cards

Once you have your logo, it's time to make your business card. Here is a sample of what my business card looks like.

On the front, I have my logo and company name. On the back, I again have my company name and logo and my name, title, and contact information. Notice all the open space that's on the front and back of the card. This keeps everything simple and helps the reader know exactly where to look.

Website or Blog

You must have an online presence. If you aren't online, you don't really exist. You can pay someone to make a website for you. You are probably going to pay $500 to $2000 for a good website. (I'm sorry for the shameless plug, but another company I've started, Real Editing & Design, designs beautiful websites for about $500.) Another option is to learn HTML and CSS and use Dreamweaver to build your own website. That's what I did for my first website. To learn how to do it, I watched hours and hours of tutorials on lynda.com. My website looked good. It was simple and professional looking. The big issue I had with it, though, is that I didn't really understand CSS (because I didn't watch all of the lessons). I knew how it worked in theory but if I messed something up, there was no way for me to figure out what I did wrong. That website was always one click away from a disaster. Although it's not what I would suggest you do, I wouldn't trade that learning process for anything. Having learned HTML and CSS now allows me to create ebooks really well (ebooks are just little websites).

I suggest that you use Adobe Muse to build your first site. From first learning how to use Muse to creating my next website and having everything ready and online took me about three days. Compared to using Dreamweaver and writing my own HTML and CSS, it was paradise. My first step was to use lynda.com's Muse Essential Training course to learn how to use the program. Then, I used a theme from muse-themes.com as a starting point. The themes are good, and they have lots of extras. For about $50, you get access to all of their themes. Check out other sites, though, to make sure you get exactly what you want. After I got the theme, I customized it and wrote the content.

The problem that I've run into with Muse, though, is that the blogging platform isn't the greatest. It's quite a pain to customize and work with. If you decide to have a blog along with or as your website, Wordpress is the best option. You should be able to find someone who can customize it for you fairly cheaply, and once it's customized, you're ready to go. The drawback to using Wordpress—unless you know PHP—is that, for major customizations, you'll have to constantly pay someone to do it. I've been changing the focus of my business every few months, so Wordpress wouldn't have been a good option for me.

Driving Traffic to Your Website

Just making a website won't ensure that anyone sees it. One of the best ways to drive traffic to your site is through your blog. Write good, thoughtful posts that add value for your readers. Don't make every post about you or about the deals you have. A good rule to follow is the 80/20 rule. Make sure that 80 percent of your posts don't deal directly with your company. If you do that, then you have earned the right to take your 20 percent and tastefully advertise yourself. If you follow this pattern, you'll be seen as a giver, not a taker, and people will want to give to you, as well.

As you begin blogging, make sure that you have an email opt-in form somewhere on your site. As people give you their email addresses, they can receive notifications of new posts and other information that can be useful for them, which will bring them to your website again and again. Building an email list is a very important part of your business, especially if you start writing books or selling products. The best free resource I've seen to create and manage your email list is MailChimp. I use it, and it is very easy and effective.

Social Media

Just like your email list, social media can be a very important part of your business. As you are building your website, make sure you include social media buttons. Hopefully a lot of the same people who will give you their email addresses will also like or follow you on social media. Follow the same 80/20 rule for social media as you do for your blog. And, don't just recycle content from your blog and put it on Facebook. Make sure you put unique material on your social media platforms.

Not all social media is created equal. I use some platforms more than or differently from others. What you decide to do depends on your needs. I describe what I do below.

My personal page on LinkedIn is the most important to me. When I hand out my business card, people don't go to my company's page to follow the company; they go to my page to learn more about me and to connect with me. I make sure that everything on my personal page is current and branded consistently with my company. I do have a company page. Company pages are great places to post helpful articles from others as well as your own blog posts and are great places to begin thoughtful discussions. You can also join writing and editing groups on LinkedIn and leave well-informed, not spammy, comments.

I post links to most of my blog posts and to other helpful resources on Facebook. When I first started using Facebook, hundreds of people would see my posts. It was great. But, then came a change in Facebook's algorithms, or something, and now maybe five people see my posts. It seems like you have to pay to play on Facebook these days, which is fine. If you set aside maybe $5 or $10 a week to promote your most important or most helpful posts, you should see your views go up quite a bit.

I have only dabbled on Twitter and Google+. You should really be on Google+, though. The number of circles you're in contributes significantly to where you are ranked through Google's search engine.

****

There you have it. That is all I thought I needed to be unimaginably successful as a freelance editor. While it's certainly not quite that *easy*, the tools that I mentioned in this chapter will build the marketing foundation you need in order to be successful. What is built on that foundation are all the meaningful relationships you develop through networking and through being sincerely concerned about the needs of others.

6

Networking and Relationships

ళ

etworking was always a vague, mysterious activity that I knew I
should be doing but never knew how to do well. I thought that
my knowing the few people I did in publishing, which I thought
was a few more than most knew, was going to provide the networking
power that I needed to be enormously successful. Just like with lots of
other things in this process, I again found that I was horribly wrong.

Since this disturbing discovery, I've learned about networking and have
figured out how to at least get started with it. And that's very fortunate for
me. While I thought that most of my business would come from traffic to
my blog and website, it actually comes from the relationships I build with
people at the meetings and conferences I attend.

Just as important as networking, and, honestly, probably more important than networking, is how you treat the people in your network, especially when they are your clients. After explaining some of the basics of
networking, I'll discuss some principles from Dale Carnegie's *How to Win
Friends and Influence People* that deal directly with how you treat the people you meet and work with as an editor.

Preparing to Network

Business Cards and LinkedIn

When you go out to meet people, you must have plenty of well-designed
business cards. To learn more about business cards, go to page xx where I
discussed them in more depth. All I will say here is that your cards must

look professional and have all the information people need to contact you or find you on LinkedIn.

I mentioned LinkedIn previously, as well, on page xx. Your personal LinkedIn page must be tailored exactly the way you'd like it. Highlight experience that will show you as a great candidate for freelance editing. Some people think that it's a good idea to post every job that they've ever had to their LinkedIn page. Their pages are cluttered with cashier and fast food positions. When you write the content of your page, think only of freelance editing and maybe a particular field in which you're an expert or have experience.

Have an Elevator Pitch

Imagine that you are a freelance editor right now. How would you describe what you do to someone you just met? How long would it take you? Try it.

It might go something like this: "I'm a freelance editor. I help correct people's spelling and grammar. I like to edit books, but I'm open to editing anything." Your description might have been longer, but it was probably something like that—weak.

What you need is an elevator pitch, or a set description of what you do that is powerful and takes no longer than the time it takes to ride the elevator with someone. Dan Miller, the author of *No More Dreaded Mondays* and *48 Days to the Work You Love*, has the best formula for an elevator pitch I've seen. Here are the elements.

1. I help _____
2. do/know/understand _____
3. so they can _____.

Here is Dan's elevator pitch that he gave on his October 18, 2013, podcast: "**I help** emerging experts such as authors, speakers, and coaches, **understand** how to leverage their unique intellectual expertise **so they can** have an expanded and more financially prosperous impact." The strength of this formula comes from how specific it is. Your new friend will know exactly whom you help, what you help them with, and, most importantly, what that means for those people.

What would be a good elevator pitch for an editor? Here's one that I use: "**I help** authors and business owners **understand** how to effectively and accurately convey their message **so they can** grow their platform and influence more people." What's great about this is that it gets people's attention. It gets them interested in you. It makes you seem like the expert you are. These feelings will prompt the person you're talking to, to ask you questions. Once you've given your pitch, you can discuss editing and exactly how you produce the results you just mentioned.

Prepare Samples

This won't be appropriate at all networking events you attend, but it might help sometimes. When I go to some functions, especially ones that I've been to before, I'll bring a copy of a book that I edited, indexed, and designed. It's a great way for people to break the ice with you. I've had a lot of people approach me and ask about the book I was holding. That gave me a chance to explain exactly what I could do for them.

Dress Professionally

Always dress professionally to networking events. If you don't know what the dress standards will be like, either call someone to find out or just overdress a little for how you think it will be. If your appearance is professional, people will view you as a professional.

Networking

Where to Go

Choosing the best venues at which to network depends on what you want to edit. I personally like nonfiction, so I go to lots of business seminars and conferences; that's what I'll discuss first. The best way that I can think of to know what business meetings to attend would be to go to a SCORE workshop. SCORE stands for "Service Corps of Retired Executives." The volunteers there are wonderful—former CEOs, marketers, financial advisors. All their help and advice is free. Go to a workshop or sign up to have a mentor (I'm meeting with mine this coming week), and talk to them about networking opportunities. Another great thing about SCORE is that they try to match you with volunteers who have the background and experience you need help with. There's a good chance that there is someone in your area who was in publishing who can teach you a lot about networking and editing in general.

If you would like to stick with fiction, I'd still visit a SCORE volunteer. There might be someone there that can help. But, you should also be attending every writing conference, workshop, and seminar in your area that you can. As a start, check your local libraries to see what events they have there and go to those. You can also do a search online. There should be a writers association in each state. Search for [your state] Writers Association. Also, here is a great list of other writer groups with specific interests that might match what you're looking for: http://goo.gl/KP9qY1. Just find out where authors go and go there.

What to Do

One of the most important aspects of networking functions is talking to everyone. I'm quite introverted and shy, so talking to everyone and wiggling my way into groups is terribly difficult. But, if you want to be successful, that is what you have to do.

When you do strike up conversations, view them as opportunities to serve. Make sure the people you're talking to know what you do, and if they need advice, give them all the help you can. Zig Ziglar, a wonderful motivational speaker and sales coach, says that if you help enough other people get what they want, you'll get everything you want. That is so true.

When you are through talking to someone, make sure that you trade business cards. If you don't, your talking to them will have been worthless, at least as it relates to networking. When you get home, use the business cards to look up each person on LinkedIn. Connect with each person (and mark the "Friend" button) and include a personal note. The personal note will do two things. First, it will make sure that LinkedIn doesn't shut down your account. If you try to add twenty-five new people to your network without a note, LinkedIn might think you are just connecting with people you don't know. That's not allowed. The personal note will show that you really do know these people. Second, and more importantly, your note will show that you valued the conversation you had with that person. Thank them for talking with you and try to include something that was specific to that conversation. This will help cement your relationship.

Good, mutually beneficial relationships are your greatest assets. If you can't develop good relationships, you will not succeed as a freelance editor. People buy from, or give their manuscripts to, people they know, like, and trust. Those types of relationships must be begun through networking and continued as those in your network become your clients. The next section will detail several key interpersonal steps that will help you begin and build meaningful relationships.

How to Win Clients and Influence Them

These fundamental principles and the other topics I discuss in this section combine my experience as a relationship builder and what is taught in Dale Carnegie's *How to Win Friends and Influence People*, a book that is required reading for beginning freelance editors. Much of what is discussed in these sections will be on how to interact with your clients, but each principle should be applied to first-time encounters, as well.

Be Sincerely Interested in People

It's easy for me to be interested in people. I am an avid people watcher. It's so bad that when Caitlin and I go out for dinner, we hardly talk to each other because we're watching and listening to everyone else. Your interest in other people doesn't have to be *that* extreme, or problematic. You might even have to force yourself to focus on the person or people you're talking to until you're genuinely interested.

To show your interest in your clients and others in your network, look them in the eye when you talk to them and especially when they talk to you. Nothing implies that you don't care more than looking around as someone is talking to you. And as you meet people and talk to them, use their names. Dale Carnegie said, "Remember that a person's name is to that person the sweetest and most important sound in any language."[5] Using someone's name in conversation will add a definite sense of closeness and interest.

Be interested in your clients' projects and manuscripts. Remember that their writing is an extension of themselves. If you're not interested in what they have to say, you are not interested in them. If you're editing nonfiction, read it with the heart of a student; learn as much as you can from the manuscript and mention a few of the points you learned. If you're editing fiction, try to get wrapped up in the story. Tell the author how suspenseful or exciting a particular section was. All of this will make your authors feel that you are sincerely interested in them, and it will make them feel appreciated.

Smile

No matter how you are communicating with someone, whether it be on the phone, online, or in person, smile. The effects of smiling are obvious

5. Dale Carnegie, *How to Win Friends and Influence People.*

in person. You seem more welcoming and friendly. You become easily approachable and likeable. But, why smile when people can't see you or even hear you? Smiling changes the way you sound, and people will pick up on that on the phone. Smiling also changes your state. What you say and how you say it will change dramatically when you smile, because smiling makes you feel different. So, smiling even when you are emailing or commenting online is a very important tool for you to win the trust and friendship of your network and clientele.

Complement; Don't Criticize

The act of producing a book and allowing the general public to read it and review it is a very emotionally vulnerable process itself for authors, but when they give it to an editor, whose job it is to critique their writing, that vulnerability becomes even more acute. Authors can be so attached to their writing that any criticism or lack of tact can be seen as an attack on them personally. Their writing becomes a part of them. That's why authors are so emotionally vulnerable during the editing process. And that is why we as editors must treat them as warmly and tactfully as we can.

The best way to help an author feel comfortable with you and your editing is to consistently complement them. Complement them in your emails and in comments on the manuscript. Don't overdo the complements, but a good complement at the beginning of the manuscript and at the end can do wonders for your relationship with authors. Also, show your appreciation for your authors. Send them thank-you notes after a project is finished. Send them a gift when they refer other clients to you. Simply show your gratitude for them—because without them, you'll really be self-employed.

But, there are still corrections to make and confusion that needs to be untangled through effective commenting. The first step in effective commenting is to not criticize. This may seem obvious, but here are some common comments that can be classified as criticisms:
- "This doesn't make any sense."
- "This citation is wrong."
- "You put periods after these bullets and commas after the ones above."

Can you just feel how tense this would make you as an author? These are very direct, strong statements, and while brevity is a good virtue, you must express yourself fully enough not to cause offense. So what would be better comments? Here are some:

- "This might be a little unclear for your readers. Could you add a couple more sentences of explanation?"
- "I looked up this citation but couldn't find it. Could you check it one more time?"
- "The bullets above ended with commas, but these end with periods. Which would you prefer?"

Can you feel how much better these questions are? Let's look at them a little closer to understand why exactly they're better. First, notice that the poorly worded comments are just statements, but the better comments combine statements and questions. This effectively tells the author what the problem may be and provides a way to fix it. You become a partner in the writing process, not an adversary.

Another important point is that the critical comments focus on the author, while the gentler comments shift the focus to the readers. Whenever possible you want to shift the focus away from you or the author. The statement "This might be a little unclear for your readers" places the focus of the change on the reader. It implies to the author that you know what he or she is saying, but there could be some very unintelligent reader out there who might struggle. It's not you criticizing the author's work; it's an unknown reader. Additionally, saying that the bullets are inconsistent shifts the focus away from the author, emotionally at least, and to the bullets. It's the bullets' fault, not the author's.

Adding *might* or *maybe* or *I think* is a great way to soften the tone of your comments. Not only does this soften your tone but it also allows the author to feel like he or she has control of the writing and editing process. Although the author could have looked at that sentence for three years without finding an issue, your using *might* or *maybe* lets him or her make the decision. You just pointed out something that was going to be fixed anyway.

Moving away from comments, there is another way that authors feel criticized during the editing process. That is through excessive deletions using Microsoft Word's Track Changes feature. Alarms start going off in authors' heads when they see the sea of red deletion bubbles on their screens. Obviously there will be deletions that authors will need to see and approve. But what about two spaces after a period or no spaces between ellipsis points or replacing en-dashes with em-dashes? Authors do not need to see or approve these changes. You should turn off Track Changes and use Word's Find and Replace feature to take care of those issues all at once. That will alleviate the stress of seeing thousands of delete bubbles surrounding the manuscript.

Don't Argue

There will be times when authors will want to make editing decisions that are just plain wrong. And that's okay. Remember that it's their manuscript and that they are responsible for what it says. If it's a minor issue, just leave it alone. But when it is something that can definitely be seen as a mistake, politely let them know what the standards are and why it would be better to adhere to those standards. Also tell them, though, that it's their choice. And if they decide to keep it the way it is, do not argue with them. Accept their decision and make sure it's consistent throughout the manuscript. Remember that most readers aren't editors, and things that you see as major problems aren't necessarily issues for normal readers.

****

Your website, your business cards, and even your editing can be average, but if you have great networking and personal skills, people will know, like, and trust you—that is, they will do business with you. Internalize the principles I've discussed in this chapter. Read Dale Carnegie's *How to Win Friends and Influence People* and practice its principles. And as you develop these skills, make sure that you are sincere. People hate fakes. Your personal skills, whether innate or learned, are the single greatest key to your success as a freelance editor.

7

Additional Marketing Strategies

໑

The marketing fundamentals discussed in chapter 5 and the networking and personal skills covered in chapter 6 are the foundation for your success. Those principles and skills must be present for you to build and run your freelance editing business. This chapter highlights a few additional ways I have used to market myself. There is almost a never-ending supply of unique and successful marketing ideas. One of the best quick-reading resources I've seen is Dan Miller's little, free booklet *48 Low or No Cost Marketing Ideas*.

Books

My main purpose with this book is to help people along the path of entrepreneurship, the same path that I'm on. But, another major part of this book is marketing; almost every author can say the same thing. When you write a book, you have one of the biggest marketing giants on your side—Amazon. And, the best part is that Amazon pays you to advertise with them. If this book gets 20,000 downloads, or maybe 200, then it's that many more people who know about me and my services. That obviously doesn't mean that you want to write a one-hundred-, or forty-, page sales book and expect people to buy your product or value your service. But, if you create content that adds value to people's lives, which is what I hope I'm doing here, your readers will appreciate you and value your business. That value helps people to know, like, and trust you.

Trust itself is a major benefit of writing a book. When you label yourself as an author, people's perception of you changes. They think that if you wrote a book about something, that you are an expert in that field. It builds their trust in you. But, if this trust is compromised by a lack of performance from you, then they will know quickly that their trust in you was misplaced. You always have to meet or exceed people's expectations of you.

Speaking

I gave my first presentation a few weeks ago on why all entrepreneurs must publish a book. It was much like the previous section. And, it was awesome. The presentation was to about twenty-five small business owners and it ran for about an hour with plenty of audience participation. Not only did it seem to improve the audience's perception of me and what I do but it also produced a number of leads that will, in the coming months, turn into major book deals.

Networking and speaking go hand in hand. You may not have the faintest idea where you could speak, but as you go to more and more networking meetings, you will be introduced to many meetings and groups that use and are dying to get speakers.

Now you might be thinking to yourself that you'd rather die than speak in front of a group of people. That's okay; you don't *have* to do any public speaking, but I do recommend it. A great way to start learning public speaking skills is by reading Dale Carnegie's *The Quick and Easy Way to Effective Speaking*. That will teach you many ways to succeed as a public speaker, and as a conversationalist. Another way to learn public speaking is through Toastmasters International. Toastmasters usually meets once a week, and you will learn about business and speaking—and have plenty of safe practice speaking in front of others.

Webinars

If you think you might need some time to get yourself emotionally ready to speak in front of a crowd, then try conducting weekly or monthly webinars. You can either do these live or recorded. The big benefit to webinars is that they geographically open up your attendance possibilities. You can conduct workshops on punctuation, flow, résumé writing, or, really, whatever else you think might add value for your customers.

8

The Boring Stuff

The boring stuff to me is the managerial work: pricing, contracts, taxes. It is so hard for me to find the motivation to complete some of these tasks, especially accounting. But, there's a good chance your business will fail if you don't do these things properly.

Pricing

Pricing can be one of the most challenging aspects of getting new projects. You first have to figure out whether you will charge per project or per hour. Making that decision isn't as hard as it sounds because I'll tell you what to do. Charge per project.

Charging per hour is just a bad idea. First, it hurts you. You do not want your income directly related to the time that you spend working. You want to be paid for the results that you produce. As you get more editing experience, your editing will improve—and get faster. Why would you want to penalize yourself for doing a better, faster job? If anything, you should be charging more because the clients are getting a better product.

Second, it can hurt your relationship with your clients. If your clients think that their project will take you fifteen hours to complete and you end up taking twenty-five, they'll think you're slow and you don't know what you're doing. On the other hand, if you take twenty-five hours on those same projects and charge per project, your clients will praise you for taking the extra time to make sure things were done right.

Now that you've decided to charge per project, how do you know what to charge? There are a few ways of doing that. To begin with, you might want to estimate how long the project should take and multiply that by what you want to earn per hour. That can be anywhere from $10 to $50 or more an hour depending on the project, the client, and your experience. To have accurate time estimates, make sure you keep track of how long each project takes you.

The way that I prefer is charging by the word. This has quite a few benefits. It makes the client happier. Most clients don't know how many words their manuscript has, so 3 cents a word seems like nothing. When they figure out it's not nothing, they will know exactly why they are paying your asking price. In the method above, it can seem like you're just throwing out a number. Stating a price per word can also make things easier for you. You will know what you charge for a normal editing project, and all you have to do is multiply that by the number of words in a project. If it looks to be more time intensive, add a half or whole cent per word to the price.

Ultimately, what you charge depends on what the client is willing to pay. I always try to charge high and leave the door open for the client to negotiate. I'll give the price, and say something like, "Is that price okay?" That is the polite thing to do, and it means that if it is too high, they'll negotiate and not go straight to your competitor. You also have to look at the type of client you're dealing with. If you know the author doesn't have any money, you really have to be compassionate. Either charge the author a lower price or send him or her to someone you know who does a good job but at a lower price. I usually just charge a lower price. But, if you're working with a business that you know has money, give them a high quote at first; then negotiate if you need to.

To see what other editors charge, you can go to the Editorial Freelancers Association's website and look under "Rates" to see their suggested rates. The rates on EFA's website tend to be quite high. If you're just starting out, you'll want to charge less until you have too much work.

Contracts

Charging per project does include some risk, though. What if the client changes everything when you're halfway through or keeps adding things you didn't agree to do? That's where contracts come in. Before you start editing anything, besides a few sample pages for your clients, discuss in detail with them exactly what they would like you to do. That should be pretty easy for editing projects, but if you are typesetting or designing the cover for a book or doing anything else, it can get a little tricky.

Once you know exactly what your client wants, you'll write the contract. Here is a contract that I've done recently: xx

Notice that I began the contract by thanking my client. You always want to be personable and grateful for the work your clients provide. I then list exactly what I plan to do and how the client should pay me. And then there's space for the client to sign. Signing the contract doesn't really mean anything; you're not going to sue your client if he doesn't pay. But, it makes your clients feel more committed to their project and, most importantly, to paying you.

The Government

One of the biggest reasons small businesses are shut down is because of tax problems. You do not want to owe the IRS money. So, to make sure you have enough money to pay your taxes at the end of the year, you have to do proper accounting.

I use a free accounting program called Wave. It's very useful. It does everything I need it to. In the beginning you might not have to use anything other than Excel or another spreadsheet program to keep track of income, expenses, taxes, and everything else. As you do your accounting, you have to keep track of income *and* expenses. At the end of the year, you can subtract your expenses from your income and pay taxes on the difference, or your net profit. You'll have to talk to a tax person to know exactly what you can count as an expense, but at least start with the obvious ones like website hosting and business card printing. You definitely don't want to pay the government more than you have to.

From what I've researched, it's best to set aside about 25 percent of net income for taxes. You'll want to have one bank account for your business and a separate bank account to deposit the tax money in. This ensures that you won't touch it.

Another thing you will have to do is get a business license. You will get this at your city or county building. Business licenses are usually fairly cheap, especially for a home-based business. Having a license will allow you to get bank accounts for your business.

Thankfully that's about the most you'll have to deal with the government.

Insurance

Insurance has gotten much more complicated and expensive in recent years. But, don't let not having insurance through your employer stop you from transitioning to freelance editing full-time. You can buy insurance either privately or through the government. Hopefully by the time you read this, things will be worked out with the government healthcare. But, as of this writing, they are not. It's a nightmare.

A different option is a company called Medi-Share. It's a specifically Christian healthcare option that meets all the government regulations and is much cheaper than normal insurance. We've looked into it and have decided it's the best option for us, but every family has different needs. There might be non-Christian options out there, as well, but I haven't found them.

****

That is all for the boring stuff. Make sure you take care of it. If you don't, you can find yourself in big trouble.

Conclusion

≪∘

There you have it. That is my advice for beginning freelance editors. I hope you have found this little guide helpful. It's certainly not an encyclopedia on how to be a freelance editor, but it will give you a head start on what you need to know to begin.

I have found the time I've spent as a freelance editor very rewarding. I love freelance editing. I hope you will, too.

47962368R00034

Made in the USA
Lexington, KY
16 December 2015